LOVE
ON
A
~~TRUTH~~
DARE

For more information, please contact Jamie Avery King at jamieaveryking.com.

Cover Art & Design: Jamie Avery King

Editor: Geri Larson Watson

Paperback 5x8: ISBN 13: 979-8-9919881-0-0

Paperback 6x9: ISBN 13: 979-8-9919881-3-1

Hardcover: ISBN 13: 979-8-9919881-1-7

Ebook: ISBN 13: 979-8-9919881-2-4

Alicia, thanks for approving of my unhingedness. Please enjoy the scene made better because of you.

LOVE
ON
A
~~TRUTH~~
DARE

JAMIE AVERY KING

Author's Note & Content Discussion

Hello reader, I want to start with a big thank you for picking up *Love on a Dare*.

Before we get too far into this, I promise you a happily ever after. And fair warning, this is a taboo romance.

Love on a Dare contains but is not limited to the following content: best friends/stepbrothers to lovers, unrequited love, rejection, ADHD representation, sexually explicit content, mild themes of sexual sadomasochism, profanity, car accident, terminal illness, grief, loss of loved ones, mention of traumas: childhood trauma and abuse, domestic violence, divorce, and remarriage.

If you want to avoid potential spoilers and don't have any concerns about the content, please feel free to continue your reading journey.

I recommend caution if you continue to read *Love on a Dare* if any of the aforementioned themes may harm your mental health and well-being.

[Heavy Spoiler Alert]

This book contains more than one supporting character death.

Please know that there are scenes of an important character suffering from a terminal illness. I tried to lighten these scenes up a little, but they may be difficult for some readers. Loss of loved ones can be extremely difficult; as someone who has lost multiple loved ones to terminal illnesses, I empathize with anyone who has suffered a loss and chooses not to read this book to avoid this content. I will admit that the scenes were tough for me to write, and they brought back many memories I'd rather keep buried.

Your mental health is more important than this book. If you feel the story is too much for you at any point, please stop reading or take a break.

If you or a loved one need support, please call or text the Suicide & Crisis Lifeline at 988 or visit 988lifeline.org. If you or someone you know needs immediate help, please call 911 (in the United States) or your country's emergency services.

Contents

May

The Beginning

Chapter 1

Ash

Message notifications chimed from my laptop.

The end of the day always brought a string of goodnight messages from my team.

Sunlight streamed through the narrow window in the small room I used as a home office. The old, tattered office chair I'd had since college creaked when I leaned back. With a sigh, I clicked open my private conversation with Rainie Bates and typed out a quick message.

Me: You did great today. You'll be off on your own before you know it.

Me: Have a good night.

Time seemed to stretch, my gaze fixed on the screen, captivated by the three dots bouncing as she typed her reply.

Rainie: Thanks for your help today. I'll catch you tomorrow.

Moments after reading the message, her status flipped to offline.

Rainie was a new employee at my company, Pix Systems. She was a software developer like me, and I was responsible for training her. People at work treated me like a shadow writing code, only allowed to see the light of day on rare occasions, so being assigned to train Rainie was the first time I had a responsibility outside of my day-to-day.

I lived in Fairfax, Virginia, where a healthy mix of private companies and government contractors resided. When I graduated from college, I found a job with a government contractor to network and gain experience. While there, I wrote code for a backend reporting system. It wasn't fun or innovative. I wasn't saving lives or making a difference. There was no fulfillment at the end of the day.

When a recruiter from Pix Systems called and offered me a cushy work-from-home job paying triple my salary—I would've been a fool to say no. With Pix, I had a chance to work on innovative software. Even though I appreciated the freedom and opportunity Pix gave me, after three years, something was still missing.

I thought the opportunity to train Rainie would mean I had growth opportunities, but it turned out that no one else knew the systems Rainie would work on. I was the only one. *My efforts would be considered* when reviews came up, but there were no promises I would see a raise for taking on the extra responsibility. I wasn't actively aiming to be a manager, but in the two weeks I'd worked with her, I realized I enjoyed helping people. A lot. I liked teaching her and sharing my knowledge. I was having fun. Legitimate. Actual. *Fun.*

I headed to my tiny apartment kitchen. It was small, with a little island that doubled as a breakfast bar, barely big enough to seat two people. Before tossing a couple pans on the stove, I grabbed fixings for dinner.

Minutes into chopping vegetables, my smartwatch buzzed to life. With the cleanest knuckle I could find, I tapped the answer icon.

"Jaz," I said, "why are you calling me after work?"

"You better bow down and kiss my feet for this one, Ashton," she said, excitement lacing her tone.

"For what? Did you finish your requirements document in time for our meeting tomorrow?"

"Not yet, but," she said, hesitating, "Rainie invited me to her birthday party in two weeks at a karaoke bar in Fairfax."

"What does this have to do with me?" I asked, tossing the chopped vegetables into a hot pan. They hissed and sizzled briefly before quieting to a low simmer. "Why am I bowing down at your feet?"

"Because you are joining me."

"I am? When did I decide this?"

"Ash, stop playing with me," she whined. "There is one condition, though."

"And what is that?"

"She made it a ladies' night, so if guys want to join. . ."

3

"What does that even mean?" I asked, slicing into the mound of raw chicken before tossing the chunks into the pan beside the simmering vegetables.

"If you want to get close to Rainie. And I know you do. You've had a crush on her since you first met her."

"Spit it out, Jasmine, or I'm hanging up on you."

I moved to the sink, washing my hands while waiting for her to respond.

"You have to be queer to get the invite."

I groaned and grabbed a wooden spoon from a drawer before pushing the veggies around in the pan. "Are you fucking kidding me?"

"I'm serious."

"I'm not pretending to be gay just to be around her." I spun around, resting my hip against the counter. "Besides, wouldn't I ruin my chance with her if she thinks I'm gay?"

"Don't be so dense. We would tell her you're bisexual."

I rubbed the bridge of my nose. I couldn't believe I was considering it. "No." I hated lying. I couldn't bring myself to do it.

"Ash, please," she begged. "I don't want to go alone. The only person I'll know will be Rainie. Please come with me?"

I dropped my hand to my side with a groan. "Fine, but I'm not the one telling this lie. This is all on you."

"I knew I could get you to agree," she squealed.

I could picture her jumping up and down, her two-toned hair bouncing as she shot me an "I told you so" look like she'd won a championship.

"Whatever," I grumbled. "Text me the details."

"Duh," she said.

I was trying to play it off, but I was happy. I liked Rainie, and if this somehow put me in a position to get closer to her, I would take it. Maybe I would bow down and kiss Jasmine's feet after all.

"So, we haven't talked about anything outside of work in a while. How's the family?" Jaz added.

I chewed the inside of my cheek while lazily stirring the food simmering on the stove. "Not much has changed since the last time you asked. Mom and Gary are as happy as ever. Angie is about to come home from her sophomore year in college, and Sam is working for a big corporation doing what he loves."

"When does Angie move back home?"

"This weekend, I think." I unlocked my phone and checked the calendar. "I'm not sure when the dorms kick her out after exam week, but she mentioned being home for my birthday."

"Speaking of your birthday, are we still going to the club on Saturday?"

"Mm-hm. You still comin'?"

"You know it," she said. "Will Angie join us, or do you not want your baby sister there?"

I chuckled, saying, "She won't be there. She doesn't need to see me like that."

"You're probably right. I'm ready to party until we're passed out in the booth of that diner near your place, shoveling food into our gut to avoid the inevitable hangover."

"Yeah, okay. You know you always end up with a hangover."

She groaned. "I'm mentally preparing myself for how shitty Sunday will be."

"Then don't drink so much. You could—I don't know—not drink the whole bar dry."

She giggled. "And that's where I exit this conversation. Ashton Emerson is trying to give me advice about drinking."

"Ha-ha. Very funny, Jaz." Flicking the stove off, I added, "Don't forget to text me the details for Rainie's thing."

"I won't forget. See ya," she said before the line went silent.

I turned back to the food and double-checked the time. It was close to six-thirty, right on time. I spun around, grabbed two plates from the cabinet, and piled the food onto them before setting the table. Once satisfied with the placement, I disappeared into my bedroom and slipped into sweatpants and a loose tank.

"Ash," Sam called as the front door clicked shut.

"Yo," I said, appearing at the edge of the kitchen.

The bags under his eyes appeared darker today, and a frown wrinkled his slender chin. Sam was an inch taller than me, but the way his shoulders slumped as he stood there made him seem inches shorter like his form had shrunk from exhaustion.

5

"Ready to eat?" I asked, then sat at the small round table in my usual spot, facing the room with my back to the wall. It was something I had done my whole life. It was hard to break the subconscious need to keep an eye on everything around me.

"I'll probably need seconds with how hungry I am," Sam said, sitting across from me. "I skipped lunch because someone didn't pay attention when scheduling an important meeting, and I didn't get the chance to eat because of it."

"What asshole did that?"

He rolled his beautiful pale blue eyes and said, "Lucinda."

"How has she managed to keep her position?"

He shrugged, releasing a rough noise: half grunt and half laugh. "The whole place is run by inept morons."

I pursed my lips. I didn't like what this job was doing to him. "You know, Sammy, you could quit. I can help pay your bills until you find something else."

His eyes softened, and his fork rested loosely between his fingers as he said, "Thanks, Ash. I'll think about it."

"Sure."

There was nothing to thank me for.

Samuel Pearce was my best friend and stepbrother. He was the most amazing person in my life. The only person I could trust unquestionably. We had been inseparable since kindergarten, and when Mom fell in love with his dad, we became a family. Becoming stepbrothers extended our bond as best friends. If we didn't look so different from each other, people would swear we were blood-related.

Sam ran his fingers through his platinum blond hair, pushing his bangs from his face before taking a bite of food.

"Your hair is getting long," I said, noting the hair on the side of his head was longer than he generally let it grow.

He tugged on his bangs with a frown. "I'm going out next Friday, so I'll have to find time to get it cut."

"Are you sticking with a low fade and keeping that top length?" I asked, knowing he would keep it the same.

Sam liked to keep his life simple, with minimal change. Some called him boring, but to me, he was everything I needed. Sam was like the most beautiful summer day: a crystal blue sky littered with fluffy white clouds and the sun beaming down, enveloping me in warmth. He was the embodiment of calm. I wanted to bottle up the tranquility he exuded and let it transport me to that vision of a summer day whenever life was too much. Whenever I felt like life wasn't worth it, I only needed to look into his kind, pale blue eyes, and those thoughts would disappear.

"How was work for you today?" he asked, taking the last bite of food from his plate.

I leaned back, adjusting the waistband of my sweatpants. "Not bad. I worked with the new girl, Nini, all day. She has another two weeks of training before I can send her off on her own."

A few girls in the office gave Rainie the nickname Nini during her first week at Pix Systems, and it ended up catching on with the whole company. I thought it was pretty cute.

Sam grabbed our empty plates, then headed to the kitchen. "The one you have a crush on?"

I nodded, rubbing my belly, and groaned. "I ate too much."

"Go sit on the couch. I'll only be a minute." He flicked on the water and started washing the dishes.

"All right," I said, hoisting myself out of the chair. "Don't worry too much about getting them perfectly clean. Shove 'em in the dishwasher."

Even though we didn't live with our parents anymore, we kept the rule that the one who cooked didn't do the cleaning. I usually cooked dinner for us on weekdays, and Sam cleaned up the dishes before we hung out in my living room for a few hours.

Mom thought we were weird for living in the same building but not in the same apartment. We wanted to be close to each other and still have our privacy. We had keys to each other's apartments and could come in any time, but the place was off-limits if the other had a partner over. It had been this way since we graduated from college and got our first jobs.

I grabbed the game controller off the coffee table and dropped onto the sofa. "It feels nice to sit on the soft cushions." I kicked my feet out, resting them on the coffee table. "That desk chair has been killing me lately."

Sam sat beside me, a slight smile dimpling his cheek. "Get a new chair. I've been telling you for years that old piece of shit needs to be replaced."

I exaggerated a gasp and nudged his shoulder with my fist. "Take it back."

He laughed, pushing my hand away before I could tickle him. "No," he said, his voice breaking into a giggle as he blocked my hands.

"How dare you disrespect my chair." I jokingly pushed him over. "That's my work buddy."

Sam's laugh was deep as he sat up, holding his stomach. "What the hell did you name that thing again? Blue?"

"Yes. Do you have a problem with the way I name my things?"

He shot me a look of disbelief. "You named your blue chair Blue." He pushed me back with another laugh. "And you had the stuffed banana toy you named Yellow. The blanket you named Blankie. And the—"

"Okay!" I covered his mouth with my hand to shut him up before he went through the entire list of every single object I had ever named. His tongue ran over my palm, and I yanked my hand away. "God, why are you so gross?"

I wiped my hand on my thigh, ignoring his chuckles, before turning on the game console and opening the newest fantasy role-playing game I'd bought.

"Is this the one with the dragons you can ride?" Sam asked.

I nodded and loaded my saved game. "Are you going to hang out for a while or heading home?"

"I'll hang out with you. It was a long day, and watching you play is fun," he said, resting his head on the armrest and curling up under my checkered gray and black fleece blanket.

"You should change out of your work clothes. That can't be comfortable."

"I'm okay. Play your game."

A few hours passed, and Sam was still on my sofa, curled up under the blanket, sound asleep. His feet ended up on my lap, and his arm hung off the side. The poor thing had been at a corporate job where they worked him to the bone, yet he still took the time to hang out with me. Since he'd gotten hired, he'd fallen asleep here like this a few times. The darker the bags under his eyes grew, and the more often he fell asleep like this on my sofa, the more concerned I became about his health.

Carefully, I shifted his feet and stood up, making an effort to minimize any noise. Kneeling beside him, I unbuttoned his dress shirt at the collar. His warm breath ran over my hands, and I stopped to look at him. We had known each other for so long, sometimes I forgot how handsome he was. His face was angular yet soft. His nose was long, with a slight curve at the tip. His lips looked smooth and curved down at the corners. I always told him he could be a model or an actor, but he dismissed me as a liar. I was serious when I said it. Sam was beautiful and had slender features with a persistent air of sadness around him, but when he smiled, he was breathtaking.

I grabbed two pillows and another blanket from my bedroom before returning to the living room. After placing a pillow and blanket where I had been sitting, I slid another pillow under his head as gently as possible to avoid waking him.

I stretched out opposite him, our feet crossing in the dim light of my paused game. The last time we slept like this, we were kids. I held in my chuckle at the memory. We were around ten, and he was at my house to watch a bunch of movies we'd rented. He'd passed out halfway through our third movie, and instead of waking him, I joined him like this.

Sometimes, I wished we could go back to those times before we grew up. Before he became my stepbrother. Not that I disliked our relationship now, but he and I were different back then. There was something I couldn't put words to, and I missed it.

Chapter 2

Sam

The alarm on my phone went off promptly at five, but I had already been awake for an hour. The screen from Ash's video game flickered on the pause menu, like he had gotten up to do something and forgotten about it.

Ash groaned when I dismissed the alarm, turning over and tangling his legs with mine. My chest flooded with warmth at the contact, but I needed to keep away from the thoughts fighting to poke through.

Ashton Emerson was my best friend and first love.

I had been hiding my feelings for him since middle school. When I was thirteen, I had finally worked up the courage to tell him, but then everything changed the night before I planned to confess my undying love for my best friend—my dad told me he had something important to discuss.

"Son," Dad said in a serious tone, standing in my bedroom doorway.

I sat on the edge of my bed, looking up at him, worried something horrible was happening—again.

His hair hadn't turned gray yet, his face was free of wrinkles, and his blue eyes sparkled with a brightness I hadn't noticed before.

"I know you and Ash have been friends your whole lives, and this may be weird for you two." He sat beside me, releasing a deep sigh. "Jane and I have been seeing a lot of each other while you boys play together. For about a year now, she and I have been dating."

My breath picked up. I wasn't sure what his confession was leading to, but I was worried.

Dad took my silence as his sign to keep going, and I hung on his every word, waiting for the punch line.

"Jane and I like each other. More than I ever thought possible." He paused, fidgeting with the seam of his pants. "After your mother, I thought I would be alone for good."

I clenched my jaw at the mention of my mother.

"Sam, I asked Jane to marry me."

The world came to a screeching halt. My plans to confess my love crumbled around me. My eyes welled with tears, but I held them back while my heart clenched in my chest, and heat burned me from the inside. I cleared my throat, fought through the tightness, and forced a huge smile for my father.

"That's amazing, Dad. What did she say?"

A few tears slipped from his eyes as he looked at me with the biggest, stupidly happy grin I had ever seen on him.

"Yes! She said yes!"

He crushed me in a hug, and I held in the devastated cry that begged to be released. It clawed at my chest and tried to climb up my throat. It wanted to be heard. It wanted the world to hear my despair, but I choked it down.

Since that day, I lived with the most crippling secret: I'm in love with my stepbrother.

In the past, I thought about telling everyone I loved Ash and couldn't live like this anymore. But how could I ruin the best thing to happen to me? Jane was the most loving and tender person I had ever known. My father was lucky to have her. I was lucky to have a mother who actually loved me. I gained a brother and sister with the marriage. Ash and I were already like brothers, so we only grew closer once our parents bought a house and moved us all under the same roof.

I was blessed to have them.

After the abuse my biological mother put me through, I couldn't destroy all of this because I wanted to be with Ash. I couldn't. So it was my secret that no one would ever know. I would take it to my grave.

Ash grew up to be broodingly sexy. Tattoos covered nearly every inch of skin on his arms, chest, back, and neck. With his black hair, it made him look dangerous. The complete opposite of me. Ash lifted weights and kept himself toned. He claimed he did it to be attractive to women, but I knew it was a part of his armor.

He kept his wavy black hair shoulder-length and often threw it up in a bun or ponytail—like now—loose strands covered his fierce-looking face as he slept.

It hurt every day that I couldn't have him. But life without him would be worse than this longing.

I need to get laid before I let these thoughts get too far.

I opened the group text with my friends and asked if we were still on for Friday night. A one-night stand usually helped curb my desire for Ash. That paired with drinking heavily.

I slipped off the couch, stretching as I walked across the small room to the front door, slid into my dress shoes, and then silently left his apartment. Ash was a night owl and undoubtedly didn't fall asleep until after midnight. It would be a while before he surfaced.

The hallway of our building was brightly lit and empty. I took the stairs up, two at a time, shaking off the last remnants of my indecent thoughts.

My apartment was empty. Cold. There was no warmth there. It was lonely and existed to remind me I couldn't have what I wanted most.

I changed into shorts, a tank, and running shoes before leaving my apartment.

The cool morning air danced over my skin, energizing me while I jogged through the park near the apartment complex. Like every morning, I started a checklist in my head. I kept a running list of everything I needed to do for the day. I planned everything from what I would wear and eat for lunch, even down to where I would park. I even made backup plans for everything, leaving nothing to chance.

I was sure I was this way because of my biological mother, but I didn't want to think too much about it. If I let her linger in my thoughts, only ugly things came to mind.

When I returned to my apartment, the soft morning rays filtered through the curtains, casting warm light through the room. The familiar routine unfolded as I prepared for the day ahead. Rushing through a shower, I couldn't stop the dread filling my chest. The exhaustion from my job was wearing on me and filling my bones like lead.

I slid into my neatly pressed slacks, the smooth fabric grazing against my skin. The crispness of the dress shirt clung to me as I buttoned it up, the faint scent of laundry detergent filling the air. With a sigh, I tightened the tie around my neck, feeling its constricting grip, a constant reminder of the stuffy office I spent my days in.

A text came through while I poured coffee into my travel mug, and I swiped open my phone to read it.

Ash: Morning. Hope you slept well.

I smiled while typing a reply.

Me: I was dead to the world. Thanks for the pillow.

Me: I'm heading to work and might not make it for dinner tonight, so eat without me.

With the coffee in hand, I checked I had everything and rushed to the parking lot when my phone pinged another notification.

Ash: Don't work too hard.

I tossed my things into the passenger seat of my run-down sedan and started my morning commute.

It took an hour and a half to get to work. It was one of the main reasons I hated this job.

The building was busy, and I had to weave through the crowd in the lobby. Some people stood around chatting with paper cups of coffee in their hands, talking about boring business nonsense. I hit the elevator call button with my knuckle and crossed my arms while I waited.

The elevator doors opened, and the crowd around me piled in, pushing and touching each other like it would be the end of the world if they didn't make it on this specific elevator at this specific time. I was shoved into the back corner, crowded so tight I could hardly move.

I already wanted to quit my job, and mornings like this made Ash's offer to help me pay my bills until I found something else that much more tempting. I didn't want to take his offer. It felt wrong to rely on him financially because I didn't like my job. As I breathed in the thick air of everyone around me, I couldn't help but think about it seriously.

I tapped the shoulder of the guy in front of me and whispered, "Do you mind hitting seven for me?"

Without a word, he bent around the person in front of him and hit the button for my floor.

"Thanks," I said.

He replied with a halfhearted, "Sure."

When the elevator lurched to a stop on my floor, I pushed through the crowd, which had only dwindled by a few people, and found myself in the narrow, vacant lobby. I sucked in a deep breath, relishing the relief washing over me in the open space before heading through the doors to my office.

The office was loud. Overpowering. The receptionists at the front greeted me like they did every morning, and I breezed past them with a quiet greeting. The aisles between the cubicles were only wide enough to fit two people shoulder to shoulder.

I glanced at my watch, checking I was on time. I had two minutes to spare. When I stepped into my cubicle at the end of the row, I flipped open my laptop and dropped into the chair.

An email came through overnight, asking me to review a company's rebranding plan and another from Lucinda, my manager, the bane of my existence. She wanted another presentation from me. God forbid she did it herself. I wanted to pass it on to someone else but knew I couldn't. I didn't have time for her presentation and my already packed workload.

I sighed, scooting my chair closer to the desk, and resigned myself to the fact that this would be my life for the foreseeable future.

Friday nights were my standing date with one of my closest friends. Sean almost had the title of best friend, but I felt weird calling anyone but Ash that. We met in a history class during our sophomore year of college and became fast friends.

Our four years of college were the only time Ash and I had been separated. We chose different universities that had been three hours away from each other. Sometimes, I thought of it as a blessing that I had the chance to be away from him. College was the first time I made friends on my own. I had found an amazing group of friends who were also queer.

Throughout my K through twelve years, kids made fun of me or bullied me. I was too quiet and didn't fit in. Ash blended in with others easily. He had a loud "I don't give a shit" persona. Ash could be larger than life, but with me, he was just Ash. My weird hermit of a best friend who would rather slay dragons in a video game for a week straight than talk to anyone but me. Why I had the privilege of being the only person he wanted to be around was still a mystery.

Sean stood on the edge of the sidewalk wearing a tight tank and loose jeans. He was taller than me, around six-four, and had muscles for days, looking like he would rip out of his shirt if he sneezed. He maintained his dark hair in a short style with a low fade and kept his goatee well-trimmed and short. He was gorgeous. Dark skin, deep brown eyes, and soft lips that I kissed once and only once. Sean and I realized quickly that we were only friends.

A shiver ran down my spine at the memory of our failed attempt at a hookup in college. We did not have the right chemistry for it. Our chemistry was purely platonic. I shivered again and shook the memory away.

A sly smile overtook him when I hopped out of the rideshare, heading straight for him.

"You're looking fine as hell," he said.

"Don't I know it?" I spun around to show off the open back of the long-sleeved black shirt. Thin strings crisscrossed over my back, leading beneath my boxers. The army green cargo pants were tight enough around the waist to stay up without a belt but fell low on my hips, exposing the waistband of my boxers. "Take me to dance with hot men." I looped my arm in Sean's, and we meandered to the line outside of the DC nightclub.

It was a small club, but one of my favorite gay clubs in the DMV. The line to get inside moved somewhat quickly, but I was beyond ready to get inside and drink and dance until I forgot what a shitty week I had.

"How was work?" Sean asked.

"Horrible. Let's not talk about work."

Sean rolled his lip between his teeth. "Why do you stay there if they drain you like this?" He brushed his thumb under my eye, likely seeing the noticeable bags that had become a permanent sign of my exhaustion.

I shrugged, moving up with the line. "Pays the bills."

"Have you tried finding something else yet?"

I shook my head. "Not yet."

The line moved up again, and the bouncers flirted a little before letting us inside. The club's lighting was themed red tonight. The small club was crowded but nowhere near capacity. Sometimes, it was wall-to-wall bodies and impossible to move without rubbing against someone else.

Along the back wall near the exit sign, the DJ booth blasted some of the best music I'd heard mixed at a club. The guy was an amazing DJ, and on more than one occasion, I had flirted with him. The DJ had his shirt off and a drink in his hand while dancing with one of the club's gogo dancers.

Sean snaked his hand around my waist and leaned close. "Want a drink?" he shouted over the music.

I shook my head. "I need a hard body to grind on," I said before weaving into the center of the crowd.

Sean followed me, settling in with me at the center of the mass. I slid my hands over Sean's chest as we danced, knowing neither of us would ever go past mild flirting.

It didn't take long for hands to touch me, pulling me against a firm chest. I went with it, letting whoever it was explore my body. If I was going to make it through Ash's birthday party tomorrow, I needed to release my pent-up sexual frustration now. I didn't care who with.

More often than not, I would call Leo, my friend-with-benefits, when I needed a release. Sean introduced us in college, and Leo was the only person in this world who knew about my feelings for Ash—not on purpose. I was wasted one night at a fraternity party with Leo, Sean, and a few of our friends. When I barely knew where I was, I almost called Ash to confess my feelings. Leo had stopped me. *Thank God.* But that night led to us complicating our friendship with sex. He knew I would never give him anything more than the physical, and I appreciated his presence.

Another guy slid between me and Sean, sliding his thigh between my legs. I tugged him closer while grinding against the man behind me.

This one was hot. Broad shoulders. Dark hair. Firm hands full of confidence roaming over my body.

I danced with them like that for a while before leaning close to the guy with his thigh between my legs and said, "Wanna take this to a hotel?"

Ash dug through his closet for "the perfect shirt" while I leaned against the doorframe, admiring his back muscles moving beneath his tattoos.

"You know," I said, adding a little bite of annoyance to my tone, "you had days to find this shirt."

Ash huffed something from the closet.

"I can't hear you through your pile of shit."

He stepped back from the closet with a midnight blue button-down in his hand and spun toward me, giving me a nice view of his sculpted chest and that sexy V that made me want to lick him from head to toe. He shoved an arm into the shirt with a scowl.

"I put the shirt in the spot for safekeeping. I can't help that I forgot where that safe keeping was," he grumbled, shoving his other arm into the shirt before starting on the buttons.

"You literally have a whole closet where it could've been hung up, and you chose to fold it and stuff it somewhere that wasn't hanging where it should."

He shrugged, rolling the sleeves up to his elbows, and I had to stop myself from biting my lip.

"If I didn't hide it from myself, I may have worn it before tonight." He smoothed the collar and added, "I like this shirt."

I scoffed, waving him off before slipping into the hallway toward his kitchen. "Whatever, Ash. Now we're late to your own party."

I tried pretending to be angry, but really, I enjoyed messing with him.

He came up behind me, wrapping his arm over my shoulder and under my chin. His lips drew close to my ear, sending goosebumps racing down my arms. "Tell me we're ordering a ride, and you're drinking with me tonight."

"I wasn't planning on it."

"Come on, Sammy. Get trashed with me. Please?"

17

I rolled my bottom lip between my teeth and pulled out of Ash's hold. "Fine, but I'm not getting trashed. That's all you."

He spun around me with a smile, strands of his long hair falling out of his bun. "I'm sure I'll get a few drinks in you to loosen up those tense shoulders of yours." His hands landed on my shoulders, and he flashed a mischievous grin. "I might even get you on the dancefloor tonight. Request from your bestie on his birthday and all. Can't deny me tonight, Sammy."

I can never deny you.

He pulled his phone from his pocket and tapped the screen as he walked to the living room and plopped on the couch.

"Our ride will be here in ten minutes," he announced.

Nearly an hour later, we stood at the entrance to a club in DC. I hovered near Ash as he spoke with the bouncer. Regular clubs weren't my scene, and Ash didn't know about my weekly trips to the local gay clubs. I chewed my lip, scanning the line of women dressed in skimpy outfits and men dressed a lot like Ash. I followed their dress code, but this wasn't me. I liked to be more sexy when I went clubbing, and this stupid black button-down was not what I would call sexy. At least on me. No, I was more of a crop top kind of guy. Not that I had ever let Ash see that side of me. He knew I was gay, but I didn't think he would appreciate the side of me I let out at the club.

"Thanks, man," Ash said, letting the guy manning the entrance stamp his hand before he did the same to me. "Let's go, Sammy." Ash winked and stepped through the doors.

Swampy humidity and the booming bass of the club hit me. We were barely inside when women gave us both looks that screamed, "You look like a snack I want to take home." Ash came to this place a lot, so I followed him to the VIP area he'd reserved for the night. I had offered to pay for it since today was his birthday, but he had refused.

It had been a while since I hung out with Ash at a club or even a bar. With work and my own plans with friends, I'd been avoiding coming with him to places like this. I knew he didn't mean anything by it when he invited me to these places, but he didn't understand that there was nothing for me there.

The VIP area was on a platform that overlooked the dance floor. The DJ booth was in perfect view, and the bar was clear across the building. In the sitting area Ash had reserved for us, Jasmine and Joe were already there. Jaz's hair was long, reaching her waist, and split down the middle. One side was orange and the other black. Joe was an average-looking guy that Ash and I met a few years ago through Jaz. The two were Ash's only friends other than me and his gaming friends he'd met online.

"Ash!" Jaz hopped off the black leather couch and leaped into Ash's arms.

His chuckle was deep and husky, sending needy chills down my spine. "How's my little demon?" he asked, setting her on her feet.

"What's up, guys," Joe shouted over the music, leaning forward to bump fists with us as we sat.

Ash sat close beside me, slinging his arm over the back cushion behind my head. He leaned forward, grabbing a menu from the glass table, pressing his leg tight against mine. He always did this. He was always touchy and closer than anyone ever dared to get. It was to the point that I didn't think he noticed he did it.

"How long have you guys been here?" Ash asked, keeping his voice loud to reach over the music, then flipped open the menu.

Jaz shrugged and shouted, "Like thirty minutes."

Joe said, "We should've known you'd be late to your own party. Damn, asshole."

Ash laughed it off and tossed the menu onto the glass table. "I don't know why I ever look at these menus. I just want a damn whiskey."

"Sometimes I think you're a country boy," Joe said, aiming a grin at Ash.

"Yeah, yeah. Whatever," Ash said. "Maybe it's the blood of my people." He snorted. "Take the family out of the country, but can't take the country out of the family."

Jaz aimed a questioning look our way. "Country?"

Ash shrugged. "According to my mom, her mom was born and raised in Kentucky. We still have family there, but we don't talk to them."

"That ain't how it works," Joe said. "Ash over here trying to make excuses for his drinking habits."

I rolled my eyes, putting on a smile, but the way Ash's leg tensed against mine at the comment made me worried. Sure, Ash indulged in alcohol occasionally, but he was always careful. His dad was a raging alcoholic with a horrific temper. Ash's biggest fear was being exactly like him. But Ash also liked to indulge and escape into the freedom he felt when drunk.

I always worried about him, but he was anything but violent when drunk. If anything, he would get clingy and flirty. There was always a point where he would be so gone that he would flirt with anyone willing to give him attention. I avoided going out with him because of his overt flirtation and lack of filter. Often, he'd direct his flirting toward me. The number of times I almost kissed him. . . Almost confessed my feelings for him. The times he would touch me openly in a way that felt like more than a friend ever would dare.

Then there were the times when I had to witness him pick up women. He would leave me to run off to a hotel or a bathroom, then come back disheveled, and I would have the constant reminder that he would never do that with *me*.

The only way for me to deal with it was to treat him like a child. I would turn off my feelings, hide my emotions deep in my heart, and pretend I felt nothing.

Chapter 3

Ash

"Thanks," Sam said, climbing out of the backseat of the rideshare. "Come on, Ash." He reached in, grabbing my hand to tug me from the car.

The world spun as I stood, and I fell against Sam. "Shit, Sammy, how much did I drink?" I slung my arm over his shoulder.

"Too much." He slid his fingers around my wrist, which hung over his shoulder, before wrapping his arm around my waist. "Let's get you to bed."

There was a joke to be made there, but every time I made gay jokes with Sam, he would get this look like his feelings were hurt. I didn't want to do that to him tonight. It was the first time in weeks, maybe months, that he came out with me. He always made excuses for why, but it felt like he was pulling away from me. Maybe it was his job, like he said, but I knew he went out with his friend Sean almost every weekend. The dummy forgot he shared his location on his phone with me. I kept it quiet. I wanted him to tell me, but it had been a year since he started brushing me off to go out with Sean instead.

I tripped into the elevator, laughing at the glare Sam aimed at me while he hit the button for my floor. "Calm down, Sammy. No need to get your panties in a twist."

"My panties are fine. How do you let yourself get this drunk?"

I hushed him, then the elevator jerked, climbing the floors. "It's my birthday, bro. No need to ruin the fun. Ya damn fun killer."

"I'm not a fun killer," he grumbled, crossing his arms and leaning against the wall.

"If you say so," I said as the elevator came to a stop and the doors slid open.

"You're such a dick." Sam shoved me against the wall and hurried toward my apartment door, disappearing without looking back.

The hallway spun with each step I took. When I reached my door, I swayed, slowly pushing it open. "I didn't say anything you don't already know." I closed the door, flipping the deadbolt with a loud click.

"Why do you always say shit like that?" Sam called, sounding annoyed and muffled. "Sam, you're so boring. Sam, you're so stiff. Sam, why don't you relax?" he mocked. I slid my fingers along the wall, finding my way down the dark hallway to my bedroom, where the nightstand light was on and the water in the bathroom was running. "Always with the same fucking shit." Another grumble of something came from the bathroom, and I leaned against the doorway. "Fucking fun killer, my ass. One of us has to be responsible enough to keep you alive."

I shoved my hand in my front pocket. "You done?"

"Maybe," he huffed, wiping his hands on the hand towel hanging over the toilet.

"You know, I'm a big boy, Sammy."

He brushed past me, walking into my bedroom.

I turned, following him. "I can take care of myself," I added.

He flipped the side table light off and said, "Fine. Do it all yourself. Glad you had a good time."

I kicked my shoes off, stifling my laugh.

"Go to bed, Ash. I'll see you tomorrow for the barbeque."

"Sammy," I whispered. He didn't answer and walked toward the door. "Sam." I grabbed his arm and tugged him back, pushing him onto the bed. "Come on. Stay with me."

"No."

I rolled my eyes, knowing he couldn't see, but the sentiment was there. "Shut up, Sammy. I like it when you're around."

I climbed onto the bed and yanked him down beside me.

"How drunk are you actually, Ash?"

I shrugged. "I don't know. The room is spinning, so drunk enough," I replied, snuggling against him. "Sleep here tonight. It's late."

"I literally live two floors up. I want to go sleep in my own bed."

I rested my arm over his chest, feeling it rise and fall with each breath. "I don't want to sleep alone tonight. Stay with me." I tightened my hold on him. "Please," I whispered.

"Fine, but you're driving home tomorrow. I don't feel like driving."

I chuckled, burying my face in the space between his shoulder and the pillow. "Deal."

Mom and Angie were in the kitchen chopping vegetables. The French doors leading to the backyard were open, and the smell of the grill floated through the air.

Angie was nineteen and a sophomore in college. She and I looked like twins, except her eyes were dark, like Mom's. Mine were more golden brown. We all shared the same wavy black hair and high cheekbones. Sam always said we looked like clones of Mom, but I couldn't help seeing my dad in us. It was the little things. My hands, eyes, facial features. Even my body type looked like him, and I hated it.

I covered myself in tattoos to cover up the skin that reminded me of him every time I looked in the mirror, but it wasn't enough. I could see it anyway.

My father was why I learned to fight. I knew enough to get out of almost any situation. I worked hard to build my muscles. Since middle school, I would work out until my body gave out. I never wanted to be in a position where I was weak again.

I'd used my skills too many times to count.

Sam had been a scrawny kid. He faced a lot of bullying when we were young. So, I became his shield the same way he rooted me to the earth.

Angie stepped around the kitchen island, wrapping her slender arms around my waist.

"Hi, piglet," I said, giving her a squeeze before releasing her.

Angie used to be obsessed with Piglet from *Winnie-the-Pooh*. For five years straight, she dressed as Piglet for Halloween. She collected anything pig-related until she was twelve. There was a time when her entire bed was covered in creepy pink pigs. Sam and I had teased her by calling her Piglet, but it turned into an affectionate pet name over the years.

Angie moved to Sam, wrapping him in a tight hug as I gave Mom a kiss.

"What's for dinner tonight? Smells like barbeque," I said with a joking tone.

"Like you don't know," Sam murmured.

I chuckled, pinching his chest, barely missing his nipple as he shoved me away. His smile lit me up as he continued pushing me through the open doors leading to the deck.

"Dad," Sam called. "Come help me beat this shit-head up."

"Oh, come on, Sammy." I hopped backward, away from him, across the deck. "I didn't even do anything."

Mom and Angie's laughs from the kitchen only fueled Sam as he got a look in his eye like he was about to chase me for real. I wasn't a runner. Compared to Sam, I was slow as shit. I built my body for strength; he was built for speed.

"Fuck, Sammy. Come on. I'm hungry. I don't wanna fuck around."

His eyebrow raised as he hiked up his basketball shorts over his knees. "Should've thought about that before you tried to fucking twist my nipple."

"Boys," Gary warned from beside the grill, "not over here."

I reached into my pocket, grabbing my phone, and said, "Heads up, Gary." Then I tossed my phone at him, praying he caught it, and darted across the deck, leaping over the steps into the grass.

I made it less than ten feet from the deck when Sam's hands clamped around my hips, latching onto my shirt. I hit the ground as his body slammed into me. His arm came around my neck, locking me in a chokehold as he straddled my back.

"Don't kill him," Gary said, returning to humming some random tune while tending the grill.

I grunted, trying to buck Sam off.

"What was that, Ash?" Sam squeezed harder, cutting off my air completely. "Can't breathe?"

I shifted my knee, finally getting enough leverage, and rolled, throwing Sam onto his back, but he only wrapped his legs around my waist and clung to me like cling wrap sticking to itself.

Sam grunted, squeezing tighter. I was nearing my limit, but I didn't want to let him win.

"Come on, Ash. Give up." His forearm loosened enough to let me suck in a breath, and I rolled us again, fighting to get him off me. "Promise no more purple nurples. Promise, or you pass out."

Sam should be thanking me for even teaching him these fucking moves. All those years of watching wrestling and mixed martial arts, practicing on each other, finally backfired on me.

I struggled against his hold, bucking and kicking. When I shifted enough to get another breath of air, I said, "Fuck you." I sucked in another breath, ready for this to continue until I actually passed out.

"Samuel," Mom yelled from the edge of the deck. "Let him go. You two aren't fifteen." She stormed off. "Fucking children. Grown-ass men acting like children!"

"Come on, Ash," Sam grunted. "Promise you won't do it again, and I'll let go. I can sit here all day."

"I raised goddamn children," Mom yelled from inside the house. "Spray them with the hose in thirty seconds if they haven't stopped."

I pushed back, forcing Sam's face to the grass, and he broke into laughter, giving me the moment I needed to slip out of his grip. I scurried back, ready to fight, but he kept laughing, not bothering to chase me.

"Jerk. Choking me out over a failed purple nurple is fuckin' crazy."

He sat up, brushing the dirt off his hands. "A twenty-five-year-old man trying to give me a purple nurple is even more crazy."

"Whatever," I grumbled. "Truce for now. I really don't want to get hit with the hose."

"Did they stop?" Mom yelled, muffled by the distance from the kitchen.

Gary chuckled. "Sure did, honey. They're like cats, afraid of the water."

Sam ripped up a handful of grass and tossed it at me. "Now I'm all dirty. Thanks for that."

I shrugged and flopped back, staring up at the sky. "Remember when we used to lay out here in the summer?"

He crawled over to me and rolled onto his back. "Yeah. Feels like it was forever ago."

25

"Do you ever wish we could go back with the knowledge we have now?"

Sam shook his head. "I'd never want to go back. If I did, we'd both have to deal with *them*."

"What if we could kill them off and then go back?"

He chewed on his lip for a second before looking at me. "Sometimes, yeah. I wonder what we could change and how it would shape us." We stared at each other for a moment before he continued, "But then I wouldn't be me anymore."

"Shit, I like *you*." I reached over and ruffled his hair. "I wouldn't want this Sam to disappear."

His smile seemed sad as he replied, "Same."

Chapter 4

Sam

Laying next to Ash in the grass, talking about going back to our past with the knowledge we had now, was weird. There were times I had wished my feelings for him away. Or for a way to change the past, but ultimately, our lives shaped us into the people we were, and I would never want to change that. I loved *him*, with all the good and bad that came with it. But my love for him was ruining me with each passing day.

I needed to squash those feelings.

I couldn't be his lover, but I could be everything else. Everything else would have to be enough.

As we lay there in the grass, staring up at the clear sky of the May afternoon, I promised myself I would move on from Ash. I would find someone to love. I would put my love for Ash away in a box and seal it because days like this, when we were with our family, sharing space, time, and memories, I needed to have this for the rest of my life.

Ash turned twenty-five last night, and I wasn't far behind him. We were on our way to thirty, the big three-o. It was time for me to move past a love that was going nowhere. Find someone who would love me back the way I needed.

I tried to fight off the frown replacing my smile, but I couldn't. When I looked at Ash lazily gazing up at the sky with a wide grin, my heart cracked into a million pieces at the thought of finding someone else. Ash knew me in ways no one else could possibly know.

I didn't want to give him up. I wanted to continue loving him forever.

"Burgers and steaks are ready," Dad said from the deck a few feet away, interrupting my internal collapse.

"Coming," I choked and shoved Ash's shoulder. "Get up, asshole."

He rubbed his arm. "Hey, what did I do?"

I chuckled and said, "Breathed." I hopped to my feet, brushing grass and dirt from my legs before jogging up the stairs to meet Dad on the deck.

Dad set a plate of burgers on the table directly beside a pile of thick, juicy-looking ribeye steaks. I licked my lips, mouth watering at the sight.

"You've done it again, Gary. Perfect as always," Ash said, brushing past me before dropping into a chair. "Ma, Angie, hurry up. Food's ready." He rubbed his hands together like he was about to feast.

I snorted and sat beside him. "Dad, feed him last."

"You all have hands. I'm not feeding anyone," Dad said, setting his expression in a fake stern glare.

"Very funny," I rolled my eyes as Jane and Angie appeared from the kitchen with bowls of sides and a huge, overflowing salad.

We sat around the table like we did every Sunday, catching each other up on our lives. Ash complained about his job and how he didn't think he would be getting any recognition for training Nini at work.

It was loud. Comfortable.

I hoped no one noticed the shift in my mood. I was good at hiding my emotions. A life full of pretending to be okay was good for something. But my heart was weeping, knowing I needed to take a step back from Ash.

My phone dinged in my pocket, and I lazily fished it out while listening to Angie talk about school.

My friend, Selena, had texted me.

Selena: You still going to Ace on Friday for Rain's party?

I smiled, shooting her a quick reply.

Me: Yep. Also, you know she totally has a crush on you. I think you should go for it.

She was fast with her response, and I smiled.

Selena: Gurl. You serious? I've been too scared she'd tell me to fuck off, and it would ruin our whole group dynamic.

Me: I swear on my life! That girl has googly eyes for you.

Me: Go for it on Friday. Promise me you'll take the chance.

When she finally replied, my heart leaped.

Selena: Okay. But if it goes to shit, it's your fault.

I knew it wouldn't.

She'd get the girl.

My jealousy bubbled up, burning my chest and the back of my throat as it climbed into my mind.

I missed my chance, and I regretted it every day.

Friday arrived in a whirlwind. I walked through the bar five minutes late, thanks to traffic. The bar was packed, but I spotted Sean and Rainie at a long rectangular table off to the side. Rainie wore a tight black dress and heels. Her cute bob was curled to perfection, and her makeup was flawlessly executed, boasting a captivating smokey eye. Sean looked sharp in his sleek black button-up and slacks; his maroon tie loosely hung around his neck. He must have come right after work as well.

The three of us had been friends since college; I would call us an odd trio. Rainie was a tiny little thing I could only call a feminine tomboy. She was conventionally gorgeous, with a sultry air about her, but damn if she wouldn't sucker punch you the moment you pissed her off. One day, we crossed paths on campus, and from there, we gravitated together.

They had already ordered a round of drinks, and fresh faces I had never met before crowded around the end of the table.

When Rainie noticed my approach, she rushed to me. "I'm glad you made it. I think you'll be interested in a couple of guys I invited tonight." She spun around, grabbed my hand, and dragged me to the table. "Everyone, this is my friend Sam," she announced, then left me to mingle with the new group.

One of the guys was cute enough, but I needed alcohol before I did anything else. I scanned the table, looking over each option Rainie had ordered, then grabbed one at random before sitting beside Sean and taking a swig of the fiery liquid.

"Sam," Sean said with a nod. "Haven't seen you in a few days. Everything okay?"

Before answering, I took another gulp, letting the alcohol coat my throat, and said, "Work was hectic this week."

Ignoring talk of work like I had asked the week prior, he eyed the table before leaning closer to whisper, "You thinking of taking one of those guys home with you? That guy on the end has been looking at you since you arrived."

I glanced at the man Sean was talking about. He was tall, had broad shoulders, dark hair, and a stern expression.

He was my type.

"I'll think about it," I said, then took a sip of my drink. "Is Leo coming tonight?"

Sean shook his head. "He had something else planned before Rain invited him. He said he'd come out with us next time to make up for missing tonight."

If Leo wouldn't be here, then I didn't need to worry about who I flirted with. And I definitely wouldn't feel bad for taking someone else home.

We fell into a simple conversation about our week. A few minutes later, a slender hand came over my shoulder, followed by a kiss on the cheek.

"Hi, love," Selena said. Her deep brown eyes shimmered as she came around and sat on my lap. "Thank you for inviting me."

"No problem," I said, holding her waist. "Rain is here too. She's been mingling."

Her long, silky black hair brushed over my hand as she twisted, looking for Rainie.

"I'll have to steal her away from them then," Selena said, hopping off my lap, heading toward Rainie.

I was on my third drink when a familiar face approached the table. Her hair was split down the middle. One side was dyed orange and the other black. Her small, round eyes landed on me with surprise.

"Jaz?" I set my drink on the table, standing to greet her.

"What are you doing here?" Jasmine asked as she came in for a hug.

"Wait," Rainie said, approaching us. "You know each other?"

I nodded and asked, "But how do you two know each other?"

"Work," Jaz said and turned her attention to Rainie.

Work? I knew Rainie had gotten a new job but didn't know it was at Pix Systems.

"Sam?" the familiar, honeyed voice tickled my ears.

I spun around, meeting Ash's cat-like gaze. Ink-black wavy bangs fell into his eyes, shadowing the beautiful champagne brown staring back at me. His hair was cut shorter than I had ever seen, styled messily into an angular fringe that faded into the sides. He wore a plain black T-shirt and form-fitting jeans. His face was clean-shaven, missing the stubble he typically kept. It gave a clear view of the scar above his lip, just under his nose, where I accidentally head-butted him in fourth grade. A stupid wrestling match turned into an emergency room visit and a lifelong scar.

"What a small world." Ash hooked his arm around my shoulder and hung off me. "You know Sammy?" he asked Rainie.

Guilt hit me. I had kept Rainie hidden from Ash because he would've tried to hook up with her, and I didn't want to see him turn on his charm like that for my friend. Since Ash and I didn't go to the same university and Rainie mostly hung out with me on her 'ladies' nights' or at gay bars, I managed to keep her away from Ash.

Rainie was bisexual but tended to prefer women, so Ash didn't have much of a chance, but there was still a chance. The last thing I ever wanted was for Ash to hook up with one of my friends.

"We went to college together," Rainie said as everyone huddled around the two of us.

"Sam and I have been best friends since we were kids. How come he never introduced us?" Ash gently bumped the side of his head against mine. He shrugged but kept hold of me. His hand rested under my chin, and the heat of his skin melted me, turning me pliant against him. "What can a guy do to get a drink around here?"

"Here," Sean said, handing Ash a glass and bumping his fist. "Been a while."

Ash released me and settled into the group effortlessly like a chameleon.

He sat beside me, chatting up the table and openly flirting with Rainie. He had been talking to me about a woman he was interested in at work, and now it all clicked. It was too bad she had a crush on Selena, and the pair were likely getting together tonight since I told Selena to go for it. Ash wouldn't care. He jumped between women like he changed clothes.

The few times he'd been in relationships, it never lasted long. His exes always said the same thing when they broke up: they felt he didn't care about them.

The one time I asked him about it, he told me they were correct. He didn't feel anything toward them. I was vaguely aware that he talked to his many therapists about it, but he mentioned nothing to me. I thought it had to do with his dad or his parents, but I couldn't be positive. I could understand if he was afraid of committing to someone because he witnessed his parents's marriage fall apart, resulting in divorce coupled with his father's abusive tendencies.

I wasn't shocked when he stopped dating and moved to meaningless hookups. I couldn't judge him. I was the same way. Divorce, abuse, and then there was the tiny little fact that I could never date anyone seriously when I was in love with him, so I kept to nameless hookups and dating apps.

I reached across the table for a shot glass in the center. When my fingers touched the glass, Ash beamed at me.

"We doing shots, Sammy?"

"Like we used to?"

Ash grabbed a glass and clinked it against mine. "Bottoms up." He threw it back, then slammed the glass on the table.

I gulped mine down, then grabbed another from the center.

I hadn't planned to get shit-faced, but I wasn't prepared for Ash to be here. Not tonight. I needed something to settle my nerves.

Chapter 5

Ash

Three hours in, I was trashed. Smashed? Inebriated. Intoxicated. Whatever the word for it, I was it. I'd lost count of how many drinks I'd had.

To say I was shocked to see Sam at the bar was the understatement of a lifetime. The other day, he had mentioned going out Friday night, but I didn't expect we would end up at the same place because of the same person. It surprised me to find that he knew Rainie, and he not only knew her but also went to college with her. They were close friends. I couldn't get over him keeping her from me. I knew all of his friends, or so I thought. There was this nagging feeling that he was hiding a part of himself from me. We knew everything about each other. Everything. Right?

I couldn't remember the last time Sam and I drank together like this. My birthday last week didn't count. He barely even drank that night. Jobs and responsibilities had taken over most of our days. We were usually exhausted when we had time to spend together. He'd often go out with his friends and leave me to play my games alone. I was never invited to nights like this. Was he with this group all those times he'd gone out without me? A wave of unease tugged at the back of my mind. I couldn't be sure he was pulling away from me, but I had a feeling that I couldn't explain.

Rainie jumped out of her chair, pointed her finger at everyone down the table, and announced, "We're gonna play Truth or Dare!"

The last time I played a game of Truth or Dare, I was fifteen, and Sam and I were at a friend's birthday party. The extent of the fun was seeing if one of us was brave enough to steal a bottle of alcohol and bring it back to the bedroom without getting caught by his parents. None of us were, but one kid left the room and made it to the top of the stairs before chickening out.

As dumb as I found this, this was my chance to flirt with Rainie. I even cut my hair and shaved for tonight. I had held in my laughter when Sam saw me. I never thought I could make someone's jaw drop, but I would never forget it.

I hoped our parents and Angie would react the same on Sunday at our family dinner. Mom had wanted me to chop off my hair for years. Who would've thought all it would take to convince me was for Jaz to tell me I would look better with short hair, which might interest Rainie?

A little crazy? Maybe.

The game of Truth or Dare started quickly, and I laughed as people answered their truths, and one guy completed his dare to flirt with the bartender. He was rejected instantly and still had to pay his tab.

"Sam," Rainie yelled, pointing at him.

"Rain," Sam yelled back at her.

"Truth," she slurred, "or dare?"

Sam rubbed his hand over his face, then said, "Truth."

"Did you come here tonight intending to kiss someone?"

He replied, "I did."

"Naughty." She giggled, then turned her attention to me. "Ashton." She giggled again. "Truth or dare?"

"Truth," I said. I was never one for the dare portion of the game.

"Are you really bi? Jaz said you're bi, but I don't believe her."

I side-eyed Jaz before looking back at Rainie.

"Bi?" Sam whispered beside me. "What are they talking about?"

"Yes," I said quickly, wanting this to pass. When it was my turn again, I would pick Dare instead.

Rainie went around the table, and everyone kept up the fun of the game, but Sam stared at me, not even trying to hide it. His eyes drilled holes into the side of my face, but I didn't want to look at him. We both hated liars and telling people I was bi was one of the worst sins in his eyes.

"Sam," Rainie said, and Sam yanked his attention away from me. "Truth or dare?"

"Truth."

She took a moment to think about her question, then said, "How long have you and Ashton known each other?"

He shook his head before replying, "I don't know. Around twenty years."

She let out a whistle before looking at me. "Ashton, truth or dare."

"Dare."

I wasn't risking the truth questions again.

Rainie leaned over the table and grabbed my face with her tiny hand. "Prove it."

"What do you mean?" I asked.

"Prove it," she said again like that somehow cleared up the confusion. "Kiss a guy." She fell back on her heels and plopped into her chair, waving her arms at everyone around us. "Lots of men to choose from."

"You want me to kiss a guy for my dare?"

I glared at Jaz, and she only returned a smile. She was getting an earful later.

"Yep," Rainie said, popping the P. "Kiss a guy."

I looked around the table, eyeing everyone. I didn't know any of them, except Sean and Sam. Both of them were gay, but Sean and I would be awkward. I didn't know him well. Not enough to randomly cross that line.

Wait, am I taking this seriously? I'm gonna kiss a guy to keep up this stupid lie?

If I backed out now, Rainie would know I lied, and that would make work awkward as fuck. What was a small kiss? I could do it.

"I'm waiting." Rainie started counting down from ten, folding her arms with a smirk.

My eyes settled on Sam, and in the moment I took to think about it, he visibly shrank away from me.

"Eight," Rainie announced.

"Ash," Sam said, "absolutely not."

"C'mere, bro. It's only a kiss," I said, grabbing his arm and pulling him to me.

"I won't," Sam said, and he actually scowled at me.

"Six," Rainie said.

Sam's face flushed to a bright red. His pale eyes grew dark, forehead wrinkling from his disapproving glare. I didn't think I had ever seen him look at me like that. Like he wanted to fight me for real.

I couldn't get enough of it. That fiery look in his eyes.

Something about it made my chest flutter, and I itched to get closer. I wanted more of that look. That deep—something. It made me want to rile him up.

"One kiss," I whispered, leaning in close to him. "No harm. It's a kiss."

"Four," Rainie yelled.

"Ash," Sam said my name with warning.

"What's the big deal? It's not like we're making out."

"Two."

I cupped the back of his head and leaned in.

Sam's breath hitched the moment I pressed my lips to his.

Warmth spread over my body, like Sam's lips had set me on fire. He was soft. The smell of alcohol tickled my nose—a little sweet. I didn't mind it in the least. In fact, I would do it again, and that thought made me nervous.

I broke the kiss, pulling away only a breath, and opened my eyes. Sam stared back at me like he wanted to punch me and hug me all at once.

My chest clenched around my heart.

I was a mess of guilt.

I knew I shouldn't have done it, but who else would I have kissed?

My fingers tightened against his scalp. I had an overwhelming desire to kiss him again. To kiss him for real.

His breath rushed over my skin, drawing my attention to his lips. His smell surrounded me: spice mixed with woodsy sweetness. A smell I had known nearly my entire life, but now it was different. It was like I saw Sam for the first time. Truly saw him. Felt him. I was experiencing his presence in a way I had never imagined.

When our eyes met again, I couldn't stop myself. I leaned in, my body buzzing with energy. Excitement. *Desire.*

Sam's breath hitched again, and I tugged on his bottom lip with my teeth, begging him to kiss me with each breath. Each touch. I wanted him to kiss me back. I didn't know what took hold of me, but I *needed* him to kiss me back.

Sam's hand pressed on my chest like he thought about pushing me away but couldn't follow through. Then he finally gave in, returning my kiss with equal need. We melted together, sinking into each other. Blended beyond the boundary of anything we'd ever had between us.

Memories of us flashed through my mind.

We were four when I first met him on the playground at our daycare. He had dirt all over his porcelain face. His platinum blond hair reflected the sun, making it look like a halo hovered over him, and I asked him, "Are you an angel?" I thought he was the most beautiful person to grace the Earth. When he jumped off the jungle gym from the spot he had claimed and flashed me a smile, there was no escaping the friendship that blossomed.

Every insignificant moment we shared raced through my mind as our mouths touched. Teeth nipped. Breath mingled. A lifetime of moments. Shared memories. Laughter. Pain. Joy. He had always been there, beside me.

I slid my fingers through his hair, tangling them in the silky strands, and pushed my tongue into his mouth, growing desperate for this connection. For him.

Heat raced through my veins, wiping out every ounce of darkness from my cells. It was like I had finally arrived at the place I had been searching for my whole life.

His fingers found their way into my hair, tugging at the roots. His other hand slid up my chest to my neck, and the sensation sent a wave of tingling warmth from the spot his hand touched.

The only thing that ripped me back to reality was my name falling from Jasmine's lips. The shock in her voice was like a punch to the chest.

Realization hit me like a fucking truck.

I broke away, blinking, only to find Sam, bright red with tears pooling in his eyes. My stomach sank to the center of the Earth, leaving me chilled to the bone with a ball of nerves tumbling in my gut. I had never seen him shed a single tear. Not even when his mom was taken away in handcuffs, so when a tear finally spilled over and rolled down his cheek, it was a knife to the heart.

To top it all off, I had a goddamn boner.

I couldn't believe it. I was so turned on. My body was burning with need. Need for Sam. For my best friend. My stepbrother. The man I'd known my whole life. The only person in this world I had ever shared my deepest, darkest thoughts with. The person who trusted me. Who I trusted with everything I had.

What do I say now?

Words couldn't form in my brain. I stared at him as everything we had crumbled around us. With that single decision, I changed our relationship. There was no going back from that.

"Oh my god," Jaz whispered behind me.

"Now that was a kiss," Rainie yelled.

But Rainie couldn't see the pained expression on Sam's face. She didn't understand that I was a ship in the middle of the ocean, and my anchor just snapped.

I was the world's biggest asshole.

"Sam," I whispered, holding firm to the back of his head, but he pulled away, wiping the tears from his cheeks.

Then he ran from me. Ran. Fucking sprinted.

I rushed after him, tripping over the chairs scattered around the table, following him into the men's bathroom.

"Sam," I yelled, pushing past someone as the end stall slammed shut. "Sammy, talk to me."

"Leave me alone."

His voice broke on the last word. It crushed my heart and left me feeling like everything I knew was evaporating, sliding through my fingers as I desperately tried to hold on. I approached the stall door and pressed my head against the cold metal.

"Sam, listen. I'm so fucking sorry."

"Go away," he said, softer this time.

"Sam, please," I begged. "I didn't mean for that to get out of hand. I'm so sorry."

The door swung open, and I fell through, catching myself on the wall moments before a fist connected with my cheek. Throbbing pain radiated from my face, and my brain tried to catch up with everything.

"Out of hand, my ass," he growled, then kneed me in the stomach.

I coughed and dropped to my knees. I deserved that one. "Fuck," I groaned, scrambling to my feet to chase after him.

Instead of finding Sam, I was met with a scowling Sean and fuming Jasmine inside the men's bathroom.

"Yo," I said, hiding my embarrassment and worry behind my smile. "This is the men's room, Jaz."

"What the hell was that, Ash?" Jaz asked, folding her arms over her chest. "You're brothers."

An awkward chuckle was the only thing to pass my lips before I pushed past them and escaped outside.

I searched the parking lot for Sam's car, but it wasn't there. I wasn't even sure if he had driven there. We were a fifteen-minute run from our apartment complex, so I ran. While running down the streets through the city, I berated myself for my actions, replaying each moment at the bar until I reached our apartment building.

Panting and gasping for air, I stumbled through the doors to our building and dashed to the elevator. I punched the button for his floor and impatiently waited at the doors, catching my breath until they opened.

When the elevator finally released me, I rushed down the hall and skidded to a halt at his door. I knocked at first, but when he didn't answer, I searched my pocket for my keys, then barged into his apartment.

It was dark. Empty. Silent.

He wasn't there.

The bed was warm, and I pulled the comforter over my face, wrapping myself in the comfort of the body beside me. As if it were the most natural thing in the world, I pulled them into my arms and buried my face in their neck, feeling a sense of ease.

"Ash," Sam's voice was muffled under the blanket.

I froze, every muscle in my body tensing.

What do I do? The person is Sam?

When I didn't respond, he rolled and climbed over me.

"G'morning," he said, trailing kisses over my abdomen.

My breath faltered, and I pushed down on his shoulder, trying to shove him away. When he didn't budge, I ripped the blanket off of us.

"What are you doing, Sammy?"

"Nothing," he said, tracing my tattoos with his fingers.

He looked up beneath his pale lashes with a crooked grin, then climbed over me until his face hovered close to mine. I couldn't tear my eyes away, completely engrossed in him. I was wholly unprepared when he pressed his body to mine and rolled his hips. Before I could react, he captured my lips, stealing my breath. His hand slid between us, tugging my boxers down until his fingers slid over my erection. He teased me until I relaxed under his touch. I clung to him, cupping the back of his head, weaving my fingers through his hair.

I wrapped my arms around him, tugging him close. Falling into the sensation of him against me. His weight on top of me. His mouth on mine. I fell into bliss.

Reality punched me awake. Ripped me from the dream that felt far too real. My boxers were wet and sticky. I sucked down a ragged breath, unable to believe what happened.

There was something wrong with me.

I grabbed my phone from the side table and navigated to my messages with Sam, quickly typing the only thing I could think to say.

Me: *I know you're angry. Probably confused as shit. So am I. I really need to talk to you about this.*

Tomorrow was Sunday, our traditional family day. He never missed it. My only hope was that if he didn't speak to me today, we could talk like adults tomorrow.

I tore off my boxers and flung them to the other side of the room. I was mortified. I had a goddamn wet dream about Sam. With a sigh, I scrubbed my hands over my face before rolling back under the covers and tapping Jaz's name on my phone screen. I put the call on speaker and set the phone on my pillow beside my head while I wallowed.

"Where the hell did you go last night?" she asked when she answered.

"Home."

"Ashton, what the fuck were you thinking?"

"I wasn't thinking."

"Your impulsive behavior is going to give me a heart attack."

It was too late. My actions had already done harm. If Sam never spoke to me again, what would I have? Sam was my best friend. My brother. Without him, I'd be lost. He was my rock. My safe place. The person who talked me down when I got too amped up. He was literally *everything* to me. Woven in my memories, my life.

My existence was so jumbled with him. I couldn't picture my life where he wasn't at my side.

Most of the memories I had of my childhood were of him. He was the white light shining through an expanse of darkness—a void of faded and forgotten.

"Have you heard from him?" Jaz asked, her voice calmer.

"No," I groaned into the pillow. "I really fucked up."

"Glad you're aware." She sighed.

"How am I going to fix this?"

She was quiet for a moment before asking, "Can you tell me something?" She paused, letting me sit with myself in the silence. "How did you feel when you kissed him?"

"You want the honest truth?" I dragged in a shaky breath and said, "Really fucking good."

Chapter 6

Sam

Ash texted and called me all night after I left the bar but hadn't contacted me since his last text yesterday morning. He thought I was angry, and maybe I was. I felt used for a split second. It hurt when he thought he could take advantage of me like that. Maybe I would've laughed it off after going along with it if I wasn't in love with him. Or if it had been a *simple* kiss with nothing behind it. But he turned it into more. He really kissed me. There was so much behind that kiss. A tenderness. Desperation.

It was confusing.

Every second of that kiss broke me down and built me back up. It confirmed my belief that Ash was my soulmate in every sense of the word.

After he kissed me, I was so shocked that the only thing I could do was run and hide in the restroom. The plan was to wipe my tears before going back to the party like nothing happened, but then Ash had to go and follow me. It was impossible for him to know why I was so unbelievably upset by that kiss, and I could never tell him.

Tightening my grip on the steering wheel, I turned down the road leading to my parent's house.

The reason I never confessed to him wasn't because I was necessarily afraid of him rejecting me. I always thought there was a fifty-fifty shot he might be into it. I had prepared for that chance before Dad told me he would marry Jane.

Ash thought he was straight, but sometimes, I questioned his claims. My running away from him at the bar wasn't about me and Ash. It wasn't that simple, no matter how much I wished it were. What held me back from trying with him was always our family. The moment our parents planned to marry, I knew I could never have a relationship with him. His sexuality had nothing to do with me as long as our parents made us family. They called him my brother. We were siblings, blood-related or not. Anything intimate and romantic between us would be *wrong*.

I came to terms with it years ago. Now it was his turn.

The smell of fresh-cut grass filled my nose when I pulled onto the long U-shaped driveway. It was a typical two-story ranch-style home with red brick around the garage and the base of the house.

I parked near the garage and ambled along the brick path toward the front door, thinking of ways to avoid Ash without looking suspicious.

Jane and Angie were in the kitchen, giggling with each other. When Angie saw me, she rushed over, wrapping me in a tight hug. Her long, wavy black hair fell around my arms when I leaned in, tugging her close.

"How're you?" she asked, pulling away and returning to the kitchen island, where Jane offered me a bright, welcoming smile.

"Good," I said, moving to Jane, kissing her cheek softly. "Another hectic week at work."

I stood with them for a while. I wasn't ready to face Ash, but after twenty minutes of chatting up my girls, I finally broke away to find Dad.

The TV grew louder when I neared the living room, blasting a news channel interrupted by boisterous laughter every few seconds. I snuck a peek from the corner of the room, taking a moment to appraise the situation before diving in. Dad laughed in his armchair, a beer bottle in hand, and Ash mirrored him with a giant grin and matching beer bottle. Ash only drank beer with my dad. He was too nice to refuse it.

Ash's eyes locked on me, and I stiffened, scared of moving another inch. The look in his eyes made me want to run away again. Something in them reached out to me and sent a shiver down my spine.

"I'll be right back, Gary," Ash said, setting the beer bottle on the side table before stalking toward me.

Dad turned, looking at us over his shoulder, and said, "Hey, Sam," before returning his attention to the screen, which had started showing a sports recap.

Before I could get a word out, Ash pointed at me as he drew closer, growl-ing, "You,"—then he pointed at his chest—"and me. Right now." He grabbed my wrist and yanked me into the hallway, dragging me up the stairs. He didn't let up and held on hard enough that I thought my wrist might bruise.

"Ash," I said, pleading with him to leave it alone, "not here."

"You won't talk to me anywhere else."

He tugged me down the hallway to his childhood bedroom. Once through the threshold, he slammed the door shut and locked it.

My heart beat erratically, pumping adrenaline-infused blood through my veins like a shot of acid.

"Ash," I said, my voice trembling.

A chill ran through me as memories of my mother came rushing back. Mom never beat me. I was lucky, but she sure knew how to hurt me in every other way that didn't leave visible bruises. Her favorite punishment was confinement. A child prisoner, locked away at her will. She would yell at me, degrading me until I was in tears. Her words, every last one, were meant to cut me deep. Meant to tell me how unwanted I was. How inconvenient I was. How disobedient I was. She would say those things to me as she gripped my arm, dragging me through the house to my bedroom. Then she would toss me inside and lock me in. It was the same every time; she wouldn't let me out until her mood settled. Sometimes, I was in my room for days before she finally released me.

Dad was always working or away on business trips, so he didn't know. And when he was home, Mom would be a different person. Happy, smiling, and loving. She would dote on me in front of him like any normal mother, but our house was a living hell when Dad left for work. The only reprieve from it was school, but at school, I had different bullies. It wasn't until I was ten that Dad finally found out about the abuse.

It was all thanks to the angry, beautiful man standing in front of me. Ash had always protected me. He would risk suspension and punishment to protect me from bullies at school, but he could never save me from *her*.

Until he did.

Mom had locked me away in my room the night before it all blew up. Her excuse that night was that I made a face when I ate the food she made. When I never came to school, Ash knew something was wrong.

That day, he snuck out of school, running nearly three miles to my house.

Why he chose to come to my house that day was a mystery. All Ash had said was, "I had a bad feeling and needed to make sure you were okay."

From my bedroom, I could hear them arguing. Mom yelled at him, cussing him out like he wasn't a child. When she came at him, Ash blew up back at her, calling her names. He was well aware of what she did to me, as much as I was aware of the reason for his broken arm months before.

My window faced the street, and I could see my front yard, but the view of the front door was out of sight, blocked by the roof over the porch. My heart sank into my stomach when Ash fell to the grass, thrown into view where I could see everything. Mom had shoved him away when he wouldn't leave. He yelled something at her. Whatever it was made her angrier than I had ever seen. She rushed him, yanked him up by the front of his shirt, and slapped him so hard I could feel the sting myself. Ash smiled, and it only infuriated her more. That was when the punches hit him. But Ash let her do it with a massive smile as if he didn't feel anything.

Mom didn't let up until the cops swarmed the house and yanked her off of him.

Because Mom beat Ash until his face was bloodied and his body bruised, the authorities discovered his own abuse suffered at the hands of his father. Because he was willing to sacrifice himself, he saved me and ultimately saved Jane and Angie from his father.

Ash was my hero.

"Fuck, I'm sorry, Sammy," he said, pulling me back to the present.

Ash's eyes softened, and his mouth turned down. Then he looked between me and the door. He ran his fingers through his hair with a sigh, his shoulders sagging as he quickly unlocked the door.

I bit my lip, wanting to thank him, but the words wouldn't come out. The tightness in my throat locked my voice away.

He dragged his palms down his face with a heavy sigh, then said, "I can't do anything right." He walked up to me and hugged me tight, resting his chin on my shoulder and rubbing his hands over my back. "I didn't mean to. That's my fault."

He held me until the memories faded. Until I could climb out of that dark pit.

"Look, Sam," he whispered, running his fingers through my hair, "I know what I did Friday night was fucked up. Please talk to me about it."

"It was nothing." I breathed the words into existence, wanting to make them true.

His breath caught, and he pulled back, eyes locked on me like I'd ripped his heart from his chest and stomped on it.

"What if I told you it was everything?" he said with a waver in his voice, breaking up that honeyed tone I loved.

Oh, God. If only our situation were different.

"You know nothing can come of it," I replied.

"It's all I've been thinking about since."

I shook my head, wishing it didn't have to be this way. "You're my brother," I whispered, the sting of tears prickling at the back of my eyes.

"By marriage, Sam. We aren't real brothers."

I shook my head again. "I won't cross that line with you and our family."

He breathed a weird grunt as he stepped back, releasing me from his hug. From his touch.

"And if I want to cross that line?"

"No. We are brothers, and that's the end of it. I will not be the cause of our family falling apart."

I clenched my jaw, wishing I didn't have to say these things. Wishing I didn't need to be the bad guy. I wanted more than anything to accept what he was saying. To let it happen.

He looked at me, wounded, with tears in his eyes.

"Do you think our family would fall apart because of this?"

I nodded. "The fact that you don't amazes me. You can be so impulsive sometimes."

"You can be too responsible and uptight sometimes," Ash snapped.

"Well, you aren't changing my mind on this. We're going to pretend Friday never happened," I said, walking past him with as much fake courage as I could pump through my chest. "We will return to normal and never speak of this again."

I looked back at him, hoping he understood I meant it. Looking back did nothing but crush my already fractured heart.

He wiped a tear from his cheek and nodded. His head was low, and his shoulders slumped forward. "Got it, Sam. I got it. Give me a minute," he whispered.

My chest clenched. I turned away and walked out of his room. I knew then that our relationship was irrevocably changed.

We would never be the same again.

Dinner was quiet. Ash was silent. His bright smiles and deep laughter that usually lit up his scornful glare were missing, and everyone noticed.

I tried to detract from it with stories about my week at work, but it didn't help.

Finally, halfway through our meal, Dad spoke up. "Ash, is everything okay?" Dad asked, leaning back in the chair and pushing his plate away from the edge of the table. "You seem down."

Ash looked up from his half-eaten plate of food and set his fork down. The anguish on his face was unmistakable, and his eyes shimmered with the threat of tears like they would pour over at any moment.

"Have you ever been in love with someone you can't have?" Ash asked, staring at his plate.

Dad leaned forward, confused and probably as shocked as I was. Ash had never used "love" when discussing anyone outside this household.

Angie grabbed his hand from the other side of the table and asked, "Are you in love with someone?"

Ash looked at me, holding my gaze for a long moment.

My heart stopped. My lungs froze mid-breath.

What is this?

What the fuck is this?

Ash pulled his hand away from Angie and croaked, "It doesn't matter. It will never happen, apparently." He stood, dropped his napkin on the table, and disappeared from the dining room.

The sound of the front door closing was like a bullet to the heart, but I was good at holding back my feelings. I was crumbling inside, but on the outside, I was stoic.

Jane set her fork on the edge of her plate and released a soft sigh. "Does anyone know what he's talking about?"

I shook my head. It wasn't a blatant lie. But I also was half in the dark and guessing by that point. I thought he had maybe liked the kiss and wanted to explore those feelings more. He probably had a bisexual awakening, and I was the first one he latched on to. There was a comfort in us being best friends that probably confused his feelings.

That was it. Confused feelings. He didn't mean it.

Chapter 7

Ash

Three weeks.

The longest three weeks of my life.

Three weeks since I kissed Sam, and realized that I might not be as straight as I thought. In fact, I might be very, very not straight. Our relationship had turned awkward as hell, and I didn't know how to handle it, so I was in pure avoidance mode.

It was the first time that I had intentionally avoided Sam like this. This wasn't like when we went to different universities. Back then, we still spoke almost every day. This was far different. We weren't texting. No phone calls. We didn't drop into each other's apartment. No weeknight dinners. The only time we were seeing each other was for Sunday dinner with our family, and even then, we weren't speaking much.

My heart was torn to pieces, leaving me empty and broken. I was a lump of flesh, bleeding on the floor. My soul was fragmented. Parts of who I was had been ripped away, leaving only an echoing void within me, accompanied by a deep ache in my chest where my heart struggled desperately to keep beating.

It took less than a day for me to realize I loved my best friend as more than a friend. After storming out of my parent's house that Sunday, I went home and combed through my thoughts. No matter how many angles I approached the situation from, I came to the same conclusion, and I was sure. More sure than about anything else in my entire life.

I'm in love with Samuel Pearce.

My best friend. My stepbrother. The only person I had ever trusted with my whole being. The only person I didn't put on a fake mask with.

He was my person.

I had been so blind.

I'd dreamed every night of him—our bodies entwined in a lustful dance. I couldn't make the thoughts leave. They refused to tame themselves and give me rest.

Staring at my phone, swiping through the contact list, I was hoping I could rid myself of thoughts of him. The name of someone who was always down for a no-strings-attached-fuck caught my eye. Made it simple.

She answered on the fifth ring.

"Ash," her smooth voice came across the phone. "Normal spot?"

"No, come to my place."

"Getting right to the fun part tonight," she purred. "I like it."

She hung up and twenty minutes later, a soft knock sounded from my door. I quickly ripped it open to find Sam standing in front of me.

Not what I wanted.

"Don't look so happy to see me, Ash." He walked in and plopped on the sofa.

"What are you doing here?" I snapped, unable to stop my frustration from showing.

I closed the door and walked over to him, but I kept my distance.

"I'm not allowed to visit anymore?" He looked hurt. My chest tightened, seeing his pained expression. "I thought we could hang out like we always do."

I clenched my jaw, holding back the words wanting to come out as my heart thudded erratically. My veins burned hot, and my stomach felt like it had buried itself underground. I was annoyed by his attempt to go back to normal. I didn't want normal. I stalked over to him and grabbed the collar of his shirt, yanking him to his feet.

"What the fuck, Ash?" His hands clamped around my wrist.

I leaned in close, ignoring the dull throb in my arm from his fingers digging into my skin.

"It might be easy for you to pretend nothing happened, but it isn't easy for me," I growled the words through gritted teeth.

This close, all I could smell was him. Spice mixed with a woodsy sweetness. His lips drew tight together, and he tried to shove me away, but I didn't budge.

When he accepted I wasn't letting go, he released my forearm from his grip and puffed out a breath that rushed over my face, and that simple, stupid moment set my body ablaze. I studied him, taking in everything about him in a new light. When our eyes locked, he swallowed, and it sent his prominent Adam's apple bobbing.

"I want to kiss you, Sam."

His brows pulled together, and his lips returned to a tight line.

I released my hold on him and turned away. He'd made it clear that nothing would change his mind. I would never have the chance to explore my feelings for him. He would never allow me to find out how he felt in return.

"Get out, Sam."

He moved to walk away, but paused, studying me. His eyes filled with pain, shining like he would cry.

"Do you think we will ever be like we used to?"

"No," I said coldly.

I needed him to know how upset I was about this whole situation. My insides felt like they were crushing in on themselves like a soda can under a car tire. I needed him to feel it with me. Hurt *with* me. If he felt anything near what I did, I would be satisfied—for a short while.

He let out a strangled breath before walking away. I dropped my gaze to the floor, unable to watch him leave. This was like a bad breakup. Like we were going our separate ways. I heard the door open, and a moment passed before it closed with a quiet click.

A shaky breath rattled through my chest. The understanding and intensity of the moment finally caught up with me.

Sam was here to ask if we could remain friends. Brothers. And I told him no. That was his peace offering, and I refused. How could I do that to him? He was my rock. My brother. My best friend. But—he was more than that to me—now that I knew he was more, how could I return to a simple friend? Or be downgraded to a brother. How could I live while watching him date someone? Fall in love with someone. Marry someone. How could I live my life pretending that I didn't care?

How can I pretend I don't love him?

Quiet knocks came from the door again, and I swung it open, hope blooming through me like a flaming chariot of joy, but it crashed as fast as it had been summoned.

Dark brown eyes shrouded by long black hair blinked up at me. Her plump lips were coated in blood-red lipstick, and a low-cut black dress formed to her tight little body.

"Lexi." I breathed through my disappointment.

"Hey, sexy," she said, sashaying past me into the apartment. "You look disappointed to see me at your door."

"It's nothing. I thought. . ." I shook my head. She didn't need to know. "Don't worry about it."

"Okay. I've never seen you look so disappointed to see me, though."

"That's my bad. It's nothing for you to worry about," I said, following her through my living room.

Lexi was twenty-seven, a few years older than me, and a successful tattoo artist. She and I met when I walked into her shop to get my first tattoo. After that, she and I hooked up from time to time, and I would go to her for all of my new tattoos. It was an uncomplicated relationship. Sex and art were all we had in common. One of which I really needed right now.

"I like the haircut," she said, kicking off her shoes when she breached the threshold of my bedroom.

"Thanks," I replied, closing in on her, shoving everything else from my mind.

I needed to clear my head, and this was the perfect way to do it. Resting my palm over the small of her back, I slid my hand down to the soft underside of her ass. She was soft and smelled like honey and cinnamon. She was warm and welcoming, leaning into the pressure of my touch.

Wrapping my arm around her chest, I pressed her close, letting her back line up flush with me. The bulge in my jeans rested against the curve of her back, pressing into her with devastating need. I traced my fingers over her abdomen, trailing the tips over her sleek dress until I reached the opening of the fabric between her breasts.

At least I could still get hard for women.

One question was answered. Maybe I was actually bisexual, and the lie Jaz told Rainie wasn't much of a lie after all.

I tugged the shoulder of her dress down and cupped her exposed breast in my palm, kneading it. Lexi moaned softly. She melded her body to mine, pressing her ass back and putting her body weight against my cock.

I bent down, running my nose over her slender neck, savoring her smell, and then the images hit me: Sam wrapped in my arms. My nose trailing over his neck. I stuck my tongue out, flattening it over his skin. A light moan sounded from Lexi as my fantasy and reality mingled.

I'm a horrible person.

I pushed the thoughts of Sam away, turning Lexi around and lifting her off her feet. I met her lips with mine, letting her touch distract me. My knees hit the edge of the bed, and I set her down. With every shift on the bed, she teased me with fleeting glimpses of what was hidden beneath her dress.

With a sly smile, she slipped out of the dress and tossed it to the floor, leaving only the tiny, barely there thong on. Her thighs were thick and naturally tan. Lexi was half-Mexican, stunning, and stood no taller than five-four.

"Take off that shirt and let me see my work as you fuck me," she said.

I climbed over her, tossing my shirt to the side. Her legs came around me, forcing me forward until her ass pressed against my thighs.

"Don't bother taking your pants off," she said, tugging the button free before unzipping my jeans faster than I could respond. "Just get inside me, Ash."

"Eager," I said and grabbed the condom from my back pocket.

She licked her lips and tugged my boxers down, exposing my throbbing erection to her eager gaze. Her eyes darkened as she took in the sight, licking her lips again.

"Hurry," she begged, wriggling out of her tiny thong while I ripped open the condom packet and slipped it on.

I slid my fingers between her thighs, finding her absolutely soaked for me.

"I haven't even done anything, Lex."

"Baby, just standing in front of me looking sexy like always is enough to get me like this."

I didn't like when people called me baby, but this wasn't the time to bring it up, so I left it alone and turned my attention to distracting my mind with the only thing I could think of.

I slipped my middle finger inside her. Her breath caught at the quick intrusion. She rocked on my finger, begging me for more. I pressed my palm to her clit as she rode my hand before slipping another finger inside her slick core.

"You're so wet. It's sexy as fuck."

With a soft groan, she tangled her fingers in my hair, pulling my face to hers.

"Shut up and kiss me."

She nipped my bottom lip before kissing me. I pulled my fingers from her and dropped my hips until the head of my cock rested against her slick entrance. Her chest rose, bumping her nipples against my skin, and I eased myself inside her.

"Ash," she groaned.

I moved slowly, letting her grow accustomed to my girth. Tingles ran up my spine when I was finally completely encased. She purred a soft moan, her body pulsing around me. I rocked my hips and settled into a rhythm that had her writhing beneath me.

As I fucked her, flashes of my dreams with Sam rushed to the forefront of my mind, and when I came, the face I saw was Sam's. It made me feel shitty. Sleazy. I couldn't even enjoy my release because it was mixed with self-hate and disgust.

Would this be my every day moving forward?

Lexi left my apartment, satisfied and unaware I'd been thinking about my best friend the whole time. I was so disgusted with myself that I stood in the shower for an hour, rinsing away my depravity.

I ran a towel over my hair before tossing it in the hamper and left the bathroom, fighting off thoughts of Sam, then sat at my gaming desk in the corner of the living room. The sound of the computer fans filled the room as I powered on the custom-built computer I had spent four months putting together. The RGB lighting was the only light in my apartment, creating a rainbow hue against the walls.

I logged into my favorite massively multiplayer online role-playing game and moved my avatar across the screen, walking until I reached the guild house. My guild was made up of a group I'd met in high school. It started with Taevon approaching me in a main town when I was level one. He offered me some help, and the next thing I knew, we talked daily. Before I knew it, we'd picked up ten others and formed a guild.

My guildmates were my only friends outside of Jaz and Sam. Joe was cool, but he only hung around me because of Jaz. In the time since the Truth or Dare game, Jaz had pulled away from me. When I told her I thought I had feelings for Sam—real feelings—she called me disgusting. I wasn't sure where we stood after that.

My whole world had collapsed because of a single choice.

A choice I didn't regret.

I opened Discord on my second monitor and clicked on my private conversation with Tae. A few days ago, he sent me a job listing. He did this every time a position I was qualified for opened up at his company in North Carolina. I never thought twice about denying him in the past, but this one. . .

I wasn't sure I could handle being close to Sam daily and simply accepting the boundary he forced upon us. Knowing me, these feelings of love and frustration would morph into resentment. I had been forced through enough therapy sessions as a teen to know where my mind would go. And it wasn't pretty.

Something like this—unrequited love where I was forced to suffer—that was a self-imposed torment I couldn't do. I was running away from my problems. There was no sugarcoating it.

I entered the message to Tae and hit send before I could think better of it.

Me: Tae, is that job opening still on the table?

Tae popped online, his status turning green shortly before the typing indicator bounced in the chat window.

Tae: Woah! Are you serious!?

Tae: Yes! It's open!

I went back and forth with Tae for an hour before reading through the job listing for another hour. It was a lead developer position at his company. Based in Raleigh, North Carolina, with some sweet ass benefits and better pay than I was getting at Pix. The bonus was that they were helping children with disabilities. I grew up with undiagnosed ADHD, which only became something I was diagnosed with after years of therapy and finally coming across a psychologist. He was trying to help me with my trauma recovery plan, and instead, I walked out with a new diagnosis and more questions than answers.

Knowing how rough life was without the support I needed growing up, the idea of working with kids to help them before life knocked them down sounded nice.

I leaned back in the chair, staring at the job application I filled out. My hand trembled on the mouse, the small arrow on my screen hovering over the submit button.

Am I doing this? Am I willing to leave my family?

How hadn't I noticed my feelings for Sam? Kissing him was an unstoppable rush. Now that I was aware of it, it was blatantly obvious I loved him. More than a friend. I really fucking loved him.

I read a lot in the days since that kiss. Joined some online forums and read through other people's stories. What I'd gathered was America pushed strict hetero-normative training, blinding me from the blatantly obvious feelings I had.

As I dissected our life together, I plucked out moments where I should've questioned our relationship. Our friends often joked that Sam and I had the best bromance ever. We were running around as best friends who were so close we could be mistaken as brothers. But when I thought back to that idea, I realized there were so many undertones to our friendship being masked by cultural expectations of us being straight. It was crystal clear that our relationship exceeded the boundaries of platonic friendship.

I thought back to the moment I met him. The first day I laid eyes on him. The sight of the boy with nearly white hair and pale blue eyes on the jungle gym was so captivating that I couldn't pull my eyes away from him. He was sent down from heaven and placed in my path. It's what I thought, at least.

What four-year-old thinks that about another boy if they aren't naturally attracted to them?

I probably loved him since back then. Of course, I was too young to understand or recognize my feelings. But looking back, it was more than thinking Sam was beautiful. It was this deep need to be near him. To never lose sight of that face that brought light into my darkness. I lived to exist under his gaze. Witness his smile. Hear his laugh.

I wanted to go back in time and punch that little punk for not seeing it. I had been completely oblivious to my own feelings. Then, our parents got married when we were thirteen.

I was twenty-five years old and as oblivious as my four-year-old self. Why would I think I was in love with my best friend when I had been trained my whole life to think every man around me was a friend and never anything else? I did exactly what my culture dictated. I believed my close friendship with Sam was simply a unique friendship. A once-in-a-lifetime friend. My lack of feelings for the women I came across was from my traumatic past of watching my mother get the shit beat out of her for breathing. Just like my therapists told me. I listened to them. Never questioned them. Never questioned myself. I trusted their reality was mine.

"You're afraid to open yourself up to your girlfriend because you don't want to end up like your father," one therapist told me when I asked why I never felt anything for a girlfriend I'd been with for months.

Fear.

Fucking bullshit.

But now that I was aware, I couldn't lie. I couldn't pretend. I was a horrible liar. Everyone knew when I was lying about something serious. Sure, a white lie here and there, whatever, but a real lie that I had to sell. . .

I tapped the mouse, hitting the submit button.

I would finally use the suggestion of one of my many therapists and remove myself from the situation because protecting myself was the only way I knew to move forward.

Chapter 8

Sam

Never in our lives had Ash and I been apart like this before. Not once had he ever told me no and meant it. But when I stood before him tonight, asking if we could ever go back to normal, that "no" crushed me. Broke me into hundreds of tattered pieces. A lifetime of friendship was thrown away. Tarnished. All because of a kiss.

Why did I let him kiss me? I could've gotten away from it that night. I wasn't that drunk. But his words and the slimy desire to kiss him had rooted me in place. I had dreamed so many times of kissing him. Of him wanting to kiss me.

Years of me pretending I didn't love him. Years of suffering in silence because I didn't want to lose him. Loneliness beyond anyone's comprehension. Longing that bore its way deep into my soul, sprouting spiny thorns that clung to my heart. Latched on, never letting go.

Now look at me. At us.

What would happen now? How could we come back from this?

Curled up in bed, I cried, memories of Ash plaguing my thoughts.

Since Ash kissed me, controlling my emotions had been difficult for the first time since I was a kid. I felt incapable of hiding my pain. He was the one person in this world I knew I could trust. The one person I could rely on no matter what happened, but now he was gone. He pushed me away. He was angry. I hurt him. The memory of his tears when I rejected him haunted me.

And now he was hurting me in return.

I struggled to remind myself of the reasons a romantic relationship between the two of us would be a horrible idea. I knew the reasons. I'd said them all to myself since I was thirteen.

We're stepbrothers. It's taboo. Our parents would think we're disgusting. Society would think we're disgusting. People would hate us. Angela would think we're creepy. My father would be angry. Jane would hate me. Our parents would divorce. Our parents would fight. I would lose my family. I would lose their love. I would lose *everything*.

Telling myself to stay away. To find someone else to love didn't help. My heart wanted no one else. It was like our souls were linked, calling to each other. That kiss had re-awoken my feelings so strongly that my coping mechanisms were failing me. The idea of being touched by someone else after having Ash's lips on me was repulsive. I didn't want someone else. I wanted Ash. I wanted those strong hands holding me. His forceful and loving kiss. I couldn't stop reliving the moment. Over and over. His warmth. His smell, bergamot and warm, musky comfort, surrounded me as his tongue slipped between my lips.

I groaned into my pillow, spreading tears across the fabric.

How would I ever move on? After so long, how could I ever fall in love with someone else?

The office was loud and busy. The usual chaotic disaster.

I adjusted my tie, leaning back in the chair. It squeaked under the movement, and I closed my eyes, trying to drown out the noise around me.

Footsteps approached my cubicle. The person was wearing heels and walked hard.

A chill ran down my spine. Lucinda.

"Samuel," she said in a shrill voice that grated on my ears and made me cringe. "I thought I told you the marketing plan was due this morning."

Opening my eyes, I righted myself. "Lucinda, good morning." I smiled the most pleasantly kind smile I knew how. "I emailed it to you at nine when I got in."

She looked me up and down before replying, "Email?" She stuck her nose up like I had shoved something disgusting in her face. "I thought I asked you to print it."

What was this, the eighties? "I emailed the document this morning."

"I didn't ask for it emailed. I need it for a meeting in ten minutes." She took a step back, crossing her arms. "Print it and bring it to my office before the meeting."

Putting my perfect smile back in place, I stood and said, "Of course. It was my mistake."

She peered at me over her metal-rimmed glasses before turning around and strutting through the aisle.

I hated my job. I had thought getting a job in marketing would be an amazing collaborative and fun experience, but instead, I was stuck under a bunch of inept computer-illiterate assholes who couldn't tell you the difference between an application and a browser. Hell, they probably didn't understand what a browser was.

I pulled open the document and set it to print at the nearby printer before stalking over to the room to wait for it to finish.

My true desire was user experience. I majored in marketing and business in school, but my dream was to start a web design and marketing company focused on user experience. I thought getting real-world experience would be a good stepping stone between college and starting a business, but I didn't expect this to be my day-to-day. Underpaid, overworked, bullied, and exhausted. What a life.

I handed Lucinda the papers and slipped out of her office before she had a single moment to complain. Halfway down the hall, my phone buzzed in my pocket. I dipped into the nearby lounge and quietly answered the phone.

"Hello," I said.

"Is this Sam?" The woman's voice was familiar, but I couldn't place it

"Yeah, who's this?"

"Jaz," she said, then continued, "I got your number from Rainie because what the hell is your brother doing?" Her voice raised into a high-pitched scream.

"What do you mean?" I asked, my heart thundering.

"Ash came back from a two-day vacation and put in his two weeks."

"What?"

"I know!" She paused, but I could hear rustling in the background. "All I know is he left on Sunday and wouldn't tell me where he was going. He said he was going to visit a friend for a short vacation before the weather gets too hot."

He was on vacation? Where did he go? He never went on vacation unless it was with our family. The only people he liked enough to see for a vacation were in North Carolina.

My stomach sank as it hit me. His gaming friend was in North Carolina. Ash would complain about how the guy always sent him job openings, trying to get him to move out there.

He wouldn't take it, would he?

July

One Year Later

Chapter 9

Ash

A soft giggle broke the silence of the cramped space. Six of us worked out of a tiny office in the heart of Raleigh, North Carolina. It was still hard to believe I accepted the job, picked up my life, and deserted my family. Other days, like today, I remembered why it was worth it.

"Taevon, stop bothering Mariam," I called, rolling my chair back and hopping up to peek over my cubicle.

"What did you just call me, Ashton?" Tae popped his face over Mariam's cubicle wall. "Why are you still here?"

"Because I can be."

"Shouldn't you be heading home?"

I dropped into my chair and threw my head back with a groan. "Shut up, don't remind me."

Moments later, Tae stood over me with a raised eyebrow and a concerned look on his far too-perfect face. His dark brown eyes glared at me as he picked up the small stress ball I kept on my desk and tossed it between his hands. His skin was dark, and he had soft facial features. Our builds were similar, but his shoulders were more broad.

"Wanna talk about it over drinks?" he asked before sitting on my desk, pushing my keyboard and mouse to the side to make room for his ass.

"Not really. You know the deal."

"Actually, I don't." He glared, squeezing the ball. "You gave me some cryptic excuse about a big argument, and that was all for the last year."

Chewing the inside of my cheek, I spun the chair around and righted myself. "You aren't getting any more than that."

"Does your family deserve the way you've been treating them? Because from where I'm sitting, you're being a brat."

Maybe I was being a brat to them, but it was the only way to protect my heart. The only way I knew how to keep myself from being consumed by my feelings.

Not that it was working.

Sam was on my mind daily. Followed me into my dreams. He never left my mind for more than a few hours.

"It's complicated, Tae."

After I moved, I lost touch with everyone. Jasmine stopped contacting me, but she had already started to pull away from me after the night I kissed Sam. Joe stopped speaking to me when Jaz backed off. Those two were the only people I spoke to other than Sam.

I lost them all. My family. My friends. Sam.

Jaz dropping me from her life hit hard. I thought she and I were friends, but it turned out she was like everyone else. Her friendship was temporary and conditional.

Sam had tried to contact me, but I stopped replying to his texts, and if he called, I never picked up.

Hearing his voice struck a nerve that sent me spiraling for days, so I simply ignored him.

Thankfully, I had Tae. We had been close before, talking through Discord or in the games we played together, but since moving to Raleigh and working with him, I could honestly call him my best friend.

Sam *was* my best friend. I didn't want him to be a friend anymore. Besides, could we even consider ourselves friends after a year apart?

The best thing to come out of this was my new job as lead developer for Tae's company, Design For Better Lives. I loved my job. For the first time ever, I felt fulfilled with what I spent my life doing. I was developing software that made a difference. Tae and Mariam were great to work for, and the tiny team had fun. We were going places.

"You know," Tae said, "I'm here if you need me. I promise to not judge you."

I sighed. He would judge me. Everyone had, and everyone would.

"Thanks, Tae, but I really don't want to talk about it."

He tossed the stress ball at my face, and I caught it.

"If you ever change your mind, you know where to find me." He placed his hand on my shoulder, giving me a solid pat before standing. "Have fun in Virginia with the family. I'll see you when you get back."

"Plan to go out and get completely trashed when I do."

"It's a date," he said, chuckling as he disappeared into his office.

I tried to avoid this trip home, but Mom complained about how I hadn't been home since Christmas and had only stayed four days before returning to Raleigh. I was glad my job was insane, and I used having only six employees as an excuse for never having time off. My family hated my new job, but it was the best cover I could have asked for.

With knots forming in my gut, I pulled the rental car into the driveway and glared at the small hybrid sedan already parked near the garage. Sam had upgraded from his run-down beater to a nice hybrid a few months back. This was my first time seeing it in person. I couldn't believe he chose the tiny ugly thing over the Jeep Wrangler he had dreamed about since we were kids.

I cut the engine off and hopped out of the car, tugging my duffle bag from the trunk before stalking up to the front door.

This would only be the third time I'd been back home since I moved to North Carolina. I wished I could've prolonged it. Every time I saw Sam, my emotions went haywire, and it was hard to control myself.

The house was quiet, but music filtered in from the backyard. Dropping my bag near the steps, I quickly made my way through the hallway and kitchen to the back of the house, where the French doors leading to the backyard were wide open, letting the midday sun pour into the house.

Angie stood on the deck, a pink soccer ball in her hands and a wide grin aimed at the angel who owned my heart and soul.

The knots twisting my gut tightened.

Sam's hair was exactly how I remembered it. A short fade on the sides and a long fringe on top. His platinum blond bangs fell into his face, and he flicked his head, tossing them out of his eyes with a devastatingly sexy grin before he grabbed the ball from Angie.

I licked my lips, trailing my gaze over his big hands covered in a glistening sheen of sweat. Thick veins in his forearms bulged, leading into the top of his hand. Those veins only showed up in him after a hard workout, and before now, I hadn't paid them any mind, but seeing them as he gripped the ball was mouthwatering.

He turned around, facing me, and lifted the hem of his shirt to his forehead, wiping the sweat away, exposing his taut stomach. The ghosting of abs led my gaze down to the white basketball shorts hanging low on his hips, revealing the band of his boxers. Brand name. Tight. Black.

Something about the dark fabric against his pale skin, hugging his body in places I dreamed of touching. . . My eyes trailed down to the outline of his dick. I'd seen it plenty of times throughout our lives, but I'd never looked at it like I wanted to devour it before.

My mouth watered at the sight. I couldn't stop looking, and my cock pressed against my pants with uncomfortable need.

The fabric of Sam's white shorts gave enough away. It was long, thick, and I knew he was cut. Would it have a thick vein that bulged like the veins in his hand?

I licked my lips, imagining what it would be like to touch that outline. Drag my hand over the head of his cock and watch his eyes flutter. Would he gasp? Whimper? Moan with those sinfully pouty lips while I stroked him?

My blood pumped to my groin, anticipating something that wouldn't happen. I vibrated with need. My muscles buzzed with energy. I was practically drooling, incapable of looking away.

Sam shifted his hips, and his dick moved to the side, begging me to look. I wanted to see it. His dick resting on those thick pillowy balls.

I swallowed a groan and tugged my lower lip between my teeth, biting down hard to distract myself from the eye candy illuminated in the afternoon sun.

Sam's gaze lifted, landing on me with surprise.

He dropped the shirt, letting it fall over his body, blocking the view of my fantasy material.

Time passed slowly while we stared each other down.

I released my lip from the pressure of my teeth, offering him a wink.

He rolled his eyes before spinning around, but that wasn't any better because it gave me a delicious view of his ass in those loose basketball shorts. The way the waistband sat over his ass. The shirt bunching up, giving me the tease of a lifetime. Sweat marked the back of his red T-shirt, showing his back outline in a way that had me wanting to run my fingers down his spine to take all that sweat—

Holy fucking shit.

I'm a sick bastard.

Stop thinking about him, Ash. Fucking dumbass. Your family is right there.

I blinked through the lust choking me, and shifted, adjusting my erection behind my waistband before stepping through the doors. Gaining some control over myself, I cleared my throat.

"Piglet," I said, tugging Angie backward and against my chest. I wrapped my arms around her tiny body and crushed her in a hug. "I've missed you."

She giggled, spinning in my hold before wrapping her arms around my waist. "Ash," she said, drawing out my name with a smile, "I'm so glad you came."

When she released me, my eyes locked with Sam's. We stared for a moment longer than would be natural, and I offered him a tense nod and said, "Yo."

He scoffed, playing off his glare before plastering a smile over his features. "Ash."

Hearing his voice made the knots in my gut turn to dancing butterflies, leaving me willing to do anything he asked of me.

I quickly tamped down my excitement and forced my indifferent expression back. As I walked past him, I purposely bumped his shoulder before joining Mom and Gary on the other side of the deck where Mom sipped on a fruity drink, likely hiding a gallon of vodka inside.

Mom and Gary greeted me with loving hugs. I sat with them, catching up about our lives until Angie brought out the fixings for s'mores. Looking at us, it was easy to forget the pain lingering in the unspoken moments.

Chapter 10

Sam

Ash was leaving in the morning, and I was torn between relief and the gut-wrenching loneliness that had been dancing around my heart since he had moved away.

"Boys," Jane called from behind the minivan.

Ash and I rounded the car, meeting her at the trunk.

"We've got it, Ma," Ash said, grabbing three camping chairs and a cooler. "Sam can get the rest."

He'd left two chairs, a small cooler, and a tote bag in the trunk for me.

"Are you sure? I can take something." Jane offered.

"Don't worry about it," I said, grabbing everything before standing beside Ash. "What direction did Dad go?"

Jane shut the trunk and pointed toward the grassy hill where Angie stood, waving her yellow hat at us amidst a growing crowd.

"I hate the fourth of July," Ash grumbled before heading toward Angie.

I followed behind him, unable to keep my eyes from trailing over his body the same way he did to me the day he came home. The only reason I knew he was standing in the kitchen was the powerful sense of being watched. When I looked up, seeing him through the open door, standing in the kitchen with a lust-filled expression—I had to look away. My whole body ached to be near him. To let that lust barrel through me unfiltered. My imagination ran wild with flashes of what it would be like to have him look at me like that without the walls I held in place. To have that needy look in his eyes while we were naked and—*fuck*.

We can't happen.

When we caught up to Angie at the top of the hill, she grabbed the tote bag from me and led us to the spot Dad had claimed in a small clearing surrounded by families with their huge square blankets spread over the grass circled by camping chairs and coolers. Some even had umbrellas with their older family members sitting under the shade.

A twinge of sadness rolled through me. Neither Ash nor I spoke to family outside of Jane, Dad, and Angie. Jane's parents died when Ash was young, and Dad's parents were in a bad car accident after the wedding. The grandparents who were alive were related to our shitty parents. There was no chance we would visit them if there was a possibility of seeing our parent. Besides, what I knew of Ash's grandad was that he was exactly like Ash's father.

There was always a pang of envy when I saw families together. Parents, grandparents, aunts and uncles. Kids running around and laughing. It was something I had always wanted and never had the chance to experience. By the time Jane and Dad married, Ash and I were older. The important formative years where we could experience family that way had already been tarnished. Our families were already trashed and broken. Jane and Dad did their best to give us the family life every child deserves, but it was too little too late for us. Angie was lucky. When Ash's dad was arrested, Angie was only four. She didn't have any memories of those years.

Dad grabbed the chairs from Ash, and I dropped everything at my feet to help them spread out the massive square blanket patterned with the American flag. It was so weird, but Dad loved this kind of thing. When everything was finally set up, I didn't even want to sit in a chair. I dropped onto the blanket and stretched my legs out under the sun. We still had about an hour before sundown, and being cooped up in an office all day didn't leave me much room for relaxing like this. I leaned back, propping myself on my hands, let my head fall back, and closed my eyes.

There was a mix of different music playing around us. Multiple families had their own little radios quietly playing their preferred music. People laughed in the distance. The whole event was loud and somehow peaceful.

A shadow loomed over me, blocking the sun from my face, making my skin cooler in an instant. I peeled my eyes open. Ash stood beside me, digging through the tote bag.

He glanced down at me with a smirk before squirting sunscreen into his palm.

I eyed him, untrusting of his next move. He and I had always fucked with each other, and even if we were pretending to be in a never-ending fight, he could never help himself when it came to messing with me.

He dropped the lotion bottle into the bag and rubbed his palms together. In a flash, his hands slid against my cheeks, spreading the thick, creamy lotion across my skin.

His warm, honeyed voice was laced with amusement when he said, "Don't want those pristine cheeks getting sunburned, Sammy."

The sensation of him touching me after a little more than a year of being completely avoidant of each other sent a fiery shot through my body, pooling in my gut with unbridled desire.

I forced an annoyed grumble from my throat when I really wanted to drag him down and direct his touch elsewhere.

Ash cackled over me, spreading the lotion over my face, then down my neck. Tingling warmth shot through me from each touch. He rubbed the lotion over my skin, teasing me with every chuckle.

When our eyes met, the same simmering lust I saw the day he came home was behind that smile.

If I let him continue touching me like this, I would be a goner. I shoved him away, and he stumbled back a short distance, chuckling as he found his balance.

"Let me help you with your legs too, bro," Ash said, kneeling beside me with a vicious grin.

I kicked at him, hitting him right in the side, sending him rolling onto his back. Then I rushed him and attacked, digging my fingers into his sides where he hated. The barking laugh he released before wrapping his legs around me sent me into a fit of laughter. It turned into a wrestling match to rival those we had as kids. Dad laughed behind us, and Angie complained about us being immature.

But this was full of tension there had never been before.

Ash chuckled beneath me while I caught my breath, straddling him. I licked my lips, and his eyes followed the movement.

"I give up," he said, heaving another breath, dropping his arms to the ground.

I didn't want to let him off yet. I needed a punishment to get him back, so I took a finger to my face, capturing a glob of sunscreen. His eyes went wide, and he shifted when he realized my plan, but I was already on him, smearing the lotion on his forehead before he could stop me.

"I'm sorry," he screamed, rolling beneath me, trying to kick me off. "I give!"

I took more lotion from my face with my palm and smeared it over his cheeks and shoulder. When his shirt rode up, exposing his abs covered in black ink, I stilled.

The man I always wanted was laughing beneath me. Wanting me the same way I wanted him.

I wanted this. More than anything.

Long fingers wrapped around my wrist. His painted black nails were a little chipped, and his tattoo-covered arms were dappled in beads of sweat. His black tank had white finger marks everywhere, and his chest heaved before he laughed again, a little softer this time.

"I'm sorry," he said, but there was a seriousness in his voice.

I wanted to ask what he was sorry for, but I was too afraid to find out. Asking would only open the can of worms I was trying to bury.

I smashed my palm over his chest, smearing the last bit of lotion over his collarbone, then pushed off him and marched toward the small cafe near the parking lot. I ducked inside, brushing past people, and stepped into the restroom. Flicking on the water at the sink, I stared at my reflection. Each place Ash had touched was bright pink and covered in a layer of white gloopy lotion.

One look at my groin told me everything I needed to know. That was too far. If anyone had looked, they would've easily seen the fucking outline in my shorts.

After cleaning off the sunscreen, I texted Angie, asking if anyone wanted a drink from the cafe, and stood in the long line. I was grateful to be away from them while the sun set and more grateful that I could use the long line as an excuse for why I was gone for nearly an hour. It gave me time to think.

When I made it back to everyone, the sun was completely gone, and they were getting ready for the fireworks to start.

Ash looked up at the sky, lying on the blanket, his arm under his head. Angie sat beside him, chatting away.

Seeing them made my decision to pull further away from Ash feel like the right thing to do. No more touching. No more joking. No more.

I handed them the burning hot cups of coffee and sat in a chair away from them.

"Did you get all the lotion off?" Ash asked, craning his head to look over at me.

"Yeah," I said, offering nothing else. My short reply gained me a look from everyone, but no one brought it up.

When the fireworks started, I couldn't help but watch Ash. It was like he had been plucked right out of a dream. This tall, handsome bad-boy player covered in tattoos gazed up at the bright lights with childlike awe.

I wanted to kiss him.

It was always moments like this when my heart tried to claw its way out of the cage I put it in. Moments where I saw the side of Ash that he rarely let anyone else see. The Ash who played with me on the playground. The Ash who, despite all his suffering, was there for me at every turn.

I miss him.

I watched the fireworks a moment longer before pulling my phone from my pocket and doing something I would regret.

Me: Want to come over later?

I sent the text, knowing I wasn't in a healthy headspace, but I needed to escape from my feelings.

Leo: What time?

I bit my lip, tugging on the skin until it hurt.

Me: Midnight?

Leo: I'll see you at midnight ;)

I had thirty minutes to shower and change before Leo arrived. After spending so much time with Ash, I was wound tight, buzzing with pent-up need. I breezed into my apartment, flicking on the floor lamp in the living room before grabbing a quick shower.

Moments after leaving the bathroom, my hair still dripping, a knock echoed through the quiet space. I grabbed the towel from my shoulder, rubbing my hair dry as I walked down the hall. When I swung the door open, dark brown eyes stared back at me.

Leonard Bradford was every parent's dream. He was the guy that families would love to have as a son-in-law. I would never be the guy who he took home to meet the parents. I could never give him more than this.

I stepped back, letting him into my apartment before closing the door.

"What made you ask me here tonight?" he asked.

I eyed him, unsure if I wanted to admit that being around Ash had driven me straight to him. I didn't want to rub it in his face that I was using him as a distraction. Friends-with-benefits was okay, but using him as a stand-in probably crossed lines I preferred to ignore.

"Long day. I need to relax," I said, tossing the towel onto the kitchen counter, and opened the fridge to grab a drink. "Thirsty? Do you want anything?"

Leo shook his head, approaching me. "Want to talk about it?" He closed in, sliding his hand over my hip, and tugging me close. "You know I'm good at listening."

"No." I shook my head, setting my drink on the counter before circling my arms around his neck, drawing myself close enough to brush my lips over his short beard. I kissed his chin, enjoying how his hair scrapped over my lips. "I'd rather just feel."

"I'll never say no to that," Leo said before kissing me.

I let him control the situation. Take from me whatever he wanted as long as it meant I could forget the crippling longing for a little while. The distraction never lasted long enough. It was always a matter of time before the emptiness and pain crept back in, shadowing me with unquenchable want.

But the momentary distractions were the only relief I had.

When I woke, I slid from bed and wandered to the kitchen for coffee. The smell of food and coffee took over my senses, making my mouth water. For a moment, I pictured Ash cooking in my apartment like he used to, but that was a fantasy. A heartbreaking fantasy.

Leo stood at the stove in his boxers and an apron. When he noticed me, he slid a mug across the counter with a smile. "Coffee," he said.

"Thanks." I took the mug and leaned my hip against the counter. "What made you do all this?" I waved my hand at the three pans on the stove full of different breakfast foods.

He shrugged, flipping slices of bacon with tongs. "I was hungry. You had the fixings."

I squinted at him. Something about him being nonchalant about making me breakfast had alarms blaring in the back of my mind. I ignored the alarms. I needed to stop holding onto Ash; maybe I could move on one day. Things like my friend cooking me breakfast after fucking me all night was totally okay, right?

I sighed, debating if my next question would be crossing a line. What was one more blurred boundary?

"Something on your mind?" Leo asked, peeking over his shoulder before returning his focus to the food.

"I'm thinking about quitting my job."

No one knew yet. I was still unsure if I would qualify for the business loan, but I had all the paperwork ready. I was mere steps away from grabbing hold of my dream.

"You should. That place is toxic."

I sipped the coffee before saying, "If I started my own business, would it be weird if I asked you to work for me?"

He spun around, eyes wide. "What?"

I cleared my throat. "I know we're a little complicated with the whole friends-with-benefits thing, but I was thinking if I got my business loan, would you want to work with me as my finance guy?"

Leo dropped the tongs on the counter and closed the distance between us. "Are you for real?"

I nodded. "Drop dead serious."

His hands slid around my waist, and he tugged me closer, brushing his nose over mine. "I'd be your finance guy any time."

"It's settled then. I'll file the paperwork and cross my fingers that the business loan is approved."

March

Two Years Later

Chapter 11

Ash

Tae's apartment was on the sixteenth floor in an expensive complex at the heart of Raleigh. He was within walking distance of the office and was only two blocks from our favorite club.

It was a nice place, but it was about a thousand dollars a month outside my price range. When there was a vacancy for a tiny one-bedroom in this building, they were asking nearly three thousand dollars a month for the thing. After seeing those numbers, my little apartment across the city for fifteen hundred bucks looked like a dream.

"Right on time!" Tae said when he swung the door open.

He wore a plain white T-shirt and sweatpants. I was similarly dressed in black sweatpants and a gray hoodie with my favorite metal band's logo on the front under my heavy winter coat. He tugged me by the collar and practically threw me inside. The door slammed shut behind me, and Tae pushed me into his massive living room where two long leather sofas were positioned across from a giant TV and a blazing fireplace.

The TV was set to a group of men in suits talking over each other while stats flashed over the screen.

"The game is about to start. Snacks are in the kitchen. Drinks are in the fridge." Tae flopped onto the sofa and slung his arm over the back of the cushions. "Oh, and pizza is on the way."

"Awesome." I shucked off my jacket before slipping into the kitchen to grab a water bottle. "Who are we rooting for tonight?" I asked when I joined him on the sofa.

I didn't have a team that I rooted for. I was usually neutral and would pick one team each game to favor at random. Sometimes, I would jump back and forth depending on who I liked more in that game. I was pretty unserious when it came to things like this.

Tae beamed at me. "My favorite team, Boston. The other team doesn't matter."

I laughed, then decided to stoke the flames when I saw who the other team was. "I feel I should be rooting for the Caps since I'm DMV born and raised."

His eyes went wide. "You will not root for any team other than Boston while in my presence," Tae replied before aiming his attention at the screen.

"Go Caps," I whispered.

"Shut up, asshole," Tae said, throwing a tan throw pillow at my face. "Just for that, you're paying for the pizza."

A stupid-sounding cackle erupted from me, and I hugged the pillow to my chest. "Whatever."

I settled in, watching the game with Tae and enjoying the comfort our friendship gave me. Tae was my closest friend now, and hanging out with him was the only thing keeping me sane. If it wasn't hockey, we'd watch baseball, football, boxing. Whatever was on. I basically lived at his place if we weren't gaming together or at work. It was actually awesome to share my hobbies like this with someone other than Sam.

Moments like these didn't make the ache in my chest disappear, but it helped. It helped a lot.

A shiver rolled through me when my fingers hit the metal handle of the glass door. Snow landed in the middle of the night, making my Monday morning that much better.

The lobby was warm and silent. I stopped in the small cafe on the basement level before hopping into the elevator. Moments later, I breezed into the tiny office space.

This place was perfect for six people a few years ago, but now, we had eighteen, making it far too cramped.

I assumed the office space was what this meeting with Tae and Mariam was about. I had asked about finding a bigger office space, but Tae kept saying, "We'll talk about it later." At least six months had passed since I last bugged him about it.

I greeted the few developers and software testers on my team who had already arrived before rushing into Tae's office. I set two to-go coffee cups on his desk, keeping the third for myself, and flopped into the chair across from him.

"'Sup," I said, waiting for him to look up from the computer.

"One second," he replied, a crease growing on his brow line.

I took the moment to sip the burning hot coffee.

Mariam rushed into the room and closed the door. "Good morning, boys," she said, shirking off her forest green jacket and flicking her red hair over her shoulder.

"Mari," I said, pointing at the coffee I left for her on Tae's desk, "that's for you."

"You're too good to me, Ash." She greedily wrapped her slender fingers around the cup, pressed her lips to the tiny opening, and sipped. "Tae, have you started yet?"

He shook his head, keeping his focus on the screen.

"Can what you're doing wait? We have things to do," she said, eying him like he was wasting her time.

I chuckled and took another sip.

"Fine," he waved his hand, then grabbed the coffee I'd left for him. "Let's start this."

Mari turned to me with a grin, clutching the coffee between her palms. "Ash, we want to first thank you for all the work you've put in over the last three years. You've been an integral part of building this dream into reality."

"I'm still shocked I got you to come here in the first place," Tae said.

Mari nodded, continuing, "And because you're so important to us and the team,"—she glanced at Tae, then back at me—"we want to promote you to Chief Information Officer and place you in charge of everything IT. As we grow, we are seeing more and more need for the position."

My jaw dropped to the floor. "You what now?"

Mari nodded, her green eyes shimmering as she said, "CIO."

"You're serious right now?" I asked, unable to believe this was real.

"Yes," Tae replied. "You're an amazing developer. You understand the needs of what we're doing. The team looks up to and respects you. Even those who know nothing about tech. And most importantly, you have vision."

"What the fuck? Vision?"

They both laughed, but I was serious.

"You may not realize it, but you fit in with Mari and me about our goals for our products. You have great ideas and think outside the box. You take the time to research and learn and then bring that back to us."

I scoffed, shrugging off their compliments.

CIO.

Never in my wildest dreams did I expect to make it that high in any company. It wasn't a goal. I thought the highest I would go was team lead or something. No higher than manager, but a CIO? *Holy shit.*

"Since that's done, let's tell the team," Tae announced as he stood.

"Now?" I asked, still stuck in a moment of shock. "I'm not ready."

Mari patted my knee with a chuckle. "You are. And it's only telling them. You don't have to give a speech or anything."

I stood with them. "Fuck, Tae,"—I looked from him to Mariam—"Mari." I grabbed them both, hugging them. "Thanks."

"We love you too," Tae said, patting my back.

The announcement to the team went better than I could have hoped. Everyone seemed happy for me. Then Tae announced we would be moving buildings. There would be enough space to grow over the next ten years. We landed huge contracts with two private schools and needed more people to handle the influx coming our way. If those projects went well, it would put us on the map.

The rest of the day turned into fucking around and taking everyone out for a late team lunch, which turned into drinking at a bar.

A few drinks in and around six o'clock, I stepped away, giddy and wanting to tell my family about my promotion. My finger hovered over Sam's name in my contact list, but I hadn't called him directly in three years. The knot that always followed my thoughts of him settled in my gut. I swiped past his name and scrolled down to my mom's contact.

She picked up immediately. I could hear the smile in her voice when she said, "Ash, I haven't heard from you in a few weeks. I'm so happy you called."

"Hey, Ma." A smile forced its way over my face, and I leaned against the wall. "Is Gary there with you? I have some news."

"He's in the living room. Hang on." I could hear her shuffling like she was rushing through the house to find him, and then she barked at him to mute the TV. A laugh erupted from me before quickly dying like it always did when I thought of why I wasn't around my family. The normal crushing regret of leaving them hit me before I pushed it away. "Okay, you're on speaker."

"I got promoted today," I said.

"You did?" Mom sounded extra excited, then asked, "What position? What will you be doing?"

"Chief Information Officer. I'll basically be leading our whole IT department."

"Congratulations," Gary said in the distance. "That's a huge accomplishment. Our boy is an executive!"

Our boy.

The words lingered in my mind.

"Thanks," I said. "It's a ton of responsibility, but Tae and Mari think I'll do the position justice."

"You will. I know you will," Mom said, assuring me.

We chatted for a few more minutes before I went back to Tae and the rest of the team, where I was handed more drinks. It was a time for celebration, but a part of me didn't feel up to celebrating. A part of me felt empty.

Hours later, my phone vibrated in my pocket. It was a message from Sam. My nerves made my hand shake as I tapped the screen, opening the message.

Sam: I'm proud of you.

Damn. I stared at the words for a while, sipping on a drink Tae had passed me. It warmed my heart to see that, yet, at the same time, it made me want to crawl into a ball and cry.

He was a better man than me. I never congratulated him on opening his company two years ago. When Mom called to tell me how Sam was approved for a business loan and could finally start his dream, I wanted to call him. I had spent days staring at his name in my phone. I'd typed out text after text, deleting every single one and never sending them. We had gone so long without contacting each other; I didn't want to be the first to reach out.

So, why would he contact me tonight? What changed to make him say something to me?

Without overthinking it, I sent a short reply.

Me: Thanks. You too.

Would he understand I was proud of him? Would he know that hearing about him running his own company like he'd always wanted was something I was so proud of him for doing that no words could express the absolute joy in my heart? When he read that text, would he know everything I left unsaid?

I love you. I miss you. I wish you were here with me.

There were so many things I wanted to say and couldn't. I wanted to hug him. Call him. God, just seeing his face would be enough.

The familiar tug of tightness in my chest hit me. Before I could let the emotions overtake me, Tae pulled me away from the bar to dance. Tae was amazing. A wonderful person. But I couldn't tell him about Sam. He couldn't know.

I wished I could talk to him about it. It would be nice to get out of my head and talk it through with someone. I had thought about seeing a therapist again, but I couldn't bring myself to start that hunt. It was hard enough to find someone I clicked with and even harder to find someone who wasn't condescending as they told me the same fucking thing over and over every session without providing me any actual guidance.

So, I danced with Tae and Mariam, drinking until we could barely stand, and pushed thoughts of blue eyes, soft blond hair, and smooth pale skin that reminded me of summer from my thoughts.

Chapter 12

Sam

When Jane and Dad called me, their excitement about Ash's promotion was contagious. I wanted to call him. I wished he had called me, but I didn't tell him when I opened my company. I didn't expect him to call me for this.

It was a crushing reality I hated.

How did we go from best friends talking every day to this? I had to hear news about him secondhand. Three years ago, he would have called me first. We would be celebrating together. It would've been a blast. Instead, I was walking out of a dark office building at eleven o'clock on a Monday night, cold and alone, texting my former best friend a fraction of what I wanted to say to him.

Some days, I wanted to give in. But I was determined to stay true to my original words. Romance between us would ruin our family. It was out of the question. I loved Jane and Angie too much to risk losing them. To risk causing my dad another divorce.

The flip of that was the loss of my best friend.

I pushed through the door leading to the skywalk from my office building and hurried to my car. It was normal for me to leave the office late. Some of my clients were in other countries and different time zones. A meeting with potential clients at ten p.m. was a typical day for me.

My car was freezing, and it took forever to warm up. I was shivering so hard I didn't want to drive, but it was late, and I was exhausted, so I flipped the radio on to listen to a random station before pulling my car out of the parking garage, praying for the heater to kick in. A thick layer of salt covered the roads. There were still little patches of ice along the edges from a storm that had hit the East Coast, blanketing the area in ice.

I turned onto a small two-lane road. It was quiet, with no other cars in sight. The weather reporter rambled about another storm coming in the next few days, possibly bringing the last of the year's snow. I passed a shopping center and a few neighborhoods before taking the ramp onto the highway.

The sound of screeching tires filled the air, interrupting the man's droning voice. Before I could find where the accident happened, my head smashed into something, turning everything into a blur of shadows and headlights.

Eerie silence shrouded me in a bubble. The ringing in my ears was the only thing I could hear. I blinked, trying to clear my vision of the darkness engulfing me.

"Sir—" the voice cut out, overpowered by the high-pitched ringing.

My head was heavy, my chest tight, and a chill blanketed my skin. I blinked repeatedly until the world gradually came into focus, the shadows receding as reality took hold. Lights blinded me from all directions. The yellow hue lit up my car. A chilly, wet dot hit my nose, sending a shiver down my spine. The windshield was gone, likely lying in pieces. Snowflakes fluttered through the broken windshield, landing on me like tiny kisses of ice.

A cough hit me when I tried to move, sending searing pain down my side.

There were voices in the distance, but I couldn't understand what they said. My phone lit up in the passenger seat. Glass covered everything, but it looked like my phone had managed to escape the disaster.

The seatbelt choked me when I leaned over, reaching for my phone.

A hand landed on my shoulder, firmly pulling me back.

I didn't know how I got it, but my phone landed in my hand, and that firm hold on my shoulder remained.

I swiped my phone open, hit the call button, and stared at the first name on my favorites list: Ash.

No.

I scrolled down until I reached Dad's contact, hit the call icon, and tapped the speaker button.

The longer I was awake, the more my body became aware of sensations. The cold slowly settled over me. My chest throbbed in so many places I didn't know if I was stabbed or broke a rib. The hand on my shoulder was growing painfully annoying, but yelling at the person made no sense. They were probably trying to keep me from doing something dumb.

"Sam," Dad's voice pierced my ears, "it's late."

"Ye—" I sputtered, but the rest wouldn't come out.

A hand reached down from the window.

Ah, that glass broke, too. Guess the car is totaled.

"Sir, your son has been in a pretty serious wreck."

"He what?" Dad sounded as if he had jumped out of bed and stumbled to the floor. "What hospital are they taking him to?"

"We don't know yet. The ambulance is on the way."

Everything after that was a blur. I was poked and prodded. Carried off into an ambulance by sexy paramedics. If I hadn't felt like such shit, I would've flirted with at least the guy giving me flirty looks. Or maybe I imagined the looks. But, hell, a guy could dream.

They rushed me into the emergency department, skipping past the entire line of people. I shouldn't have felt special getting to cut in line, but at the time, it was cool.

Nurses and a doctor looked me over, patched me up, and gave me some really awesome drugs that made all the pain not exactly go away, but more like made my brain not care that I hurt.

"Sam!" Dad flew into the room, worry all over his face as he rushed toward me.

Jane was close behind him, clutching her purse to her chest, her knuckles white like she held onto the strap for balance.

"Hey," I croaked.

Dad wrapped his arms around me, careful of the bandages and my left arm which had been placed in a sling. It wasn't broken, but it was banged up. My ribs were bruised. Felt like they broke in half, but I was lucky to escape with minor injuries.

"We spoke with the police," Jane said, her lips turning down with a frown. "A drunk driver lost control on a patch of ice and hit you and another car."

"Don't tell Ash."

They exchanged a look before Dad asked, "Why?"

"I don't want him to worry."

If Ash knew I was in the hospital and had been in a bad wreck, he would be on the next flight home and wouldn't care about anything but getting to me. It was how he had always been with me. He had too much going on in his own life to need to worry about me. Plus, ruining the night of celebrating his promotion with this kind of news would be unfair to him.

Leo held the door to the karaoke bar open, letting me pass him. "Thanks," I said.

"Anytime, cripple," he replied teasingly.

I knew he meant it as a joke because of my injured arm, but I couldn't bring myself to laugh.

We weaved through the crowded bar to the back near the stage, where someone was already slurring their words, singing along to a popular song.

Sean lifted his glass at our approach and yelled, "He lives!"

Rainie and Selena laughed, tapping the base of their shot glasses on the table.

"How's the arm?" Rainie asked, then downed her shot.

"Better." I lifted my arm, showing off my newfound freedom. "Today's the first day I didn't need the sling, but my ribs are still sore."

I slid carefully into a chair across from her, and Leo sat to my right, putting himself between me and Sean.

Sean leaned in. "At least you have Leo to drive you places." He slapped Leo on the back. "How's being your boss's chauffeur going?"

Leo laughed, shoving Sean. "Shut up."

"I'm waiting on the insurance companies to decide how much I'll get from the wreck before I buy anything, but they haven't given me a rental yet."

"Want to borrow my car?" Selena asked, leaning against Rainie. "I barely use it since I commute on the metro. Rain could always drive me somewhere if I need a ride until you get a car."

Selena and Rainie had moved in together a year ago. Their relationship started out hot and kept the momentum. I was sure they'd marry and ask me to be their bridesmaid. Bridesperson? I wondered which of them I would stand with. Selena because I told her to go for it, or Rainie because I'd known her the longest?

"Thank you, Selena, but I can't take your car. I'll be fine."

Leo scoffed, nudging my elbow. "Yeah, 'cause you're using me."

I glared at him. "Now you're taking Sean's side? I'll get a rideshare home tonight if you're gonna be sour about it."

His smile dropped, then he leaned close to my ear and whispered, "Don't do that. I had plans for you now that you don't have that sling on."

I rolled my eyes but smiled.

It was nice to be out with my friends. They were great distractions when life chose to drag me down.

May

One Year Later

Chapter 13

Ash

The dim room was filled with the sounds of grunts and skin slapping skin. The man beneath me released a deep, satisfied groan as he came. Moments later, I joined him in the momentary full-body sensation of pleasure.

Without a care, I pulled out of him and removed the condom. Strutting across the hotel room, I dropped the condom in the trash can and disappeared into the bathroom to clean up.

When I stepped back into the room, the guy was still on the bed in the same position I had left him.

"Oh my god," he said. "That was—"

"You don't have to finish whatever you're going to say," I said, sliding into my jeans. "The room's paid for. Stay the whole night if you want." I slipped into my plain white T-shirt, then my shoes, and headed for the door, grabbing my leather jacket and motorcycle helmet on the way.

"What's your name?" the guy called from his position on the bed.

I smiled at him and said, "You don't get to know that."

He groaned, probably frustrated, but I wasn't here for a relationship. Relationships weren't in my sights. I pulled open the door and strolled through the hotel halls, leisurely making my way to the parking lot. I did this at least once a week. Met up with random people, fucked their brains out before ditching them to go home empty and unsatisfied.

In the four years since I moved to Raleigh to work with Tae, my taste in sexual partners had grown—different. Once I discovered how much I liked being with men while trying to get Sam out of my head, it only made it worse. It started as experimenting to see if I genuinely was bi. Experimenting turned into wanting.

The dating apps made it easy to find a partner for the night. Most of the time, finding a one-night stand on the fly was simple. I never saw the same person twice. While I enjoyed whoring around, fulfilling wouldn't be the way to describe it. It wasn't even satisfying anymore.

I was going through the motions. Living, but not feeling, unless feeling an ever-present longing for my best friend counted. *I'm sure a therapist would tell me it does. I'm sure a therapist would tell me a lot of things.*

Mom, Gary, and Angela thought I was happy in Raleigh, living out this new, exciting dream. It wasn't that I was unhappy; it was that a huge part of me was missing, and the pain of that emptiness was crushing. I told my family lies about why I couldn't make it to holidays. Why I came around once or twice a year and only stayed a few days at most.

When I was back home, I would stay at my parent's house and sleep in my childhood room. Sam and I avoided each other, but after four years, I was still hung up on him. I tried to move on. I did. Each time someone tried to get close, I ended it. I couldn't do it. I couldn't handle trusting someone. Giving myself to someone when the only person I wanted was burned into my memories and unattainable was cruel to everyone involved, so I avoided it like I avoided everything.

My foot hit the pavement, and I marched toward my motorcycle. I slipped on my helmet, started it up, then took off into the night toward my next destination.

The bar's tiny parking lot was packed, so I pulled up onto the sidewalk and parked alongside the building under a large tree. It was an older bar, inherited by Tae's friend Jeff when his dad passed away two years ago. He refused to renovate the place, said it had "character," and wanted to keep the old southern biker bar charm. I tugged off my helmet and glided through the sea of people crowding around the outdoor patio.

Yellowish, warm lights barely lit the shadowed bar. The tang of spilled beer and sweat filled the musty air.

Tae leaned on the corner of the bar, resting his forearm on the old, worn wooden countertop. He wore slim-fit, light gray slacks with black and white plaid stripes, a black T-shirt, and a simple silver necklace. He shoved a hand in his pocket, his forearm catching the light on his dark skin, showing off his tattoo. Last year, I'd taken him to meet Lexi, and he walked away with a forearm piece and a crush.

I dropped onto the barstool beside Tae and tapped my fingers on the bar top, winking at the bartender. "Give me your best whiskey."

The guy nodded and started fixing my drink.

"Sorry I'm late," I said, facing Tae. "I was busy."

He rolled his eyes. "I know you were getting your dick wet. I hope you showered before coming here."

I chuckled, shaking my head. "Not a drop of water touched this body. I came here right away."

"Gross, dude," he said, waving his hand in my direction like I stank. "Did you at least wash your hands?"

I tilted my head with a smile. "Nah." I was joking to make him uncomfortable. It made me warm inside to watch him squirm.

"Why the fuck am I friends with you?" He looked at me, exasperated. "Don't touch anything. God. I hope she was hot."

I pursed my lips, acting like I was thinking about it. "I guess they were."

"I'm pretending this part of the conversation never happened." He grabbed his drink, took a big swig, and wiped his mouth with the back of his hand before setting the glass on the bar. "Are you still going home before your birthday?"

I nodded as the bartender slid my drink toward me. "I'm driving up on Sunday. Angela has her graduation the day after my birthday."

"Damn, guess we have to celebrate you turning twenty-nine when you get back."

"You don't have to plan anything. I'd rather pretend I'm young forever."

"Fine, but I'm going all out for your thirtieth."

I bit my lip and pulled my phone from my pocket. Angela had texted me four days ago, asking when I was coming home, but each time I went to reply, I couldn't bring myself to do it.

"Look, Ash, I know something happened between you and Sam, and things haven't been the same since, but maybe this two-week visit home can be like a new beginning for the two of you."

I locked my phone and hastily tucked it away in my pocket. "Yeah, I don't think so." I chugged the whiskey, letting the burn distract my memories of Sam.

"I know I say this every time you go home, and you're probably tired of me saying it, but I'm here if and when you want to talk."

I dropped my hand onto his shoulder and said, "Thanks, Tae, but like every time you offer, I'd rather not talk about it."

While Sam wasn't my actual brother, people had strong opinions.

I was afraid. Afraid that the one friend I had left in this world would run far away from me if he knew my secret.

"Suit yourself, man."

"Did you get a chance to look over the proposal I sent to you this morning?" I asked.

"Not yet. I'll probably read through it in the morning when I have coffee in front of me."

"I expect you to love it."

He scoffed and chugged his drink, slamming the glass on the countertop. "You don't get special treatment just because we're friends."

"Yeah, yeah. Big bad boss-man, I hear you. You'll still love it."

My favorite team in the research and development department of Design For Better Lives was looking into ways to turn our teaching software into an application for tablets and phones. My other proposal was to create a video game to help kids with learning disabilities in subjects taught in K through twelve.

With Tae and Mariam trusting me as the CIO of DFBL, I was finally in a position where I knew I could make a difference. I was empowered, and the fulfillment I gained from that knowledge fed me. It kept the darkness in my heart from consuming me and was one of the reasons I was grateful my life had fallen apart. If I had never taken the job Tae offered me, I would've missed the opportunity to be here today.

Changing the subject, I leaned in close to Tae and said, "How does it feel to know my team kicked your team's ass this year?"

Because of Tae, I'd grown to like sports. I lived to root for the team opposite his so I could piss him off when his teams lost. This time, the Washington Capitals knocked Boston out of the Stanley Cup playoffs, and I was about to rub it in his face all night.

"Fuck off! The Caps only won because our best defenseman is injured!"

I laughed, waving down the bartender for another drink. "Keep dreaming."

Chapter 14

Sam

Angie's graduation from her master's program should have been filled with happiness and pride, but it shrouded me in dread. Ash planned to stay in town for two weeks. Dad thought it would be a great idea to spend the first week as a family helping Angie move into her new apartment and attend her graduation ceremony. That would be expected. Normal. But then he had to bring up an idea for us all to go on a family vacation to celebrate her accomplishment. Not any vacation, either. I would have thought we would go to the beach. No. Since Dad and Angie loved camping in the woods and exploring mountains, we had to go to the woods.

I hated camping. Hated the woods.

Ticks. Dirt. Sweat, and not the good kind of sweat. It wasn't my thing. Sleeping in a tent was the last thing I wanted to do for a vacation. I would need a vacation after my vacation.

My office door swung open, and Autumn walked in with a stern glare aimed my way.

Since I opened my company, she'd been my assistant, and I put a ton of pressure on her shoulders. She had to make sure I was doing what I needed, and today, I had been avoiding all of it to wallow in dread.

"Sam," she said, dragging her finger over her tablet's screen, "you missed a meeting at one o'clock. It was important, and they were not happy."

Her dark curls bounced in her face as she strutted toward me and roughly set the tablet on my desk, positioned so I could see the schedule. Her deep brown eyes peered at me like she wanted to shove a dagger through my heart. Her impeccably manicured nails captivated me. They were so long and elegant that it seemed impossible to function with them. She took one of those long nails and aimed it at my face.

"You are giving me a damn ulcer."

I bit back my grin and leaned forward, glancing at the tablet's screen.

"Autumn, I'm sorry I missed the meeting. I didn't realize it was time for it."

She waved her hand like she was flicking my words away, her gold bracelets jingling over her smooth brown skin with the motion.

"I fixed it, but you better not put me in that position again."

"I'll be more careful moving forward."

She pulled back, taking the tablet back into her grasp with a dangerous smirk, then said, "Good, because you are busy next week. I'll refresh your memory."

"No need. We can worry about it on Monday."

Her smirk morphed into a grin shrouded with the spark of revenge. "Ahem." She fake cleared her throat and started rattling off everything I needed to do promptly on Monday morning.

I sat back, taking my punishment, listening to her list every single thing down to the tiniest details.

Ten minutes into my punishment, she finally made it through Tuesday, which I had dedicated to moving Angie into her apartment.

"Starting on Wednesday, I have you set to unavailable, but one of our international clients wants to hold a meeting at eight p.m. to discuss opportunities. I told him I needed to speak with you before confirming."

She glanced up from the tablet, waiting for my response.

It didn't matter what I would be doing with my family at that time. I needed to make room for my client.

"Approve the meeting."

She nodded and continued down the list.

"Thursday, you will be one hundred percent unreachable, correct?" I nodded, and she continued, "Starting Saturday, you will be off the grid until Thursday, when you will drive back to Virginia. I've ensured Everly and Imogene are prepared to take over your responsibilities while you're away."

"Sounds like you have everything handled," I said. "I feel better knowing Victory X will be in your capable hands."

Her features softened, and she moved closer to my desk. "On the topic, how are you feeling about spending that much time with your brother?"

Autumn and I had grown close since I opened Victory X. I considered her a friend.

"Not great, but we are very good at pretending to be fine around our family."

She pulled back, reverting to her stern glare, and said, "Well, maybe this is the punishment I've been praying you get."

I gasped and said, "Punishment? You're asking God to punish me?" She nodded with a huge smile, then I asked, "For what?"

"Like I said earlier, you're giving me an ulcer. Maybe now you'll be the one to have an ulcer, and I can laugh at your suffering."

"Rude." I shook my head.

She flipped the protective cover over her tablet and headed for the door, leaving me with a laughter-filled goodbye.

When Autumn was out of sight, I sunk further into my chair, letting it hug me while I returned to my thoughts. This would be the longest stay since Ash moved away. I had so many mixed feelings about being around him. His moving away four years ago left me feeling lost. I didn't know how to function without him, but I attributed my success to his leaving. His leaving gave me the need to focus on something, and that something was starting my dream. I couldn't tell him that, though. I didn't want him to think I was happy he left.

At first, I was angry he ran away. It hurt, but I understood. If nothing could come of his feelings, Ash would only grow to hate me. I knew that. It surprised me I hadn't grown to hate him. Resent him. But was the situation we were in any better? I didn't think so. I would rather he hate me.

When Jane and Dad asked why Ash would suddenly uproot his life, he said his gaming buddy offered him a job he couldn't refuse. The timing was too coincidental, though.

After he left and started coming home only for one or two holidays a year, our family became curious about what happened between us. They'd noticed the shift, and neither of us explained it. We didn't even come up with a lie. I explained that we had a fight and hadn't resolved it, but that was never enough to satisfy them.

I thought the distance would be good for us. Expected we would move past it. I hoped I would slowly move on and find it easier to get over him. That wasn't the case. He flittered through my thoughts daily. I was cursed to pine after him for the rest of my life.

My office door opened again, and Leo waltzed in. He closed the door, turning the lock. "You look tense," he said, loosening his tie as he approached my desk.

I rolled my eyes and huffed, "Because I am."

He slipped his tie off, dropping it on my desk as he sat and slid his leg between my thighs. "I can help with that." His light brown hair fell into his eyes when he leaned closer, bringing his lips inches from mine. "If you want."

"You want to fuck in my office?" I asked, my breath picking up.

Leo and I had grown complicated since he started working for me. He came around more when he found out Ash had moved away, and I never turned him away. I craved being wanted. Some days, I tried to picture a future with him. I knew he liked me. His crush had been obvious for years, but whenever I considered it, my thoughts always turned back to Ash.

Leo licked his lips, then said, "You'll be alone with him for two weeks. Think you can last that long?"

I chuckled, dragging my fingers down his chest. "Thanks for thinking so highly of me." I leaned in, closing the distance between us until my lips brushed over his stubbled jaw. I nipped the hair and smiled. "I'll take you up on your offer, but not here."

He pouted. "After work?"

"Want to come with me and Sean to a club in DC?"

"The one you two always go to?"

I nodded.

"I'll meet you there."

I leaned back in my chair, creating distance between us. "Good. I'll see you tonight."

When Leo left my office, unease settled over me that he was hoping for more from me. A relationship wasn't something I was willing to give him. I couldn't.

Maybe it was time to end things with him. I was worried it would be awkward with him being my Chief Financial Officer, but if he wanted what I couldn't give, it could cause drama I didn't want to deal with. None of our friends knew about us. We'd kept it quiet. I liked the freedom of being able to be with anyone I wanted. But there was a comfort in Leo being a friend that I leaned into a little too much.

Chapter 15

Ash

I pulled into the driveway leading to my parents' house and parked my bike near the garage before cutting the engine. The ride home was filled with loud music to drown out the little voice in my head screaming to turn back. These two weeks around Sam would be the exact torture I had run away from. I was terrified I would do something I couldn't take back. Terrified of myself. Of my impulsiveness.

There were times when the impulses screamed so loudly it was impossible to keep from acting on them.

I often wondered if that's what drove my father to violence. I wasn't a violent person, but I was quick to anger in the right situation. It was why I'd gotten into so many fights as a kid and ended up in detention or suspended. If someone threatened the people I cared about, I didn't stop to think—I acted. I was afraid that if I lost control, I would end up like my father: a violent alcoholic, hurting the people he was supposed to cherish. A man consumed with rage and the inability to control his actions.

I was afraid of the man I knew I could be.

Some days, I felt like I was on the edge of that darkness, and hands were reaching up from the abyss to tug me into that hell.

After withdrawing the key from the ignition, I stared at the side of the house, not wanting to go inside to face the questions that always came when I was home.

Why haven't you and Sam fixed things? How could it be that bad? Don't you guys want to be friends again?

The questions were never-ending.

Sam was probably at his apartment since his car wasn't in the driveway. The idea of seeing him consumed my thoughts. I wanted to see him. Hug him. Simply be near him. I missed talking with him. Hanging out. Having dinner in my shitty apartment. I missed him. I had half expected the resentment to hit me at some point, but it never did. Instead, I dreaded being around him because it was a reminder of everything we used to be and could never be.

I finally lifted myself off the bike, taking off my helmet as I approached the door.

The smell of cookies filled the foyer, reminding me of the days Mom used to bake when I was young. Angie didn't remember, but I did. Dad would go on a rampage, beat the crap out of Mom, or me, or both of us until he passed out from the alcohol, then Mom would cope by baking something. The house would fill with the smell of cookies, cakes, and confections—a sweet contrast to the horrors committed in the home where my innocence perished. The next morning, Dad would act like nothing happened, praising Mom for the sweets and the delicious smell of the fresh desserts. He would kiss her on the cheek, whispering of his love for her as he ignored the bruises, the tears, and the house filled with fear.

I hated the smell of sweets because of it.

"Anybody home?" I called. "It's quiet today."

I set my helmet, jacket, and gloves on the floor near the door and walked through the hallway leading to the kitchen.

"Hi, honey," Mom replied from the kitchen.

Her long black hair hung in a loose ponytail, and little white finger marks and palm prints littered her apron.

"Did you get into a fight with the flour?" I asked, approaching her.

She looked down at her clothes and snorted before pulling me into a hug. I slumped against her, letting the comfort of her embrace envelop me.

"I dropped the new bag of flour when I was trying to open it," she said, pulling away.

"Show me that bag. I'll have a word with it for you, Ma."

She playfully smacked my shoulder and went back to rolling the cookie dough into perfect balls.

"Where are Angie and Gary?" I asked, leaning my hip against the counter while she rolled another ball and placed it on the mountainous pile in front of her.

Her eyes lit up, and she glanced at the back door. "Getting the camping gear ready for next week. The pair of them are so excited for the trip."

Angie deserved to have a nice trip where her family celebrated her accomplishment. I knew it wouldn't be what she wanted when Sam and I were in the same room, but I would try to give her the best two weeks I could manage.

"I'll go say hi before I hop in the shower."

Mom nodded, and I set my backpack on a chair before sneaking outside. I pushed the door open as silently as possible. I was lucky because Angie and Gary were laughing, hovering around the camping equipment. There was no way they'd heard me.

I tiptoed, coming up behind them, then lunged forward and wrapped my arms around Angie's waist. She screeched as I lifted her into the air, her feet flying forward. Her laugh filled my chest with warmth, and I squeezed her tight.

"Hi, piglet," I said, nuzzling my nose in her back. "I missed you."

"Ash!" she squealed before wriggling out of my grasp and wrapping her arms around me.

"Hey, Ash," Gary said, giving me a firm pat on the shoulder.

I spent an hour catching up with them. They told me about the camping gear, plans for grilling over a firepit, and how Mom and Gary would share a tent, and then the rest of us would each have a tent to ourselves. Angie was packing them up, and while they were tiny individual tents, it was better than the three of us sharing one.

"Now, remember, we won't be on those sissy campgrounds," Angie said. "We're doing real camping. Our bathroom will be nature." Her evil smile sent a chill down my spine.

"Are you kidding me?" I groaned teasingly.

Gary and Angie always dragged us camping once Mom and Gary were married. Every summer, they would take us out into the middle of nowhere and call it being "one with nature." I didn't mind it, but Sam hated it.

"By the way," Angie said, twirling a stick in her hands, "Sam is coming for dinner."

"Cool. I'm gonna hop in the shower since I spent half the day on a motorcycle in this heat."

Angie squinted at me but left it alone. None of them knew what happened, and Sam and I would keep it that way. This was a "to the grave" kind of secret. Unless he changed his mind, then I would happily parade him around as mine to anyone willing to listen. I still hoped he would realize our family wasn't as fragile as he thought.

"And later on, I'll need you two to help me with some boxes."

I backed away, saluting her, and said, "Got it, boss."

My room was the same as it had been since high school. Over the years since I'd lived in Raleigh, I'd left some clothes here so I could stay without needing to bring luggage. When I bought the motorcycle, I figured keeping clothes back home would be better than buying a whole car or renting something to drive up here.

I pulled open the bathroom door inside my bedroom and flicked on the light. The house was a four-bedroom, three-and-a-half-bath, where two bedrooms shared a connected bathroom. Sam and I had the two bedrooms with the shared bathroom, and Angie had the other bathroom to herself and the larger private room down the hall.

The bathroom was pristine. Decorated the same as it had been for years: dark blue shower curtain, black towels, and bath mat. The door to Sam's room was open, exposing the shadows to the bright light. His twin bed sat in the center of his room, facing the bathroom with the headboard against the wall. When our parents offered to upgrade him to a bigger bed, he refused it and said, "This is enough for me."

After a long, steamy shower, I changed into sweatpants and a black tank before heading downstairs.

Sam's smooth voice hit me from the kitchen before I turned the corner. My stomach flipped into my throat, and I paused, leaning against the wall, listening to him talk.

Mom chuckled, murmuring something I couldn't decipher.

"Autumn was furious with me. She's praying for something bad to happen to me while I'm in the woods," Sam said with a tone I was familiar with. He was joking but tense.

"Poor Sammy," Angie said, a slight snort mixed with her words. "I'll keep you safe out there."

"Son," Gary chimed in, "you can't treat your employees like you don't care. You have to show them you'll do whatever it takes to keep your company afloat, and part of that is being on time for meetings."

And this was where I needed to step in. Before Gary got on his soapbox, saying things he didn't need to. Sam cared about his employees. He didn't need a lecture.

I rolled off the wall and popped into the kitchen. "Did you guys miss me while I was gone?" I dropped into a chair across from Sam at the table, aiming a smile at him that said, "You're welcome for the save."

"Ash," Sam said.

He looked nice. His hair was shorter than I was used to seeing. It looked good on him, but I liked his regular length more, where his bangs fell into his eyes.

"You cut your hair," I said.

He tilted his head, giving me a once-over. "I figured I would cut it shorter for camping."

"Smart plan, Sammy," Angie said, patting his shoulder as she stood to help Mom at the stove.

The room was silent for a while before Gary dropped into the chair beside Sam and glanced between the pair of us.

"Can I ask you boys something?" Gary asked.

"What's up?" I said, sinking lower in the chair.

The tip of my toe bumped Sam's shoe, and I almost jerked away, but when he only looked at me and turned his attention back to his dad, I chose to stay put.

"Will you boys ever tell us what happened between you?" Gary asked, his eyes bouncing between me and Sam. "I know you both have said you don't want to talk about it, but it's been four years. Was it that bad that a lifetime of friendship was worth losing?"

Mom jumped in, adding, "I never understood how you two could drift apart so quickly."

"Give it a rest," I warned.

Sam shifted, his gaze dropping to the table like it used to when we were kids, and he didn't want to be in a situation anymore.

Angie marched over, determination oozing from her smile. "You two used to be attached at the hip, and now you can't stand to be in the same room."

You have it so damn wrong, guys.

Sam shifted again, his gaze flicking toward me for a brief moment before looking back at the table.

"I said to leave it the fuck alone," I growled.

"Fine, fine," Angie said, raising her hands up in surrender and winked at Gary. "So grumpy."

When Angie asked Sam and me to help her move into her new apartment, the last thing I expected was a building in Alexandria and for her apartment to be on the fifth floor. I also never expected there to be no elevator.

"Angela," I growled from the curb, "I'm going to strangle you and bury you in those campgrounds you love."

"Count me in," Sam said.

I looked at him, an eyebrow raised, surprised he was joining in.

He shrugged. "What?"

"Nothing," I said, unlocking the back of the moving truck, and stared at the packed space. "Angie, the least you could have done was invite some friends."

She pouted and grabbed my arm. "But I wanted my brothers to help me."

Sam released a gruff laugh and climbed into the truck, wedging between a dresser and a mattress. "You could've had your brothers and friends." He grabbed the mattress and slid it toward me. "Now we're both going to be spent."

I grunted my agreement, taking the mattress and pulling it down. "Fucking preach, bro."

I knew he hated when I called him bro, but I couldn't help myself. I loved pushing his buttons.

The mattress flew at me, knocking me back a step. I bit my lip, holding back my laugh. "Piglet, I better see you lifting and sweating when we come back down these stairs."

She groaned with a cute pout.

"I expect to see your hands full," I added.

"Forehead dripping with sweat," Sam said, hopping to the ground and pushing me back toward the stairs with the mattress between us. "I also expect you to feed me a mountain of food for this."

"Don't worry. Dad and I already have dinner planned."

"Good." I took the first step backward and groaned, knowing how shit this was going to be.

Five hours later, Sam and I set the dresser down in Angie's bedroom. It was the last thing to bring in. We were soaked in sweat. My legs felt like jello. My shirt was suctioned to my chest, and all I wanted to do was collapse.

"Finally," I said, blowing out a breath before dropping to the floor and rolling onto my back.

Sam was less exaggerated about it but joined me. "I don't think I have the energy to leave this room," he huffed.

I chuckled and looked over at him. "Think she would let us shower here?"

"We don't have clothes."

"Fuck."

He grunted, then yelled, "Piglet!"

She rushed into the room and hovered over us. "You guys look dead."

"I feel it," I said.

"Guess I'll be burying you both in the woods." She giggled. "Oh, how the tables turn."

"Angie," Sam whispered, like he was too tired to speak, "get us something to drink, or you might actually have to follow through with the burial."

A moment later, Angie returned with two ice-cold water bottles and Gary.

"You both look like hell." Gary laughed, then tossed a bag dead center on my chest. "Hop in the shower while Angie and I take the truck back."

With a grunt, I pushed the bag off my chest. "I don't wanna move."

Gary hurried away and called, "Reservations are in an hour and a half. I know you're both hungry."

Hungry was nowhere near describing the state of my stomach. It felt like it was trying to claw its way out of my body and turn into a Venus Flytrap.

I shoved the bag at Sam and said, "You first."

He took it, rolling onto his side before crawling to the bathroom. In moments, the shower was running, and I was left knowing he was naked and soapy in the next room. How had I gone most of my life with him doing this exact thing from our shared bathroom and never once acted on it? Never once thought about it, yet now, it was all I could think about.

Passing the time, I scrolled through my phone and watched a few videos. My attention was fixed on some guy talking about bonsai trees. How I got there, I wasn't sure. The algorithm was its own animal, but I was having fun until my eyes wandered to the looming figure above me with a pink towel wrapped around his waist. Water rolled down his exposed skin. One hand held the towel in place and the other clutched a bundle of clothes.

I cleared my throat and set my phone on the ground. "Done?"

He nodded, walked past me, and tossed the clothes on the bed.

Before I could make things awkward—well, more awkward—I shifted to my feet and fled the room.

Even an icy shower couldn't erase the images of Sam dripping wet. And when I heard Gary's booming chuckle, I rushed to dress and join them.

Chapter 16

Sam

Ash's birthday dinner was almost normal—*almost.*

Angie sat beside Ash, keeping close to him while she talked with Dad, who sat at the head of the table. Jane sat on my right, keeping Ash and me locked in conversation with her the whole time.

Across from me, Ash looked delicious in a black button-up and tight jeans tucked into black boots. And the glare he aimed my way did everything but scare me. It twisted my insides. Exciting me in ways that would make anyone blush. It was downright predatory.

Ash was like a cat deciding the best way to hunt his prey.

He had noticed I caught him staring, and instead of looking away, he smirked. *The cocky jerk.*

I swallowed, and his eyes trailed down my neck before returning to my face.

Jane leaned over, bringing her lips close to my ear, and whispered, "Come back to the house when we leave here. We want to give Ash his gifts and have cake, but don't tell him."

I chuckled, asking, "Does he not know he's getting these things?"

She shook her head. "He told us not to bother. Apparently, his birthday is now a reminder that he's getting old."

What a weirdo. "I have a business call at eight, but otherwise, I'm free," I whispered.

Jane checked her watch with a nod. "We better get home then. We can probably get everything done before you need to take your call."

"Sounds good to me."

Jane nodded and tapped Dad on the arm. "Time to go."

Dad hopped up from the table and grabbed Angie by the shoulder, continuing their conversation as they walked out of the restaurant together.

Ash smiled the entire time he was forced to open gifts and eat cake, but there was an emptiness behind his smile that I'd seen since he moved to North Carolina. He would put on his smiles and force his laughs. The ever-changing chameleon blending into the needs of those around him.

He was good at pretending with people, but I saw through it. He was sad, and I was part of it, if not the whole reason.

The reminder on my phone went off, and I quickly excused myself, jogging up the stairs to my childhood room. I closed my bedroom door behind me and turned on the dim desk lamp before lying on the bed. I was grateful it was a phone call and not a video conference as I dropped onto the bed and dialed the number.

"Hello, this is Samuel Pearce from Victory X," I said, introducing myself to the man on the other end.

His accent was heavy, and I pressed the phone to my ear with the volume up as loud as it would go.

The sound of others joining the call came through the phone, and Imogene, the president of my company, and Everly, my vice president, introduced themselves.

A few others joined before I started the discussion.

Twenty minutes into my meeting, the bathroom light flicked on, and Ash appeared like a shadow. I was silent, listening to the man and his accountant discuss the logistics of my offer.

The sound of a zipper dropping had me springing up. I had the perfect view of Ash pulling his dick out while standing over the toilet. I dropped the phone and fumbled with it to find the mute icon before his release echoed through my ears.

My heart pounded, climbing up my throat.

"Ash!"

His head snapped up, eyes landing on me.

"Seriously?" I said, pointing to my phone.

"My bad. Didn't realize you were in there." He reached over, closing the door with a soft click.

I breathed through my anxiety, wrapping up my call moments before Ash sauntered in from the bathroom and flopped onto the bed, sprawling out like he owned the place. The sound of my sigh filled the room before I placed my phone on the corner of the bed.

"Why are you in here?" I asked.

"Sorry about whipping it out in front of you. I seriously didn't realize you were just chillin' in here."

"It's whatever," I said. "Thankfully, no one on my call heard you."

Ash rolled onto his back, grabbed my shirt collar, and tugged me down beside him.

"Can we call a temporary truce?" Ash asked, a bit of hesitance in his voice. "At least until I leave, and then we can go back to pretending we hate each other."

I scoffed. "Who's pretending to hate who?"

"Maybe you're right." Ash sighed. "We aren't pretending to hate each other. We're avoiding each other."

"You do a pretty good job of avoiding me."

He ran his hand over his five o'clock shadow; his scruffy look was my favorite. It looked so good on him. If I tried to grow out my facial hair, I looked like an old man who had already gone gray because my hair was so close to white.

"Look, I want to give Angie the good time she deserves. She deserves to have a happy, loving family celebrating her big moment," he replied.

"I wasn't disagreeing with you, Ash."

"Well, it felt like you were about to start something."

"Really?" I shot him a glare, then fixed my attention on the ceiling.

"We'll be trapped together for five days. Do you think you're ready for that?" he asked, but it sounded more like a question for himself than for me.

"Can you manage to be normal? Because I know I can."

"I'll try."

"Only try?"

"We have a lot of unspoken and unresolved feelings floating around, Sam." He rolled onto his side to look at me.

"And?"

"I want to talk about it."

"I don't."

"Then listen while I talk," he said, letting the silence hang between us for a while. "I've been with a lot of people in the last four years. A lot."

"Is this going somewhere?" I swallowed. Afraid. Nervous. Anticipating something—anything. When it came to Ash, I could usually read him, but sometimes he was impossible to predict.

"Remember how this all started? With Jaz lying about me being bi to Rainie?"

"How could I forget, Ash? Get to the point."

When our eyes locked, my heart jumped, kicking up speed until I was dizzy. I wanted to reach out and touch his face. Smooth his frown. Slide my fingers through his hair. I wanted him so badly it hurt to look at him. His cologne filled the space, warming me with notes of sandalwood and jasmine. I was lost in his eyes, the browns too shadowed in the dim light to show off the golden flecks that reminded me of champagne.

"I've figured out I'm actually bisexual," he said. Before I had a moment to realize what was happening, he straddled me, lips brushing my ear as he spoke. "If someone has a hole, I'll fill it."

Electricity raced down my spine, snapping my body to life. My heart thundered, and my dick twitched to life like a traitor.

"Get off of me," I warned.

He didn't budge. Then he dropped his hips until his ass settled over my growing erection.

"Wanna know something else, Sammy?" he asked, grinding on me, sending a burst of lust through me. "I think about you every time I come."

I bit back the breathy groan threatening to escape my lips and pushed hard against Ash's chest.

He stumbled back with a smirk. "Wanna jerk each other off now that we're like this?"

I kicked his stomach, knocking him back further.

"What the fuck is wrong with you?" I shouted.

He chuckled, righting himself like nothing happened. "Guess not." He moved back into my space, leaning close, brushing his lips over my ear again, sending a wave of chills down my arms. "Sammy, one of my worst fears came true."

He kissed my cheek. The caress of his lips lit up my insides like a bonfire. I wanted to pull him down until his body was flush with mine and give in.

I knew better. Suffering in silence was the only way.

"I'm just like my father," he whispered before backing away.

I blinked a few times, watching him disappear through our shared bathroom. The sound of the bathroom door closing jerked me out of my shock.

What the fuck was he thinking? Was he trying to make me hate him?

I stilled. That would be something he would do. A last resort to protect himself from something painful. Push me away so I couldn't hurt him. It was the same reason he ran away to a different state. Was being around me that hard for him?

I had been pining after Ash for more than half my life, so I was used to the pining. The intense longing. But I had to admit, since that kiss, it was harder to pretend and ignore my feelings. Maybe I was lucky since I was used to telling myself no when it came to Ash, but Ash never had to do that before.

I stared at the bathroom doorway like it would show me what to do.

Do I go talk to him or leave him be?

Talking to him could make it worse, but leaving him alone showed that I didn't care about his feelings, and I was positive he was having big feelings after that show he put on.

I stood, resigning myself to talking with him even if it meant talking about the exact things I didn't want to. I passed through the bathroom to his door and swung it open, thankful he didn't lock it.

Surrounded by shadows, he stood, focused on the view outside his window. Moonlight poured in, casting a soft white light over his now shirtless form. His eyes shimmered when he looked at me, a deep frown marring his beautiful face.

I'm just like my father. His words echoed through my mind with a gut-wrenching chill.

"What does that mean, Ash?" I marched toward him, grabbing his face with both hands, forcing him to look at me. "You are nothing like *that* man."

He smiled, but it barely made a dent in his frown. "It's kind of you to say that, but you don't know me anymore."

"Ash, how dare you say that? You haven't changed that much."

"You'd be surprised how much someone can change." His fingers curled around my wrists, lifting my palms away from his face. "I'm sorry I fucked with you like that. I won't do it again." He pushed my hands to my sides and stepped away from me.

"Ash, don't be like this. Don't make me walk away from you when you're like this." I took a step toward him, and he shrank from me.

"What gives you the right to care anymore?"

Was he serious?

"Ash, come on. I care about you more than anyone."

"You have a funny way of showing it, *bro*."

I hated when he used "bro" as an insult, like a dig.

"Stop calling me that."

"What's wrong, bro? You don't like being my brother anymore?" He stepped back again.

"Ash," I said, moving closer. "You are not your father."

"Thanks. I know I'm not him. It would be impossible."

"You're being so fucking difficult." I pressed my palm to his chest and shoved him back a step. His eyes blazed to life with the fight I had always seen directed at others. My heart lurched. He had never looked at me with such anger before. "Why are you acting like this?" I pushed him again, and he barely moved. "Pushing me away. Pulling me in."

His face morphed into a crooked smile, flashing his teeth. It was beautiful and menacing. "Do you hate me yet, Sammy?"

"Hate you? I could never hate you."

"Why not? It would be easier for us both if you did."

"Why do you want me to hate you? Do I hurt you so much that you want us to fight for real? Do you want me to resent you? Wish you what? Didn't exist?"

"It would be better than living like this," he shouted. His whole body tensed, and his eyes widened like he was cracking, ready to break down.

"What the hell does that mean?" I pleaded. "I need you to give me something here, Ash. Anything. I'm begging you."

"I can't." He sounded tired, like he was giving up. His back hit the wall, and he slid to the floor, rubbing his hands over his face. "What I want from you, you won't give." He curled in on himself, shrinking, and released a heavy breath. His fingers curled into his hair, tugging at the roots.

For the first time in years, I saw him. Truly saw him. He was still the little boy who beat up my bullies. The boy who cried when I couldn't. Who shielded me from pain. Who took it all on to protect others but forgot to protect himself. Behind his hard exterior was a fragile little boy still looking for someone to see him.

I dropped to my knees and hugged him, sliding between his thighs, closing the space between us. Gripping the back of his head, I held him against me. His breath stuttered, hot against my chest. When he wrapped his arms around me, it was like the last four years vanished.

"What the hell is wrong with me?" Ash asked, tugging on my shirt as he pulled me closer.

"Nothing is wrong with you." I ran my fingers through his hair, staring at the wall, blinking away the tears threatening to surface. "Nothing."

"I feel broken. I'm tired and losing my grip."

"No, you're not broken." I squeezed him, taking in a deep breath. "You're the strongest person I know. You would never lose your grip. Never."

"You're a bad liar, or did you forget?"

"You're a much worse liar than I am, but I'm not lying. You are not broken, Ash. Don't think that."

"I don't trust myself anymore," he whispered, his voice shaking while his body shuddered.

"Why not?" I stroked my fingers through his hair, holding him tight with my other. I feared if I let go, he would disappear.

He shook his head, refusing to answer me.

"You aren't like your father, Ash. Please tell me you know that."

He shook his head again, curling his fingers into my back. "I may not be violent, but I'm exactly like him. I try so hard not to be, but I am." A broken cry released from him, and his arms squeezed me tighter. "I can't trust myself, Sammy. Especially around you."

I curled over him, wrapping my arms around his neck like I could protect him from himself. "Don't say that," I whispered, hushing his worries. "I trust you implicitly, Ash. You would never hurt me."

A strangled cry escaped him, and he buried his face in my stomach. "I have hurt you. I'm hurting you right now."

"No," I whispered. "No, no. You aren't."

"Don't lie."

He sucked in a shaky breath, pulling back from me to look into my eyes. Tears streamed down his cheeks like falling stars catching the moonlight. He was beautiful even when crying, and I wanted nothing more than to kiss his tears away. Take his pain away.

Why weren't we allowed to be together again? I'd almost forgotten because seeing him vulnerable and falling apart like this made me question my decision.

Is it worth it? Is it worth this?

Ash lifted his hand, bringing it to my face, and cupped my cheek. "I should've never gone to that bar," he whispered so quietly I could barely hear him.

His thumb slid along my jaw before tracing my lips.

Tears burned my eyes, trying to force their way out. A lump climbed up my throat, choking me. I drew my lips into a tight line, shaking my head. I wanted to say something. Anything, but it wouldn't come out. My voice was trapped behind the ball in my throat. What lie was I trying to speak? What was I trying to say? Only the truth wanted to come out.

I'm glad you kissed me because I'm in love with you.

I couldn't say that. If I said those words now, then what had I done for four years? The suffering I put us both through would be worthless.

Is it worth suffering more?

It was too late. The decision had been made long ago. Back when I was a thirteen-year-old boy who desperately wanted a family who loved me.

I dropped my hand to his shoulder. "Look, I'll tell everyone I'll stay the night, okay?"

"No," he said. "Go home."

"I don't want to leave you like this, Ash."

"I've lasted four years alone. I can manage."

My breath left me at his words. I used to be his support system. We were Ash and Sam, best friends. He used to rely on me for everything. Now, I wasn't allowed to be there for him? I wasn't allowed to support him?

I bit my lip, gripping his shoulder, digging my fingers into his tight muscles.

"I'm not leaving you alone tonight," I whispered. "Not tonight."

"Why?" he asked. "Why now?"

I brushed my thumb over his forehead, smoothing the creases, and said, "Because as much as you like to act like we don't care about each other, it doesn't make it true."

I pulled myself from his arms and rummaged through his dresser for a change of clothes. I didn't trust he would let me back in his room if I left. I dropped my pants and slid on a pair of shorts, then shed my dress shirt and folded it before setting it on the dresser.

"Been a while since we shared a bed, but you're not escaping this," I said.

Ash rose to his feet, his eyes raking over my mostly bare body. "I don't think that's very smart of you."

"Try anything funny, and I'm cutting off your hands."

"What a fucking asshole," he grumbled, unbuttoning his jeans before climbing into bed in only his boxers.

Who was I kidding? The rule applied to me, too.

Unlike me, Ash took it when our parents offered a bigger bed. It was a queen, and far better than my twin in the other room. I pulled back the covers and slid in beside him.

Once settled, we lay there in silence, staring at the ceiling. I was too afraid to talk. Too afraid of the emotional rollercoaster we were on.

"Can I kiss you?" Ash asked, breaking the silence.

"Go to sleep."

"Sam," he whispered, "I want to do way more than kiss you."

"Go to sleep."

"Let loose with me."

"No," I grumbled.

"Fine." Ash rolled over, facing away from me. "You're no fun."

"Good. Sleep."

I woke up tangled in bed with Ash. He had his face buried in my shoulder and his arm slung over my chest, but I couldn't savor the moment. If I let myself enjoy it, there would be no way to resist him. I was stupid for staying, but the way he looked last night, I was worried he would do something he couldn't undo.

"Ash," I whispered.

He groaned.

"We have to get ready for Angie's graduation."

"It's too early," he whined.

"It starts at noon. We have to leave soon."

I slid out of his grasp and moved to the bathroom, fighting every desire to break my rules and let us fall into something we couldn't take back.

Slipping into my room, I rumpled the sheets on my bed to make it appear I slept in it, changed into my clothes from the day before, then headed to the kitchen. The smell of breakfast hit me, making my stomach rumble. Jane stood over the sink rinsing a bowl filled with potatoes, and Dad glued his eyes to the coffeemaker, waiting for it to bless him with his morning pick-me-up.

"What are you still doing here?" Jane asked.

"I uh—" I paused, thinking up my excuse. "After my meeting last night, I was too tired and fell asleep."

She eyed me but said nothing.

I didn't think she noticed I hadn't actually been in my bed. My bedroom door had been closed.

The morning went by quickly, and before I knew it, I sat on a wooden bench in a massive auditorium, watching the college graduates walk up to the stage in their navy blue caps and gowns. Angie was graduating with a mark of distinction and had a cream chord pinned to her graduation gown. She was brilliant among her peers. Her makeup was done perfectly. Her hair was curled and styled, flowing down her back with tiny white pearl-like beads tied in among her silky black strands. She looked as if she was wearing jewels.

She was radiant beyond imagination, and the pride overflowing me made my heart swell with love for the beautiful, intelligent woman I had known my whole life, who I had the privilege of calling my sister.

Ash pressed his knee against mine in the cramped space. The families here to watch their kids were packed in like sardines, and I swore I caught Ash grinning when he and I ended up shoved against the wall and pushed as tight as we could fit.

When his thigh pressed harder against mine, I turned, glaring at him. "Can you stop doing that?"

"Doing what?" he asked, a teasing gleam in his eyes.

"Touching me," I said, pointing to his leg.

He shrugged and looked away.

"Ash," I said, using my leg to shove him.

His eyes turned on me with a cat-like glare. "Sam," he growled my name through his clenched jaw, sending my stomach flipping and fluttering into the clouds.

Oh, what I would give for him to do that again.

He leaned closer and whispered, "Are you trying to pick a fight to turn me on, or are you annoying for no reason?"

I swallowed, staring at him, trying desperately to hide my interest.

"Cat got your tongue?"

He sure does.

I forced my attention back to the stage where Angie was coming up behind four others.

"Do I make you nervous?" Ash whispered inches from my ear, his warm breath running over my skin.

I ran my palms over my thighs, trying to ignore the tension building between us. "Dream on."

Angie's name was called, and she walked across the stage, holding her head high. It was hard to believe she was graduating from her master's program. I could still picture the days she was running around in a diaper while Ash and I played in his family's backyard or hung out in his bedroom. Her little face would poke in through his bedroom door, asking if we wanted a snack. Sometimes, she would sneak in and curl up on the floor beside us while we played video games or watched a movie.

It was beginning to hit me that we were all grown up and living our lives separately.

Chapter 17

Ash

Birds chirped from nearby trees, welcoming the morning. Mom and Angie rushed out of the house carrying more bags. Gary appeared from the garage with a cooler rolling behind him. His graying hair was combed back, and his beard was freshly shaved. I hadn't gone camping with them in over five years, but it was comforting to see that some things never changed. Gary always shaved off his beard before a camping trip. He said it was his good luck charm. I never understood the reason behind it, but I never questioned it either.

Sam was running late, which was unlike him, and the minivan was overflowing with camping gear and supplies, leaving us with a problem: not everyone would fit. I shoved the last of the camping gear into the trunk before closing it.

"How are all of us getting there?" I said.

"What do you mean?" Angie asked, appearing beside me. "Sam's driving his car."

"He is?"

As the words left my lips, an orange Jeep Wrangler pulled up and parked behind the van.

"What the hell is this?" I asked, walking up to the driver's side, unable to believe my eyes.

Sam grinned from the driver's seat, leaning through the open window. "My weekend car," he replied.

"Weekend car? Are you a big shot now and have multiple cars?"

Sam shrugged. "The hybrid is for daily driving. This," he said, sliding his fingers along the steering wheel, "is for having fun."

"Wow. Okay," I said, rolling my eyes.

"You guys go ahead. I have the GPS pulled up already," Sam said to Gary, who was standing at the front of the minivan.

"See you at the rest stop at our halfway point," Gary called back and ushered Mom and Angie into the van. "You boys better behave." He climbed in and took off down the driveway, leaving me completely alone with Sam.

"Why did no one tell me this was the plan?" I asked.

Sam chuckled. "Does it matter?"

"Guess not," I said, walking around the Jeep. "When did you get this thing?" I climbed into the passenger side and buckled up.

"About six months ago." Sam put the car in drive, glancing at me with a slight smile.

No one told me.

Knowing I was out of the loop stung more than I cared to admit.

It was my own fault for pulling away from them and only coming home a few times a year at best. Whenever I asked about Sam, my family's responses were short. Nothing was ever offered up unless I directly asked, and I assumed it was the same for him.

Sometimes, I regretted how things turned out. The way we put our family between us. The lie that we were fighting—it killed me. I hated that we had drifted so far apart. I fucking hated it.

"What made you get this thing?" I asked.

He shrugged and turned onto the road. "Remember how much I wanted one as a kid?"

"No," I lied.

When he turned eight, Gary gave Sam a Jeep Wrangler model kit. Sam spent a week building it. He loved that thing. When we got jobs fresh out of college, Sam had hunted for a Jeep, but they were too far out of his price range, so he settled on a crappy used sedan. Then, when that finally died, he traded up for a hybrid to have a better commute to work. I thought his dream of owning a wrangler had been lost.

I was such an asshole for lying to him, but something told me to pretend I'd forgotten. Who would remember such a small thing, anyway? Only an obsessed jerk like me.

"I really wanted one and could finally afford it," Sam said, tapping the power button for the radio. The warm May air whipped through the cabin, drowning out the music.

I didn't say anything. I didn't know what to say or how to act. *Do I say, "Cool, I'm glad you finally realized a dream of yours," and then what?*

It was better to leave it alone.

"By the way, we have about an eight-hour drive, and we're only stopping at one rest station. Snacks are in the back seat." He motioned behind us with his thumb, then added, "Soda and water are in a small cooler back there. If you need to take a piss, we aren't stopping."

"I can always use a bottle."

"Absolutely not!"

I glared, shifting to face him. "You said we only get one stop along the way. Do you want me to piss out the window as you drive or a bottle?"

He groaned and gripped the steering wheel harder. "Bottle."

"That's right, jerk."

"Whatever," he said, mumbling something I couldn't hear under his breath.

I held in my laugh, watching the passing trees lining the highway. This visit home was weird. Since my birthday, it felt almost like we were closer to normal. Not quite normal, but we hadn't bickered and joked like this in years. It was nice to have these brief moments again.

The bright orange evening sun dipped behind the treetops as we pulled into the Ohio National Park and drove down a path to our camping plot. The campground was next to a river and had decent hiking trails that Gary and Angie had already made plans for. Angie even scheduled to take a break from camp one day and visit Lake Erie.

Ahead, Gary pulled the minivan into a clearing next to a fire pit and a worn picnic table. Sam quickly followed and parked beside the van under the thick canopy of a tree.

I hopped out of the car, stretching as I walked around the back to look around. The clearing could easily fit two or three more cars, and a small pathway led through a grouping of bushes into an open, grassy area beside a river.

"Boys, come help unload the van before it gets dark," Mom called from beside the van where she and Angie were unloading the smaller things we had shoved in the back seats.

"Sure, Ma," I said, approaching them.

"We should set up the tents first," Angie said, pointing to a stack of long bags in the trunk. "Those are them. We should have four."

"Okay." I grabbed the one on top and then kept going, unloading the trunk until everything was piled near the cars, but we had a problem. Angie said we should have four tents, but I only found three. "Piglet," I said, checking the van for signs of another tent bag. "We don't have four tents unless I'm completely blind."

"What do you mean? I packed four." She rushed over and counted the same pile of tent bags I had already checked ten times. "Oh," she whispered, "did I leave one behind?"

"I bet you did," I said, spinning toward the firepit where Gary and Sam were stacking wood for a fire. "Looks like we've got a problem. Angie miscounted the tents. We have three instead of four."

Gary stood, lighter in hand, and said, "Looks like you boys are sleeping together."

"Dad," Sam half-shouted.

It took every ounce of maturity I owned not to laugh.

"Well, your mom and I have a tent. Angie gets a tent. You boys will get the third." Gary bent down and lit a piece of newspaper he'd shoved between a section of wood. "You used to share a tent all the time. You'll be sleeping. It isn't that big of a deal," he said with a deep chuckle.

An hour later, the three tents were set up. Two tents were between the cars and a wall of trees. The tent Sam and I would share took the remaining spot on the opposite side of the firepit. It was closer to the path leading to the river, leaving us with a nice view of the water if we opened the little window flap on the side of the tent. And behind our tent was the shower tent. I didn't even know they made a tent for showers, but Angie gave me a full tutorial on how they work while she made me set it up.

Mom set out the last chair around the fire pit, plopped into one, and said, "Who has the cooler with the beer?"

"In the van, honey," Gary shouted from inside their tent.

"I'll get it," Sam replied, disappearing behind the van.

I dropped into the chair beside Mom. The weird material tightened under my body weight and strained with an odd groan as I relaxed. "Do you need me to do anything else?"

"I think we got everything," Mom said. "Perfect timing." She pointed to the sun creeping lower in the sky by the second.

Sam set the cooler beside Mom and sank into a chair across from us on the other side of the fire pit. The flames danced, lighting his face with different hues of orange. His eyes flicked up, locking with mine. My chest clenched, the deep pang of longing hitting me as the last remnants of sunlight disappeared.

Something was different in the way Sam looked at me. Was he angry? Thinking of the best way to divide our tiny tent? Maybe a list of rules?

"I hope you two can get along while we're here," Mom said.

"We'll be fine, Ma."

"Had to check. I don't need you two fighting the whole time."

"Shut up, Ma." I leaned forward and eyed the cooler. "Did you bring the whiskey I asked for?"

She rolled her eyes and pointed to a tote bag to the left of her chair. "Of course I did."

I dug through the bag and pulled out a bottle of whiskey, but there weren't any cups.

When I held up the bag and the bottle, Mom shrugged and said, "You're the only one who drinks it. Have at it."

I could feel Sam's gaze lingering on me when I took a swig from the bottle. Desire settled in my abdomen when our eyes locked through the flames.

When Gary and Angie finally joined us around the fire pit, we sat around chatting about random crap, our conversation interrupting the sound of nature and the crackle of wood.

After a while, Sam stood and sauntered toward me. A rush of nerves filled my chest at his approach. He grabbed the whiskey bottle from my hand and pressed the rim to his lips, keeping his gaze fixed on me.

"I'm having some," he said and took a sip, then knocked back a few more before handing it back to me.

"I don't have a problem sharing, but why not bring your chair so you aren't hovering over me?"

He looked back at his chair and shook his head. "Anyone hungry?"

In response to a unanimous yes, Sam rummaged through the cooler in the van before returning with a pack of hotdogs and buns. He flipped the handle of the metal grill plate attached to the firepit and let the flames lick against the grill for a minute, then ripped open the package of hotdogs and set them across the metal bars.

Everything was so *normal*. Though the tension between Sam and me always existed, this was the most normal our family had felt since I kissed him. I wasn't sure how sleeping in the same tent would go, but I hoped we didn't argue. I hoped it would be like the night of my birthday. That night had been the best sleep I'd had in four years.

"Angie," Mom said, sipping her beer, "when does your new job start?"

"Three weeks."

"Is that a bad thing?" Sam asked, turning the hot dogs on the grill with big metal tongs.

He rested a knee on the ground, hovering over the firepit to make his perfect hot dogs. He had to turn them at whatever he thought the precise moment was to make them perfect on all sides. I held back my chuckle as he fought with one, trying to turn it over to the exact side he thought wasn't getting enough flame.

"Not bad. I wanted to start it sooner, but I had to put in my two weeks at my current place and then take a two-week vacation with you guys, and that put a kink in HR's timing for a start date." She slumped back in the chair and waved her hand. "Something about lining up payroll with a start date."

When the hotdogs were finally to Sam's liking, he divvied them up, and we sat around the fire, stuffing our faces. Hearing Angie talk about her plans for the future, her friends, and hobbies—all things I had missed out on since moving away—made me feel excluded from my family. They had a whole life I wasn't a part of anymore.

It felt isolating.

Gary finished the last bit of his sixth hot dog, then rubbed his belly with a sleepy groan. "Ten o'clock already?" he said, glancing at his watch. "Time whizzed by today."

"Sure did," Mom said, packing up the beer cooler before asking Sam to put it back in the van.

He hopped up and disappeared with the cooler.

"I'm calling it a night. Some of us were up at four to start the day, unlike a couple slackers I know," Angie said in a teasing tone and winked at me.

The wink felt a little exaggerated. She and Gary had been acting odd since the morning, but I couldn't pinpoint what was different with them.

Mom stretched as she walked past the firepit. "Us too." She reached for Gary, lacing their fingers together before saying, "Good night, kids. Love you."

"See you in the morning," Gary said.

Mom blew us a kiss before she and Gary disappeared into their tent.

Angie stood, eyeing Sam and me. "Be nice to each other, please."

Sam and I exchanged a glance, and I said, "Don't worry about us. Get some rest."

She gave us both a hug before climbing into her tent.

Silence hovered between Sam and me, interrupted by the chirps of insects. Occasionally, I would catch Sam watching me through the flames.

I was unsure what was going on between us. In four years, we hadn't spent this much time alone together, so whatever it was, it was new.

"Why not come over here and share some of this drink with me?" I asked, holding up the bottle I'd been nursing.

He glanced away from the fire and fixed his gaze on me. "Are you trying to get me drunk?"

"No, it's weird with you sitting all the way over there while we're alone."

He bit his lip, nibbling on the skin as he looked around. Then he rose to his feet and approached me. "Give me the bottle." He pulled a chair closer and sat, stretching out his legs before taking a swig of the whiskey.

"We haven't really sat and talked like this in a while," I said, taking the bottle back and swallowing a huge mouthful.

"Yeah," Sam replied, staring at the flames.

"How's your company doing? I haven't asked about it much."

"It's good."

"Is that all you're gonna give me?" I chuckled, then mocked, "It's good."

He whipped his attention to me with a glare. "What do you want me to say?"

"I don't know. Something other than that."

He scoffed and ripped the bottle from my grasp. "How about you?" He threw his head back, gulping down more than he should have.

"Take it easy, Sammy." I grabbed the neck of the bottle and yanked it away from him. "Fuckin' greedy."

"Asshole," Sam snapped, leaning back in the chair and closed his eyes.

"So I've been told," I said, chuckling, and took another sip from the bottle. "I'll tell you first, then you tell me. 'Kay?"

I paused, taking a peek at his lax figure. His legs were spread wide apart, and his jeans hung low on his waist. His T-shirt was loose and riding up, exposing his belly. He was scrumptious, and I couldn't believe how I'd gone my whole life not realizing my attraction to him.

"I'm helping kids with disabilities," I said, handing him the bottle again. "I'm trying to change the world of education with technology."

Sam swallowed and passed the bottle back to me. "How so?"

"I submitted a proposal before I left to come here. I want to turn our education platform into a video game that any kid anywhere can use from a phone or tablet."

"That doesn't already exist?"

I shoved the bottle back at him. "It does, kind of." I shrugged and slumped down in the chair. "It doesn't exist in the way I want it to. We aim our software and teaching model at helping children who struggle. If I had this shit as a kid, I probably would've graduated with more than a C average."

"But you have ADHD. It can't be helped."

I huffed out a breath. "That's the point. I needed help, but no one knew how to give it to me. No one understood how to help me learn or succeed. The software my company makes is to help people like me."

124

Silence hovered between us while Sam continued to drink the whiskey, keeping his eyes fixed on the fire pit.

"I'm making enemies in my industry," he finally said. "Victory X is my dream to put the user experience ahead of anything else. If we take care of the consumers, they will recommend the product or the company. The companies I work with need to consider them as more than numbers or dollar signs."

"How does that get you enemies?"

"Companies don't think about more than the numbers, so when I tell them to think differently, or it won't work, they get angry and bash me to their CEO buddies. I've lost contracts because of it."

"Savage."

He laughed and handed me the whiskey. It was half gone already. I hadn't realized we'd drank that much. While searching for the cap, I managed to catch his attention.

"What are you doing?"

"Cutting us off." I held up the bottle, letting the light from the flames hit the glass. "We've had a lot."

"It's fine," he said with a crooked grin. "And the cap is on your lap."

I grabbed the cap and screwed it on before putting it away in the tote bag Mom had brought it in.

"Should we put out the fire?" Sam asked.

I stood, shoving my hands in my pockets. "I guess we should. I don't know how we're supposed to do this, though."

"I don't know. Water should work," he said, stumbling toward the area we'd designated as food prep and found a small bucket. "Should do it." He headed toward the small clearing that led to the river.

"Sam, what are you doing?" I rushed to catch up to him. "We're drunk, and you're going toward a body of water."

"You act like I'm gonna drown," he slurred.

"You could."

He ignored me and kept going until we left the treeline. The moon lit the riverbank so brightly I could see perfectly. Taking a moment to enjoy the sight, I lost track of Sam, who wobbled, reaching the water's edge, then dipped the bucket. When he swayed, I rushed to him, grabbing his waist, yanking him away from the water.

"I swear to fucking God, if you don't get away from the water—"

He erupted in laughter and swirled around, sloshing water everywhere. "C'mon, let's put out the fire and go to bed." He swayed and wobbled all the way back to the fire pit, then doused the flames with his half-empty bucket. "Stupid fire," he said and turned on his heels, aiming his wobbly self toward the river again.

"Sam, stop. I'll do it."

I pried the bucket from his grasp and jogged to the water, filling the bucket to the rim. When I made it back, Sam stood in the same spot, staring at the firepit, looking like someone had hurt his feelings in my absence. I dumped the water over the pit and watched the fire die out.

"You okay?" I asked.

He grunted halfheartedly.

We stood there until the last ember cooled, then headed for the tent. Sam unzipped the door of the tiny tent and ducked inside. I quickly followed, tripping over his foot in the dark.

"Jesus, Sam. Are you trying to kill me?"

He groaned and pushed me.

"Fuck off," I said, wobbling before catching my balance. "I can't see shit. Find the flashlight or a glow stick."

"Do it yourself," he whined, and the air mattress bounced as he flopped down.

"I need to close the fucking door."

"Feel for it."

"You feel for it," I grumbled before kneeling at the flappy door and feeling around for the zipper. When my fingers landed on the little metal piece, I quickly zipped up the door before crawling around in search of the mattress and a place to put my shoes. The cramped tent made it difficult to move around, but it was better than sleeping in the open air where bugs would eat me alive. Setting my sneakers off to the side, I found my duffle bag and stripped down to my boxers, tossing the clothes on top of the bag. "Sam, are you changing? Or are you sleeping in your clothes?"

He groaned, and I could barely make out the outline of his body as he sat up and ripped off his shirt. His belt clinked as he released the clasp and shimmied out of his jeans. The clothes landed on the floor. Then he flopped back with a sigh.

How am I supposed to last five days like this?

"Happy?" he grumbled.

"You're so drunk, Sammy."

"Only a little."

"A lot." I climbed onto the makeshift bed and snuggled under the giant sleeping bag. We had unfolded one to make a sheet and used the other as the blanket. I was surprised by how comfortable the setup was.

The air mattress dipped, ripping me out of the limbo between sleep and reality.

"Sam, if you don't st—"

"Shut up," Sam whispered, inches from my face.

His breath ran over my skin. The heat of his body settled over me.

"What are you doing?" My words were faint, almost like I didn't speak them.

"Giving in."

His hair tickled my forehead. His breath lingered over my lips, and the smell of whiskey mixed with smoke from the fire hung between us.

"I'll ask again to be sure," I said through a rush of nerves. "Are you drunk?"

"A little," Sam said. "I know what I'm doing, Ash."

"Then why are you doing it?"

The sound of him swallowing above me sent my heart racing and blood pumping straight to my groin.

"I've thought about this since we were thirteen."

"Thirteen?"

Don't tell me that, Sam. How am I supposed to ignore this?

Do you love me? The same way I love you?

I couldn't ask it. I was afraid. I wanted him to tell me yes. To tell me he loved me as more than a friend. But he set the rules four years ago. He told me it would never be. He would never be *mine*.

The air mattress dipped again as he moved, brushing his arm against my shoulder.

"Now here you are, nearly naked in bed with me for the second time since you've been home," he said. His breath puffed over my skin with each word, teasing me with everything I knew I couldn't have.

"And?" I asked, wanting to touch him but knowing I shouldn't.

"I'm tired of telling myself no."

"Sammy," I whispered, "you're drunk."

"Shut up," he replied quietly, then his lips brushed mine, silencing any words I would've said.

My chest tightened and warmed. I knew this wasn't like him.

And yet, I couldn't stop.

I grabbed the back of his head and wrapped my other arm around his waist, pulling him flush against me.

His teeth nipped at my lower lip, tugging the soft skin into his mouth. My tongue darted between his lips, tasting him, dancing with him. I slid my hand under the fabric of his boxers, gripping his ass, and rolled my hips. Our erections rubbed over each other through the thin material, sending a rush of lust through me.

I tangled my fingers in his hair, tugging his face back. "I didn't bring condoms," I whispered against his lips.

"Neither did I." He kissed me, then pulled back again. "I didn't really plan for this. I only have lube."

"You brought lube?"

He kissed me, trailing his soft lips over my jaw until he reached my ear. "I planned to be well acquainted with my hand this week."

I chuckled, curling my fingers in his hair, bringing his face back to mine. "I always use condoms. I know I'm clear," I whispered between panting breaths. "Also, I'm on PrEP and get tested regularly."

"Same."

Sam's breathing was erratic as he lifted himself and disappeared under the makeshift blanket. His lips trailed down my chest, then over my abs. When his mouth reached the band of my boxers, his fingers curled under the fabric.

This isn't right.

He's drunk. I'm drunk.

Last time, we were drunk, and it ruined everything.

I gripped his shoulders, pushing him away even though it went against every desire. Every want. I needed Sam back in my life like he was oxygen, but this wasn't the way to do it.

"Stop," I breathed, letting the word fall from my lips like a guilty plea. "Sam, stop."

I pushed him back, moving from beneath him. When his hands fell from my waist, my chest filled with ice.

"You're drunk," I whispered, straining to see his face in the dark.

"So what?" he said, leaning into my grip on his shoulders. "You act like neither of us has ever had drunk sex before."

"Would you have kissed me if you were sober? Would you have climbed on me if you weren't drunk?"

He didn't answer, but his silence was my answer.

No.

"Thought so," I said, sliding to the edge of the air mattress.

I ran my fingers through my hair, tugging at the roots as I clawed through the pain boiling in my heart. He was right there. But it was wrong.

"Fuck," I yelled.

I needed to escape.

My chest burned. The familiar pain raced in, erasing anything resembling joy as it settled back in its place, coiled around my heart.

I stood, fumbling in the mass of crap beside the bed until my fingers landed on the cold metal flashlight. I flicked it on and found a pair of shorts before tossing the flashlight on the bed and leaving the tent.

Chapter 18

Sam

Ash stumbled through the stupid floppy door of the tent, yanking his shorts on as he walked away. It stung, having him reject me, but he was right. I was the one who set the rule. I told him nothing could happen between us. I rejected him every single time he made any advance on me.

It was always me who said no.

So why was I the one ready to jump him with our family twenty feet away?

It was the little moments since his birthday that were getting to me. A look here and there. His laugh. Our bickering like we used to. His existence was taking over my thoughts like he had never left. But he had left, and I had forgotten what it was like to be near him every day. What it was like to hold a suffocating amount of control over my desires.

I had forgotten the reality of my feelings.

Sitting there in the dark, the reality finally came back. I wished it didn't have to be this way. I wanted to return to the past, to the time before our parents married. Back when we could be together without the chains weighing us down that we had now. Back when we didn't understand our feelings. When we fit together perfectly. I wanted to transport myself back to when simply being with Ash filled me with the purest form of joy I had ever known.

He was my savior.

A god among demons, and I worshiped the ground he walked on.

Perhaps our feelings were clouded by a lifetime of baggage. Maybe I loved him because he was there when no one else was. I wasn't sure, but questioning it didn't make my love for him any less real. Any less consuming.

The morning light blinded me when I climbed through the flap called a door. My head pounded, and I rubbed my temples before looking around for Ash. Angie and Jane hovered around the food prep area, and Dad placed the fishing tackle in the van as he hummed a tune.

I hoped they didn't hear Ash and me last night, though I was sure they at least heard him yell "fuck" before climbing out of the tent. After he left, I half expected him to come back. I was disappointed when he didn't.

"Oh, good," Jane said at my approach. "Is Ash still asleep?"

My immediate reaction was to look away, shame filling my chest, clawing at my heart.

"We had an argument last night, and he didn't sleep in the tent," I said.

Her brows dipped, and she chewed her lip, exchanging a glance with Angie, who eyed me with the same worry.

"Don't worry, I'll go find him." I headed toward the river. I doubted he would go into the woods, but he loved being near the water.

When I broke away from the canopy of trees hanging over the narrow, worn pathway, it opened up to the riverbank we came to last night.

Ash was on his back, arm propped under his head, staring at the sky.

"Aren't you cold?" I asked, sitting beside him.

He looked at me with a frown, then said, "Not really."

"Did you sleep at all?" I picked up a twig from the ground and rolled it between my fingers.

"No." Ash shifted until his head rested on my lap.

"What are you doing?" I dropped the twig and flattened my palms on the ground. It was cold and wet. The mud was mixed with a sandy texture and stuck to my skin like glue.

He looked up at me through wavy strands of black hair. His eyes caught the rays of morning light creeping over the trees, making them look like tiny orbs of gold.

"I think it's time we talked about it," he said in a hushed whisper.

"I don't want to." My voice trembled through my words.

"If we don't talk about it, do you think we can live the rest of our lives like this?" He reached up, grabbing the front of my shirt with enough force to pull me down until I was only inches from his face. "I miss my best friend," he said, his voice cracking. "I hate what we've become." His hand fell away, dropping to the muddy ground, but his eyes stayed trained on my face. I felt naked under his gaze. Like he could see through me to the core of who I was. "I'll go first," he said, reminding me of our conversation around the fire pit. "I admit, when I kissed you at the bar because of that dare, I chose you because it would be the least awkward."

"Worked out great," I mumbled.

"I never regretted that kiss. I only regret what happened afterward." He took a deep breath. I was captivated, wondering where he was going with this. "It took a few days to realize my feelings and what that meant for our friendship, but I can't pretend it never happened. I can't act like friends when I know what I really want is far more intimate than simple friendship."

"I. . ." *I don't want to lose my family.*

"I'm not talking sex," he said. "Okay, yes to sex, but it's more than that. You know it."

I did. I knew what he meant. It was an effortless feeling we had our whole lives. We clicked. We were drawn to each other from the beginning. Ash was the only person in my life where I had experienced that easy connection. An instant comfort. It was why I had called him my soulmate since I was a teen. It was like he was born to be in my life. To be the parts of me I was missing. To support me in the exact ways I needed.

I breathed in, holding my breath while I debated speaking my truth. My secret. Releasing the breath, I gave in.

"When we were thirteen, I planned to confess my feelings for you," I said, my heart pounding, vision narrowing. "I figured I had a fifty-fifty shot at rejection. I was prepared to take the risk."

I said it. I said it aloud. To him. To Ash.

Oh my god.

His breath hitched before he asked, "What stopped you?"

"Our parents." I bit my lip. My heart raced, and I felt light for the first time. Like simply saying this was a release. "The night before I planned to tell you, my dad told me he had asked Jane to marry him. That was when I swore I would take my feelings to the grave. You would never know."

"Why?" He looked up at me like I had betrayed him. "Why would you hide it from me for so long?"

"My dad was so happy. They were both so happy. How could I ruin it with my selfish feelings? I was thirteen and had never seen my dad that happy. We had never had what your family offered us."

Ash rolled over, lifting himself up to kneel in front of me with a frown. "Do you think my mom will stop loving Gary because we love each other?"

"How can we be together when you're my brother? It isn't right."

"Says who?" He reached for me, gripping my chin. "You aren't my brother. We aren't related." His thumb ran over my chin. "We don't share the same last name. The only thing making us a family is that our parents married each other. That's all."

"It's wrong," I whispered. "People will think we're disgusting."

"Have we ever cared what other people think?"

I shook my head. But how could I pretend I didn't know what society would say about us? Being queer and stepbrothers was asking for hate and disgust from others. Our parents were fine with me coming out as gay, but how would they feel if Ash and I announced we were together? How could they accept their sons being lovers?

Ash leaned in, brushing his lips over my ear, sending a wave of warmth down my spine.

"Think about it. If you wanted me right now, you could have me." He pulled back and rose to his feet with a sly grin as he backed away toward the water. "No limits. No rules." He untied the string on his shorts and let them slide to the ground before spinning around and running into the water.

"It's not that easy," I yelled after him.

After a few paces, he launched into a dive, disappearing beneath the surface.

"What isn't easy?" Angie appeared next to me, and my soul left my body at the sight of her.

"Jesus fucking Christ, Angela!" I pressed my hand to my chest, feeling my heart thunder from the shot of fear racing through my burning veins. "Tell someone when you're behind them." I focused on my breathing, letting it slow. "You gave me a heart attack."

She frowned, walking around me like she was inspecting something. "What was that just now?"

I rubbed my hands together, brushing away some of the mud. "What was what?"

"That whole thing with you and Ash for the last few minutes." She pursed her lips and locked her hands behind her back.

"Spying on people is rude."

"It may have been rude to watch you guys, but I've been curious." She squatted in front of me, scanning me with her big, round eyes. "You and Ash seemed much closer than you've led us to believe. Do you really hate each other, or is something else going on?"

"It's a private matter between me and Ash," I said, standing and stepping away from her curious stare.

"Angie," Ash called, jogging toward us, "when did you get here?"

She shielded her eyes with a screech. "Oh my god. Why are you only wearing boxers?" She looked back at me, horrified by the sight of Ash dripping wet like an ad for a men's underwear brand.

"Don't be so dramatic," Ash said, chuckling as he slipped his shorts back on. "What are you doing over here, anyway?"

She peeked through her fingers, making sure he was decent, before straightening up to face him. "Breakfast is ready," she said, glancing between us like she was looking for a clue.

"Don't lie. You were being nosy," I said.

"Nosy, about what?" Ash asked, striding past us. "Walk and talk. I'm starving."

Angie rushed to catch up to his already disappearing form and said, "Nothing. I wasn't being nosy."

She kept eyeing us while we wandered back to camp, which had Ash glancing between Angie and me.

When we entered the clearing, Dad beckoned us over to the picnic table. "Good timing."

Jane set out paper plates and sat next to him. "Dig in. There's plenty here."

"After breakfast, we're heading to Lake Erie. I'd love it if you two fish with me while we're there." Dad said when Ash and I sat.

"Sure," Ash said, piling food on his plate. "I'd love to fish with you, Gary."
What a liar. You hate fishing.

Dad parked the van, and Ash hopped through the side door first. I quickly followed him. He seemed far too excited. He hated fishing. He thought catch and release was cruel and was a major advocate against hunting.

"You're excited," I whispered as I came up behind him.

"Am I?"

"I thought you hate people hunting for sport."

His face scrunched like I said something dumb. "Gary doesn't hunt for sport. Even I know that."

"I thought. . ."

"I know we're eating whatever we catch today. I don't have a problem with that." He winked and rounded the van to the trunk. "Gary, do we need fishing licenses?"

Dad grabbed a tackle box from the trunk with a twinkle in his eyes. "That building over there will give them to us." He pointed to a small building next to a long pier.

"Cool," Ash said, grabbing a fishing pole. "Angie, let's go get our licenses. You ready to catch some fish?" The two of them headed into the building, leaving the rest of us behind.

Dad and Jane approached me. "You going to watch us fish, or are you getting your hands dirty today?" Dad asked.

I chewed the corner of my lip. I didn't really do this kind of thing. "I'll get a license just in case."

After getting us all set up with fishing licenses, the lady at the counter told us which fish we were likely to catch off the pier, and I had no idea what she was talking about. She explained we could keep our catches as long as the fish we caught were in season.

Seemed complicated. I didn't want to bother with it.

It was a gorgeous day to be on the water. The water was calm, and the sky was clear. We walked along the pier. I carried a couple camping chairs on my back and a cooler in one hand. Ash walked beside me with a fishing pole and tackle box. I couldn't tell if he was actually happy or pretending. The look he had was weird. I couldn't decipher it at all.

Dad stopped at the end of the pier and set down his fishing gear before pointing to an area and said, "Sam, put my chair here. This is a good spot to get started."

I placed his chair, then unpacked and set up the others before lining up the chairs beside each other and taking a seat next to Dad. When Ash stood next to me, my stomach did a little flip, and I immediately tamped it down.

We still had too much to talk about. He wanted more from me.

A relationship. A future.

But this was our future. Here with our family.

Was it so wrong of me to want a family? To keep what we had?

Moments like this. Family vacations and joking around. I didn't want to lose any of this.

Ash sunk into his chair and flipped the tackle box open on his lap to search for the bait he wanted to use.

He was so relaxed. A little upbeat.

When he found the bait he wanted, he plucked it from the box, then weaved it onto the hook.

A gust of wind hit us, pushing his curls into his eyes. I wanted to reach over and push them away. Trail my fingers over his cheek. See the sun light up his beautiful brown eyes like golden champagne.

He looked up from his lap, his eyes locking with mine, hitting the sun just right to give me exactly the picture I had hoped for. His smile reached his eyes, crinkling the corners into lines.

We were getting so much older. To think we'd known each other for so long. . . I could picture him at every stage of our lives.

I swallowed down the growing tightness in my throat.

Thinking about the upcoming stages of our lives where I would watch him marry someone. Have some kids. Maybe even grandkids—all without me—it left an ache in my chest so deep I wasn't sure how to pretend it wasn't there.

Chapter 19

Ash

Sam looked at me with a frown. His gorgeous blue eyes sparkled from the reflection of the water. His lips parted, then he closed his mouth and looked away from me.

Did he want to say something? Between last night and our talk that morning, there was a lot left unsaid between us, but to hear him say he had feelings for me since we were kids was like a beacon of hope in my heart. I had a chance. I needed to take my chance and show him what we could be. Everything I could be for him. With him. I needed him to know what we could have if he stopped being afraid.

The bond our family had was built on a solid foundation. Our parents loved us unconditionally. They wanted only the best for us. Sam had to know that. He had to know our being together wouldn't break that.

I cast the fishing line into the water and leaned back in the camping chair that creaked and groaned under every move I made.

It wasn't my first time fishing with Gary, but the few times I had, I never caught anything.

"Ash," Angie said, placing her hands on my shoulders.

I tilted my head back, looking up at her.

"Mom and I are going to walk down the street to this cute little shopping area."

"Have fun," I said.

She kissed my forehead and spun around. "See ya. Have fun fishing and not catching anything."

Gary and Sam laughed.

"I will. It will be tons of fun," I called after her.

After an hour, I hadn't caught anything, but Gary had caught three decently sized Smallmouth Bass. I sighed when he reeled in another fish.

"Am I doing something wrong, Gary?" I leaned on the armrest of the flimsy chair, hoping I didn't fall flat on my face. "Did I use the wrong bait?"

Gary unhooked the fish and put it in the cooler with the others he'd caught before strutting toward me. "Bring your line in, son."

I did as he instructed, taking the chance to peek at Sam, who smirked at me.

Yeah, yeah. I'm a failure at this.

Gary held my hook up with the bait I'd chosen and laughed. "No wonder you aren't getting any bites." He took the bait off, rummaged through the tackle box, and pulled out something else, then slid the new bait onto the hook. "This should get you some Bass." He put his hand heavily on my shoulder, tapping a couple times before returning to his chair.

"Thanks." I cast my line and leaned back.

"Daddy," a young kid rushed past us, running down the pier toward a man fishing like us.

The kid's dad stood up and scooped him into his arms before spinning around like he hadn't seen his son in ages. Like he was happy to see him.

A pang of envy tugged at my heart.

I didn't know what that was like. I didn't know what it was like to have a father who loved me. Who hugged me. There was never a tender touch or a bear hug. Nothing of the sort. I only ever knew what his fists felt like.

My father only ever taught me pain.

Sometimes, I dreamed about a future where I had a kid to teach. A kid to bring fishing. A little devil spawn of my own to bring into this cruel world.

It would never happen. The chance of being like my father was too high. I didn't need to risk being like him. The dream was cute, though.

The fishing pole rumbled, tugging in my hand. I jumped to my feet. "Shit," I said with way too much enthusiasm and tugged.

"Oh my god, he got a bite?" Sam said. "Dad, you worked a miracle."

Gary chuckled, and the two of them watched me struggle to reel in the fish. When I pulled it out of the water, it was another Bass. It was definitely big enough to eat, even if it was on the smaller side.

"Everyone ready?" Mom asked, grabbing her backpack off the ground. "We have water and snacks. Sunscreen and. . ." She patted her pockets and glanced around the campsite again.

"We have everything, Ma," I said, slinging my backpack over my shoulder.

Gary, Angie, and Sam stood at the edge of the campsite near the trail leading to the hiking path. Mom had triple and quadruple-checked that everything was in order for an hour, delaying our hike. We all wore jeans and hiking boots, even though it was in the mid-seventies. Poison Ivy was no joke, and none of us wanted to rub against it inadvertently with bare ankles. That would be one way to ruin a trip.

"Let's go," I said, tugging her backpack over her shoulders and turning her toward our waiting family. "We aren't leaving and never coming back."

"But if I forgot something we need while we're gone—"

"Then we can get it when we come back."

I pushed her forward against her protests. She often thought she forgot something when she didn't. If I let her check one more time, it would never end.

Two hours into the hike, we were around the halfway mark on our planned trail. Gary had been needing frequent breaks, which was unlike him. Out of the whole family, he was the healthiest. He loved the outdoors. Hiking, rock climbing, all of it. I had always attributed Sam's love for running outside to his father taking him on runs and hikes as a kid. I may have been strong and packed with muscle from lifting weights, but my stamina was nothing compared to the two of them.

"I'll be back in a minute," Sam said before turning around and heading into the dense tree line at the edge of the footpath.

"Don't get lost!" I called, leaning against a large rock beside the pathway.

"Why do you always pick on him?" Angie asked, crossing her arms with a glare.

I poked her forehead, nudging her. "I'm not picking on him."

She rolled her eyes. "You are. You do it all the time, ever since we were kids."

I went to speak, but telling her it was my way of flirting with him and that I liked getting him riled up probably wouldn't go well.

Angie and Mom fell into conversation about their plans for the upcoming days before we headed home, but after a few minutes, I started to worry about Sam.

"Guys, why isn't he back yet? He was only taking a piss, right?" I said, failing to hide the concern in my voice.

"I'm sure he's fine," Gary replied.

Pushing off the rock, I walked over to the edge of the trail where Sam had entered the woods. There was no sign of him, not that I could see far.

"Sam!" I called, hoping he was nearby, but my chest tightened, restricting my air when he didn't respond.

"Relax, he's probably, you know," Angie said with a wiggle of her brows and held up two fingers. She mouthed, "Going number two."

I glanced back at the woods and grumbled, "Could be." I stared at the tree line, scanning the dense forest for any sign of Sam. "Why don't you guys go on ahead? I'll wait for him, and we can jog to catch up."

"Are you sure?" Mom asked, but she seemed okay with the idea.

"Yeah. I'm sure." I returned to leaning against the rock. "If anything happens, or we get lost, I'll call you."

"What if you lose reception?" Gary asked.

"We're adults. We can figure it out."

They eyed me with a flash of concern before continuing down the trail with a wave.

I stared at my watch, watching another five minutes pass.

This isn't like him.

I tugged my phone from my pack and tapped Sam's name in my favorites. It rang until the voicemail connected. I called again and again, only to get his voicemail. I sent him a text and waited a minute. Still nothing.

Something happened.

I dropped my pack, pulled out a thin yellow rope, and tied it around a narrow tree trunk near where Sam had entered the forest. I pulled out my hunting knife and cut the end before taking a red flag and tying it to the rope, marking the starting point. This was our family's safety plan. When Sam and I were about fourteen, we went on a camping trip in Montana. Angie got lost after disappearing from the campsite. Because we had to call a search and rescue team to find her,

Gary devised a safety plan if we were ever lost in the woods again. It looked like Sam had forgotten those important details today.

He had gone straight back, but then, about ten feet in, I'd lost sight of him. Every ten feet, I tied the yellow rope around a tree and called for Sam before pushing forward. I tracked disturbed branches and leaf litter, but some of it was too hard to tell if it was human or animal. I wasn't an expert at tracking. My skills were minimal at best.

Nearly thirty minutes into my search, my shirt was drenched with sweat, and my body surged with adrenaline. I was focused. Determined to find him. Praying he didn't fall somewhere.

"Sam," I bellowed, approaching a wall of moss-covered stone reaching up through the forest more than twenty feet. Tall trees branched above the narrow path, filtering the sunlight. It was clear that this part of the forest was rarely explored. There was no evidence of a path having been created naturally by foot traffic. I wasn't sure I was heading the right way, but some broken branches were leading this way. Stopping at another tree near the moss wall, I tied another yellow rope, this time with a blue flag.

The rocks bowed, narrowing the path, forcing me to take off my pack. I shimmied sideways, dragging my bag through the tight squeeze. After a few feet, it opened up, and standing only fifteen feet away was the man I would do anything for. The person I loved more than myself.

His hair was slicked with sweat, and his backpack rested by his feet at the edge of a natural spring.

Ragged rock walls surrounded us and curved over the clearing. Trees lined the edges above the opening, shrouding the cove from a clear view of the sky. Ferns, vines, and moss covered the rocks, creating a lush oasis. Straight back at the center was a narrow waterfall spilling into a pool of clear blue water.

Dropping my pack, I rushed toward Sam. Relief and frustration mixed in my chest. When I reached him, I yanked him back and crushed him to my chest. The sound of the waterfall drowned his gasp before he relaxed, leaning into my hold.

"You fucker," I said, shoving my nose in the crook of his neck. He was sweaty, smelling like a mix of musk and dirt. "I was worried you were hurt."

"Not hurt, but lost," he replied. "How did you find me here?"

"Luck and more luck," I said, releasing him.

He faced me with a smile. "I'm glad you found me. I got turned around, and then by the time I realized how lost I was, I had come across this place."

"You didn't 'come across' this place. You actively found this place." I pointed back to where I had squeezed my body through as proof.

He shrugged and turned back to the water. "I was curious what was back here."

"Mr. Responsible risked his life over curiosity? Who are you, and what have you done with Sammy?" I closed the gap between us again, slinging my arm around his chest, tugging him back. I pressed my lips to his ear and whispered, "Don't ever do that again."

"I won't."

"I don't believe you," I growled.

"I promise, Ash."

"Do you understand what went through my head while I searched for you?" I hugged him tighter and gripped his jaw with my other hand, turning his face so he looked into my eyes.

"I can imagine," he said through gritted teeth. "Now, let go."

I didn't want to, but I did as he asked before approaching the water's edge. "This is a good find though. Who would've expected this to be here?"

I yanked off my sweat-soaked shirt and tossed it to the ground, then unbuckled my jeans while kicking off my shoes.

"What are you doing?"

"Taking a dip." I smiled at him over my shoulder, then asked, "Do you think humans have ever been here before?"

"How would I know?" he asked, walking toward me with a scowl. "You shouldn't swim here. You don't know if it's safe."

"Let loose sometimes. You were fine risking your life to find this place, but you're afraid of a little water?"

I dropped my pants and slipped out of my boxers before touching the water with my toes. It was cool but refreshing.

"God, seriously? Naked?"

"Come join me, bro," I called, goading him as I waded into the water, letting the chill soothe my skin.

He shook his head from the edge of the water. His face was beet red, and he refused to look at me.

"Don't you get tired of being in control all the time?" I asked, leaning back, letting my body float to the surface. "Let yourself relax once in a while, Sammy. It won't kill you."

Chapter 20

Sam

Ash was an absolute temptation. He teased me, floating in the water like a prize I could have if I wanted it. If I was willing to break my self-imposed rules.

I grabbed my backpack and turned away.

"Where are you going?" Ash called from the center of the spring. "Wait for me."

I halted near the exit, my chest tight. Mouth dry. My pulse surged, knowing Ash was running around exposed behind me. And I wanted nothing more than to run over and kiss him. He was pushing me too close to the edge. The way he touched me when he arrived set my nerves on fire. When he scolded me while holding me tight, it took every last drop of self-control not to kiss him. I wanted to let him break through my walls. I wanted him to force his way in. I wanted to give in.

I held in my frustrated groan.

A part of me questioned my reasoning. Was I making excuses? Was this not a big deal to others? Did I blow it out of proportion?

I can't give in. I have to stay strong.

"Come on, Sammy. We have a two-and-a-half-hour hike back to camp," Ash said, striding past me.

His hair was messy and dripping, leaving wet spots on the fabric over his shoulders. I chewed the inside of my cheek to keep from smiling like an idiot. When he looked back at me, a surge of heat bubbled in my gut.

"You good?" he asked, looking me over.

I nodded, unable to trust my voice, and stayed close to him, squeezing through the narrow path. As soon as we reached the other side, my attention fixed on a tree with a yellow rope tied around it and a blue flag dancing on the gentle breeze.

"You remembered to do that?" I pointed to the rope.

Ash approached it, setting his bag on the ground, pulling out a green flag before cutting off the blue with a hunting knife.

"Of course I remembered to do it," he said, glancing back at me. "Unlike someone who got lost and had the same training I did."

I couldn't remember exactly when Dad taught us this survival trick, but we had been young. I barely paid attention, so I was surprised to see Ash had taken it seriously.

"It tracks all the way back to the trail." He stood and motioned for me to follow. "I placed these every ten feet."

The line of trees tied with a yellow rope was methodical. Not once on the way back through the forest did I question the direction. He had taken every precaution to ensure each tree would be visible on the return or if someone had followed it through. There was even a point where he had gone in another direction, and when he chose to backtrack, he tied an orange flag to each tree he came back to. Exactly as my father had instructed all those years ago.

"Why aren't we taking them down?" I asked.

Ash stepped over a fallen branch and said, "We're coming back here before we go home."

"We are?"

He beamed, spinning toward me. "Can you imagine that place at night?"

I had to admit, I was curious.

Hours later, we found ourselves at the edge of camp. Tension filled the air as we approached. Jane's voice shook with each word said to the person over the phone. Angela and Dad had their packs placed in chairs next to the fire pit, shoving in fresh supplies.

"We made it," Ash said, carelessly dropping his pack on the ground and rushing to a chair near the fire pit. "It's so nice to sit."

"Ash. Sam," Jane screamed when she realized we had returned. She quickly apologized to the person on the phone and thanked them for their help before hanging up.

Dad hurried toward me, tugging me into a hug. "We were about to start the search party for you boys."

When Dad released me, Angie and Jane crowded around me, squeezing me tight.

"We're so glad you're okay," Jane said, resting her cheek on my chest.

Dad stood behind Ash and placed his hand on his shoulder, giving him a solid pat. "Good job, bud."

Ash nodded, then leaned back in the chair, closing his eyes. "It was nothing."

Nothing?

Was that how he thought about his actions? Did he think every time he helped me that it was nothing? A simple action that deserved no thanks?

"Well," Dad said, marching toward the cooler in the van and flipped the top open. "Does anyone want some dinner?"

The campsite grew loud with dinner preparations. I started the fire, and we all gathered around as our food cooked over the open flame. There was something different about tonight. I couldn't put my finger on it, and maybe it was me who felt different. Not from being lost in the woods. I could have found my way back, eventually. There was something different between me and Ash. He wasn't putting on his pretend anger. We were both calm—relaxed.

After everyone went to bed, Ash and I stayed, sitting beside each other watching the fire. Hours passed without a word passing between us. The pop of the burning logs occasionally jolted me from my thoughts. I'd caught Ash watching me a few times, but he would hold my gaze a moment, then look back at the fire.

Ash finally broke the silence and said, "We should call it a night." He stood, searching for something near the fire pit. The flames were nearly gone. Only a few embers smoldered. "Where's that bucket Gary brought over?"

I pointed to where it sat behind his chair.

He grabbed it, then doused the fire. The wood let out an angry hiss, and the area filled with the intense smell of smoke and burned wood before the last ember disappeared.

We made our way to our tent and climbed in. I grabbed an unused glow stick and snapped it before hanging it from the tent's ceiling, giving us barely enough light to see.

I changed into cotton shorts, then quickly crawled into bed, welcoming the sweet, relaxing sleep I knew would come after a long day of hiking. Ash was close behind, pulling the covers up and snuggling next to me like he used to.

His warmth settled on my skin, heating me to my core.

"Why are you touching me?" I asked.

"Shut up, Sam. Relax, for once in your life, relax," he said, slinging his arm over my chest. "I'm not planning anything. Just sleep."

"But you're hot and making me sweat."

"Yeah, well, you stink, and I'm still here."

"I stink?"

"Very bad," he said, chuckling as he moved closer, placing his head on my shoulder.

"Why are you touching me, then?"

"You made me look for you and think I would find you half dead or worse. My compensation is a cuddle."

"Fine."

Ash chuckled, vibrating my skin. His breath ran over my chest, sending a lustful shiver rushing down my spine. He pressed his nose against my neck, taking a deep breath. "I wanna eat you up," he said, nuzzling his face in my neck.

"I will fight you," I warned.

"I'm not doing anything," he whined, and I could hear the smile in his voice.

I would be a liar if I said I didn't enjoy it.

It was our last night at the campsite. Angie grabbed the trash from another meal cooked over an open flame, and Dad was off somewhere packing up.

Ash approached me from our tent with a crooked grin. He wore dark jeans, a gray long-sleeved shirt, and his hiking boots like he was heading somewhere. "Do me a favor. Change into the clothes I put on the bed and grab your backpack."

"What?" I replied, "For what?"

"Remember how I wanted to see that spring at night before we leave?"

I nodded, worried about where this was going.

147

"We're going now."

"But it's a two-hour hike to get there, then we have to trek through the woods."

He nodded and gripped my shoulders. "Sam, go get changed."

Jane looked up from a book she had been engrossed in. "Where are you two heading?"

Ash waved me away as he walked over to her, kissing the top of her head. "Going for a bit of a walk," he said.

A bit? Try, we'll be gone all night.

On the air mattress, Ash had set out jeans, hiking boots, and a white long-sleeved shirt I liked to wear on my morning runs. After quickly changing, I grabbed the backpack, which was fully stocked with everything needed for the hike, including snacks and water.

When I found myself at the center of camp again, everyone was gathered around the fire pit. The flames were at their peak, and Ash was talking Jane down from her worry.

"Ma," he said, "I swear we won't get lost. I know exactly where I'm going."

Her gaze flicked to me when I approached before focusing on Ash again, worry lines forming on her forehead.

"If you wake up in the morning and we aren't here, then you can worry," Ash said, spinning toward me. "Let's go before they tie us up." He chuckled and grabbed his backpack from the ground, then rushed through the camp.

"Have fun," Angie called.

When I looked back, she wore a cheesy grin, whispering to my dad like she had fresh gossip.

"Get your hustle on, Sammy. We have barely enough time to get there before it's dark."

I jogged toward him, grumbling, "Great. Everything I've dreamed of."

The two-hour hike wasn't horrible, but Ash kept a fast pace the whole way. He released a frustrated groan when we reached the place on the trail we had stopped at the other day. He bent over, resting his hands on his knees, aiming his glare at the ground.

"Some asshole cut my marker."

The frayed yellow rope and red flag were in a dirty pile on the ground.

"Do you think they cut them all?" I asked, picking it up and tying it to my backpack. "They could have at least taken it with them instead of leaving it on the ground."

"Doubtful," Ash said, marching into the woods.

About ten feet in, we found the next marker untouched.

"Maybe they only noticed the one next to the path."

Ash spun back around and quickly tied a new rope with a red flag on the same tree. Dad and Jane would use it as their starting point if we never returned to camp.

It was a long thirty minutes finding our way back to the hidden spring. My breath was ragged as I squeezed through the narrow path, but the moment I emerged, the sound of the waterfall filled my ears.

Ash grunted behind me as he escaped the grasp of the rocks, then stumbled past me with a breathy chuckle.

"We made it," he said, dropping his backpack on the ground before walking to the water's edge. "And just in time." He pointed to the darkening sky, turning to me with a grin. "I have things to do, but you need to get changed."

"Changed? What is it this time?"

He sifted through his pack, then pulled out swimming trunks. They were mine. White with blue trim. I didn't think I had ever used them.

"Why?" I asked, marching up to him and ripping them from his hands.

"We're swimming."

He returned to his backpack and pulled out a small bag of floating pool lights. Jane had bought them for a party, thinking they were string lights, so they had sat in a closet, forgotten and unused.

"Why did you even bring those?"

He shrugged. "I figured we might use them near the river, but we never went swimming in the dark. What better time to use them than now?"

He reached into the white mesh bag, pressing the power button on each baseball-sized globe light. A rainbow lit in his hands before he tossed them into the water, not aiming in any specific direction. They landed with tiny splashes, illuminating the deep water.

"Get changed. Hurry up," Ash said, lifting off his shirt and hanging it from a nearby tree.

I quickly changed, folding my clothes and shoving them in my backpack before joining Ash by the water's edge. He was barefoot and still in his jeans, gazing at the water like it was a work of art.

"What are we doing here?"

He looked at me, tilting his head, and said, "Enjoying life."

"Don't we enjoy life every day?"

"Do you?" he asked, unbuckling his belt and popping the button of his jeans. "Because I don't. To be honest, life fucking sucks. Sleep, eat, work, and do it all again the next day. What are we living for? What am I enjoying?" He slipped out of his jeans and tossed them with his shirt. "Or do you think getting drunk and fucking strangers in cheap hotels is enjoying life?"

"Everyone's version of happiness is different," I said, but I couldn't stop the flood of memories racing through my mind of the times I went to a club to take someone home for the night. There was always loneliness mixed with the physical intimacy. They left me after they used me. They took from me but never gave me what I truly needed. The crushing despair of knowing that no matter how many people wanted my body, I could never find someone who filled the emptiness in my chest.

Was that how Ash lived his life, too?

Unease crept into my chest like a smoldering weight.

Ash hooked his fingers under the waistband of his boxers and stalked toward me. "What's your version of happiness?" He pushed the waistband down, slipping out of the fabric.

I swallowed, trying to ignore his blatant attempt to get to me.

"Put some pants on," I said.

Ignoring my request, he tossed the material over his jeans and waded into the water. He was a work of art—his body—the tattoos were their own. Ash's body was something he had spent years perfecting, and I appreciated every inch of it as he sunk deeper into the water.

"Let loose once in a while, Sam. Come feel what it's like to step out of the rigidity you hold yourself to."

I followed him into the water; it was cool, sending a wave of goosebumps over my skin. With every step, my sense of vulnerability grew, as if the water stripped away my safety net.

Ash disappeared beneath the surface. I stood there, heart pounding, watching the water for any sign of movement. When he popped up for air, he was far. A slight pang of disappointment rolled through me.

Was I waiting for him to come closer? Did I really want that?

Yes.

"God, you look so fucking stiff over there."

Ash swam toward me. His eyes reflected the lights as he passed them. I swallowed down the swirling nerves in my chest. I could have anyone else, and it wouldn't be a problem, so why did I want him?

When Ash reached me, I was a confused mess. After all these years, my love for him hadn't faded.

"Am I going to regret coming here with you?" I asked.

He closed the gap between us, wrapping his arm around my waist, and whispered, "You don't have to regret it."

"You know we can't do this."

The floating lights were our only light source as the last trace of sunlight disappeared. My pulse pounded, vibrating every inch of my body, making my skin buzz. His hand pressed against my lower back, bringing us closer.

"We can," he whispered. "It's only you and me here."

"But when we leave. . ."

"Does that matter?" he asked, pressing his body against mine.

My breath caught, and electricity raced beneath my skin. The cool water did nothing to temper the tension spreading between us.

Ash rested his forehead on mine. Droplets of water fell from his hair, dripping onto my cheeks. "Haven't you ever thought about what it would feel like to be with me?" he asked before biting his lip.

More often than I can count.

"What it would be like to let ourselves do what we want," he said, his breath heavy, mixing with mine. "No one but us needs to know."

His deep, honeyed voice added to his tempting words.

151

I should refuse. It could get messy if we did anything more than this. Hell, it was already messy. But I wanted him. Longed for him for so long. It was wearing on me.

"What if someone found out?"

"Fuck 'em," he said, bringing his other hand to my face, stroking my chin with his thumb. "All you need to know is that I love you more than life, Sam."

"Impossible," I whispered, leaning closer, my heart leaping and thumping.

"You are my life," he replied. "Without you, I'm nothing."

"You're exaggerating," I said, closing the gap until my lips brushed his.

"I mean every word," he whispered.

I knew it was wrong. I was breaking every rule I had ever set for myself, but I ached for him. Needed him with every fiber of my being. I was tired of holding back. Of following the rules. Of telling myself I couldn't have the only person I had ever loved so deeply that being without him in any capacity left me filled with pain and loneliness. The day he moved away, he took every part of me with him that made me—me. The only thing I had left was work. Everything else in my life was dull and empty.

I missed him. Us.

Our time together since he came home had reminded me of everything we used to be. Everything I missed out on because I refused him. Rejected him. He had stood there four years ago, willing to risk it all to have me, but I was too worried about losing our family. I was still worried about losing them because of this. If they called us disgusting. Depraved. I didn't think I could handle it. If my father never spoke to me again. Or it caused our parents to divorce. If Jane hated me. If Angie never wanted to see me again—it would break me.

"Don't disappear into your head, Sammy," Ash whispered, his voice deep and filled with lust, yanking me back to his body pressed against mine. His hand flattened against my lower back, burning my skin beneath the cool water.

"If our world falls apart because we can't keep it in our pants. . ." I wasn't sure how to end the sentence.

There were too many variables. Too many possible outcomes. And to be fair, it wasn't only about sex. My feelings for him were so ingrained in me that it was like he was a part of my body. Encoded in my DNA. Ash was the oxygen I breathed. The ground I stood on. He was with me in my dreams and my waking thoughts. His smile from across a room was enough to ignite my heart with the deepest feelings of love I had ever experienced.

He was my soulmate.

I had always called him that, but I truly believed he and I were meant for each other.

Ash was my other half. He filled in all the missing parts of me. Lifted me up. Gave me everything I ever wanted. Prioritized me over anything else, even himself.

He proved time and time again that if I needed him, he would always be there. Not once had he failed me. Not once did he betray me. Not once did I ever think he would abandon me.

Not until he moved to Raleigh. But that, I understood. I pushed him away, and I didn't chase him. It was my fault four years passed with a chasm between us. Yet, after four years, it only took a few days for us to fall into place. For us to fit together again.

"Sam, I think you underestimate what I would give up to have you back," he said with a heart-stopping grin. "What I would give to call you my lover."

"Stop. That's enough."

His fingers slid under my chin, and the pad of his thumb pressed against my skin with force. "If God came down and told me that I had a choice to be with you for one night and die the next or never see you again but live forever, can you guess which one I would choose?"

"Stop," I whispered. Of course, I knew which one he would choose, but saying something like that. . . how could he say that?

"Every single time, Sam. I choose you. Every. Time."

My eyes pricked, tears welling and wanting to spill over. My chest was warm and tight. I was conflicted, so fucking conflicted.

Family or the love of my life.

He was standing right there, confessing his love for me. Telling me that he would choose me even if it meant death.

How could I say no to that?

I wasn't sure where this would go, and I really didn't know how we would handle a relationship. Our family. If we would even come out of this unscathed, but there was no more running away. I couldn't do that to us anymore.

I'm tired of resisting my feelings.

Tilting my head the remaining distance, I pressed my lips to his, letting his warmth envelop me. Savoring the sensation of his soft lips against mine, breathing him in as I finally gave in. He smelled of spice and nature and sweat. His smell invaded my space.

I broke away, listening to his heavy breaths puff against my face. "I love you too," I whispered against his lips.

I kissed him again, moving my hands around his waist, and tugged him toward me until my chest was flush with his, and his erection slid against my abdomen. Ash whimpered and dug his fingers into my back, clawing at me like we weren't close enough. I took the opportunity to slip my tongue into his mouth. He tasted sweet with a hint of cherry from the sports drinks we had on the hike.

Ash moved his hands, searching until he found his way under the waistband of my swim trunks. His hands flattened around my ass, and he squeezed, aiming my hips toward him. His arousal glided against mine over the fabric of my swim trunks, and he rolled his hips again. My dick strained against the soft mesh inside the shorts, and all I wanted was to see him and touch him without the water in the way.

I broke our kiss, and he chased after me.

"Out of the water," I ordered through heavy breaths. "Now."

Ash bit his lip, holding back a sexy smirk as he rushed to the edge of the water before rummaging through his bag, pulling out a giant beach towel and lube.

"Who are you, Mary Poppins?" I asked, laughing while I approached him.

"I'm better because I brought lube."

He tossed the bottle into the air before loosely catching it. His wide grin sent my heart fluttering as he stood there, naked, with a raging boner and lube in his hand in the middle of the woods, as if this was merely another day in the life of Ashton Emerson.

Fuck. I'm a goner.

"Anything else in that bag of tricks?"

He laid out the towel before aiming his stupidly wide smile at me and said, "All you need is right here." He motioned toward his body and wiggled his eyebrows.

I licked my lips before closing the short distance between us. "Yeah," I said, sliding my hand behind his head and pulling him close. His grin disappeared, replaced by a lustful gaze. "What do you prefer?" I asked.

"I prefer a lot of things. I need you to be specific."

I cleared my throat, staring into his smoldering eyes before dropping to his lips. "I'm verse, but prefer to bottom."

He bit his lip, releasing a slight groan. "I've kept my ass for you, but I'm going to fuck you silly today."

"Kept your. . . you what?"

"My ass has never been touched, saved exclusively for you." He rolled his tongue over his top lip before biting his bottom lip. "I mean, toys have been there, but," he said with a throaty groan, "right now, I'm gonna fill you until—"

I placed my hand over his mouth, stopping whatever filthy thing he was about to say from entering the world.

Chapter 21

Ash

My heart tried to climb up my throat while I stared into Sam's eyes, his palm resting over my lips.

"It's settled then," he said, sliding his hand from my mouth.

I licked my lips at the prospect of sinking into his warmth. I'd dreamed of it for years, and now he was right in front of me while I clutched the lube bottle like it anchored me to reality.

"We're doing this for real? This isn't a dream?" I asked, my voice cracking.

His hands dropped to his waist, untying the string on his swim trunks with a nervous smile. He tugged the shorts down, letting them fall to his feet.

I tossed the lube onto the towel before drinking him in, slowly raising my gaze over his toned calves. Up his thighs with only a light dusting of visible muscle, to his delectable balls hanging there looking perfect for licking. And his fucking perfect cock, standing tall with a thick vein running down the shaft. I swallowed hard, nearly forgetting where I was before forcing my gaze to the sexy V leading to his tight stomach, dusted with the light outline of a six-pack. I bit my lip when I reached his beautiful face, gazing back at me with lust in his eyes.

I'd never wanted to dive inside someone before. The logistics of it didn't make sense, but the need to climb over him and somehow sink my whole body inside him spurred me forward. It was only a step, but it felt like miles. I crashed against him, desperate and needy, kissing him, running my fingers through his soft hair. My other hand gripped his waist, sliding over his smooth skin, pulling him flush with me. Our erections met with delicious friction when I crushed him to me.

A breathy moan escaped Sam between kisses and lip-biting. I backed up, tugging him with me until my feet hit the towel, then I released him and dropped to my knees.

"This is something I've wanted to do for a long time," I said before kissing his thigh, moving my lips slowly over his skin.

Sam released a breath, resting his palm on my head, his fingers curling when I inched closer. "Ash," he whimpered.

The sound of his whimper made me lightheaded, my chest tight, and the need to bury myself inside him and let him swallow me whole grew stronger.

Trailing my nose up his length, I fell into the sensation of his soft skin. Each gasp he took was because of me. Each time his grip on my hair tightened, I was filled with something I couldn't put words to.

I kissed his length before licking him from base to tip. The heady taste of his sweat landed on my tongue, leaving me lusting after the flavor. The mix of earthy nature from swimming in the spring only added to everything. I licked over the tip, tasting the salty tang of pre-cum before sinking my mouth over him until he hit the back of my throat with a moan.

"Fuck," Sam said, "Ash." His grip tightened in my hair when I moved, licking and sucking, dragging gasps and moans from him. "More," he begged, thrusting into my mouth.

He didn't need to explain. I released him for only long enough to suck on my finger, soaking it before returning my mouth to his throbbing cock. I gripped his ass with one hand, enjoying the fullness of his tensed muscles as he fought to stand. With my other hand, I slid my fingers down his crease until I reached his soft hole and rubbed my finger around the rim, teasing him and forcing a moan to sing through the air. He moved back like he was begging me to push inside before he pressed his cock to the back of my throat again.

It was so fucking hot. I wanted to throw him to the ground and sink into him. I wanted to live inside him. I wanted him to consume me until our bodies fused.

I pressed the tip of my middle finger inside, testing how far I could get with only my saliva. I didn't get past the first knuckle; I needed lube to do anything meaningful, but it must've been enough because the tight ring of muscles clamped around my finger, and Sam shuddered.

My heart fluttered each time I stroked his cock with my tongue, swallowing him deep until my nose pressed against his skin. Sam's reactions kept me going, working to drag gasps and moans from his lips. I was sure the only thing keeping him standing was the hold I had on his ass.

"Ash," he groaned, "I'm—"

I pulled off of him and held tight so he wouldn't fall at the sudden release of pressure. "No, you don't. Not yet."

Sam released a soft whimper, and his hand fell from my hair.

"Face down, ass up," I ordered, pointing to the towel.

He was dazed as he kneeled and leaned forward, giving me the world's best view. Even in the dark, he was perfect.

"You're so fucking sexy," I said, settling behind him, resting on my heels.

"Right back at you." He chuckled and rested his forehead on his arm.

I bent over him, pressing my erection to his ass, and brushed my lips over his ear. "I'm going to fuck you until your legs shake and you beg to come." I kissed the soft skin behind his ear.

Sam's quiet gasp left me wanting.

"Then we're gonna walk our happy asses back to camp, and I'll cuddle you until morning." I rolled my hips, sliding my cock over his skin, and said, "You can back out." I lifted myself up, staring down at his ass under my length, and warm shivers ran through me like electricity.

"I'm not backing out," he said.

"Good," I groaned happily.

Sliding my palms down his back, I took in the sight of him, bent over with his ass in the air, and spread for me before positioning my lips so close to his hole I could feel the warmth of his skin.

"Mm, Sammy," I hummed. "I'm gonna eat you up."

He made a noise like he was stifling a whimper when I flicked the tip of my tongue over his hole. I gripped his hips, holding him in place, and licked a line down to his balls where I paid close attention to each one, sucking and licking them before trailing my tongue back to his tight hole. I teased the area before pressing the tip of my tongue inside, flicking and swirling my tongue over him.

Sam released a breathy groan and whispered my name, pushing back so my tongue moved deeper.

The taste of him was indescribable, sending my brain down a path so clouded with desire that I couldn't even call the state I was in consciousness.

I pushed my tongue deeper, thrusting and licking until the muscles loosened, and Sam was a needy mess.

My fingers landed on the lube near my knee, and I flipped the cap open, pouring a glob onto my fingers before rubbing over his hole with gentle circles.

"More," Sam whispered. "Please."

I chuckled, then said, "So demanding, Angel," and pressed the tip of my finger inside his soft warmth.

I moved slowly, letting his body grow accustomed to the intrusion before focusing on loosening the tight ring of muscles. The breathy sounds coming from Sam had my body taut and aching. My abdomen was tight against his ass, and my cock rested under him, rubbing against his balls and the base of his length. It was amazing to have his touch—a full-body ecstasy like no other. Sliding my finger from him, I admired the view before pressing two fingers in, continuing to give him pleasure while prepping him.

When I slid a third finger in, he pushed back like he was begging for more. His hand wrapped around my length and pressed me tight against his arousal.

"Ash, please," he whined.

"Sammy," I said through gritted teeth, his hand stroking me with a tight hold. "You aren't ready yet."

"I am," he whispered. "I swear I am."

"I don't want to hurt you."

"Please, Ash."

Ah, fuck.

I pulled my fingers from him, provoking a soft groan, and grabbed the lube, lathering myself before tossing the bottle to the side.

Grabbing his hips, I pulled his ass back, biting my lip as all my fantasies finally turned into reality. I slid the tip of my cock over his slicked hole, rubbing around the rim.

Sam moaned and pushed back. "Stop teasing me."

I leaned in, flicking my tongue over his earlobe. "I want you to face me."

"Why," Sam whined, wiggling his ass.

I kissed his neck, chuckling against his skin before resting my head on his and whispered, "Because I want to see your face when I sink all the way inside you." I bit my lip, releasing a soft grunt. "While I fuck you."

"Fine," Sam groaned.

I smiled, pulling away from him. He lifted off the ground and spun toward me. The lust in his eyes stole my breath. He grabbed the back of my head, tangling his fingers in the curly strands. His forceful grip stung, but it was quickly overtaken with pleasure. He leaned in, capturing me with a forceful kiss. His free hand explored my body, sending goosebumps over every inch of skin he touched. I slid my tongue between his lips, plunging inside to taste him. Wrapping my arms around his waist, I crushed him against me, lining our bodies up perfectly.

I guided him back until he was flat on the ground, looking up at me with needy eyes. I nudged his thighs further apart, dropping my hips until my cock found his hole. "Sure I stretched you enough?"

He nodded, then said, "Fuck me already."

"Whatever you want," I whispered, pressing a kiss to his jaw.

I pushed in, slow, easing myself inside him. He threw his head back and puffed out a groan. When his legs wrapped around me, I pushed deeper, continuing my slow entrance to his delectable warmth. It took every ounce of willpower not to drive in hard and fast, but I wanted this. This heightened sensual feeling where every millimeter was like an explosion of nerves sending pleasure through every part of my body. Sam's arms enveloped my shoulders, and his fingers found their way into my hair. The sensation was pure heaven. I drove deeper into his body, savoring every ounce of contact and breath between us.

He lifted his hips, trying to push against me like he was begging me to move faster. I took the invitation and dropped to my elbows, taking his mouth with mine. When I was completely buried inside him, I held myself there, letting his body pulse around me.

Sam moaned and said, "Holy fuck, Ash."

Same.

I made slow movements at first, reveling in the feeling of us united, sharing our bodies in a way I never anticipated would be reality. Being inside Sam, being with him like this, was like coming home. There was a connection between us. A pull. Something I couldn't explain, and this only intensified it.

"Ash," Sam whined, tugging my hair and moving his hips, "move faster."

I kissed him, pumping into him harder, rolling my hips, consumed by him. I tried to keep myself on the edge, holding off my release, but each gasp and moan pouring from Sam had me struggling to hold out. My chest rubbed on his, and sweat pooled between us. I reached for his length as I rolled my hips, hitting that little spot that made his body shake and his head fall back. He was thick and leaking in my hand, on the edge like I was.

He whimpered, tightening his hold on my hair as his lips found my neck.

My first thought was to let him do whatever he wanted, but if we appeared in front of our family with hickeys, they would know immediately.

"No marks."

He released a frustrated groan, burying his face in my neck.

I ran my hand over his length, rubbing my thumb over his leaking slit. I didn't want it to end, but I smiled when his legs started shaking around me.

"Come for me, Angel," I whispered and kissed him, savoring the feeling of him around me. Consuming me. Owning me. Owning my pleasure. My body. My soul.

With one last stroke over his cock, he released in my hand with a sexy fucking moan, and the warmth of his cum in my palm was the last straw for me. I lifted off of him, pulling out, and with the hand covered in his cum, I gripped my cock. It was a full-body pleasure. Different than I was used to. My head rushed, and an electrical buzzing raced under my skin. I gave myself a tug before releasing over Sam's chest.

I held his gaze as our breathing came down.

I couldn't believe that happened.

The sight of our cum coating my hand was such a turn-on. I lifted my hand covered in our release and licked. It was salty and heady. But the hottest part was the look on Sam's face while he watched me. Like he wanted to devour me whole. It sent a shiver down my spine. It was like he knew I wanted to be consumed.

"Ash," he said, sitting up and reaching for my hand. "Don't do that."

"Why not?" I twisted out of his reach.

"You're making me want to fuck you again."

I licked more of our cum from my fingers. "Mmm," I moaned. "Sounds like everything I've ever wanted in life." He pounced on me, pushing me to the ground. "Fuck," I said, laughing, "you'll get me all wound up again."

Sam climbed over me, surrounding me with his body and showering me in kisses all over my face and neck before straddling me.

The look on his face grew serious, and he pressed his palm to my chest as he sat back.

"What are we doing, Ash?"

He sounded worried, like if I said the wrong thing, this would be the one and only time we would be together like this.

"To be honest," I said, sighing and sliding my hands over his thighs, "I'm hoping this means we're together now."

"You want to date me?" he asked, like it was a crazy concept.

"Is it so wrong to want a relationship?" I sat up, holding him tight, and kissed his chin. "I love you," I whispered, kissing his neck, then his collarbone. "I want to be with you."

He rested his forehead on mine, then said, "Even if that means everyone we know and love hates us or thinks we're disgusting?"

"Even if," I said, squeezing him tighter. "I don't think you truly understand how much you mean to me, Sammy. The entire world could be against us, and I would still choose you."

"Here you go again."

I kissed him before pulling away. "One day, you'll understand."

"Maybe."

I cupped the sides of his face with both hands and tugged him down, kissing his forehead. When I pulled away, with only a fraction of space between us, I whispered, "You are my everything."

"Fuck," he groaned, squeezing me in a tight hug. "I love you, Ash. I fucking love you."

"Mmm," I hummed. "I could stay like this forever."

When we finally pulled ourselves apart, we cleaned off in the spring, and I gathered up all the pool lights before packing everything up and getting dressed. I was light on my feet on the hike back to camp, but as the hours and miles wore on, our high faded, and by the time we made it to our tent, it was three, and we had about two hours before our alarms were set to go off.

I didn't care, though.

The moment we hit the bed, I pulled Sam close and cuddled him like I promised. We smelled like dirt, earthy spring water, and sweat. It was glorious, and I fell asleep holding the one person I never wanted to live without again. Nothing else mattered.

The alarm blared through the quiet morning, and I quickly hit the snooze icon on my phone, silencing it for another five minutes.

Sam groaned into the pillow and wiggled closer to me. I wrapped my arms around him, holding him tight, pressing every inch of my body to him that I could, including my morning hard-on.

"Morning," he said, muffled by the pillow.

"Mornin'," I whispered into the back of his head, nuzzling my nose in his hair. "I don't want to get up."

He groaned and spun around to face me. "Neither do I."

"I wish we could teleport to your bed and stay there for a few days."

"Sounds perfect. Go invent the tech so we can do that."

"If only I was smart enough to come up with that kind of thing," I said, chuckling and kissing him. "We should get up."

He whined and buried his face in my chest.

I was full of giddy happiness. My chest bloomed with warmth, enveloping the broken pieces of my heart the longer I had Sam in my arms. The only downside was we hadn't discussed how to tell our family, so while I wanted to kiss him and hug him like this all day, there would be a point where we had to pretend we were only friends again. Well, stepbrothers and friends. Best friends.

Didn't people say to marry your best friend? *Sounds like the perfect plan to me.*

My alarm went off again, but this time, I dismissed it and rolled on top of Sam while the sound of our family coming to life surrounded us.

"Sam," I whispered and ground my erection over his thigh, "If you don't get up, I might have us do something about this."

"Ashton," he scolded me, "our family is right there."

"And?"

He shot up, shoving me away, and I burst out laughing at the terrified yet horny look he shot me.

"Glad to see my boys made it back to camp safely," Mom called from what seemed a good distance away.

"Mornin', Ma," I called back, shoving Sam back down with one hand square on his chest. "Mmm, Sammy, you look good enough to eat," I whispered, holding back my laugh as I ran a hand down his stomach and hooked a finger in the waistband of his shorts.

"Ash," he pleaded, "don't."

His little whimper had me wanting to do it for real, so I pulled off him with a smile. "Don't worry, I was joking until you looked at me like that. Jesus. When we get home, I need you to take me to your bed ASAP." I glanced down at the bulge in my shorts. "Though this is a real problem."

He smacked my chest and hopped off the air mattress. "You'll figure it out, bro."

"Bro? You never call me bro, bro."

He shot me a wink before dropping his pants. He was as hard as me, and I licked my lips, watching him slide into jeans and a T-shirt.

"Tease," I said, pushing him aside and finding my clothes. "Just wait for later. Payback's a bitch, bro." I winked and dropped my pants, making sure to bend down perfectly in his view to see all of my ass before I covered myself in jeans.

His stifled grunt was everything I needed before emerging from our tent to greet the day.

"Did you two have fun last night?" Mom asked, folding a blanket and shoving it in a duffle bag.

I marched happily toward her and planted a kiss on her cheek. "Loads of fun." I glanced over my shoulder with a grin. Sam stood at the edge of the fire pit, aiming a death glare at me. "Didn't we, bro?"

"Take all that energy you seem to be wound up with this fine morning and help me get these tents taken down," Gary said, appearing from the other side of the van.

"You got it, Gary." I walked around Mom and made myself useful. "Where do you need me? Direct, and I will do."

Gary loaded me up with a list of things to do, from taking down tents to packing up the van. Sam and I worked together as easily as we used to. The stiffness we'd had when we first arrived was gone, replaced with our old antics and bickering.

While tearing our tent down, I caught a glimpse of Angie watching me. I knew that look. She was seeing something but wasn't sure what it meant.

Sam and I really needed to have that talk, but I wasn't ready for it. I had a feeling it would bring back some of the tension I worked hard to eliminate last night.

When the cars were packed up, I hugged Mom and Angie, said goodbye to Gary, and rushed to the Jeep with Sam close on my heels. I closed the door, buckling up, unable to keep the smile from my lips. The minivan was first to leave camp, and before Sam could shift the car into drive, I grabbed the back of his head, leaned over the center console, and kissed him.

Pulling away, I said, "Now we can go." I rested my hand on his thigh, settling back in the seat, and added, "Let me know if you want to take turns so you can nap."

With a wide grin, he held my gaze a moment before driving off.

There was no way we would hide this for long. One look at the two of us would give it away.

Sam pulled into the driveway close behind Gary's minivan. The girls had already hopped out, and Gary marched through the garage, opening the door.

Sam took a deep breath and turned to me. "Best behavior, Ash."

"Will I get a reward if I'm good?"

"Sure." He nodded, biting back his smile.

"Tell me what it is so I work hard for it."

He leaned in, his eyes flicking over my face before landing on my lips. "It's a two-fer." He leaned closer, whispering, "First, if you're really good and don't say anything suspicious, you can fuck my face."

"Mm," I groaned. "What else?"

"After you fuck my face, I'm taking your ass."

"Oh, fuck, Sammy. I'll be the goodest boy," I said, half-jokingly, and grabbed his hand. Sam may not have realized it, but he was the *only* person I would ever give myself to like that. The only person. I didn't trust anyone else. "I wanna kiss you so fucking bad right now."

He chuckled, shushing me, and hopped out of the car. I quickly followed him because the faster the cars were unpacked, the faster we could get to his apartment.

Halfway through unloading the cars, Sam's phone rang. He answered, walking away a few feet. Sam said something before laughing, glancing over at me with a twinkle in his eyes. His grin was breathtaking.

Angie bumped her shoulder against my arm, looking up at me curiously. "What happened to you two out in the woods?" she asked, tilting her head to the side, eyeing me.

I swallowed. "Nothing," I said, hoping my voice was smooth and untelling before turning back to the van, grabbing a few things, and heading into the house.

"Nothing?" she whispered, following me. "I don't believe you."

I cleared my throat, shoving a bag at her. "Put this away, nosy."

She took it, squinting before walking up the stairs.

When I returned to the van, Sam finally hung up the phone and walked over to me, his shoulders tense behind a smile.

"Everything okay?" I asked.

His worried expression had me concerned.

"How do you feel about dinner at a bar?"

"What?" I set down the bag I was holding. "Why?"

"That was Rainie," he said, running his fingers through his hair. "Inviting me to dinner with her, Sean, and a few of our friends."

I pursed my lips, remembering the last time I went out with Rainie, though, now that Sam and I were together, maybe she deserved my thanks.

Sam continued, "We don't have to go, but tonight is karaoke night at this bar we all go to a lot." He chewed the inside of his cheek. "I can say no." His head tilted to the side as he frowned. "It's okay if you don't want to."

I gripped the back of his neck, pulling him close. Brushing my lips over his ear, I whispered, "I'll go wherever you want."

"Will you sing for me?" Sam asked, resting his hand on my chest.

I chuckled. "Not a chance."

He patted my chest before dropping his hand and backing away from me. I wanted to complain about the distance, but I also didn't want to get caught by Angie.

"We have two hours before we meet them. We should hurry and shower."

I pulled away, sliding my hand from his neck and running my thumb along his jaw.

"Guys!" Angie called from the garage, and I slowly dropped my hand from Sam's face before she could see anything.

I jogged toward Angie. "What's up, piglet?"

She eyed me, then glanced over my shoulder where Sam was walking toward us, the bag I'd dropped clutched in his hand.

"Is that the last bag?" She pointed to it. "Mom wants to know if Sam is staying for dinner."

"Nope. We're going out after we get cleaned up."

Her face scrunched up like I said something disgusting. "Where to?"

"Sean and Rainie invited me out," Sam said, moving past us and into the house.

"The phone call from earlier?" she asked, following him.

"Yeah," he replied and disappeared down the hall.

She stood next to me while I closed the door.

"That's a bummer. I wanted to spend more time with you guys," she said, pouting and crossing her arms. "So you're invited with him? Did you two make up?"

I pinched her cheek and dashed away.

"I knew something happened," she squealed in a hushed voice as she chased me through the house until I spun into the living room and flopped onto the sofa.

Her tiny body landed on me, and her hair fell around my head as she leaned her face next to mine. "Tell me, Ash. Are you guys back to normal?"

I chuckled. "Maybe," I teased. "But do me a favor and stop doing whatever you and Gary are up to."

She gasped and leaned back. "We aren't up to anything,"—her eyes shifted, and a smirk dimpled her cheek—"much."

"I knew you two were plotting something," I said, holding in my chuckle. The pair of them were about as unsubtle as a horse prancing through a living room.

She leaned close to my ear again and whispered, "The fourth tent getting left behind was part of the plan, but honestly, we were hoping you two would fix it on your own by being trapped in the woods for almost a week." She cackled as she pushed off of me and darted from the living room before I could get to my feet and tackle her. Torture by tickles sounded perfect. "Dad!" she screamed somewhere in the house. "Ash figured us out! Hide!"

Laughing, I rose from the sofa, listening to her charge through the house, screaming for Gary to save her. I stopped by the kitchen, where Mom already started dinner. When she looked up, I rounded the island and kissed her cheek.

"Don't worry about me and Sam, Ma. We're gonna shower, then go out with some friends."

"Together?" she asked. A sad smile formed on her lips when she wiped her hands on her apron. "Honey, did you two finally fix things?"

I nodded and crushed her in a hug. "You don't have to worry about us. We're fine." I released her and stole a slice of bread she'd put off to the side. "I'm probably crashing at his place tonight, so don't freak out if I'm not home until tomorrow."

She patted my back, giving me a reassuring rub. "Okay, sweetie."

I felt slimy giving her only half-truths, but before Sam and I fell apart because of my decision to take that dare, sleeping at each other's places was normal. We could get away with it easily. Thinking about it, the only difference in our relationship from then and now was sex.

My room was dark, but the shower was already running in my shared bathroom with Sam, and a devious idea came to mind. I walked back into the hallway, snuck down the hall to his room, locked the door, closed it and returned to my room, locking my door too.

After shedding my clothes, I opened the bathroom door. "So many years we could've done this, and only now can it come true," I said.

"What are you doing?" Sam asked.

"Mmm, the shower is already nice and warm for me. That's so kind of you, Sammy." I pulled the shower curtain back and stepped into the tub where the man of my literal dreams stood covered in soap. I licked my lips, closed the shower curtain, then slid my hand over his hip. "Wanna help me get all cleaned up?"

"Is this a dirty thing or a real thing?" he asked, stepping into the stream of water, washing away the suds covering his body.

"Can it be both?" I asked, gliding my hands over his stomach. "C'mere," I whispered, pulling him flush with me, aligning our bodies perfectly. I stroked my fingers over his hair, down his neck, and kissed him.

Sam broke our kiss, whispering, "This isn't the place to fool around."

I nodded against him, tugging his bottom lip with my teeth. "I know." My hands slid over his body, loving every second of contact. I backed him up until we both stood under the stream of water, then returned to kissing him. "I want to be near you right now."

"This is more than being near me."

I stepped away to grab the shampoo. "Think of it as a promise for later."

"What does that mean?" he asked with a smile.

"Exactly what I said," I whispered, pouring the cool liquid into my palm and setting the bottle down. "Come here."

Sam stepped out of the stream, his pale blue eyes following my every move. I melted under his gaze. Wanting nothing more than to give him anything and everything he could ever want.

When he was mere inches from me again, I rubbed my palms together. Then I gripped the back of his head with both hands, staring into his eyes, and massaged his scalp in slow swirls.

A soft groan rumbled through his chest, and his eyes fluttered closed. I kept going for a while, letting him lean against me, melting under my touch.

I wouldn't take it anywhere. Not here, but I needed him like this. With me. After so many years of avoiding each other. I needed this.

Chapter 22

Sam

The engine cut off, and I slipped out of my Jeep. Ash rounded the back of the car. He wore a black button-down with the sleeves rolled up to his elbows, showing off both sleeve tattoos. The top four buttons were left undone, giving me a peek at his mouth-watering neckline, where more tattoos climbed his skin, stopping at his jawline. He shoved his left hand lazily into the front pocket of his jeans, which hugged his ass tight, leaving nothing to the imagination. When I met his eyes surrounded by black eyeliner, staring at me with desire, it took every last bit of self-control not to shove him against the car and kiss him for anyone to see.

With his free hand, he ran his fingers over the back of my neck and asked, "You okay, Angel?"

It was the second time he had called me that, and I wasn't sure where it came from, but it sent a rush of anticipation through me when he did.

I nodded, turning toward the bar. We had agreed to keep our relationship quiet for now. These were my friends, but I wasn't ready to tell them yet. I was scared they would judge me. Us.

My nerves heightened when the bar's door shut behind me.

The hostess smiled, grabbing two menus. "Two?" she asked, dragging her stare over Ash.

"We're here with a group. I think they're already here," I replied, inching closer to Ash.

Her smile wavered, then she said, "Feel free to look for them."

Walking through the bar, I felt too visible. I half expected them to know I was with Ash. I waited for their knowing glares laced with judgment. The reality of the situation finally sank in. I had to continue hiding. Always hiding. I was so tired of pretending. The lies. The half-truths. Avoiding situations or people.

They'll know. They'll hate me. What if they never speak to me again?

Ash slung his arm over my shoulder, his lips brushing over my ear as he said, "Sammy, don't stay in your head like that."

I glanced at him, knowing that no matter what happened, he would be there. That knowledge tempered my fears.

Ash followed me while I scanned the building for the familiar faces of my friends. When I found them posted up in a back corner of the bar, my stomach knotted, sending burning heat racing up my throat.

How do I explain why Ash is with me? Will they believe me if I say we made up?

"He made it!" Rainie yelled, leaping to her feet and rushing toward me. Her short bob bounced with each step, then her arms were around me, crushing me against her.

I forced out a laugh, then said, "Hey, Rain. It's good to see you."

She pulled back, leaning against me. Her mouth opened like she was about to say something, but she froze when her attention landed on Ash. "Ashton?"

Ash slung his arm over my shoulder like he always did, but this time, it felt like more. Like he was doing it to tell me he was here and we were in this together.

"How goes it, Nini?" Ash said. His honeyed tone was playful as if he was enjoying her reaction to seeing him with me.

"Uh, well," Rainie stammered. "You two are talking again?"

I nodded and said, "Turns out a few days in the woods can clear up any argument."

I chuckled through my unease. Everyone here knew about the Truth or Dare kiss and how it had led to Ash and me "fighting." My nerves took hold in my stomach, twisting until I tasted bile.

"Oh, thank God you're here," Autumn said from the end of the table. "Leo has been talking about work, and I didn't come here to work."

I forced a smile and said, "How about we fix that right now?"

Rainie released me, and I stepped around her, heading to the only two open chairs, and sat in the one beside Leo.

172

"Hey, Sam," Leo said, low enough that others couldn't hear him. "How was the trip?"

"It was great." I avoided eye contact, shifting in my chair.

There was a part of me hoping I could've avoided him until after Ash went home—that clearly wasn't my luck.

Ash sunk into the chair on my right between me and Sean, fist-bumping Sean before placing his arm over the back of my chair.

Autumn cleared her throat, eyeing me while glancing between me and Ash.

I chuckled, then said, "Autumn, this is Ashton." I motioned to Ash. "Ash, this is Autumn, my friend and assistant at Victory X."

She looked him up and down the way women always did, but this time, it made me more uncomfortable than ever. "Hello, Ashton," Autumn purred.

I wanted to tell her to back off, but I was too afraid. The memory of the disgust on Jasmine's face when Ash kissed me for that dare rushed to the forefront of my mind, sending my heart slamming against my ribs. Jaz knew we weren't blood-related and still had the exact reaction I expected. I didn't think I could recover if Autumn looked at me the same way.

"Autumn," Ash said, shaking her hand. "I hear you've been taking care of Sammy. Make sure he doesn't overwork himself. He doesn't know when to relax."

"Don't I know it," she said, looking Ash up and down.

Leo leaned over the table, getting far too close to me, extending his hand to Ash. "I don't think we've ever met."

Ash cocked his head to the side, his eyes flicking to me for a brief moment. "Don't think we have."

"Leo Bradford," Leo said, shaking Ash's hand with a grip that looked painful. "Sam's friend and CFO at Victory X."

Ash's eyes flicked to me again, and the muscle in his jaw rolled under his skin. "Nice to meet you, Leo."

The tension between them could be cut with a knife. I sensed they both knew who each other was, which worsened the nervous twisting in my stomach.

I cared about Leo, but Ash was the love of my life. The only person in this world I ever truly wanted. Sitting between them while they aimed death glares at each other like I was some possession they owned was not something I had planned for.

I sighed, pushing away from the table. "I'll be right back."

Ash's brows creased with worry, but he didn't say anything.

When I was a few feet away, I chanced a look back at the table. Rainie and Sean had descended on Ash, crowding him, likely asking him far too personal questions.

Laughter filled the crowded bar. On the stage where live performances happened on the weekends, someone was setting up the Karaoke machine, preparing for the weekly shitshow of drunken idiots singing their hearts out to random songs. I turned the corner, ducking into the narrow hallway leading to the restrooms, and quickly dipped into the men's room.

I should've prepared myself ahead of time for my fuck buddy and boyfriend to meet, but I hadn't thought it would happen the night after Ash and I stopped running from our feelings. I groaned, locking myself in one of the empty stalls, and scrubbed my hands over my face.

Act cool. We agreed that no one would find out. Not tonight. Not any time soon. I just need to get through this night without giving it away.

The bathroom door opened, letting the music from the bar pour in.

I flushed the toilet before leaving the stall, thinking it would be awkward if I had been standing in the stall doing exactly what I had been.

My steps faltered when I came face to face with Leo's soft brown eyes and crooked smile.

"So, that's the brother?" he said, wiggling his eyebrows, and he leaned his hip against the counter.

I approached, trying to school my expression. "Obviously." I flicked on the water and pumped the soap into my palm. "Also, stepbrother. Not actually my brother, Leo." He knew how much I hated people calling Ash my brother.

"Why'd you bring him with you? Did you two start talking again or something?"

Or something. "Yeah, we're cool now. We had a long talk and worked our shit out."

He raised an eyebrow. "Really?"

"Really," I replied, running my hands under the warm stream of water.

"So, how horny are you after being around him for two weeks straight? Want me to come over tonight?"

My breath hitched, and without looking him in the eye, I turned to the towel dispenser and focused on drying my hands. "Not tonight."

"What, you going to be with him the whole night?"

I tossed the balled-up paper towels into the trash and spun around. "Actually, yeah. We're hanging out tonight."

His hands fell to his sides, and he pushed off the counter. "Wait, seriously?"

"Yes. Seriously."

"So what? Just like that, and you two are best friends again?" He grabbed my arm, keeping me from walking off.

"What is your problem, Leo?" I yanked my arm away from him.

"My problem?" He scoffed. "You've been pining after your brother for years, and I'm the one with the problem?"

"Clearly." I looked him up and down. "You're the one cornering me in the bathroom asking why my best friend is hanging out with me tonight."

"Because it's fucking weird, Sam," he said, raising his voice. "You've been avoiding each other for years, and now, all of a sudden, he's here hanging out with us, and you're blowing me off tonight to hang with him instead."

I shrugged, stepping around Leo, needing this conversation to be over.

"Don't walk away from me, Sam." He grabbed the back of my shirt, yanking me back. "What happened while you were in Ohio?" He spun me around, gripping my arms hard enough to make me grit my teeth.

"Nothing. Let go of me," I warned.

"Oh my god, you didn't?" His lip curled into a snarl. "Did you?"

I shoved him away, scared that if I said anything more, I would confirm it.

"Holy shit. You did." Leo's laugh was laced with anger, sending my stomach swirling.

"Stop. We're done, Leo. You and I,"—I motioned between us—"we're done."

His eyes went wide, his laugh cutting off. "Why now?"

I chewed the inside of my cheek, staring at the floor.

"It's true then? Little Sammy, in love with his brother, finally got what he wanted. How much did you have to beg? Did you have to get him drunk?"

"Shut the fuck up!" I shoved him. "You don't know what you're talking about!"

"You sick fuck," he said. His voice sounded like acid to my ears. "I hope his dick was worth it."

"Shut up! You don't understand anything!" I shoved him again. "Leave me the fuck alone about this. It's none of your business."

He laughed, raking his fingers through his hair. "That's where you're wrong, Sam. It is my business. You're not only my boss, but you're my friend. Hell, I've been in love with you since I met you. I thought you'd come around and realize your feelings for that fucking asshole were useless." He tugged on his hair, eyes glistening as he looked at me like I was his worst enemy. "I've loved you for seven fucking years. Seven years. I thought you were finally over your stupid crush. But I guess I was the idiot here."

"I told you from the start that I could never love you, Leo." I had never lied to him. He knew. He fucking knew.

"You sure did, didn't you? You're going to run away from my feelings the same way you run away from everything that gets too hard. Right?"

"I'm not running away from you," I snarled. "I will never love you. I love—" I cut myself off.

"Say it, Sam. Fucking say it. I dare you." He stepped toward me, crowding my space. "You let me think I had a fucking chance." He pointed at his chest, his hand shaking like he couldn't contain his rage. "I thought I had a goddamn chance," he roared, and his face grew deep shades of red.

"You're not my boyfriend," I shouted. "You were never my boyfriend. I—" My breath heaved, lungs constricting like Leo had stolen all the air.

"No, I'm not your boyfriend, but I thought you cared about me enough to treat me better than this."

I stepped back. I didn't know what to do or say.

"You know what," he said, brushing past me, "have a nice life with your incestuous family. I hope you're happy together."

"Fuck off," I mumbled, slumping against the bathroom stall as the door slammed shut.

I stood in the restroom for a few minutes before finding the courage to face everyone. I was sure Leo had stormed out, telling everyone the news. When I neared the table, they were drinking and laughing as if I hadn't disappeared to the bathroom for fifteen minutes.

Leo was nowhere in sight.

When I sat next to Ash, his hand found my thigh, and he gently squeezed before locking his eyes with mine. I could practically hear him asking if I was okay. I flattened my hand over his, offering a smile I knew looked fake and broken.

Ash leaned in, drawing his lips to my ear. "Everything okay?"

I shook my head and said, "Later."

When the person singing karaoke on the small stage finished, Rainie jumped up, dragging Sean with her to sing.

I couldn't enjoy it. It was like I was on the outside looking in, watching my friends have fun and live their lives while wondering how mine would implode. What was Leo going to do? When morning came, would he have told the world? Would I wake to find my personal life blasted all over the internet? Would I find texts and missed calls from everyone I knew?

By the time Ash and I walked out of the bar, I was ready to crawl into bed and hide from the world. When Ash's hand touched the small of my back, his presence pushed everything away. We were together. We still needed to talk through everything and figure out what *us* meant, but he was here. Ash was back in my life. He was *mine*. That should be the only thing that I cared about.

My hand shook as I pulled my keys from my pocket and hit the button to unlock the car.

"Are you gonna tell me what happened in the bathroom and why Leo stormed out of the bar without saying anything to anyone?"

My gaze dropped to my feet, and I kicked at a loose rock. "Don't be mad."

He moved closer, sliding his finger over my belt loop before hooking it through. "Mad? Why would I be mad?"

I sighed, lifting my chin to look into his eyes. "I could think of a few reasons."

"Sammy, just say it. I don't know if I'll be angry. Upset. Hurt. I can't know that, but I do know that nothing could ever compare to the time I walked away from you. Nothing could ever hurt me as much as that decision hurt. So say it. Whatever it is, we can face it together, okay?"

My heart stuttered, and my chest warmed, but it didn't erase my fear. It wasn't like I had cheated on him. It wasn't like Ash and I didn't sleep with people all these years, but something about the friends-with-benefits relationship I had with Leo made it different from those meaningless hookups.

Ash stepped closer, pushing me against the passenger door of the Jeep. "Tell me what has you looking so worried."

His body closed around me. Grounded me.

"There's something you need to know about Leo and me." I released a shaky breath before continuing, "Since college, he and I would occasionally hook up, but after you left. . ." I trailed off, not wanting to say the words. I didn't want it to become real for Ash. For me.

Ash tilted his head, staying silent, giving me room to speak.

"We've been friends-with-benefits for years."

"Okay. And what does that have to do with tonight?" He sounded calm, scarily calm.

"He guessed that you and I are together." My breath caught on a garbled laugh. "Actually, he thinks we fucked, and I must've gotten you drunk for it to happen. He said we're *incestuous*." I dragged in a deep breath, my body shaking under the weight of everything. "He's known about my feelings for you since we met." I shook my head. "It doesn't matter. I'm just upset. After our argument, I don't think he'll want to work at Victory X."

Ash pulled me into a tight hug, gripping the back of my head, and I went with it, burying my face in his shoulder.

"We knew things like this would happen," Ash said, stroking his fingers over my scalp. "Friends-with-benefits is complicated. Do you have feelings for him?"

I shook my head. "No. That was his problem. He thought he had a chance with me when he didn't. He was just a friend I shared orgasms with sometimes."

Ash chuckled.

"I like him as a friend. Never anything more than that."

"I'm sorry," Ash whispered.

"It's not on you to be sorry, Ash. This one is all me." I pulled back, running my fingers through my hair. "That's enough of that. No reason to let this ruin our night. Right?"

Ash laughed before kissing my cheek. "Right."

"Ready to go back to my place?" I asked, pulling the door open for him before rounding the back of the Jeep and hopping into the driver's seat.

"Where are you living these days?" he asked as he buckled in.

"I'm actually only a few miles from my office in Herndon."

"Why'd you move? I thought you liked your apartment."

I shrugged, turning on the car. "I wanted to be closer to the office, so I moved out there about a year ago. After the car accident, I didn't want to drive between Herndon and Fairfax anymore."

His face scrunched up. "Car accident? What the hell are you talking about, Sam?"

"Uhh." I'd forgotten he didn't know about it. When the accident happened, I had asked everyone not to tell him because I didn't want him to fly up here and worry about me, but then we never told him it happened, and it ended up being a secret I didn't mean to keep. "Last March, I was leaving the office late, and someone hit me. Totaled my car."

"Are you fucking kidding me?" He half shouted. "And none of you fucking told me?"

A nervous laugh bubbled up my throat. "I told everyone not to tell you that night because I didn't want to ruin your promotion. I knew you'd get on the first flight or drive up here as soon as you heard. I didn't mean for you to be kept in the dark this long. I forgot you didn't know."

"Y-you didn't want to ruin my promotion? Sam, what the fuck?"

His breathing was heavy, face red, eyes glistening with the threat of tears.

I grabbed his wrist, a deep sense of fear rolling through me.

I hurt him. Oh fuck, I hurt him so bad.

"Ash, don't be upset."

"Do-don—" The words died on his lips. "That's why you got that new car? The new hybrid thing?"

I nodded, running my fingers through his hair. "Please don't be upset. I—we were in a dark place. We weren't talking. Sending that text to you that night was more than I should've done, so when Dad and Jane came to my room in the ER, I asked them not to tell you. I didn't want to burden you."

"You were in the ER?" His voice wavered, and a tear slid down his cheek.

I moved my hand from his hair to his neck, running my thumb over his skin, wiping away the tear. "I know I should've told you. I know." I swallowed through the tightening in my throat. "I'm sorry."

Ash nodded, placing his hand over mine. Another tear rolled down his face. "I can't believe you didn't tell me," he whispered with a heavy shake in his voice.

"I'm so sorry," I whispered, stroking his cheek with my thumb again. "We're here now. All we can do is move forward."

Ash lifted my hand away from his face and kissed my palm. "You're right about that." He kissed my palm again. "Let's get out of here." He cleared his throat. "Show me this apartment of yours."

My apartment was on the eighth floor and had two bedrooms, a small kitchen, one bathroom, and a decently sized living and dining room combo. It was nothing extravagant. The extra bedroom acted as a guest room for friends to sleep in, but it had never been used.

"Nice little place you've got here, Angel," Ash said, wandering through the kitchen.

"Can I ask you something?"

"Shoot," he said and leaned against the kitchen counter.

"Why are you calling me that?"

He cocked his head to the side and smirked. "What? Angel?"

I responded with only a nod, prompting him to push off the counter.

When he reached me, he ran his fingers through my hair, studying the pale strands like they were gold sliding between his fingers. "Do you remember when we first met?"

I tried to think about it, but nothing came to mind. "No. We met at daycare or something, right?"

His smile grew wider, and he continued playing with my hair.

"I remember it like it was yesterday," he said in a soft, rumbly tone. "This white-haired boy stood on top of the jungle gym like he owned it. The sun was so bright that day. There were barely any clouds in the sky." He released my hair and trailed his fingers over my jaw. "That boy looked down at me with a smile brighter than the sun and asked if I wanted to join him at the top. I was so taken in by his beautiful face covered in dirt, and the sun lighting him up like heaven had placed him before me that I didn't know how to answer him. All I could do was ask him if he was an angel."

"No way," I said, chuckling. "That for sure never happened."

"Mm-hm, it did, and I'll never forget it. It's one of the few memories I have from back then, and I'll treasure it forever."

My cheeks flushed with warmth.

"I've had a lot of time to think about it, and I think I've loved you since we were kids. You and I,"—he moved his thumb over my cheek—"we were meant to be from the moment we met. My little ignorant self knew it then, and I know it now."

I leaned into his touch, closing my eyes. "I wish I told you when I had planned. I wish my dad hadn't come to me that night when we were kids. I wish I had gone to school the next day and confessed my feelings anyway."

"I don't think I would've been ready then," he said, bringing his face closer. "You and I both know how fucked up I was. I don't know if it would've hit me the same. When we were younger, I was fighting my demons in the worst way and you were there for me. You were always there. Now, we've evolved into something even better. Don't wish our past could change because even if we were only best friends, you were still everything to me. You always will be."

Resting my palm over his heart, I smiled. "You talk too much," I whispered, sliding my hand up and over his shoulder before sinking my fingers into his hair and pulling him into a rough kiss. His stubble scraped over my skin, igniting the need building inside me.

Ash's hands slid over my hips, and he tugged me toward him, pressing my chest to his. I traced his lips with my tongue, teasing him even after he opened his mouth, waiting for me. He whimpered when I flicked my tongue over his lip, grazing the tip of his tongue.

"Sam," he whined, leaning toward me, chasing my lips.

I smiled and stepped back. "Bedroom."

He followed me down the dark hallway into my bedroom, where I had a king-size mattress looking out over a manmade lake through enormous windows spanning the length of the walls.

"Damn, this is a view if I ever saw one."

"Wanna know something?" I asked, pointing to the curtainless windows. "No one can see in."

Ash bit his lip. "Even if the lights are on?"

I nodded in the dark space, lit only by the lights outside. "They have some kind of special film on them. It was a selling point for this apartment."

He held my gaze, watching me.

"Baby," I whispered, testing the term of endearment I'd always wanted to use but never could. It sent a wave of goosebumps over my skin at hearing it from my lips directed at the person I had wanted to be mine for so long.

His eyes widened. "Call me that again," he rumbled.

"Baby," I whispered, then bit my lip.

"Yes, Angel?"

"Take your clothes off."

He moved slowly. Anticipation buzzed through my veins. When his fingers hit the first button on his shirt, I swallowed, moving closer. Our eyes locked together, electricity vibrated my body. I popped the next button for him, and the fabric fell away from his tattooed skin. I licked my lips and leaned in until my lips touched his collarbone and the images embedded in his skin.

A soft groan filled the room, and Ash's hand ran over my hair.

"Sam, please. . ." he whispered, his breath wavering.

"Please, what, baby?" I asked.

He tangled his fingers in my hair and squeezed. "Don't judge me."

"I would never." I kissed his skin and unbuttoned his shirt the rest of the way. "Tell me what you want." I kissed him again, lower, then again, even lower.

Ash whimpered again, holding my hair firmly but never hurting me. "I can't believe I'm saying this," he said through a string of rapid breaths. "Bite me. Bite me really hard."

I smiled against his skin, trailing my fingers over his body before kissing his abdomen. "Do you want me to bite you somewhere specific?"

"Anywhere."

I dropped to my knees and looked up at him, biting my lip through a smile. "Are you sure?" I asked, leaving a line of soft kisses down his abdomen until I reached the waistband of his jeans.

He looked so vulnerable as he nodded.

Ash kept his guard up with people. He rarely let them in. Rarely trusted them. His trust in me was intoxicating. I would do anything to ensure I kept it forever.

I unbuttoned his jeans, then slowly eased the zipper down before sliding his boxers and jeans down his legs. My mouth watered at the sight of his erection. I grabbed his length, sliding my palm over his heated, firm skin.

Ash gasped, pressing closer.

I flicked my tongue over the tip, tasting the salty drop of pre-cum. "Mmm, where am I going to bite you?" I teased him with another long drag of my tongue over his erection. "Somewhere you don't have a tattoo?" I kissed his thigh.

Ash groaned, tightening his hold on my hair. "Yes."

Trailing more kisses over his thigh, I searched for a spot I wanted while stroking my palm lazily over his length. When I reached an area high on his thigh below the last line of his tattoos, I licked the skin and wrapped my arm around him, holding him tight, then I closed my mouth around the skin and bit.

A deep groan filled the room, and Ash leaned back, letting me hold most of his weight while I continued to bite and stroke him. When I released my hold on his skin, I ran my tongue over the area before I moved to kiss the tip of his length. I slid lower, dragging my tongue over his balls, sucking them into my mouth.

Ash groaned, his body shaking.

Moving back up, I traced my nose over his length until I brushed my lips over the head of his cock. My tongue darted out, dragging over the bead of pre-cum, hitting me with the salty headiness of Ash. His musky cologne and the smell of his sweat hit me, and I took him into my mouth, sucking him down with a soft groan. I grabbed his ass with one hand, holding him close as I took him like he was my last meal.

Ash held the back of my head with one hand while my mouth consumed him. His fingers tightened on my scalp before he thrust into my mouth. His grunts and tortured moans filled the room, sending goosebumps across my skin.

I groaned around him when his fingers tightened in my hair even more, sending a spark of pain down my spine.

Ash whimpered, rolling his hips and fucking my mouth until his balls dripped with my saliva.

"My God, Sam," Ash said, grunting and rocking his hips, sliding in and out of my mouth.

I loved seeing him let go. Watching him surrender to me gave me a high that could never be replicated.

I palmed my erection through my pants, enjoying every sound he made.

"As much as I love this," Ash said, "I really want you inside me." He pulled away from me, and I released him with a grin.

"Lay on the bed."

He slid his arms out of his shirt, dropped it to the floor, then kicked off his shoes and pants before laying face down across the bed.

I grabbed the lube from the bedside table and stripped out of my clothes before climbing over him, sliding between his legs.

"What a sight," I groaned, running my hand down his spine and grabbed a handful of his ass. He grunted and pushed against my hand. I trailed my finger down his crease, stopping when my finger brushed over his hole. "I don't do this for anyone."

"Am I about to get exclusive treatment?" He laughed. "Exclusive ass gets exclusive treatment."

I chuckled and bent over him, kissing his lower back before moving to his hole. "Exactly."

Ash never letting anyone fuck him like this didn't come as a surprise. Between his trust issues and hate of feeling vulnerable, I could never imagine him letting some random hookup put him in this position, and knowing that, I wanted to let him have the best experience I could give.

I spread his ass, opening his hole to me, and dropped my face close before swiping my tongue over the sensitive rim.

Ash gasped and pressed back. "Oh, shit. Do that again."

I did as he asked, dragging my tongue over his hole, then I flattened my tongue and pressed against him.

Ash moaned, pushing back, and I pressed the tip of my tongue inside him. His muscles tightened around me, and his breaths came rapidly, filling the room. He rocked back, so I pressed in further. He released a moan, rocking his hips again.

I popped the top of the lube and coated a finger, then pressed my finger beside my tongue and slowly pushed inside him.

"More, Sam. Holy fuck, more."

When my finger was buried, I licked around his rim and slowly moved my finger out before pressing back in. Ash pushed against me, forcing me deeper. I poured more lube over his hole and moved a second finger through it, coating myself to the knuckle before sliding out of him and pressing both fingers inside.

I worked him until he could take three fingers easily.

When I thought he was ready, I whispered, "You ready for me," and climbed over him, kissing his shoulder.

He pressed his ass back until he brushed against my aching cock. "Yes," he whispered. His voice was rough and thick with lust. It was different from when we were at the spring in Ohio. He sounded husky and demanding then, but laying here, he was breathy and unraveled.

I wanted to savor the vulnerability he showed me and only me.

Before settling behind Ash, I grabbed the bottle of lube, poured a generous amount into my palm, and coated my erection. Lowering myself over his back, I pressed a kiss between his shoulder blades, then nudged the tip of my cock at his hole. The pressure of touching him sent warmth tingling down my spine.

"Baby," I said, my voice shaking with need, "tell me if it hurts."

His response was to push back, forcing me to enter him. The pressure made my mind fuzzy. Everything disappeared. All I saw was Ash beneath me, begging me to take him. All I felt was his body, giving me something he would never give easily. I pressed my hips forward, inching inside him, until I was encased in his tight body, barely clinging to reality.

I sat there for a moment, unmoving, while I took in the feeling of Ash around me. A shudder rolled through him, and I collapsed to my elbows, crushing Ash beneath my weight.

"Oh my god," I whispered, barely coherent enough to get the words out.

"How does it feel so good when we haven't even done anything?" Ash asked through rapid, panting breaths.

I buried my face in his back and said, "I don't know."

He rolled his hips, giving us a fraction of friction, sending tingles racing over my skin as we both moaned. I rocked, barely pulling back, and then pressed tight against his ass. I was in absolute bliss. With long, slow movements, I moved again, taking in every single nerve lighting up as our bodies moved together. When I rolled my hips, rocking inside him, Ash groaned and pushed against me through a shiver.

"Do that again," he begged and rocked back on my cock. "You hit my—"

I didn't let him finish, rocking the same way I had, and his whole body shuddered. He grabbed my hand, lacing our fingers together as he pushed back in time with me.

"I want to turn you over, but this feels so good. I don't want to stop," I said, rolling my hips again.

"Don't turn me over," Ash whimpered. "My cock is fucking your bed right now, and it feels amazing."

"Are you leaking all over my blanket?"

"Yeah," he breathed.

"That's so hot." I rocked my hips faster, making sure to hit the angle that made him shudder. I kissed the nape of his neck and breathed him in, loving the scent of his sweat mixed with the warm notes of his cologne. "I want you to stain my bed. Do it for me."

Ash moaned, squeezing my hand harder.

"Come for me, baby," I whispered against his hair.

Ash whimpered, and I picked up my pace.

He came on a breathy moan, rocking his hips in time with me. His body pulsed around me, gripping my erection until I spilled over the edge. A deep groan poured from me as I rocked through my release before collapsing on top of Ash, littering kisses along his neck.

I tightened my hold on his hand, smiling at our interlocking fingers.

"Ash," I whispered.

He grunted beneath me, flattened on the bed.

"I love you." I kissed his shoulder, then relaxed against him.

He squeezed my fingers, bringing my hand to his lips, and kissed my knuckles. "I love you too."

Chapter 23

Ash

My body was pliant, pressed against Sam's bed. His weight rested over me. His cock was still inside me, but neither of us moved.

"I could fall asleep like this," I said, wiggling my ass. I was sure I'd be sore later, but damn, it was worth it.

"Me too," Sam replied, kissing my neck. "But we should go clean up."

I groaned when he pulled away. Rolling onto my back, I propped my head on my hand. He smiled when our eyes locked. Warmth settled in my chest, wrapping around every cell. Climbing through me, filling me with breathtaking affection.

Is this what it means to feel fulfilled? To have the person I love beside me, sharing my space?

The desperate need to hold him close. To watch him. My chest was ready to burst with this building feeling.

His fingers raked through the curls falling into my eyes as he said, "Come shower with me, then we can cuddle."

"Mmm, that sounds perfect," I hummed, blinking up at him through my half-closed lids. "I think I need more incentive to move."

Sam leaned in and kissed me. "I'll drag you to the shower if you don't get up in three seconds."

I groaned. "Not that kind of incentive."

He laughed and backed away. "Three."

He stood at the edge of the bed. Behind him was the lake, reflecting lights from the nearby trail and buildings.

"Two."

I had always thought of him as the sun, but in the dark with the backdrop, he was like a full moon pulling me to him. He controlled me like the moon controlled the tides.

"One."

He reached for my ankles, but I moved out of his grasp and pulled him down beside me, kissing him.

"I don't want to go home tomorrow," I said, brushing my lips over his.

"Then don't."

I pulled back, scanning his face. "What do you mean?"

"Stay for a few days. You don't go back to work until Monday, right?"

I nodded. "Yeah, so what? I pretend to leave and come here instead."

Sam bit his lip. "Do you not want to?"

I squeezed him tighter, realizing this was our reality for now. "How are we going to tell our family?"

He shook his head. "I honestly don't know, and I'm afraid of their reactions."

"So we keep it secret until we're ready." I kissed his cheek, then trailed my nose down his neck. "Drop me off at their house tomorrow. I'll grab my bike and come back here."

"I'll give you a key."

"Good. I'll be able to drop in any time I want."

He hummed, vibrating my lips still pressed against his throat. "We really do need to shower and sleep."

I climbed away from him, feeling the loss of his touch like it would burn me. "Come on then," I offered him my hand and pulled him up when he took it.

After a quick steamy shower, where we were a little too handsy, we crawled into bed and snuggled. Sam nuzzled his face in my neck and rested his arm over my chest while I stared through the windows at the lights reflecting off the lake.

It felt like I was dreaming, and at any moment, I'd wake up to find out none of this was real.

Fingers stroked my hair. Lips traced my jaw. I leaned into the touch, soaking in the tenderness. When I opened my eyes, Sam was awash in sunshine, radiant under the light. His neck was littered with red marks, and his hair was messy. He was beautiful. Even more so because he was mine.

"Mornin', Angel," I whispered, running my fingers over his cheek.

"Did you sleep well?"

"I slept like the dead. Is that what it takes to make me so relaxed that I don't dream?"

Sam chuckled and planted a kiss on my forehead. "We were exhausted, but it isn't realistic to do that every night."

I pulled him close, hugging him tight. "What? You don't want to run on two hours of sleep and come our brains out until we pass out every day?"

"Exactly."

I buried my nose in his hair and took a deep breath. "What time are you going into work?"

He sighed and glanced at the clock on the side table. "Two hours."

"Okay, that's plenty of time to make you breakfast."

"I've missed your cooking."

"Aren't you lucky I'm here and willing to feed you?"

He nodded with a wide grin. "How come you never became a chef?"

"Too much effort. I can be your personal chef instead."

"Sounds divine."

I pulled away and headed for his kitchen.

"Cooking naked? I love my new reality," he called.

I chuckled and quickly found bacon, eggs, and all the fixings for pancakes. By the time he appeared in the kitchen, he was dressed in black suit pants and a white dress shirt. His hair was combed and styled with his bangs out of his face.

I whistled at him before saying, "You look fine as hell in your work clothes."

"Stop, I'm so average like this," he said, glancing down at his feet.

I set his plate on the table and kissed his temple. "There's nothing average about you."

I motioned for him to sit before making my way to the bedroom, dressing in the clothes I wore the night before, and joined Sam at the table. A key lay next to my plate. I picked it up, sliding the cool metal between my fingers. It had been four years since we shared keys. Four years of having less than a friendship. And now, we were racing to a place beyond anything we had ever shared.

I wondered what we would be like in a year. Two years. Five. Whatever it looked like, I hoped we were as happy as I was now. Was it possible to be happier than this?

Sam pulled his Jeep up the driveway to our parent's home, resting his hand on my thigh with a smile. "What time will you be back at my place?" he asked.

"I'm not sure. What time are you getting off work?"

He stopped the car near the front door. "I don't know. Depends on what meetings I have today. Maybe five o'clock. I'll text you when I know more."

"Sure," I replied, leaning toward him. "I wish I could kiss you right now."

He leaned close, barely a breath away from me. "Be a good boy today, and you'll get all the kisses you could ever want later."

"Mmm, I love this incentive you're giving me."

I hopped out of the car before I let my wants get the better of me. Sam wasn't ready for us to tell our family, and I respected that. I also worried about what they would think, but I didn't believe they would judge us. Anyone who knew us knew our history. They knew how close we used to be. The other side of me, the pessimistic side, thought everything would fall apart if anyone knew, so I would keep us secret for as long as Sam wanted.

I unlocked the door and breezed into the house. "Mornin'," I called.

There was rustling from the kitchen, then Mom replied, "Sweetheart, do you want breakfast?"

"Nope. Sam and I ate." I kissed her cheek and hugged her on my way through the kitchen. "Is Angie here already?"

"She and Gary are in the living room."

"I'll say hi before changing."

Her expression turned serious. "Did you have a good time with Sam?"

I smiled and said, "The best," then I headed through the short hallway to the living room, interrupting Gary and Angie's movie before heading to my bedroom. I cleaned up and changed before tossing a change of clothes into my backpack and headed back downstairs.

"I'm heading home," I said, joining my family in the living room, hoping I didn't sound like I was lying through my teeth.

Mom stood from the sofa and said, "Text us when you get home." She wrapped me in a hug. "I'm so glad you came."

"Me too," I said, squeezing her tight. "Love you."

Angie looked me over before hopping into my arms, wrapping her legs around my waist. "I'll miss you, Ash. Please come visit more often."

I kissed her temple and spun around with her. "I promise you'll see more of me."

Gary patted me on the back, half hugging me. "See you next time, son. Maybe we can all come visit you and make a trip to the beach down there."

I cocked my head to the side. "That would be nice, Gary."

When I finally made it outside, the summer air was muggy and hot. I slipped my helmet on and climbed onto my bike, plugging Sam's address into my GPS. We had until Sunday morning to figure out how to do this long-distance thing. We were both in important positions at work, making it difficult to pick up and leave. I couldn't abandon Tae and my team, not when I had only recently been able to start working on my goals. Sam owned Victory X. Picking up and moving an entire company would be difficult and risky.

I expected we'd be taking flights to and from for the foreseeable future. I was sure Tae would let me work from home more often if I told him it was because Sam and I fixed things, but I suspected asking for that would come with questions I wasn't ready to answer. I was willing to figure it out as we went, but being away from Sam now would be a worse hell than when we were avoiding each other.

Chapter 24

Sam

My time with Ash went by far too quickly. Sunday morning arrived in the blink of an eye, leaving me desperate to stop time. Ash sat on my couch reading a book on his phone while sipping coffee, wearing my sweatpants and no shirt.

We spent all of Friday night enjoying each other's bodies and woke up Saturday to do it again. Last night, it finally hit us that it was our last night together, and instead of sex, we snuggled and had a movie marathon. That was until Ash brought up the elephant in the room. We were in a long-distance relationship. He had clearly thought about it, and while I didn't like being away from him, he was right. For now, we had to visit each other on weekends. Flying back and forth would be our most efficient option to save time. We both lived close to an airport, and Ash mentioned testing the waters with his company about working from home some days so that he could stay with me longer when he came to visit.

I didn't love the plan, but it was all we had for now.

"Baby," I said, taking his coffee mug from his grasp and setting it on the table before straddling his lap.

"Yes, Angel?" He wrapped his arms around my waist and leaned back.

I braced my hands on the back of the couch and settled over him, burying my face in his neck. "I don't want you to leave."

"I don't want to go either, but I have to." His arms tightened around me, and he pressed his lips to the side of my head, lingering before asking, "Want to check flights for Friday?" He picked his phone up from the seat cushion. "Let's find you an afternoon flight. I can leave the office early and work from home the rest of the day. How does that sound?"

I nodded, shifting in his lap to look at his phone. "Autumn will scold me, but that will be a small price to pay."

He chuckled and clicked through the flights until he found one that fit what we wanted.

"A little expensive," he said.

"You're worth the extra money, Ash. Book it."

"I feel so special," he mocked, running his hand down my back before squeezing my hip.

Once the flight was booked, Ash put his phone down, and our eyes locked.

"I love you." I leaned in and kissed him. "I'll miss you."

He cupped my face with both hands and inched closer until his lips were almost touching mine. "I love you too, Angel. This is going to be the longest five days of my life." He kissed me, tender and loving at first, then it turned needy and desperate as we clung to each other.

I wanted to freeze time and stay with Ash like this for eternity.

"Oh, thank God you're here," Autumn said from the end of the hallway when I reached my office door.

"Did I miss something?" I asked, pushing the door open and flicking on the light.

My office wasn't extravagant, but it had a small seating area near the door, with a couch and two chairs circling a round coffee table and an L-shaped desk against the left wall facing the door. Floor-to-ceiling windows lined the entire wall facing the grassy courtyard between the four office buildings that made up this area. Behind my desk was a wall-to-wall bookshelf, mostly filled with fake plants, family photos, and business-related books.

Autumn rushed toward me, clutching her tablet to her chest with a raised eyebrow. "Did you not see the email from Leo?"

My stomach dropped to my feet. "No. I was busy this weekend and turned off my notifications." I tugged my phone from my pocket, set it on my desk, then dropped into the chair.

She worked her lip between her teeth before saying, "He emailed his resignation this morning."

I couldn't say I was surprised, but it still stung. We would likely never speak again, at least not on purpose. Sure, it was mostly my fault, but a part of me still thought he should've known better than to fall for me and hold on. I never kept my feelings for Ash a secret from him. Leo had been the one to stop me from drunkenly calling Ash to confess my feelings in college.

I paused on that memory.

We had gotten home from a frat party. I was so drunk I could barely stand. I was complaining about missing Ash when I let it slip that I was in love with him. Leo laughed at me. He thought I was joking, but then I pulled out my phone and tried to call Ash to tell him I loved him. Leo had taken my phone away and wouldn't give it back, claiming he would return it when I was sober.

He said, "You're too drunk to be allowed to talk to anyone in this state."

That night, I confessed everything to Leo. When he kissed me, I was so damn trashed I barely registered what we were doing. After that night, I would fall into bed with him as a distraction. It was comforting to have someone want me like that.

Did Leo stop me from making that call because he didn't want me to get hurt or because he wanted me for himself?

The thought sent my mind racing through every interaction Leo and I ever had. Moments where he would convince me to lean a certain way. Times when he advised me against something. Was he manipulating me the whole time?

I groaned, leaning back in the chair.

I had trusted Leo with everything. *Everything*. More than any other friend because he had seemed so supportive of me. I thought he cared.

He did care, dumbass. He's in love with you.

Knowing he loved me that whole time had a sinking weight settling in my chest. Did he come to work with me here at Victory X because he thought I would fall for him? Did everything he ever did for me or with me come with the hope that it would make me love him back?

Bile rose in my throat, and I quickly swallowed it down.

A slimy coating of unease blanketed my body. I knew what it was like to be in love with someone who didn't love me back. Being around Ash had been selfish, but that was where my selfish actions ended. I did things with Ash because I loved our friendship. I treasured the time we had together. I never expected he would turn around and love me. The idea that Leo may have stayed my friend to get something from me unsettled me to my core.

"Where are Imogene and Everly?" I asked Autumn, who was still standing across from my desk, patiently waiting for me to process the news.

"I can have the entire executive team in the conference room in ten minutes," she replied.

I nodded. "Ten minutes."

She offered a stiff smile and turned on her heels, leaving my office in an eerie silence. I pulled up the email from Leo on my computer and read through it. It was generic, thanking us for the time he spent at Victory X, but a rush of adrenaline hit me when I read the last paragraph.

During my time at Victory X, Samuel Pearce and I had a sexual relationship that I didn't feel I could decline. I've contacted a lawyer and will be filing a claim of sexual harassment and coercion. Due to this, please refrain from contacting me directly. I've provided my lawyer's information below.

"I fucking what?" I yelled, standing from my desk. "You goddamn son of a bitch."

I spun toward the bookshelf and dropped my forehead against the edge of a shelf. I expected he would quit, but this—this was a new low. How did he expect to prove something so blatantly wrong? Was this to defame me? Tarnish my reputation? Or pure revenge?

"Sam," Autumn's soft whisper brought me back to the present.

"I'm coming," I whispered, sucking in a deep breath that did nothing to calm my nerves.

I pushed away from the bookshelf and followed her through the hallway, receiving curious looks from some employees, but they hadn't seen the resignation letter. No. The group I was about to face in the conference room had. They all had. Sure, they all knew I was gay, but Leo and I had kept our friends-with-benefits relationship quiet. Not even Rainie or Sean knew about it. It was my word against his, and that terrified me.

When Autumn and I reached the closed door to the conference room, my nerves were in overdrive, overwhelming my senses until my hands shook.

Autumn pushed the door open, leaving me behind to stand at the threshold like I was walking the plank over an ocean full of starving sharks.

I can do this. Leo's claims are lies.

I straightened, rolling my shoulders back, and stepped inside, closing the door behind me. "Good morning, everyone," I said, facing the room full of concerned expressions.

"Good morning," they all replied.

I took my seat at the head of the table and placed my hands in my lap, where I tried desperately not to fidget, but I needed an outlet for my nerves, and when my finger found a loose string on my pants, it became the only thing grounding me.

"I assume you've read the resignation letter by now?" Imogene, the president of my company, asked, leaning forward to rest her elbows on the table.

She was an abrasive woman with sharp features, but she helped me stand this company up from the ground. I respected her immensely, and though my trust in everyone was wavering, I knew my fears were unfounded. The people in this room were my closest partners.

However, I had thought the same about Leo.

"I have," I said, somehow managing to keep my voice even and calm. "The allegations of coercion and sexual harassment are a lie."

Everly, my vice president, smiled. Her long brown hair was pulled back in her usual bun, and she wore new rectangular glasses with hot pink edges. "Can you please elaborate on your relationship with Leo and why he might say these things about you?"

I scanned their faces. These were my employees. Advisors. Head of Human Resources. Lawyers. Marketing. IT. Sales. Did all of them need to know about my sex life?

I cleared my throat and rolled the string on my pants between my fingers.

"As you are all well aware, I'm gay."

Everyone responded with their murmurs of acknowledgment.

"I met Leo in college. We—" I glanced at Hannah, the lawyer who ran everything at Victory X. "Hannah, do I really need to go into detail?"

Jeff, the head of marketing, sat a little straighter. "Sam, I'll be honest with you. I get that this is personal, but all of us are here because we need to know your side of the story. If you're a dick and did force Leo into a sexual relationship, then I'm out. Today."

The room filled with agreement and nodding.

Jesus Christ.

"And if it isn't true?" I asked.

"Then we're here to help in whatever way we can," Jeff replied.

I swallowed before continuing. "Leo and I have been hooking up since college. This didn't start recently. We're talking seven-ish years of him and I having a friends-with-benefits relationship. We were never anything more than that."

Jeff whistled, then asked, "So what changed?"

I rolled my bottom lip between my teeth and released a choked laugh. "I got a boyfriend."

Everly sighed. "And I assume that boyfriend isn't Leo."

"You'd be correct."

"So what do we do now?" Imogene asked, glancing at everyone around the table.

Hannah leaned forward and connected her laptop to the projector. "We figure out a plan of action."

My flight landed in Raleigh thirty minutes late. When the man over the speaker told us we could turn our phones back on, I quickly texted Ash, informing him I had landed.

He immediately responded, and I smiled when I saw his message.

Ash: I'm standing near the baggage claim with a sign that says, "Have you seen an angel?". I bet you didn't see that coming.

Ash: I've been standing here for an hour looking like a dumbass.

Me: How is standing there waiting making you look like a dumbass?

I grabbed my bag from the overhead compartment and rushed off the plane before checking my phone again.

Ash: This teenage girl is waiting for my girlfriend to arrive. She's been watching me and believes I'm being stood up.

Me: Why on earth would you think she cares about you at all?

Ash: She asked if I was waiting for someone. When I told her I was waiting for my partner, she laughed at me! Laughed! She told me how she watched a guy wait for three hours to find out his girlfriend wasn't coming. Then she said, and I quote, "Fifty bucks says your girlfriend is never showing up."

I giggled, gaining the attention of others nearby while I shot off another text.

Me: Would the bet still count if it was a boyfriend?

Ash: I called you my partner. Never specified a gender.

Me: Well, we're about to be fifty dollars richer. I'll be at the baggage claim in two minutes.

Ash: Should I make bets like this more often? I think the fifty bucks will pay for five percent of the fees for the flight.

I laughed again and breezed down a flight of stairs, bypassing the escalators.

After my week at work dealing with Leo's accusations and starting the search for a new CFO for Victory X, I needed this weekend with Ash. Ash always joked about me being uptight and needing to relax, but right now, it was the absolute truth. I was stressed out of my mind. Every morning, I woke up with my heart racing. My thoughts were flooded with what-ifs and planning. I never stopped planning. I tried to think of every situation that I could possibly come across. Hannah, Victory X's lawyer, had advised me on how to proceed, but there wasn't much we could do until Leo surfaced with an actual accusation backed by lawyers. Until that happened, they were all useless threats.

When I rounded the corner at the baggage claim, I found Ash standing next to a seating area with a sign at his side. He wasn't joking about the stupid sign. A girl, no taller than five feet, was laughing at him while he scowled.

"I'm not a liar," Ash said. "Why are you in my business, anyway?"

He wore dark jeans, motorcycle boots, and a leather jacket. Two motorcycle helmets sat on a nearby chair with his gloves and another jacket.

"I'm bored," the girl said and stuck her tongue out.

Ash cocked his head, looking disgusted.

I approached them, unable to keep my smile at bay. "Ash."

Ash spun toward me, and an enormous grin replaced his scowl. "Angel." He crossed the few feet separating us and lifted me into his arms. I clung to him, wrapping my arms and legs around him before capturing him in a deep kiss that sent my heart fluttering into the sky.

"There goes fifty bucks," the girl said.

When I broke our kiss, I pressed my forehead to Ash's. "I missed you."

"I missed you more," Ash said, kissing me. "I can't believe you're here." He set me on my feet and laced our fingers together.

"I can," I winked and grabbed the sign from him. "I can't believe you actually made a sign."

He chuckled. "I thought it would be cute, but it ended up biting me in the ass." He turned toward the girl. "Hey, what's your name?"

She chewed her lip, eying us before she finally spoke. "Nora."

"What are you doing here, Nora?" Ash asked. "You've been here four hours or so if I'm to believe what you've told me."

She glanced around. "I'm waiting for my dad."

"When does his flight arrive?"

She shrugged. "Who knows."

"What do you mean, 'who knows'?" Ash looked around. "Do you not have a flight number?"

She smiled, clearly trying to hold in a laugh.

"What?" Ash asked. "What the hell is funny?"

"You," she said and flopped into a chair. "I come here every day to people watch."

"So the dad thing is what? A dumb joke?"

She shrugged. "I like to think he'll walk through here, but that's a bet I'll lose."

Ash's expression turned sympathetic, and he sat beside her. "So what, you come here and watch random strangers for fun?"

She nodded. "People are fun to watch."

I folded my arms, watching them for a moment. "Where is your mother?" I asked.

She shrugged.

"Who takes care of you?" Ash asked, glancing at me with concern etched on his stern face.

She chewed her lip again. "My grandma, but she's old and still working."

I checked my watch. It was only two-thirty. "Aren't you supposed to be in school?"

She aimed a perplexed look at us, then said, "Y'all must be older than you look. It's summer break."

Ash and I exchanged glances before laughing, and I said, "Wow, I feel really old right now."

"How old are you," Ash asked.

"Thirteen."

Ash stood, crossing his arms with a little sway of his hips. "You shouldn't be hanging out in an airport. Creepy old men might try to take advantage of you."

She snorted out a breath and rolled her eyes.

"How did you get here?" Ash asked her.

"My bike."

"Where's your bike?"

I had to hold in my laughter because this was a serious moment, and I knew Ash was concerned about this girl, but seeing him act parental with a teenager was kind of adorable.

"Parking lot B."

Ash grabbed the jacket and extra helmet from the chair and gave them to me. "Good. My bike is also in lot B." He grabbed his gloves and helmet from the chair before resting his hand on Nora's shoulder, leading her toward the exit. "Angel, you have everything?" Ash crumpled the sign and tossed it in a nearby trash can.

I nodded, lifting the strap of my bag with a smile. "Right here."

"You call him angel?" Nora asked, glancing at me over her shoulder.

"It's not your business. How close is your house?" Ash replied to her.

She narrowed her eyes. "It's not your business."

"Oof. She got you there, babe," I said, chuckling.

Ash shot me a look that said, "If you say one more thing, I'm going to hurt you," so I stifled my laugh as Nora led us through the parking lot to the bike rack.

"Now, go home. You should be hanging out with friends, not people-watching at an airport. It's dangerous."

She unlocked the chain connecting her bike to the rack and laughed at him, mumbling, "Whatever, old man," before swinging her leg over her bike. She looked back at us with a smile. "It was nice meeting you, Angel." She dug through her pocket and pulled out a small ball of crumpled cash. "A bet is a bet."

Ash and I both pushed it away.

"Keep it," Ash said. "We're *old* and have jobs. We don't need your money for a dumb bet."

She eyed us, then shoved the cash back into her pocket. "Your loss." She pushed off and waved as she rode her bike down the sidewalk, disappearing through a tree line where a bike trail started.

"That was interesting," I said, pulling on the motorcycle jacket Ash had handed me earlier. "Think she's okay?"

Ash shrugged, tugging on his gloves. "Probably." He reached for my hand, wrapping me in his hold. "She kind of reminds me of us when we were kids."

I nodded, glancing back at the tree line. "She's probably in a similar situation, but there isn't much we can do."

He released my hand when we reached his bike. "I hope she gets home safe."

I kissed his cheek, knowing he'd think about it for days. "Don't worry. You did good."

Ash helped me get the helmet on and set up the communication thing so we could hear each other through the little speakers inside the helmet before putting on his own.

He tapped the top of my helmet and said, "Let's get out of here." It was weird knowing he was standing next to me while hearing his voice through the speaker like we were on a phone call. "I've never had a backpack before."

"A backpack?"

He sat on his all-black sports bike and offered me his hand. "A passenger."

"Never?"

He chuckled. "Not once."

His appearance in all his gear was incredibly attractive. I'd never thought about it before, but motorcycle helmets were sexy. Actually, the entire outfit was sexy.

I held onto his hand, using it to steady myself as I settled onto the back of his motorcycle. My chest pressed against his back, and Ash positioned my hands on his stomach, giving my hands a little pat before he leaned forward and gripped the handles.

I slid my palms up and down his tight abdomen, feeling the zipper of his jacket catch under my fingers. His muscles tensed when he started the bike, and the vibration climbed over my skin.

"Ready, Angel?" His honeyed voice came through the speaker in my helmet, sending a wave of goosebumps down my arms.

I tapped his stomach, reassuring him. "Ready."

"Don't let go."

"Wouldn't dream of it."

Ash's back moved, and the bike slowly took off through the parking lot.

A small bump sent me leaning forward, pressing harder against his back. I tightened my hold on his abdomen, realizing how intimate this was.

Ash navigated through the streets of Raleigh until we ended up at a red light. I couldn't stop myself from having roaming hands. I was crushed against him, holding him tight, feeling his back move against me. It was such a tease.

I wiggled a little, pretending to get more comfortable, and slid my hand up his chest while dropping the other low. Ash tensed, but he didn't move, so I lowered my hand further, bumping his belt buckle.

"Angel," he warned.

The sound of him scolding me through the stupid speaker sent warm chills racing down my spine. Knowing the cars surrounding us could see what I was doing only spurred me on. I slid my hand to his groin, feeling his semi-hard length beneath my palm.

"Do you think they know what we're doing?" I asked, rubbing my palm over the head of his dick.

"Sam, stop," Ash warned, but he sounded more needy than angry and didn't make a move to stop me.

"Do you think I could make you come before we get home?" I asked, stroking him through his jeans.

He leaned forward and whimpered as the light turned green. "Fuck, Angel," he groaned and took off from the light.

While we were moving, I didn't tease him too badly, but I kept my hand pressed against his cock. Each bump. Each shift. He would release a soft whimper. When Ash pulled the bike into a parking garage next to an apartment complex, we were both needy messes.

"Baby," I whispered when Ash cut the engine. I was still pressed against him. It was dark and quiet. No one could hear us through the helmets. It felt oddly private. "I think I've discovered a kink I like." I rubbed my palm over his length, and he stifled a moan. "Fuck me with your gear on."

He shuddered and lifted off his bike, grabbing my hand and leading me through the garage to an elevator.

"Do you want me to be rough?" Ash asked, punching the button to call the elevator. His voice was husky and deep through the speaker in my ear.

A tingly chill ran over me, sparking the heat bubbling in my abdomen. I'd never had sex where I wanted anything like this. Was this considered role play? I didn't know, but I did know I wanted Ash to be rough with me while he wore that black helmet, those tight jeans, and that sexy jacket. I licked my lips.

"Yes," I whispered.

Ash stepped close, resting his helmet against mine. "Do you want to keep your helmet on or only me?"

"On." I wanted to hear him in my ear. I wanted every whimper and breath to come through the speaker.

The elevator doors slid open, and Ash backed me up until my back hit the wall. He reached back, pressing the button to his floor before caging me in against the wall. Heat raced to my groin, and my breath grew rapid. Ash pressed his abdomen to mine, grinding his cock over mine through our jeans.

"I'm gonna take you as soon as we get through the door," he whispered.

He sounded growly and claiming. I shivered, picturing him fucking me in his entryway. I slid my hands over his chest, biting my lip as he rocked his hips, teasing me through our clothes.

When the elevator doors opened, Ash dragged me through them and down the hall in a blur of movement and shadows. The helmet visor made everything dark. I felt closed in, but not in a way that made me nervous. Instead, I was eager. Anticipating it with every cell in my body.

Ash pushed his door open and didn't bother turning on the lights. The door snapped shut as he shoved me against the wall and made quick work of my pants. I was undressed from the waist down in moments. Ash threw his gloves to the floor and took a step back.

"Don't you dare move from that spot," he growled before disappearing around a corner.

When Ash appeared again, he had a small bottle in his hand.

"Turn around," he ordered, and I quickly did as he asked, spinning around, splaying my palms over the wall, and arching my back.

I had been prepping myself all week in anticipation of the weekend so we wouldn't have to spend too much time prepping me in the heat of the moment.

Ash ran his palm over my ass before digging his fingers into my skin with biting pain. The top on the lube clicked open a moment before my hole was hit with a cold glob. He didn't give my brain time to react. His fingers swirled over my hole, chasing away my thoughts of how cold it had been or how much my skin hurt where he'd gripped me tight. He didn't let me enjoy that either before his finger breached me, pushing inside.

"Did you like teasing me, Angel?" Ash asked, pressing his chest over my back. I released an unintelligible noise as he pressed another finger inside me. "Did you like knowing people could see you?" He pulled his fingers back before sliding them back inside. Heat spread over my skin with each thrust. "Did you want them to watch us fuck?"

Another noise escaped me, followed by a moan.

"You did, didn't you? You were getting off on them watching us."

I braced myself against the wall, pushing my ass back into Ash's hand.

"Say it, Angel. Tell me how much you liked being the center of attention. How much you liked that strangers knew what you were doing to me." He pulled his fingers away, and the sound of his zipper sliding down filled my ears. His helmet bumped mine, and he closed himself around me. "Say it. Tell me how much you liked it."

I groaned as the head of his cock rubbed over my hole.

"If you don't say it, I won't fuck you."

I whimpered and pressed back. "I liked it, Ash." I gasped as he pushed his fingers back inside me. "I wanted to fuck on your bike where everyone could see."

"Good boy, Angel," he praised. His deep, rumbly tone had my body coming to life, sending a warm, tingling heat shooting down my spine.

Ash rubbed the head of his length down my crevice, sliding through the lube until he was slicked, and I was a whimpering mess.

"Baby, please," I whispered.

"Please, what?"

I pressed back, feeling his heat rub over my hole. "Enter me, please."

His hand slid up my back under my shirt, resting on the back of my neck, slightly below the edge of the helmet.

"Because you asked nicely," Ash whispered.

He pressed me against the wall with significant force, then pushed himself inside me. It wasn't like the other times we'd had sex. He didn't move slowly. He didn't give me time to adjust. The burn took my breath away. Ash filled me in seconds, stretching me with a sting that had me gasping.

"That's a good boy. My angel takes me so well."

I melted at his praise. Ash turned me into a puddle on the floor. He could do anything to me, and I would welcome it.

Ash rocked his hips, sliding out of me, leaving burning heat behind before thrusting back inside, filling me until the burn turned to pleasure.

"Look at you," Ash growled, sending a wave of desire through me. "Your greedy ass is sucking me in."

He slid a hand over my hip while keeping his grip on my neck. When he rocked his hips again, he ran over my prostate, and my whole body shuddered. A deep moan poured from me, and Ash pressed me harder against the wall, picking up his pace. A whispery grunt danced through the speaker, tickling my ears, and I pushed back, meeting him in his thrust. Ash's heavy breaths came through my helmet, surrounding me. He grunted as he pushed inside me again. I felt like I was being surrounded by him. He took over every touch and sound. My mind and body were filled with only him.

A deep moan escaped me when Ash dragged over my prostate again. "I'm so close," I whispered.

Ash slid his hand around my waist, dragging his fingers over my stomach. I was practically mewling for him. He hit my prostate and gripped my length in his palm, bringing me to the edge while I listened to his grunts and moans through the helmet. It was sensory overload, and my body was in heaven.

Even though he was rough, it still felt like he was worshipping me. There was still a sense of security and tenderness. As he rocked his hips, pressing deep inside me, working my cock with his hand, it was all too much. My back arched as a rush of heat barreled through me.

"That's it, Angel. Come for me."

My release tore through me, blurring my vision as I cried out.

Ash grunted, and a moment later, his release warmed me, heating me inside. We leaned against the wall for a moment, catching our breath.

He pulled back and fumbled with his helmet before setting it on the floor and helping me with mine. With the helmet off, colors were back to normal. Sunlight streamed into his living room from a square window. His walls were plain white, and the couch was dark gray. It was so like him I almost laughed.

"Is that what you were looking for, Angel?" he asked, kissing my cheek.

I turned around, putting all my weight on the wall, and cupped his face, pulling him closer. "That was exactly what I needed." I kissed him and wrapped my arms around his neck.

Chapter 25

Ash

Sam shifted next to me, moving closer. The movie we put on was one we'd seen a million times. It was comforting to be home snuggled up with him. I was so happy with Sam at my side that the thought of going out and giving other people, even friends, my time instead of Sam was like my idea of a living hell. Spending time with him was my highest priority, so I hesitated when Tae sent a text inviting me to his place to watch a baseball game.

I hadn't told Tae anything yet. The biggest question with anyone finding out was how they would take the news. Would they be okay with it? Would they hate me? Hate Sam? How would we explain to people that we were together? Explaining to strangers was easy. All we had to say was, "This is my partner." No other explanation would be required. Explaining to friends and family was what worried us.

People had the notion that because our parents were married, it immediately meant we saw our step-siblings as siblings, but that wasn't the case. I didn't think I had ever viewed Sam as a brother. I simply felt like we were closer than anyone else I knew. I called him my brother because that's what was expected of me, but I never felt it. Not once.

Going to Tae's meant questions would be asked. Questions I wasn't ready to answer. If I blew him off, he'd let it go the first time, but if I continued to avoid him on weekends, there would be questions.

"Angel," I said, kissing the top of Sam's head.

"Hmm?"

"Tae invited me to his place to watch a game. What do you wanna do?"

He peeled himself away from my side with a slight smile. I almost tugged him back to my side, hating the loss of his touch.

"Do you want to go?"

"Only if you go with me."

"What would you do if I wasn't here with you?"

I pursed my lips, lacing our fingers together so I could touch him again. "I would go." I brought his knuckles to my lips and kissed his skin, rubbing my thumb over his fingers. "Do we tell Tae about us?"

Sam shrugged. "Maybe?"

"He doesn't even know you're in town. Seeing you with me will start the questions." I chewed my lip. "He doesn't know I'm bi. I never correct him when he talks about my hookups as women."

"Does he know about Lexi?"

I nodded. "She's the only one he knows by name and has met. Everyone else was nothing."

He placed his palm on my chest, tugging his hand from mine. "Are you saying Lexi was something?"

I scoffed. "No."

He tilted his head and pressed me into the cushions with a darkness in his eyes I'd never seen before. "No?"

"Lexi is a friend, Angel. She and I haven't seen each other like that in years."

"You promise?"

He looked so worried. I wasn't sure what would make him think that I would want anyone but him after all this time. It made me want to ask, but I was worried I wouldn't like the answer.

I cupped his face and said, "I swear on my life. Lex and I aren't like that anymore." I kissed him. "But Tae has a huge crush on her since I took him for his first tattoo."

"He does?"

I nodded, then kissed him again. "Huge crush, but she told him to go die in a ditch, so I think his chances are slim."

Sam laughed and kissed my forehead. "Okay, let's go. This can be a test run for telling people about us." He rubbed his thumb under my eye and added, "Wear that eyeliner again." He bit his lip and stood. "It does it for me."

I stared at his ass as he hurried to my bedroom. Since we'd started dating, I'd seen parts of Sam he had hidden away from me. These little glimpses were hitting me in all the right places. It was sexy, seeing him open up to me in a way he never had. The whole motorcycle thing came out of nowhere, and I wondered if it was a one-time thing or if it was only the beginning.

I wore a simple black T-shirt and jeans, ready to lounge on the sofa for hours while eating junk food and watching baseball, but Sam had whipped out a tight red crop top from his bag, and ever since he pulled that thing over his head and it suctioned to his chest I could barely contain myself. He looked delectable. The red long-sleeved crop top stopped inches above his navel, and the dark baggy jeans riding low on his hips exposed the waistband of his boxers in a deliberate fashion choice. He looked snuggly and sexy all rolled into one. I couldn't decide if I wanted to stay or go home and rip his clothes off.

I couldn't keep my eyes off him. Each shift of his hips had my gaze wandering. I licked my lips when the elevator doors slid open and motioned for him to go ahead of me.

"Thanks, baby."

"Any time," I said, lowering my voice.

"You just want to look at my ass."

"Caught me." I tapped his ass and followed him out of the elevator. "You're a real tease, you know that?"

"Not a tease," he said, glancing over his shoulder at me with a sly smile. "I'm promising for later."

"Oh, promises? You giving me incentive?"

He spun on his toes and tapped his finger to his lips like he was thinking about it. "I'll surprise you later."

"I grunted a laugh. "I like surprises, but what if I don't want the surprise?"

"You'll want it."

"So sure of yourself." I kissed the side of his head and walked around him toward the hall that led to Tae's apartment.

When we reached Tae's door, I tapped my knuckles to a random beat against it and waited, too scared to look at Sam now that we were standing there. This was the moment of truth I dreaded. The reaction Sam and I feared. I was wound tight with nerves. Sam said we would gauge the mood, and if it felt right, we would tell Tae about us, but I was panicking a little.

The door swung open, and Tae pulled me into a hug. "'Sup, man"

"Hey," I said, patting his back.

When we pulled away from each other, he hurried me inside before finally noticing Sam. Tae glanced between us before saying, "You should've told me you were bringing someone."

I released a halfhearted chuckle and rubbed the back of my neck. "This is Sam." I motioned for Sam to come inside.

Tae's eyes went wide. "It's nice to finally meet you," he said, shaking Sam's hand. "Took long enough. I thought I'd never get the chance."

Sam laughed, moving closer to me. "Ash isn't very good at sharing."

"What's that supposed to mean?" I said.

Sam aimed a wink my way. "You never mentioned Tae is hot."

Tae looked down at his worn gray T-shirt and white shorts before looking back at Sam and said, "I am?"

"Oh, honey, if you ever want a man, do I have a friend for you."

"Sam," I yelled, a little louder than planned.

He aimed an innocent "what" at me.

Tae laughed. "I'm not gay."

Sam winked, giving Tae a very obvious once-over. "That's too bad."

"On that note." I put an arm around each of their shoulders and turned them toward the living room. "Baseball time."

"Kitchen first, then we can relax," Tae said, pulling away from my hold to breeze into the kitchen. He grabbed his phone off the white marble kitchen island and slid bottles of water across the counter toward us. "Is pizza cool with you both?"

I shrugged. "Sure."

"As long as you don't do pineapple and ham." Sam shivered and made a gagging noise.

Tae laughed, shaking his head. "Pepperoni?"

Sam hopped onto a barstool at the island and leaned forward. "Mind if we get a cheese with jalapenos?" He looked around the kitchen. "And do you have Tabasco?"

I raised an eyebrow at him. "I guess my surprise isn't what I thought it would be."

Sam laughed. "Look, I rarely eat pizza, and this is the only way I like it, so you'll be all right, baby." Sam winked and leaned on the island with his elbows.

Tae aimed a confused look at me and tilted his head to the side as if asking, "What the fuck was that?"

I shook my head with a forced smile, hoping he wouldn't think too deeply about it. I didn't think Sam said it on purpose, but using 'baby' was suspicious.

"How does two pepperoni and one cheese with jalapenos sound?" Tae asked, then reached into a cabinet and pulled out a giant bottle of Tabasco sauce that was half empty.

"Sounds good, but can we also get some wings? Buffalo?" If Sam was going to fuck up his stomach, then I would, too. We could share in the pain later.

"Oh, joining me in the spice-filled night?" Sam wiggled in his seat.

I approached him and caught him in a headlock. "Shut up, dumbass."

"Oh, it's on," Sam grumbled, grabbing my forearm and pushing away from the chair.

"Do you really wanna do this in that cute little outfit?" I said, walking us back.

Tae locked eyes with me but didn't say a word. I didn't think I'd ever seen him look so confused. I'd never been playful like this around him—well, anyone except my family.

"You started it," Sam muttered, walking us back until my legs hit the back of the sofa across from the giant ass TV. I sat on it, forcing Sam to arch his back to follow me. "If you wanted me in this position, you could've asked." He sat on my lap, pressing his weight against me until we tumbled over the sofa and landed on the cushions, tangled together and laughing.

"Do you two do this a lot?" Tae asked as he sat on the other sofa diagonal from us.

I shrugged. "Kinda?"

Sam sat up, shoving my head into the cushion one last time, then added, "How do you think he got that scar above his lip?"

I huffed and sat up, shifting until I found a comfortable position that was touching Sam but not in an obvious "we're fucking" kind of way. It was something I hadn't noticed until after I kissed him for the first time, but I had always ensured I would be close to him, and if I could touch him, I would. My favorite go-to was pressing our thighs together. That touch alone was enough to keep me grounded in any situation.

"Wait, that was you?" Tae asked Sam.

"Yeah, the asshole head-butted me when we were like eight."

"It was an accident," Sam added.

Tae laughed and leaned back, turning on the TV. "Sooo," he said, eyeing us, "when did you two make up? Last I heard, you weren't talking."

Had he caught on? I laid my arm across the back of the sofa behind Sam's head and crossed my ankle over my knee before replying, "That camping trip was great for us."

"Oh, yeah?" Tae's eyes locked with mine. I could imagine him saying, "Do tell," in a snarky and expectant tone.

"Angie left a tent at home, so we ended up with three. Sam and I had to sleep in the same tent, so we kind of worked our shit out."

"To be fair, you were persistent," Sam added.

I chuckled and, without thinking, ran my hand up the back of Sam's neck, curling my fingers in his hair.

"And you're cool now? Just like that?" Tae asked.

"I wouldn't say that, but we talked through it, and now we're good."

"*Talked*." Sam nodded beside me. "Yep. *Good*."

"Is this what we're doin', Sammy?"

Sam replied with a shrug.

I was saved by a knock at the door, and Tae hopped up to answer it before the conversation went down a more awkward path.

"What are you up to, Angel?"

He leaned close, turning his face so his nose almost touched mine. "Testing the waters."

"And how's that working for you?"

"I think he suspects something but seems more confused than anything."

"I have a feeling we aren't as subtle as we think we are," I whispered.

"I'd say," Tae said, rounding the sofa carrying the pizza boxes and a bottle of bourbon.

"Busted." Sam chuckled.

"Were you two even trying to act normal?" Tae asked before dropping onto the sofa with a slice of pizza.

"This is normal for us," I replied, scooting forward and grabbing a slice of pizza from the open box on the coffee table. I took a bite, nearly burning my tongue off. I swallowed down the scorching bite, then blew on the end of the slice before taking another.

Sam joined in, grabbing the whole pizza box and Tabasco bottle before sliding back against the cushions with a huge grin. "We're always touchy if that's what gave it away."

"Wait, can I get a clear definition of what I'm seeing here?"

I shrugged, "Sam and I are dating."

Tae nodded, setting his pizza slice on a napkin. "I think I need more information."

This was my friend. My closest friend, other than Sam. I had to trust him with this. If I couldn't trust someone who claimed to be my friend, then who could I trust?

I recounted everything from the night I kissed Sam for the dare to the moment we showed up at Tae's door. Tae was quiet the whole time, listening with a blank expression. When I was done, Tae leaned back, crossing his arms over his chest.

The sound of the announcers over the TV giving a play-by-play of the game while the crowd cheered filled the silence.

"All these years," Tae said, glaring at me. "I've known you for fifteen fucking years, and you didn't think you could tell me about this?"

I glanced at Sam, who had put on his brave face for this. To everyone else, he looked fine, but I could see the panic. The fear. Tension in his body coiled, waiting.

I rested my hand on his thigh, gently squeezing it.

"Don't put it all on Ash," Sam said. "I had a lot to do with why it was kept secret and why nothing ever came of us back then."

"Speaking of," Tae said, glaring at Sam. "What made you change your mind? What's so different?"

My memories rushed back to our camping trip. The time I spent around Sam leading up to taking him back to that spring. The embarrassing things I said to him. The moment he gave in. God, I wished I could relive it over and over. It was the happiest moment of my life.

"You have to understand something, Tae," Sam said, finding my hand and wrapping me in his warmth. "I've been in love with Ash since we were kids. The only reason I never crossed the line is because of our family. So, nothing was different." He looked at me and smiled. "I finally let my happiness be my priority."

I squeezed his hand, bringing his knuckles to my lips. "Took a lot of convincing."

"We have a lot to lose," Sam whispered.

My eyes lifted, locking with his. "Do we?"

Tae erupted with laughter and dragged his hands down his face. "Holy shit. How has no one seen it?"

We both looked at him, confused.

He glanced between us with a smile. "Is this how you two always are with each other?"

Sam and I exchanged a look before shrugging. "Yeah, minus the kissing," I replied.

Tae's look of shock was quickly overtaken by another round of laughter. "Come on!" He laughed. "How have people not asked if you two are an item? Are you kidding me?"

We both slumped back. "People always said we have a bromance, but they assumed we were platonic," I said.

"God, your family has to know." Tae chuckled. "They have to. If they don't, then they're blind."

"I'm thinking they're blind. Everyone always looked at us as best friends and brothers. . ." Sam trailed off, tipping the Tabasco bottle and dousing his pizza slice in the sauce before taking a huge bite.

I cringed. "Please don't ever call me your brother again." I exaggerated a shiver and grabbed my half-eaten slice of pizza, then shoved it into my mouth.

"But you are, by marriage," Tae added before eating his pizza too.

"Nope!" I put my hand up, stopping Tae. "Not a fucking word. Nope. I don't claim it. There is no relation. No one was adopted. Last names are still different. Nope."

"I'm not judging you."

"Feels like you are."

"You never told me you were into guys."

My leg bounced, releasing some of the anxiety clawing at me. "It isn't something I like to come out and talk about." I glanced at Sam. "I only realized because of that night we kissed, and then I've barely held it together since then."

"So all this time, you used me to run away from your problems?"

"Come on, Tae, you know that isn't how it is." I sighed. "Honestly, if it was anyone else, I would've quit, moved home, and never looked back the moment Sam and I made it official."

"Coming from you, bud, that makes me feel special." Tae grinned. "So, how is this working, anyway?" He motioned between us. "The long-distance thing?"

"For now?" Sam said, "Weekend flights."

"What? So you're here until when?"

Sam shrugged. "I fly out tomorrow afternoon."

Tae's eyebrows lifted. "And when did you get in?"

"Friday afternoon," I said. "It fucking sucks, Tae, but we'll figure it out."

"Man, that's rough, guys." Tae rubbed his palm over his short hair. "I could never."

"For the right—" Sam and I said at the same time, and we exchanged a look before laughing.

Tae joined in, shaking his head through his laugh. "How in the actual fuck has no one been like 'they're for sure fucking'?"

We shrugged, then crushed the rest of the pizzas while watching the game.

Chapter 26

Sam

Fingers stroked my hair. The quiet murmur of deep voices tugged me from my dream. My eyes were heavy, and I was unbelievably comfortable. Warm. Surrounded by the safety that Ash's presence always brought.

Ash's honeyed, deep voice caressed my skin when he spoke. "Don't worry about us. We'll figure it out."

"When do you plan to tell your family?" Tae asked, sounding concerned.

Ash's fingers slid over my scalp. "I'm not sure. We'll probably play it by ear. Sam's worried about their reactions."

"No kidding?" Tae said. "You really love him like that?"

Ash's breath caught, and his fingers stilled. "Sam is the only person other than Mom and Angie that I can say I truly love." He was quiet for a moment. "And to be honest, Tae, Sam is at the top of that list."

"Shit, man. You don't love me?"

Ash quietly laughed like he was trying not to wake me. "Shut up. I care about you, but that's all you get."

"You're such a dick," Tae said.

"I don't give my love to just anyone."

"Again, you're a dick. Does our friendship mean nothing to you?"

Ash chuckled again. "You are one of my favorite people on this earth, Tae, but you won't get the L-word out of me if that's what you're fishing for."

Tae snorted, then said, "Why don't you sleep in the guest room? We can hang out in the morning before you head back to your place."

Ash slid his fingers through my hair, playing with the strands. "Sure." They were quiet for a while before Ash added, "Thanks for not freaking out on us."

"I was surprised to see you show up here with someone without telling me. I was trying to figure out why Ashton, loner extraordinaire, had someone with him, and honestly, I couldn't come up with anything."

Ash chuckled. "Am I that sad of a person?"

"Nah. You're an amazing person, Ash. Just hard to get close to you, is all."

Ash chuckled, then said, "By design."

"I'm sure it is." Tae sighed, and the sound of his clothes rustling as he walked away filled the quiet space. "You know where everything is."

"Sleep tight, boo," Ash said with a high-pitched tone.

Tae laughed, then said, "You too, sweetheart. Also, you owe me a hundred bucks since my team won."

Ash groaned. "I'll transfer the money in the morning."

"You better."

"Go to bed." Silence descended on us. Ash's breathing was steady, and his fingers returned to my hair. "You can stop pretending to be asleep."

I smiled and looked up at him. "But your lap is so comfy."

"The bed is better."

"Doubtful," I said, lifting the hem of his shirt and kissed his stomach.

"Playful after having a nice nap?"

I bit my lip. "Maybe."

Ash gently pushed me away and stood. "Come on." He offered his hand, and I took it. "We'll have to be quiet if we want to play."

"This is like sneaking around while our parents are asleep."

Ash shook his head, then led me down the hall to a small room with a queen bed against the wall and a tiny TV on top of a dresser.

"We have an attached bathroom with spare toothbrushes and stuff."

"Does Tae have visitors often?"

Ash shrugged. "His parents come to stay sometimes, and I stay here a lot."

I shut the door, letting my eyes adjust to the dark, before grabbing Ash by the shirt and pushing him against the wall.

"Turn on a light, Angel," Ash whispered.

I felt along the wall near the door until my fingers landed on the light switch. It turned on a side table lamp, giving us plenty of light to work with.

"Better?" I asked.

Ash nodded, sliding his hands over my hips, pulling me against him. His lips brushed mine. Teasing me with a brief touch. I closed in, crowding him, and traced his lips with my tongue.

Ash pulled away, whispering, "You taste like hot sauce."

I laughed and kissed him, purposely dragging my tongue over his lips again. "Delicious."

"Can we brush our teeth?" he asked.

I shook my head. "If you can't love me when I taste like hot sauce, do you really love me?"

He groaned. "That's not a thing."

"I just made it a thing, baby." I kissed him, sliding my hands over his body, and pressed tight against him.

"Please don't spit on our dicks with that mouth." He smiled against my lips.

"Who needs spit when I'm leaking for you?" I bit his lip, tugging the soft flesh.

"Leaking, huh?" His fingers tightened on my hips, holding me as close as we could get.

"Soaking."

Ash groaned into my mouth. "I fucking love you."

"I fucking love you too," I said, then kissed him, savoring the feeling of his lips before deepening our kiss and sliding my tongue into his mouth.

He released his hold on my hips and unhooked the button on my pants. I mirrored him, popping the button of his jeans open, then dragged the zipper down. I hooked my finger under the waistband of his tight black boxers and tugged, letting his dick spring loose.

"You said no spit, so I assume sucking you off is not allowed?"

"No way in hell, Sam. I don't need a hot sauce burn on my dick."

I laughed, and he tugged my boxers down, exposing me to his hungry gaze. "Fine." My smile widened when his eyes raked over my body like he wanted to eat me alive.

I kissed him, wrapping my hand around his length. His hand pressed on my lower back, forcing me closer until our erections aligned. His hand joined mine, holding us both together. The sensation of his velvety skin sent a wave of lust rushing through me. I kissed him, stroking us, mixing our pre-cum together. Ash broke our kiss, trailing his lips down my neck.

"You're so perfect," he whispered, rocking his hips, sliding his cock against mine.

I didn't know what to say to someone calling me perfect. I was far from it.

Maybe perfect was the right word for *us*. I was willing to believe that together, we were perfect. Together, we were fate.

Ash thrust in my hand, digging his fingers into my back while our tongues tangled in our desperate need to be closer. Like we couldn't get enough of each other.

I rocked my hips in time with him, sliding in my palm. The friction was intense. The tension hovering between us was like a cloud. We were sloppy and somehow coordinated.

With one hand, I lifted Ash's shirt up, exposing his beautiful tattooed stomach.

"I love your tattoos," I whispered.

He released me and tugged his shirt off, tossing it to the floor. "Wanna show them how much?"

I squeezed our cocks, forcing him to grunt before I dipped my face to his collarbone and sunk my teeth into his skin. Ash fell back, pulling me with him. His head lolled against the wall as he moaned and thrust his hips, sliding his length over mine. Ash's pre-cum dripped down my knuckles. I licked over the area I bit and found another spot higher on his shoulder and bit again. The whimper Ash released had my heart fluttering. I pressed closer, crowding him against the wall, and gripped the back of his head with my free hand.

"Sammy," Ash breathed my name like a plea, "do it again."

I kissed him and rocked my hips, bringing us closer to the edge with each slide of skin on skin. I kissed a trail down his neck until I reached the top of his shoulder and licked along the firm muscle. I kept one hand stroking us and moved the other down his neck, forcing his chin up until his head tilted back, exposing his throat to me. I licked along his skin, enjoying the panty breaths he released each time I licked him. I moved to his earlobe and bit while swiping my thumb over the head of his cock.

I covered us with my hand, catching his cum in my palm, and stifled his moan with a kiss. Rocking my hips, I rubbed against him, sliding through his release. I melted against Ash, kissing him to silence my groan as I came, releasing spurts of cum over his abdomen.

We stood there a while, holding each other, exchanging kisses, and catching our breath as we came down from our lustful high. When Ash pulled back, he lifted my palm to his lips while keeping eye contact and licked our cum from my fingers.

It took me back to our time at the spring in Ohio, and I grabbed his wrist, tugging him close, holding his heated stare. "How do I get you out of my system so I don't want to fuck twenty-four-seven?" I asked.

"I never want you out of my system." Ash licked his lips, then kissed me.

My eyes went blurry from staring at my phone screen for too long. Hannah had sent an email detailing the lawsuit from Leo. He was filing the claim against Victory X and naming me. He wanted millions in a settlement. Millions. I couldn't believe it. He claimed I did irreparable damage to him emotionally.

I clicked on my favorite music playlist before dropping my phone on the end of my bed and dumping the basket of clean laundry out. I couldn't bring myself to reply to Hannah. Not tonight. Not when Ash was on his way to make me forget that anything else in this life existed outside of the two of us. This was Ash's weekend to fly up, and he told me he'd take a rideshare instead of having me pick him up. He couldn't get an afternoon flight, so he didn't land until after six. Right at the height of rush hour. He texted me when he landed nearly an hour ago, and I was growing worried. The airport was only a few miles from my apartment, but sometimes Northern Virginia traffic could be a parking lot. Especially if there was an accident.

Relief flooded me when I heard the front door close. I hit pause on my music and opened a food delivery app on my phone before shouting, "Baby, do you want food? We can order in tonight." I wandered into the hallway, scrolling through restaurants. "I don't want to make you cook after that flight and fucking with traff—" I froze at the edge of my living room, "—ic," I said as the last bit of breath escaped my body.

My heart stopped.

I didn't know what to do.

"Baby?" Angie said, walking toward me with a bright smile. "Sammy, are you dating someone?"

My heart kicked up, going from zero to one hundred with a single breath.

"Why do you look so shocked to see me?" she asked, passing me and heading toward my bedroom. "Am I interrupting? Is he coming over?" She disappeared into my room.

"Uh," I said, unable to form an actual word. A moment passed, and I hurried after her, trying to think up an excuse or anything to say at all. "Actually, yeah. I'm seeing someone."

"I thought I could stop by on my way to see Mom and Dad," she said, flopping onto my bed with a huff. "I really need my brother's opinion on this guy at work who's treating me like an idiot."

"Oh, um—okay." I sat beside her, shoving some of the clothes away, and quickly sent a text to Ash, letting him know Angie was in my apartment.

She rolled onto her stomach and started sorting through my laundry, helping me sort and fold my clothes. "So, his name is Izayah, and he's only a few years older than me, but he's acting like I have no idea how to do my job. Even though—"

"Jesus," Ash's voice boomed down the hall.

Angie's hand froze over a shirt she'd been reaching for, and her eyes flicked up, aiming toward my open bedroom door.

"Traffic was horrible," Ash continued. "You'd think the airport was forty miles from here."

His heavy footsteps echoed through my apartment, and I froze, unable to stop the train wreck that was about to ensue.

"I'm fucking starving. Can we order something?" His footsteps drew closer. "You're being super quiet. Is everything. . ."

Watching him round the corner into my room was like watching a movie in slow motion. I saw it coming. I knew it was happening, but my voice wouldn't come out, and my mind went blank.

He halted in the doorway, eyes landing on Angie.

Angie sat up and was the first to break the silent standoff. "Ash, what are you doing here?"

He finally looked at me, pure terror in his eyes.

I slowly shook my head, unable to explain this. I was sure my expression matched his.

"I texted you," I whispered.

"I didn't see it."

We hadn't talked about telling our family in weeks. We were simply enjoying each other, going with the flow.

"Guys?" Angie stood. "Is this what I think it is?"

I glanced up at her sheepishly. "What, um." I paused, eyeing her. "What do you think it is?"

"Sam is waiting for his boyfriend. And now you're here. Both talking about ordering food." She looked between us. "What the hell is going on?" She glared at Ash. "You never come home, but you flew in randomly on a Friday night? You didn't tell us you were coming home but came directly to Sam's?"

Busted.

"And you,"—she turned toward me, pointing with a long finger—"you knew he was coming. Were you lying about a boyfriend? Did you want me to leave and what, not see my brother?" She turned back to Ash, pain spreading over her delicate features. "Why wouldn't you tell me you were coming home? I want to see you. I never see or talk to you, but here you are."

Ash swallowed.

"Will either of you say something?" Angie's voice raised to a squeak.

"I don't really know where to start," Ash replied.

She roughly moved her hands to her hips. "Start with why you're standing in front of me right now."

Ash nodded, swallowing so hard his Adam's apple bobbed violently. "To see Sam." He glanced at me a second before looking back at Angie.

"Okay. Were you going to tell the rest of us you're home?"

His gaze flicked to his toes. "No," he whispered.

"No?" She shifted. "And why not?"

223

"He came to see me," I said.

She whirled on me. "And why would he come to see you and only you, Sam? Aren't you two fighting?" Realization seemed to hit her. "No, because you two made up back in May."

A painfully awkward silence descended on us.

"I think we should sit and talk," Ash finally said, backing into the hallway and disappearing toward the living room.

Angie shot me an exasperated glance before marching after him. I rushed after them, nearly stumbling on my way through the hall. Ash sat at my kitchen table, staring at Angie across from him.

It was a small square glass table with four chairs and a cute flower center-piece I'd put together the day before, knowing Ash would be there. Ash didn't care much about decorations, but I liked having the fresh flowers on the table when we sat there eating his delicious home-cooked meals.

I sat between Ash and Angie, wanting to shrink into the shadows.

"I'm waiting," Angie said with a snarky tone.

"Sam didn't lie about his boyfriend. He's seeing someone."

"Were you all going to party this weekend or something? You didn't want your annoying little sister getting in the way of your fun? Fucking typical of you two. I swear, it's like when we were kids. It was always Ash and Sam. No one else could ever come between you two. God, I'm shocked you even date people with the way you two act. How could anyone ever compare to—"

My heart jumped into my throat, and my stomach twisted into millions of knots. My eyes met Ash's, and it was like we were silently trying to calm each other down with a single look.

"You two. . ." She trailed off, watching us. "You two are dating?" she screamed, half jumping out of her seat as she slammed her hands on the table. "Are you fucking with me right now?" She kept scanning us like the answer would appear magically, but neither of us spoke or confirmed her suspicions. "Ash is baby? Are you serious?"

"What's she talking about?" Ash asked.

"When I heard the door, I thought it was. . . I said, "baby." She heard me."

LOVE ON A DARE

He cupped the side of my face, stroking my cheek with his thumb. "It was bound to happen. It just happened before we were ready."

Angie dropped back into the chair. "I'm right?"

Ash moved his hand to my thigh and said, "Yes, piglet, you're right."

"Since when?"

"The camping trip."

"Three months? You've been together for three months and didn't tell me?" Her voice cracked.

"It's so much more complicated than that, Angela," Ash said. "You have to understand that."

"Comp-complicated? Sure. But you couldn't tell me?"

"Angie," I said, trying to soothe her, "Ash and I—we tried to avoid our feelings. We tried. For years, we tried."

She looked at me with shimmering eyes. "Is that why Ash moved away and everything changed?"

Ash and I nodded.

"How long have you two had feelings for each other?"

We were silent, letting the seconds pass by.

Eventually, I cleared my throat. "I've been in love with Ash since we were kids."

Her jaw fell slack and her dark, chocolaty eyes held me in an odd trance. "That long, huh?" She ripped her gaze away from me to train her attention on Ash. "And you?"

Ash shifted and squinted like he was in pain. "I kissed Sam a little over four years ago." He rubbed the back of his neck, shifting in his seat again. "Sam was the one who was worried about our family and what it would do to us all, so he told me we couldn't be anything more than what we had always been—friends."

"Oh," she breathed, a lone tear sliding down her cheek. She rubbed her hand over her mouth before she sighed and closed her eyes. "If it wasn't for the marriage, when would this have come out?"

I dropped my gaze to the table, and Ash rubbed my thigh.

I guess my super big secret is coming out.

"When we were thirteen."

Angie choked through a breath. "That was a long time ago."

"The night before I planned to tell Ash about my feelings, Dad told me your mom had agreed to marry him," I admitted. I lifted my eyes, meeting hers.

Tears ran down her cheeks, and her lip quivered.

Seeing her upset hit me, gripping my heart and tearing me to pieces. Angie was my family. I loved her like she was my real sister. I'd do anything for her. Seeing her cry because of me was breaking my resolve. It hit me in places not many people on this earth could reach.

"You, um," she said, her voice wavering. "You have to tell them."

A tear finally slipped past my shield, and I shook my head. "I'm not ready to lose everyone."

Ash's hand clamped over the nape of my neck, and he drew me close until our foreheads pressed tight together. He looked into my eyes, pleading with me to hear him. "We aren't losing anyone here. You understand me?"

"But, Ash..." I couldn't speak the rest of it. It was all things I had thought before. I closed my eyes, picturing it all.

They'll think we're disgusting. Hate us. Tell us to get out of their lives.

"Angel," he said, "they are not *her*."

My eyes flashed open, meeting his.

He was right. Dad and Jane were kind people. They loved with everything they had. They were the opposite of my mother. The opposite of his father. But would that be true when they found out we were together? Would Jane still love me if she knew I was fucking her son? Would she think my dad was the same degenerate as me and be unable to—

"Sammy, come back from your head," Ash whispered. "I'm here. We're in this together. No matter what." His fingers tightened on the base of my neck. His breath passed over my lips.

It should've calmed me. His presence should've been everything I needed, but it couldn't touch the terror building in my heart. The fear that had kept me away from him for so long. The fear of losing everything and everyone I'd ever loved. Of the rejection. The judgment. Failure.

I blinked through the tears now streaming down my face. I couldn't believe I was crying. Ash kissed my forehead, and a sob escaped me. My whole world was on the edge of collapse, and I couldn't stop it.

Angie made a soft sound, reminding me we weren't alone. "I," she said, pausing on a sob, "I should've seen it. Oh my god. We all should've seen it."

Ash released me from his hold and turned to her, sliding his hand down my arm until his hand clamped around mine with a squeeze. "What do you mean?"

She leaned back, wiping her tears. "It's so obvious now. You two were always so close. I was always so jealous of your relationship. I wanted a friend I could be like you with. I never could find that person who gave me what you two have." She laughed, wiping more tears away. "God, now it all makes sense." She laughed again between a sob. "Brothers." She broke into more laughter.

I visibly cringed at hearing *brothers*.

She laughed harder when she saw my reaction. "Now I know why you hate him calling you bro," she said, more laughter pouring from her.

Ash's grip on my hand loosened, letting the blood flow freely. Then he joined Angie in the weird laughing fit.

"What's happening right now?" I asked.

Angie stood and threw herself at me, falling into my lap. "Sammy." She kissed my cheek. "I love you so much." She tightened her arms around my neck and held me tight. "So much."

I was stunned, unable to move.

"You don't hate me?" I asked.

Her head shook against me, and she squeezed tighter. "Never."

My arms wrapped around her slender body, and I held tight, burying my face in her shoulder.

Ash stood, moving behind my chair, and touched my shoulder. I couldn't see it, but I could feel him pat Angie's head before he bent over us and kissed the top of my head. The action had my heart pounding while sending a wave of warmth through me.

He didn't have to speak the words. I could feel what he was telling me.

I told you, Angel. You're loved.

Without warning, Angie flew off of my lap and screeched. "Oh, my god! You guys fucked while we were camping!"

The blood drained from my body in an instant, and Ash bent over, laughing.

"Jesus Christ," I mumbled.

She screeched again. "You did! Didn't you?"

Ash righted himself and bit his lip. "Best night of my life," he said with a satisfied grunt.

Her eyes flew wide open like she was running through the whole trip in her mind. When her mouth opened to say something, Ash stopped her.

"Piglet, there is no need to announce it. Both of us were there. We remember it clearly."

Her mouth clamped shut, and she eyed us, biting back a smile. "Well, I'm happy for you both. Dad and I were so happy you two had finally made up after being miserable for so long. Guess you made up a lot more than we ever expected, but I'm glad either way."

"On that note," Ash said, "Who's hungry?"

We ordered Thai from my favorite local restaurant and sat with Angie until midnight. Her finding out was terrifying but gave me hope. We'd promised to drop by the house to tell everyone in the morning, which had my nerves on edge.

While Ash finished washing his face, I rinsed the last bit of toothpaste from my mouth.

"Baby," I said, and his muffled "huh" came through the towel covering his face. "I don't think I can sleep like this. I'm way too nervous. What if they're angry with us?"

His eyes peeked over the towel a moment before he walked over and wiped my face with it.

I pressed my palm against his bare chest and said, "What are you doing?"

He tossed the towel on the counter before squatting, wrapping his arms around my waist, and hoisting me over his shoulder. An involuntary yelp escaped me, and he laughed. I smacked his ass when he flicked off the bathroom light, carrying me to the bedroom.

"What the fuck? Ash!"

He tossed me onto the bed before breezing over to the side table, flipping off the light so my room was cast in shadows and we could see the lights outside over the lake.

"Ash, what—" His mouth crashed against mine, effectively shutting me up.

He pulled back, leaving us a breath of space. "You worry too much. How about you focus on us?" He kissed me long and slow. Speaking against my lips, he said, "I've missed you. I've been thinking about you since I watched your sexy ass get on that damn plane." He kissed me again, then pulled back. "I planned to come home, fill my belly, and then fill you, but that plan was shot to hell."

I chuckled as desire flooded me. "That was my plan, too."

He hovered above me with a sly smile. "Tell me, Angel, did you prep yourself today?" His warm breath ran over my lips, sending desire rushing straight to my dick.

"I did. I had a plug in until recently."

Ash groaned. "God, I love you." He kissed me, crowding my body as he straddled me.

I chuckled, sinking into the distraction he offered. It wouldn't last, but it would be enough to let me sleep.

He drew me into a lazy kiss. "Mmm," he hummed. "You taste divine. Truly a gift from God."

Chapter 27
Ash

Angie's car was already parked in the driveway of our parents' home. I pulled Sam's Jeep beside her car and cut the engine before turning to Sam. He was in complete freak-out mode. His anxiety was through the roof, and he was one wrong move away from bolting. Convincing him to come with me was a major task. I thought I had done enough to help relax him last night, but the second he woke up, he was right back to a wound-tight ball of anxiety.

He had it in his head that our family would fall apart the moment this came out and called Angie's reaction a "fluke." I was struggling to ground him. I didn't think Mom would be angry, but Sam had a sinking feeling that Gary would lose it. Maybe not with anger, but he had a gut feeling his dad wouldn't like what he heard.

What could we do, though? Hide it from them forever? Angie finding out the way she did helped me come to terms with the need to tell them. Good or bad, they needed to know. If our parents found out the way Angie did, I didn't think it would go well.

"Come on," I said, sliding my hand under Sam's. "I'm right here with you. We'll be okay. No matter what. You have me."

His worried eyes landed on my face. "Do we have to? I don't have a good feeling."

"I think we have to. If not today, it will have to happen eventually and the longer we wait, the more likely they are to be angry that we didn't tell them sooner." I released his hand and cupped his face, running my thumb over his cheek. "Do you want to rip the Band-Aid off now or later?"

He sighed, then said, "Now." Turning to open the car door, he grumbled, "Kill me now."

We knocked on the door since our coming was a surprise. Angie promised not to tell them, so we stood outside, waiting like we didn't have keys.

When no one came to the door, Sam grew fidgety, so I pulled my keys from my pocket and opened the door.

"Ma," I called, "Sam and I stopped by to visit."

The sound of chairs scratching against the wood floor in the kitchen echoed through the silence. When we rounded the corner, we were met with teary eyes and piles of used tissues on the table. Gary had Angie wrapped in his arms, tears pouring down their cheeks, and Mom wiped her nose with a fresh tissue.

My stomach dropped, unease settling in my gut.

"What the hell is happening?" I asked.

They looked about as confused as I felt.

"Why's everyone crying?" Sam said, stepping toward the table like a stiff robot. "Angie, did you tell?"

She glanced over her shoulder at us, sniffing and shaking her head. "No."

"Tell us what?" Mom asked.

"Wait," I said, Sam's sinking feeling now valid. I would have to tell him he may be clairvoyant. "What's going on?"

"Ash, why are you in town?" Mom's brows pulled together, and she looked between me and Sam.

"I have a feeling we're missing something," I said. "What the fuck are you all crying over? Who died?"

Mom and Gary exchanged a look. One they'd shared so many times in my life. I knew it as the "should we tell them" look, and I never liked what came after it.

"Don't do that. Clearly, Angie knows," I said, my voice growing louder with my nerves, and I pointed to Angie, who was still clinging to Gary like she'd never see him again.

"Sit down, boys," Mom said, pointing to the chairs around the kitchen table.

I grabbed Sam's hand, scared he would try to run off, and sat beside Mom. Sam sank into the chair beside me, and I kept hold of his hand as if he anchored me to the chair.

Gary patted Angie's arm, squeezing her a little, then said, "A few months ago, I went to see a doctor about my shortness of breath. I noticed it when we were hiking during our trip." He rubbed Angie's back and looked at Mom. "The doctors ran some tests, and we finally have an answer." He looked somber, sending fear shooting through my chest. Sam's grip on my hand tightened, his palm growing clammy. "I have lung cancer."

Sam gasped, barely audible even in this silence.

"Stage three," Gary continued. "I have more tests scheduled for this week. I'm seeing some reputable doctors. Some of them have hope that we can still fight this thing."

I swallowed. "Stage three? How bad is that?"

His eyes softened with a slight tilt of his head. "The cancer has started spreading, but not far. If I start treatment now, I have a shot."

Sam's hand dug into mine, cutting off the circulation.

I looked at him, consumed with worry. "Angel, look at me," I whispered.

When he didn't move, I reached over with the hand he didn't have a vise grip on and held his chin in my fingers, forcing him to look at me. His eyes shimmered with tears, his lip trembled, and he quickly bit it.

His mother had done a number on him. He had always called me a crybaby when we were younger because I would openly cry over something while he held it all in, an ever-stoic mask of masculinity. It wasn't until we were teens that I'd found out why. His mother would call him a little girl when he cried, then lock him away in his room to learn how to deal with his emotions like a *real man*. He told me of a time she'd locked him in his room because he'd cried at his great-grandfather's funeral.

How no one knew what she did to him was always shocking to me, but who was I to question people's ability to ignore what was directly in front of them? I'd show up at school with bruises and broken bones, but no one questioned it. I heard the easy excuses far too many times. My father would say, "Oh, you know, boys will be boys," or "He plays too hard" to excuse the proof of his drunken pastime. No one ever questioned the excuses.

Sam rose quickly, releasing my hand. "I need a moment," he said with a chill that permeated my bones.

He was closing off. Shutting down.

I couldn't let him get that far, or getting him back to the bright sunshine of a man I adored would be one hell of a journey. I scanned the table, taking in my family's concerned expressions before rushing after him. He'd made it halfway up the stairs when I caught up to him.

"Angel, talk to me."

His shoulders tensed, but he kept walking. His room was at the end of the hall, so I grabbed him by the waist and dragged him into my room, kicking the door shut behind me. It was dark. My one lone window let in a sliver of sunlight through the dark curtains. I rushed to the bathroom door and closed it, giving Sam the privacy he was searching for. Most days, he didn't like closed doors, but when he wanted to get away, he would lock himself in his room to think.

"Come on, Sammy. I'm here. Lean on me." I approached him like he was an animal, backed into a corner, and his eyes finally lifted, locking on me with despair. My heart shattered at the sight. "Please, Angel."

I opened my arms for him, and he crashed against me with such force that I stumbled back as I wrapped him in my arms. His hands clung to my back, digging into my skin. I kissed the side of his head, whispering reassurances, hoping it would ease the pain even a fraction.

He shuddered in my hold as a sob rocked through him, filled with the purest form of pain I had ever seen from him. I gripped him tighter, wishing I could merge us together. Wishing I could take his sorrow from him. I cared about Gary, but my relationship with him was never as close as Angie's. And to Sam, Gary was all he had left. His only remaining family. His only blood relative. His support system. Especially after Sam's mom was arrested. That was when Gary stopped traveling for work and became more involved in Sam's life. They did everything together. Shared hobbies and lifelong memories. My heart ached for him. I couldn't begin to imagine how I would feel if it was Mom.

A part of me was glad it wasn't Mom, but the thought felt sour before I pushed it from my mind.

"This can't be real," Sam cried.

"I wish it wasn't." I buried my face in his neck. "I wish it wasn't," I repeated.

I was helpless, only able to offer him my presence and nothing else. I was used to taking away the thing causing him pain, but I couldn't take this away.

Sam stood wrapped in my arms for what felt like hours while he cried. When he finally calmed down, he pulled away, looking at me with sad, puffy eyes.

"I don't know what to do," he whispered.

I tightened my grip on his waist and dropped my forehead to his, looking him in the eyes like I could grab his heart and protect it.

"We go downstairs, and you spend time with him. You help him fight this like I know you can." I kissed his nose. "You support him. You love him." I dropped a soft kiss on his lips, barely a touch. "And I'll be right beside you the whole way through."

He bit his lip, biting back a strangled sob as he nodded.

"We can get through this."

He nodded again, then pulled away, saying, "Let me wash my face," and then disappeared into the bathroom.

I pulled my phone from my pocket and opened my favorites, hitting Tae's name.

He picked up immediately. "Ash, you okay?"

I cleared my throat. "I have a family emergency. I'll fly home Sunday, but I'll need to work from Virginia, and I don't know how long it will take."

He was silent a moment before replying, "What's going on? Did someone get hurt?"

"It's Gary. He has cancer."

Tae's sigh on the other end of the line made my chest tighten around my heart. "Shit, man. I'm so sorry. Is Sam okay?"

I glanced back at the closed bathroom door. "He's doing about as good as anyone could in his situation."

"All right, so stop by the office on Monday and we can get you all set up and let the team know you'll be remote for a while. We can keep you remote for as long as you need, but I may need you to fly out sometimes. I'll try to keep my requests minimal."

I released a heavy breath, running my fingers through my hair. "Thanks, Tae."

"Don't mention it, bud. Take care of your family."

A half-hearted laugh escaped me. "Yeah, I'll do my best."

"And Ash."

"Yeah?"

"Take care of yourself. Call me if you need anything."

I thanked him before hanging up and slipping my phone into my pocket.

When Sam finally returned from the bathroom, he looked a little better. His eyes were glossy and red from crying.

I gripped the back of his neck, dragged his face close to mine, and said, "Let's get back down there." I slid my hand down his spine. "Angie might come looking for us thinking we're busy fucking up here. Can't have that now, can we?"

He laughed and nudged my shoulder. "Dummy."

We found our family in the living room, huddled together on the sofa, watching a sports reporting channel. I leaned against the doorframe, crossing my arms as Sam came up beside me.

"Angel, I talked to Tae. I'll be staying here with you."

He turned, his eyes wide as he asked, "What about work?"

"Remote unless I'm asked to come in for something specific, but Tae said it would be minimal. For now, I want you to look at this right in front of us and enjoy it."

He scanned the living room, observing the normalcy of our family. "We have something to do first," he said, tugging my hand free from my chest and lacing our fingers together. "We need to share this before anything else."

I nodded and let him lead me into the room.

We sat on the loveseat facing the larger sofa where our family was perched, enjoying the sports channel.

"Guys," Sam said, and all eyes focused on him.

Angie's eyes landed on our hands, and she smiled, scooting closer to Gary.

"Ash and I—"

Mom threw up her hand. "Hang on." She eyed us. "Before you say anything. Ashton, why are you home, and why didn't you tell me you were in town?" She aimed a scowl at me.

"Well, Ma, if you had let Sam speak, you would know. Now we have to do this instead of you already knowing the reason."

Her brows furrowed, and then she released a huff. "Fine, continue, Sam." She waved her hand at him, encouraging him to speak.

I chuckled and squeezed Sam's hand.

"So, like I was saying, Ash and I have something important for you to hear, and we need you to hear us out completely before passing judgment."

"Did you do drugs?" Gary asked, and that absolutely sent me over the edge. I erupted with laughter and leaned into Sam's shoulder, unable to contain myself.

"Dad, I'm serious!"

"Okay, fine, sorry," Gary said, patting Angie on the shoulder.

"Ash and I," Sam glanced at me, nerves clear in his shaking voice, "we're partners."

The blank look from Mom and Gary told me everything I needed to know: they didn't get it.

"Really, guys?" I scoffed. "You don't know what partners means?"

"What, partners in crime? Boys, I need you to be more specific here," Mom said in an annoyed tone.

I chuckled and faced Sam. "Sammy," I whispered, and he turned his face to me. I ran my fingers over his jaw, then leaned in and kissed him.

Angie squealed, and Mom gasped.

"Oh, partners," Gary said.

"Wait, Ashton," Mom said, "since when are you gay? Did you lie to me all these years? Because I swore up and down when you were fourteen that you were a little gay, but then you started dating girls, and I thought maybe you gave off that vibe but didn't actually like boys."

"Mom!" Angie yelled, slapping Mom on the thigh. "I cannot believe you said that."

Mom shrunk back. "What the hell, Angela! Why'd you smack me?"

Sam chuckled beside me, warm and deep. The kind of chuckle that warmed my soul.

"And I was worried they'd think it was disgusting. Instead, you're in trouble for not coming out sooner." He flashed his beautiful smile and aimed a wink at me. "Good luck explaining this one, baby."

Gary clasped his hands together and leaned forward, resting his elbows on his knees. "Girls, stop the arguing. Sam, Ash," he looked us both square in the eyes, dressing us down with a single look, "since when and why now?"

There it is.

I kissed Sam's knuckles before starting the explanation, thankful they were willing to hear us out. More than grateful that they didn't get angry. Most of all, blessed that they were still sitting across from us with overwhelming love for us both.

Chapter 28

Sam

I left the conference room after dropping the bombshell of all bombshells. I told my executive team I wanted to move Victory X to Raleigh, North Carolina.

I'd never seen Imogene stunned into silence until today.

The idea had been swirling around in my head for weeks. Ash leaving his job that he loved didn't make sense and we couldn't keep up with the traveling forever once Dad was better.

The best solution I came up with was to move Victory X.

It wouldn't be easy, and it asked a lot of my team to pick up their lives and move. I was willing to offer one hell of a severance if someone didn't want to move, or I would pay for their moving expenses if they followed Victory X. I knew it was a lot to ask of people, but I needed to do this. I needed to know that at the end of the day, Ash and I could have a life together. I wanted to go home to him every day, not every weekend. I needed him, and if that meant sacrificing on my part, I would do it.

Autumn matched my pace, holding her tablet to her chest. "Are you sure about this, Sam?" Autumn twisted her finger in her hair, tugging a long curl. "This is a major change. It could cause us a lot of trouble. Retaining employees and the—"

I lifted my hand, cutting her off. "All things I've considered, but this is the right move for me. Victory X isn't going to fail because of this."

She chewed her lip like she was keeping her opinions to herself.

I sighed. "Say it. You always do. Why hold back now?"

When we reached my office door, she closed it behind us before turning to me with a worried frown. "So you and Ash. . ."

Another sigh poured from me as I dropped onto the couch across from my desk. "Yeah. Me and Ash."

She sat across from me in an armchair. "I'm sorry you felt you couldn't tell me before." She rubbed her palms over her legs. "I'm also sorry I was fucking him with my eyes when I first met him. That probably made you feel like shit."

"It didn't. I promise," I said, laughing. "Ash was a complete whore in the past, so don't think you ogling him with your eyes is any worse than what I've witnessed him do firsthand."

Her face contorted before she snorted, "What an asshole."

I smiled and replied, "That he is."

Her expression turned serious, and she set her tablet on the coffee table between us. "How's your dad doing?"

I swallowed, working through the immediate lump in my throat that appeared every time Dad was mentioned since his cancer announcement. "He started chemo a few weeks ago, but we won't know anything for a while."

Autumn leaned back, closing her eyes. "I'm rooting for him."

"Thanks," I replied, sliding my laptop over and flipped it open. "Now, let's take a look at locations. Wanna help me shop?"

Her eyes flew open, and she popped out of the chair to sit beside me. "You're telling me I can help you spend millions, and it won't come out of my pocket? Count me in."

After an hour of looking into corporate office spaces for lease, Autumn and I were over it. They all started blending, and it felt like none of them were what I was looking for.

"Okay," Autumn said, "this is harder than I thought."

I chuckled, closing the laptop. "Maybe I should hire a realtor to make this entire process easier."

She nudged my shoulder with a smile. "Sounds like a good plan."

My phone came to life beside the laptop, buzzing on the coffee table. I grabbed it and hit answer without looking at the contact. "This is Sam Pearce."

"Sammy!" Rainie's voice hit me like a string yanking me by the chest out of the darkness I'd found myself in.

"Rain, holy shit," I said, taking a peek at the caller ID to make sure I wasn't hallucinating. "How long has it been?"

"Oh, we will talk about that later, but right now, I want you to agree you'll come out tonight. Nine o'clock at the karaoke bar."

I glanced at the clock on the wall. It was almost six, and Ash would be getting home with Dad from an appointment in a few minutes.

"I have a lot to tell you, Rain, so I'll be there, but I'm also bringing my partner. Is that okay?"

"Sean!" Rain yelled. "Holy shit, Sean! It happened! The world is ending! Sam has a boyfriend!"

I laughed, my chest filling with warmth.

"He what?" Sean's deep voice was distant but loud.

"So we'll see you at nine?" Rain asked.

"Yeah, you'll see us at nine."

"Sweeeeet," she said, "See you in a bit." The line went silent, and I chuckled, setting my phone on the table.

Autumn stood, picking up her tablet. "I'll leave you to it then."

"Hey, Autumn," I called before she could leave my office.

She turned with a smile. "Yeah?"

"Thank you for everything you do."

With a nod, she opened the door. "What are friends for?"

Ash and I climbed out of the rideshare and marched up to the familiar karaoke bar. The first time we were there, he kissed me, and it sparked one hell of a journey.

I slid my hand into Ash's as we approached the doors. "Ready for the rest of the world to know about us?"

He leaned in, kissing my cheek. "I've been ready. I've been waiting for you."

"Oh, hush," I whispered, then pushed open the door.

In a back corner of the bar, Rainie sat with Selena, Sean, and Jasmine. A vibrant array of drinks covered the table, mixed between pitchers of beer. Music blasted. The lights were dimmed to a soft yellow hue, making the atmosphere cozy.

It wasn't until Rainie noticed me that a shot of adrenaline hit me. Her eyes flicked to Ash and then back to me, surely recalling how I said I was bringing my partner. The hand-holding was likely the next giveaway.

Ash leaned in when I halted, my heart beating so hard I swore it would give out. "No matter what. . ." He squeezed my hand.

No matter what, you always have me.

I sucked in a deep breath and breezed across the room with a blip of mustered confidence.

"Hey, guys," I said, smiling at my friends. Jaz's eyes bulged from her head, and Sean and Rainie looked at us like we'd sprouted wings.

"Ash?" Jaz said, looking between us. "You can't be serious?"

Ash smiled at Jaz. "Good to see you, too."

They hadn't spoken since he moved to Raleigh. I wasn't in the loop about what happened, but from what Rainie had told me, Jaz freaked about Ash's feelings for me and wanted nothing to do with him after that.

"I haven't seen you in ages," she said. Her uncomfortable gaze flicked to me, then she said, "Hey, stranger."

"Hey, right back," I replied. Sean and Rainie stood, approaching Ash and me. "Guys, this is my partner, Ash. Ash, you've met them before."

Ash gave Sean a fist bump like they always did. But Rainie stood there staring like she couldn't believe her eyes. Selena pushed past her and hugged me before introducing herself to Ash.

"I think we met once," Ash said, "but you were all over the girl I had a crush on, so you probably don't remember me."

Selena laughed and agreed with him before sitting back down beside Jaz.

"So, a lot has happened," I said, squeezing Ash's hand. "A lot."

Ash smacked Sean on the shoulder. "Don't worry. The family knows. You don't have to act so surprised." Ash looked Sean in the eyes like he was daring him to say something Ash didn't like.

Sean nodded, then said, "It's good to see you, Ash."

Rainie finally spoke, and it hit me in an odd way that I couldn't place. "Is this my fault? It's because of that stupid Truth or Dare game, isn't it?"

"Rainie, I have to thank you for that, actually," Ash said. "If Jaz hadn't convinced me to go that night and if I hadn't agreed to lie about being bi, then I wouldn't be standing here with the love of my life, so thank you."

Her jaw fell open. "W-well, um. . ."

A nervous laugh escaped me. "Ash and I are together. Our family is aware and supports us, so why don't we all have a seat and catch up?"

Rain and Sean nodded, sitting back down in their seats, and Ash and I joined them. We ordered drinks and caught up with everyone. Eventually, we all moved to the center of the bar where a large group danced. Ash pulled me close and kissed me.

"How crazy is it that everything changed in this very place?" Ash said, his lips brushing over mine. "Now we can come back here, and I can think fondly of that moment. Of this place. The place that opened my eyes to my feelings for you." He kissed me again. "The moment I realized how much I truly love you."

I wrapped my arms around his neck, sliding my fingers through his hair, and brushed my lips over his. "I still can't believe you lied to come that night. Even more unbelievable was you actually kissing me."

"Mmm, there was this look in your eyes," he said, running his hands down my spine. "You got all red and angry. I wanted to eat you alive on the spot."

"You still deserved that punch I gave you." I chuckled.

"I fucking did, but I wish you had let me take you home that night and fuck you into oblivion. We could've saved ourselves years of suffering."

I tugged his hair, pressing our foreheads together as he drew his hips closer to mine. "Sometimes I wish I hadn't let fear take over me."

"Mm-hm, but God, Angel, that camping trip was the highlight of my life. I'll never forget making love to you under the moon beside that waterfall. That was straight out of a goddamn dream."

I bit my lip. Remembering our time only four short months ago like it was yesterday. "Yeah, that was life-altering."

Ash rocked his hips, swaying us to the music. "Or the motorcycle. I think we need to play with the motorcycle more, Sammy."

"Maybe we can start by having some fun in the bathroom here." I laughed. "Maybe we can make new memories in the stall I punched you in?"

He groaned, then kissed me. "I'd like that a lot." He kissed me again.

"Wanna go make those new memories right now?"

"Hell yes," he said, pulling back and grabbing my hand.

We pushed through the crowd, passing our table where Rainie had Selena on her lap, lip-locked and oblivious to everyone watching them.

"You made it," Sean called from the end of the table with a wave aimed at someone behind us.

I glanced over my shoulder, only for the blood to drain from my body. My feet locked up, and I stopped moving. My sudden stop nearly ripped Ash's arm from his shoulder.

"Angel, what the hell?" He spun toward me, his smile faltering when our eyes locked.

Sauntering toward the table was Leo.

I have to go. I can't be near him in the middle of our legal battle.

I took a step back, watching as he approached the table and did his stupid handshake with Sean that they'd done since college. He looked impeccably put together, like always. Light brown hair perfectly styled back and lined up. Deep-set brown eyes shadowed beneath his pronounced brow line. His stupidly perfect square jaw was covered in a perfectly maintained short beard. He came tonight in his usual workwear: an expensive as fuck suit.

"Sorry, traffic was terrible getting here," Leo's voice was loud and commanding over the music. "How long have you been here?"

Ash's hand slid around my waist, pulling me close. His lips brushed over my ear as he whispered, "Ignore him."

I nodded, unable to break my eyes away from the man I had called a friend. The man I had trusted with my company's finances. I hadn't spoken to anyone except Ash about it, but Sean knew Leo had left Victory X. I had asked him to tell me if Leo was ever coming to anything so I could ensure we didn't cross paths. Maybe it was my mistake for not telling him why, but I expected my friend to extend me the courtesy of informing me like I had asked.

"Sean, what the hell is he doing here?" I snapped.

"What do you mean?" Sean asked with a frown. "I invited him."

"Why didn't you tell me he would be here?"

Sean shrugged but didn't say anything to explain himself.

Leo finally looked at me, and disdain filled his expression. "Sam," he said with a tense nod.

I ripped my gaze away from him and turned to my friends sitting around the table. "We're out. It was great to see everyone."

Ash's hand rested on my hip as he leaned over and whispered something in Jasmine's ear.

"Good to see you, Ash," Sean said.

"You too, man."

"You're all cool with this?" Leo asked, his eyes raking over Ash with venom.

Ash rose to his full height beside me, his hand still on my hip. "Why wouldn't they be?" Ash asked, sounding like he was looking for a reason to fight Leo. "Sam, let's go before I get the urge to hurt someone." Ash glared at Leo and stepped forward.

"Oh, big scary brother, is here to defend you, Sam?"

Keeping my mouth shut, I fell into step with Ash as we headed for the door.

"Is your brother everything you always dreamed he would be?" Leo called from behind us, and Ash spun to face him. "Does your family know you're fucking?" Leo laughed. "God, how desperate must you be that you have to go after your own brother?"

Ash's face took on the look he always got when he was about to fight. He used to get that way when kids at school would pick on me. It was always that look that led to him getting suspended. In this case, it could lead to an assault charge. I had a feeling Leo was baiting us to help his legal case.

Leo's laugh grated on my ears. "Look at you two. Fucking made for each other. I bet you fuck your sister, too. Do you make it a threesome?"

Ash's nostrils flared, and he stepped forward. I reached for him, pressing my hand firmly against his chest. "Stop, Ash." I stepped in front of him. If looks could kill, Leo would've dropped dead on the spot. "He's doing it on purpose."

Ash's eyes found mine. "But he—"

"Ash," I whispered, pressing harder, trying to get him to back up. "I have a legal team going after him right now. If anything happens tonight, it can ruin everything I've been doing for months."

He rolled his lip between his teeth so hard I expected it to bleed. "Fine." He backed up, grabbed my hand on his chest, and eyed Leo. "Fine, Angel." His voice was rough and growly like it was taking every ounce of willpower not to kill my former friend.

"I appreciate that you would risk going to jail on an assault charge for me, Ash, but it isn't necessary."

He cracked a smile and kissed my hand. "Let's go home." He slung his arm over my shoulder, tugging me close, and whispered, "He has one thing right."

"What's that?" I asked as we stepped outside.

"We are made for each other." He smiled and kissed the side of my head.

Chapter 29

Ash

The smell of coffee wafted through the air, and I poured a packet of sugar into Sam's mug before turning back to the pan of sizzling bacon and flipping the strips over to ensure they didn't burn on either side.

"You don't have to do this every morning," Sam said as he appeared from the hallway.

I pointed to the coffee mug and said, "I want to."

He picked up the cup and took a sip, releasing a soft, satisfied groan. "Thank you."

"You're welcome, Sammy, but you don't have to thank me." I plucked the slices of bacon out of the pan and set them on a plate. "Any word from Hannah?"

Sam frowned, then took another sip. "There's some kind of mediation date scheduled with the judge, then a few additional private things where the witnesses and everyone will be brought in. She said something about the police investigation will be presented." He sighed, setting the cup on the counter. "I tuned her out after she said I would be interviewed and have to tell my side of everything in front of the judge and Leo."

I moved toward him, sliding my hands around his waist. "You're almost done."

"It feels like it's taking a lifetime, and with everything going on with Dad," he looked at me, "I'm tired."

"I know." I kissed his forehead and crushed him in a hug.

We were all tired, but Sam's legal battle was an extra burden he could do without.

To keep up with work and Gary's chemo schedule, I had to spend a lot of late nights getting things done that I couldn't do during the day. It was exhausting, and

I wasn't sure how long I could keep it up before I started falling behind at work. If it was a choice between being there for my family and work. . . I liked to think it was obvious what my choice would be.

Releasing Sam, I slid the plate of bacon next to the plate of freshly made blueberry pancakes and kissed his cheek. "I'm off to pick up your dad."

"Thank you for breakfast," he called after me.

I pulled Sam's Jeep into the driveway and parked as close as possible to the front door. I left the Jeep running, and jogged up the steps to the door. It opened before I hit the top step. Gary aimed a tired smile my way.

"You look like shit," I said, offering my hand for him to put his weight on me.

He coughed and reached for me, steadying himself. "I feel like shit, so at least it tracks."

"Were you able to keep any food down yesterday? Mom didn't text me her usual updates."

He shrugged and headed down the stairs, leaning on me with each step. "I told her I kept it down, but don't rat me out."

I sighed. "Gary, you know she knows." We reached the passenger door, and I tugged it open, helping Gary in. "Don't take her for a fool."

He choked out another cough. "I know." His voice was hoarse as he covered his mouth, shuddering through a fit of coughs. "I don't want her to worry too much."

I frowned, closed the door, rounded the front of the car, and hopped into the driver's side. "Don't rat me out, Gary." I chuckled, winking at him. "But I can get you some weed. I've done some reading, and it can help with the symptoms and this pain you're in."

His eyes widened, and his lips parted, leaving us in silence as he stared at me like I'd offered him some crazy hard drugs.

"I'm just saying. If you ask, I will get it."

"Ashton, I always worried you did drugs. Are you a druggie?"

I curled forward, leaning over the steering wheel, releasing a deep laugh. "Oh, fuck, Gary. No!" I put the car in drive and took off. "I'm just saying I know some people who could get what we need. They've even offered to bake it into some cookies or brownies." I looked at him before turning down a street leading to the highway. "We could get you feeling a little better than you are now." I glanced at him again, watching him go from horrified to considering it. "Maybe enough to get you eating some food and feeling a little more human."

He sighed, looking through the window. "I never thought we'd be having this conversation, Ash." His hands folded over his lap, and he sighed again. "You really think it could help?"

The tight pain building in my chest constricted even more, and I swallowed it down. "Yeah, I think it would."

A few minutes of silence hovered between us before he said, "Get me those brownies, and this stays between you and me."

"I've got you. I promise."

While Gary was in the chair receiving his round of chemo, I took the opportunity to step out into the hall and scroll through my contacts, quickly hitting her name. The phone only rang a couple times before she picked up.

"You coming to see me for another tattoo?" Lexi's sultry voice rang over the line.

"You only wish." I laughed. "Do you remember what we talked about a few days ago?"

"You want it?"

"Can you make some brownies?"

"Swing by tonight. I'll have them."

"Thanks, Lex."

We went silent a moment, then she said, "How's he doing?"

I glanced back at the doorway with about twelve people sitting through their round of chemo for the day. Gary was talking with a girl no older than fourteen. "Not great, Lex. It's progressing fast, even with the chemo."

"I'm sorry," she said. "Be here around seven. I'll have your brownies."

"Thanks," I said, watching Gary laugh with the girl as I hung up. His eyes were sparkling, and he kept leaning toward her like they were whispering, sharing some secret. His eyes met mine. Then the girl turned her head, and all the blood in my body drained to the floor.

She wore a T-shirt and sweatpants. Her hair was short and dark. But those big brown eyes landed on me with nothing but joy.

Nora?

Tucking my phone in my pocket, I dipped past a nurse before reaching Gary and Nora. "Gary, I see you've made a friend." I crossed my arms, aiming an inquisitive look at Nora.

Nora smirked and said, "Hey, old man, what brings you to my home away from home?"

I smiled to hide my concern, opting to follow her lead. "This is Sam's dad," I said, pointing to Gary. "What are you doing here, delinquent? You people watching in a new venue?"

She scrunched her face up. "You mean Angel?"

I offered a half smile. "Yeah, this is Angel's dad."

Nora turned to Gary. "Aren't you glad you're here with me instead of with those two old men?"

Gary laughed. "My sons are old men?"

She nodded vigorously. "You wouldn't believe how they acted when they found out I was sitting at the airport people watching." She aimed a glare at me. "This one,"—she pointed at me with fingernails covered in dark purple nail polish and yellow smiley faces—"made me leave because it was too dangerous," she mocked. "They walked me to my bike like they were my parents." She crossed her arms and released a deep, exaggerated breath.

"My boys?" Gary looked between us.

"Yeah, but that was in Raleigh. What are you doing here, Nora?"

She shrugged. "My doctors weren't able to give me the treatments I need. My grandma and I are up here going between this place and some big shot place in Baltimore."

My heart lurched. This young girl was. . . I swallowed. *She's barely lived.*

"What are you doing after this? Where's your grandma?"

"Probably going home." She shrugged, pointing to a tiny woman with short gray hair in the waiting room. "She waits over there."

I nodded. "Okay. I'll be right back."

I approached Nora's grandmother and sat beside her. She shifted, eyeing me, and I almost laughed because a lot of people took one look at me with my tattoos and eyeliner and judged me. They all thought I was some drug addict or degenerate.

"Ma'am," I said, offering her the warmest smile I could. "This is gonna sound weird, but I met your granddaughter at an airport a few months ago." I pointed to Nora, who was back to giggling with Gary. "See, I live in Raleigh and was picking up my partner at the airport. I ran into her there."

She smiled and looked at Nora like her heart was utterly broken. "I hope she didn't bother you too much. I think she's lonely and likes to meet new people."

I shook my head. "Honestly, she was a peach. You can imagine my surprise seeing her here."

She nodded. "I had to sell our home." Her lip quivered. "The treatment is getting so expensive, and the doctors in Raleigh have tried everything, but it isn't making a difference."

My heart broke for this woman. Sam and I were struggling ourselves, and Gary's battle had only begun.

"How long has she been fighting?"

"Two years." Her fingers twisted in the strap of her purse. "We thought she was in remission, but it came back."

I grabbed her hand, unable to find the words both of us knew couldn't change anything.

"I was wondering if you and Nora would like to come to my parents' home after this?" She looked confused, glancing between me and the rest of the waiting room.

"Why would you want to do that?"

I aimed my gaze at Gary. "You see that man Nora's talking to?"

She nodded.

"That's my partner's dad, and he's having a rough go of it lately. I think having Nora with him might keep that spark in his eyes that's there right now."

We watched Nora and Gary for a few minutes before she finally spoke again. "Young man, what is your name?"

"Ashton, but call me Ash."

"Ash," she said. "It's nice to meet you." She shook my hand. "Regina."

"Regina, what kind of food do you both like?"

Regina and I spoke for a while longer before I excused myself to the restroom. Dragging my hands over my face while taking deep breaths, I tried to push the thoughts rushing through my mind away. They were nothing but worst-case scenarios. Conjured images of Gary's death. A man who acted as a father to me. A man who raised and loved my best friend. The most amazing person I had ever known. The man who was a father to Angela. As far as our family was concerned, our biological father was nothing. No one. To Angie, Gary was her dad. And Mom, suffering once more. I couldn't. . . I pulled my phone from my pocket, my fingers shaking as I hit Sam's contact.

It barely had time to ring before Sam picked up.

"Babe, is everything okay?" His voice instantly soothed me, and I wanted to wrap myself in his arms.

"Hi, Angel," I said, my voice cracking.

"Baby?" I could hear the worry in his voice. "What's wrong?"

I bit my lip, fighting through the emotion trying to crush my throat. "Can you stop by the nice little Italian restaurant by your office on your way home? I'll text you what to order."

"Sure, but why do you sound like you're crying?"

A tear slid down my cheek. "Because I am, Angel."

"Is Dad okay?"

I swallowed past the tightening lump. "He's fine. I'm um, I'm okay. We're having some guests over tonight, okay?"

"Ash, you're worrying me."

"Don't, we're fine. I swear. I'm just feeling a lot right now."

"Do you need anything? Should I go there? You're still at the cancer center, right?"

"Don't come."

His voice shook as he said, "You don't have to be brave for me."

I sucked in a deep breath before letting it out. "I know I don't, but Gary doesn't need me crying."

"Where are you right now?"

"Bathroom." I chuckled. "I'm hiding in the fucking bathroom."

"I'm sorry," he whispered.

"Don't. You're the one who always grounds me. We can't both fall apart."

He laughed, but it was strained. "Okay, Ash. We can only fall apart on alternating days. You get today, and I'll get tomorrow."

"Sounds perfect."

"Compromise for the win."

I chuckled. "Thanks, Sammy."

"Always, my love."

"I'm good now. I'm gonna head back to Gary."

"Okay. I love you, Ash."

"Love you too."

I hung up, then stared at myself in the mirror. My eyes were a little glossy, but thankfully, it wasn't easy to tell I'd been crying. I turned on the water and leaned over the sink, watching the water rush down the drain.

You can be strong. You can hold on.

I cupped my hands together, gathering water, then splashed it over my face.

Hours later, I parked near the front door of the house, and Regina pulled up behind me. I hopped out, moving around the car to help Gary out. We made it up the stairs seconds before Nora and Regina.

"Wow, Gary, you have a nice place," Nora said.

He laughed as I opened the door, letting everyone in.

Mom rounded the corner from the living room, taking in the sight of everyone. "Hey, Ma. We have some friends for dinner, and Sam is bringing food, so don't worry about cooking tonight."

"What is this?"

"Jane, I have a story for you. Let's sit in the living room," Gary said, swapping my arm for Mom's.

Mom glanced back at me, her eyebrow raised in a questioning manner as she followed Gary.

"Nora, Regina," I said, backing away from them toward the front door, "I've got a bit of an errand to run, but I'll be back. Promise not to cause too much trouble." I winked at Nora, then added, "Angel will be here with dinner soon."

Chapter 30

Sam

When I finally pulled up to the house, I parked beside Angie's car, directly behind a little blue sedan. My Jeep, which Ash had been driving, was nowhere to be found. I shut my car off, grabbed the bags of food Ash had asked for, and hopped out. Pulling my phone from my pocket, I glanced at the notifications and swiped open my phone as I headed for the door. Ash had sent me a text, so I opened it, hoping he'd explained what I was walking into.

Ash: Everyone is in the house. I had to see Lex for something. I'll be home in twenty minutes.

Lex? A pang of jealousy twisted my stomach. The lawsuit with Leo and my dad fighting for his life had me on edge. I knew Ash would never cheat on me. He wouldn't do that, but sometimes the thought crept in anyway.

I shoved my phone back in my pocket and breezed through the front door. The overhead light in the foyer was on, and laughter filled the house.

There was something about hearing so many voices that both warmed my chest and sent a cold shot of terror through my veins.

I slipped into the kitchen, setting all the to-go containers on the counter before I found myself in the living room where my family sat, chatting with a random old lady and a teenager.

"What's going on?" I asked, stepping into the room.

All eyes turned to me, and Dad smiled. It was warm and filled with love. It almost made me forget he was in pain.

"Son," he said, beckoning me closer. "You've met Nora, but this is her grandmother, Regina."

"Nora?" I searched my memories for the name or even her face, but I had nothing. I was blank. She looked up at me expectantly. "I'm sorry, I don't remember." I shook her hand like it was our first time meeting because, for me, it was. I turned to Regina and took her hand. "Nice to meet you."

Nora flopped onto the loveseat across from Dad and Jane, where Angie sat on the floor between them.

"So rude, Sammy, not remembering someone you met," Angie said in a condescending tone.

I aimed a glare at her because I was horrible at remembering people.

"It's okay if you don't remember me, Angel," Nora said.

I spun so fast to look at her that I almost pulled a muscle in my neck. "What did you call me?"

She sat forward, shrugging her shoulders like it was nothing. "Angel."

My face pulled together, holding her stare with mine. "Only Ash calls me that. How do you know about that?"

"Wait, Sam, Ash calls you angel?" Angie laughed. "Are you serious?"

"Stop it, Angela," Jane chided. "I think it's cute."

I ignored them and stepped closer to Nora, squinting at her and finally taking her in. She was young, but definitely a teen. Her hair was short and appeared brittle. Her eyes were like Dad's, dull like she never slept. Where her cheeks should've been plump, they were sunken. She was thin and frail-looking. Her tiny wrists poked out of the baggy sleeves of her hoodie. Her fingers were thin and bony as they curled into a fist.

Is she sick, too?

"Where did we meet the first time? I don't remember," I said, moving my attention away from her possible illness.

She leaned back and smiled wide, showing her teeth. "The airport in Raleigh. Ash was waiting for you, and I bet him that his girlfriend would ghost him like this other guy I'd seen that morning."

Something at the back of my mind tried to poke its way into my consciousness as I sat beside Jane and tried to push through the cloud of faded memories.

Nora continued, "Anyway, he won the bet because you showed up and made out like a couple of weirdos."

Angie exaggerated a gasp, mocking me. "Angel made out with Ash in public and in front of a child?" She clutched her chest, feigning horror. "A child!"

Nora giggled. "Oh my god, no, because it's burned into my memories forever." She slipped off the couch and crawled to Angie, the pair of them cackling. "There was tongue. I saw tongue."

I threw my head back with a groan, rubbing my hands down my face.

"Then," Nora said, laughing, "they lectured me about being in the airport alone and walked me outside to my bike. I got this whole spiel about hanging out with people my age and avoiding dangerous situations." She cackled again. "Then they both go and get on a motorcycle. Talk about dangerous."

My stomach dropped as the memories flooded me. The first time I flew to Raleigh to see Ash. How I'd asked him to keep his motorcycle gear on while he. . . "Okay, so that's enough of that conversation," I said. "How about we eat?"

"Oh no, you aren't getting out of this one, Sammy." Angie clamped down on my knee with her clawlike fingers. "You were flying down to see Ash?"

Ash and I hadn't told our family much about our relationship. They didn't know we had been flying back and forth every weekend for months, only that we'd been seeing each other and visiting when we could. I had been the reason to keep the fact from them because if they had known how many times Ash was in town and didn't stop in to see them, they'd be insanely upset.

I stood, marching into the kitchen, hoping to escape the awkwardness of the situation. When I rounded the corner from the hall into the kitchen, Ash sauntered in with a clear container in his hand and a grin that lit up my heart.

"My love," I said, almost pleading as he neared me. "Please save me from them."

He set the container on the counter before wrapping me in his arms. "What's wrong?"

I groaned and dropped my forehead on his shoulder, soaking in the comfort he always filled me with. I pulled back and said, "They're just so—"

"Sam," Angie yelled as she charged into the room. She halted, quickly changing the target of her—whatever emotion she was dancing around. "Ash." She approached us with a scowl. "How come you let *Angel* ride your bike with you, but you told me no one is allowed to be your backpack?"

Ash tightened his hold on my back as he beamed with a twinkle in his eyes. "Angel is special."

"Angel is special," she mocked. She reached around us, grabbing the container off the counter. "What's this? Brownies?" She moved to open the container, but Ash snatched it from her before she could. "Hey!"

"This isn't for you." He hugged the container to his chest like he was protecting something precious.

"Who is it for?" She crossed her arms, glaring at me.

"Don't look at me like that. It's not mine." *I hope.*

Ash nodded. "It's specially made for Gary. None of you can have any." He winked and disappeared into the hallway. Moments later, laughter erupted from the living room while Angie continued staring me down like I'd somehow done something to her.

"Angie, why are you looking at me like that?"

She stepped forward, gazing up at me. "Why are you suddenly all special?"

I laughed and grabbed her shoulders. "Are you jealous?"

She shrugged, pouting. "Maybe a little."

I pulled her tight. "No need to be jealous. Ash loves you and spoils you more than you deserve."

Her gasp was followed by a gentle punch to my stomach. "You're such a jerk."

"Yeah, yeah." I released her and rounded the counter to grab plates. "Help me set the table so we can get everyone fed. Dad has to be starving."

Her face drooped. "You know he's lost five more pounds since this time last week. Mom says the doctors are worried."

"I know."

I swallowed. I didn't like talking about Dad and his deteriorating health. The cancer was spreading even with the chemo. Next week, he was supposed to have more tests run to check in on the spread, but from what I'd read online, his type of lung cancer didn't have great outlooks.

Angie and I set the table before forcing everyone into the kitchen. Dad was downing the last bite of a brownie while talking with Ash at the edge of the couch. They whispered to each other like they were the only ones in on a secret. While everyone filtered into the kitchen, I neared them.

"Everything okay?" I asked.

Dad nodded and rose from the couch. "Just great, Sam." He rested his hand on my shoulder, giving me a squeeze.

He walked away, leaving Ash and me alone.

Ash closed the container with at least ten more brownies, rising to his feet with a grunt. "Damn, I'm gettin' old." He brushed past me with a chuckle. "My damn knees hurt from kneeling for only a few minutes."

I shoved him playfully. "We aren't even thirty yet. Don't talk like that."

He slung his arm around my waist and tugged me close. "Careful, Angel, you'll have me thinking you want a repeat of the time you asked me to be rough with you."

I bit my lip, shooting a glance toward the kitchen. "I wouldn't mind a repeat, but you don't have your bike."

He leaned closer, his lips nearly touching mine. His breath brushed over my lips as he smiled. "I don't need my bike to give you what you want."

"I-I—"

"Ash, Sam," Jane called. "Come eat."

Ash kissed me before dragging me into the kitchen, where our table was packed so tight a folding chair had to be brought out of storage, and Angie, Ash, and I had to squeeze together on one side.

Ash grabbed a container with three pounds of spaghetti—which cost a small fortune—and piled his plate high. "I'm starved."

He turned and hovered the container over my plate before pushing a huge pile over the edge. The ball of noodles hit my plate with a splat, sending red sauce everywhere. A glob hit my cheek and neck. I was positive my shirt was speckled with little orange dots.

"Babe." I pushed Ash's arm away. "Why?"

He laughed and set the container down with a devilish smirk. "Sorry," he said, licking sauce off his thumb. "Didn't mean to splash you with it." He leaned closer and added, "Here, let me help." Before I could register his actions, his warm, wet tongue hit my cheek.

Panic hit me, overshadowing anything about it that I could've enjoyed. We were in front of our family, a teenage girl, and a grandmother.

This is so inappropriate.

I scanned the table, but no one seemed to notice. They were all engrossed in their own worlds, talking amongst themselves.

Ash pulled back, his eyes bright with laughter. It had been a few weeks since he'd smiled like this.

"Stop it," I whispered. "Nora is a child."

He bit his lip. "Fine, but you have a little—" he swiped his thumb over my neck and brought it to his lips—"sauce." His tongue darted over the sauce as he held my gaze.

I threw my forearm up, catching his throat. "Stop it."

He laughed, pulling away as he raised my hand, pressed it against his lips, and kissed my knuckles.

"Boys, stop behaving like children," Jane said without looking at us.

"Yes, ma'am," I said, shoving Ash again.

The sun bathed the room in light, but I couldn't fully enjoy it. My mind was consumed with anxiety while I impatiently waited for the room to fill. I was a wreck. I would finally hear the decision about my lawsuit with Leo. The police had interviewed me multiple times. They turned Victory X and my personal life upside down. The police and lawyers had dragged my friends into giving interviews. Sean stopped speaking to me. Rainie claimed she didn't want to pick sides and told me not to speak to her until my name was cleared, but fuck, my friends honestly thought Leo was telling the truth, and that hurt more than all of this bullshit.

My employees at Victory X had more faith that I didn't do what Leo claimed than my closest friends. It was a special kind of betrayal.

Ash did his best to comfort and support me through this, but having Rainie and Sean flat-out tell me they thought I was some kind of sexual predator only left me feeling more alone than ever. I should've known better. I never should have expected people to stand by me when they didn't have to. My mother had been the worst of them all. She was the life lesson I should've kept in mind.

It was fine. I had Imogene, Hannah, and the rest of my team at Victory X. Most importantly, I had Ash and our family.

They never believed a word from Leo. Not for a second.

Our family had embraced my relationship with Ash and supported me through this farce of a lawsuit, all while supporting Dad through chemo.

I knew I would get through this. Still didn't stop the pang of betrayal. And definitely didn't settle the anxiety swirling through me at every second of the day.

Hannah and our team of lawyers had been hard at work for months, but we expected to win. It helped that I had messages from Leo from before he worked at Victory X about setting up a time to get together. The old dick pic they found in my camera reel from a random accidental upload to cloud storage from my phone to my computer helped a lot. The picture was sent to me two years before I created Victory X.

Phone records. Social media posts. It was all helping my case.

But most of the whole claim was based on Leo's word. He didn't have proof.

Hannah expected the whole case would be dismissed and that we would win our countersuit for malicious prosecution since this was clearly revenge.

The door creaked open, and Imogene popped into the room. "Hello, Sam," she said, placing a folder on the table before sitting on my left. "Did you manage to get some sleep last night?"

"A couple hours."

Hannah stepped through the open door a moment later. Her curly black hair bounced around her round face. "Morning." She adjusted the collar of her dress shirt and sat on my right before rolling her sleeves up her dark skin, where a fresh scab trailed over her forearm.

I pointed to it and asked, "Cat got you again?"

She ran her fingers over the raised scab. "Little jerk tried to fight me for my dinner last night."

"You're really convincing me to get a cat here," I said.

Hannah had tried talking me into getting a cat a few different times over the years, but I didn't think a cat was meant for me. Seeing her come in beat up with random scratches only added to the cons list I was keeping in my head.

"He's a peach, I swear." She flashed a fake smile. "I promise I would never ever trade him in." Her fake smile grew bigger, and her eyes widened. "I love Mr. Muffins with all my heart."

I chuckled. "Say it enough, and it will be true?"

Our laughter died when the judge, an older gray-haired man, stepped into the room. He looked no younger than seventy but was kind the few times I had spoken with him.

A woman, the stenographer, slipped into the room shortly after him and took her position at the corner. Watching her type, never missing a beat, had been the most impressive part of this entire process.

The judge sank into the leather chair at the head of the table and cleared his throat. "Mr. Bradford and his lawyer are absent?"

Hannah nodded, "We have not seen them yet, sir."

The judge glanced at his watch, then said, "I'll give them five minutes."

I dropped my hands to my lap, wringing them to release my nerves. It would benefit me if Leo and his lawyer never showed up. Hell, a minute after the five-minute limit would be a blessing. But as the minutes passed, and we neared the time limit arbitrarily set by the judge, Leo and his lawyer, Rick Gibson, walked through the door with their smug grins.

"You're late," the judge snapped.

They apologized as they sat across the table from me, their stupid smirks fraying my nerves.

"Let's get started since Mr. Bradford and Mr. Gibson thought it acceptable to waste our time this morning."

The room was silent, and I could feel Leo's eyes on me. I couldn't bring myself to look at him.

"I have reviewed the statements and heard your arguments, but I can not, in good faith, accept the claim Mr. Bradford has brought forth against Mr. Pearce and his company, Victory X."

He leaned back, looking between the two sides of the table. I was careful to keep my face as plain and emotionless as possible.

"With that said, I do agree that Mr. Bradford filed his claim with malicious intent against Mr. Pearce." He directed his pointed gaze to Leo. "Mr. Bradford,

Mr. Pearce's malicious prosecution claim, I believe, is valid based solely on the information presented to this court by the police, Mr. Bradford, and Mr. Pearce's team. I'm hereby ordering you to pay the full sum of damages outlined by Mr. Pearce and his company, Victory X." He turned his attention to me. "Please provide Mr. Bradford and Mr. Gibson with the paperwork you provided my office this morning."

Hannah nodded and slid a packet of papers toward Rick and Leo. "This outlines the fees incurred by Victory X and Mr. Pearce, loss of contracts because of these claims, as well as the terms of the restraining order as requested by Mr. Pearce and his partner Mr. Emerson."

"If I'm not mistaken, there was a request for a non-disclosure agreement?" The judge asked.

"Yes, sir," I replied.

The judge nodded, motioning for Hannah to continue.

Hannah slid another paper toward Leo. "This is the non-disclosure agreement, outlining the proprietary information Mr. Bradford was privy to during his time at Victory X. This agreement states you may not disclose or discuss any information you are aware of for four years, given you were aware of important projects which have not gone public."

Leo glanced at his lawyer before nodding to Hannah. His face was completely blank, but I had a feeling he was shitting bricks.

Hannah added, "Another clause within this NDA is that Mr. Bradford will withhold from recruiting, hiring, or discussing business with all Victory X employees for one year."

Leo pinched his lips together in a tight line.

"Will there be any problems?" the judge asked.

"None from us," Rick said.

I wanted to laugh in their faces. I'd heard the rumors about him trying to poach a couple of my best-performing developers. Leo couldn't offer them a better deal than I was already giving. Instead, they told on him like a kid tattling on the school bully.

"It's settled then," the judge said.

The judge dismissed us, forcing us to file into the hallway as a group.

"Let's go," I said to Hannah and Imogene, placing my hand on their backs to direct them to the exit down the hall.

We were silent, walking through the building. I could feel Rick and Leo following behind us. It had my shoulders tensing with an uncomfortable prickle crawling up my spine.

Imogene opened the door, letting Hannah through, and I followed closely. The cool breeze hit me when we stepped outside, where the building led to steps near a road and parking garage.

October had arrived in the blink of an eye, and with it, the muggy summer heat finally faded to a comfortable high sixties filled with brisk breezes and autumn colors.

Relief flooded me, easing my tense muscles when Ash looked up from his phone with a crooked grin. He pushed off the brick half-wall he'd been leaning on and walked toward me.

"Tell me good news," he said, wrapping me in his arms.

"What are you doing here?" I asked, holding him, settling into the comfort his crushing hold gave me.

"I'm here for this exact moment, Sammy." He kissed the side of my head. "Now tell me. What happened?"

Leo and his lawyer breezed past us, keeping their eyes averted.

I smiled, then looked back at Ash. "We won. They signed every document."

"Wasn't very hard," Hannah said, giggling. "We're going to the coffee shop around the corner. When you two are done smooching in public, join us."

I laughed at her before mouthing, "Thank you," and returned my focus to Ash. "Victory X is free of him."

"No," Ash whispered, "you're free of him."

I bit my lip, holding back the pain clawing at my heart.

"What is it?" Ash asked, pressing our foreheads together.

I worked my lip between my teeth before saying, "Why do people always hurt me?"

Ash's hands cupped my face. "I don't have an answer for you, Angel, but you'll always have me."

263

I kissed him, hoping he knew how much that meant to me. How much he meant to me.

Ash pulled away and spun to stand at my side and said, "Let's go celebrate with the girls at that coffee shop. Come on, sexy." He smacked my ass and started walking toward the street corner.

I shook my head and followed him before pulling my phone from my pocket. I opened my last conversation with Rainie and Sean, rereading the last messages from them.

Rainie: I'm sorry, Sam, but after everything Leo has told us, I can't believe you. Besides, what you did is fucked up.

Sean: I'm with Rain on this one. I can't believe you were using Leo like that. He has feelings, too. Even if he's lying, you still hurt him. You hurt us by never telling us. I don't even know who you are anymore.

I didn't bother replying to them. It felt like they weren't willing to listen to anything I had to say. I tried to meet up with them to tell them my side of the story, but they refused.

Ash slung his arm over my shoulder and leaned in close. "Whatcha doin'?"

"Texting them."

He peered down at my phone with a frown. "Say your peace, then whatever they decide is on them."

I nodded, sucking in a deep breath before letting my fingers race across my phone screen. When I hit send, I was both terrified and relieved.

Me: I want you both to know I won the court case. I hope you can find it in yourselves to hear me when I say this. I'm sorry that I treated Leo like he's disposable. I'm sorry that I never told you we were friends with benefits. And I'm so fucking sorry that it caused this riff between us. While I am sorry about those things, none of that changes that I'm in love with Ash. My offer to have a conversation is still on the table, but I refuse to accept that I'm a horrible person when I never once lied to Leo. Maybe that makes it worse in your eyes. I'm not sure. If you ever want to talk, you know how to find me.

I pocketed my phone and slid my hand into Ash's. "So, coffee with Imogene and Hannah, then home to celebrate?" I grinned at him.

"I like this plan," Ash said, tugging me down the street toward the coffee shop. "This time, I have a surprise for you." His smile was so wide his cheeks dimpled, and his eyes creased.

"I like surprises. Does it involve your body?"

He pursed his lips to the side like he was thinking about it. "It might involve my body." He winked and squeezed my hand. "And someone else's body might be required."

We laughed, ambling through the coffee shop doors like we didn't have a care in the world. We found Imogene and Hannah sitting near the street view window at a round table with two coffee mugs waiting for me and Ash.

While I was upset that my friends had walked away from me, I was happy with where I ended up because my relationships with those who had stuck by my side only flourished.

With the loss, I had found myself a few new beginnings.

Chapter 31
Ash

Nora and Regina had been coming by often since the first night I invited them over. Gary seemed to enjoy having them around, though he wasn't one to voice it. Angie treated Nora like a little sister. It was adorable to see them together. Mom loved having two more mouths to stuff full of cakes and cookies every weekend—not that either of them appeared unhappy about the arrangement. Mom and Regina had grown close, even exchanging family recipes.

After Mom's parents passed, she had been alone except for our tiny little family. Having Nora and Regina around had shown me what my family could have been. I didn't remember much about my extended family. There were some blips of memories here and there. They were mostly fuzzy and dark. No matter how hard I tried to remember family holidays and events—my mind was blank. I had nothing.

Maybe it was better that way.

When Regina called yesterday to tell me Nora had gone into remission, it took all of my willpower to keep the secret from my family. Happy couldn't even describe the fullness in my chest. The girl was too young to fight so hard for a shot at life. I desperately wanted her to be okay. I wanted her to have a future where she could grow up. See the world. Find love. Whatever she wanted, she deserved it.

While I was happy for Nora, standing in front of Gary, handing him a chocolate chip cookie infused with weed so he could eat dinner, tore me apart. Gary's condition was worsening. The doctors were worried his cancer was too aggressive for his current treatment. We were in a holding pattern, waiting on more test results before we could do anything else.

"Eat it fast before Angie sees it," I said. "She'll be upset that I'm sneaking you treats again."

His frail laugh before he shoved it into his mouth, hiding it from everyone's view, added one more fracture to my cracking heart.

My chest ached when I took Gary's thin arm and led him to the minivan, where our family climbed in, filling the air with laughter. None of them had any clue where I planned to take them, yet the excitement that filled them when I said I had a surprise was reminiscent of Christmas morning moments before opening the first gift under the tree.

Once Gary was secured in the back with Angie and Mom, I hopped into the driver's seat and planted my hand on Sam's thigh. He wrapped his hand around mine and squeezed.

"So, do we get to know where you're taking us?" Angie asked, leaning over the center console to rest her chin on my arm.

"Do you not understand the definition of a surprise?" I said, turning the van down the driveway and onto the road. "Now, sit back."

"I like to know things. What if I want to invite Zay?"

"Maybe he isn't invited," I said jokingly.

Izayah was invited. He was Regina and Nora's ride. Angie's work enemy had turned boyfriend a few weeks ago. I still wasn't sure about Izayah, but it was too soon to tell.

Twenty minutes later, I pulled into the handicapped parking space in front of a far too expensive restaurant. I ignored the questions from the peanut gallery in the back seats and hopped out of the van to help Gary.

Sam appeared beside me and said, "What did you do?"

"What could you possibly be referring to?" I grinned like an idiot, opening the van's side door to help Gary out.

"Ash," Sam whispered my name like he was both angry and curious.

"You'll see," I said. "Now help your dad so I can talk to the people inside."

Sam took Gary's arm, and I escaped into the building.

The only reason I could afford this place was because I'd backed out of my lease for my apartment, sold most of my things, and had been splitting bills with Sam, allowing me to put all that extra money into savings.

The host at the front greeted me when I approached them.

"Hi, I have a reservation for the patio under Emerson."

They nodded and scanned the computer screen before saying, "You can go through those doors over there." They pointed to massive French doors that looked out onto a sleek dark brown patio with lush flowers potted around the railing that overlooked an enormous manmade lake.

"Perfect," I said, rushing outside to corral my family through the restaurant to the back patio, where I hoped we could all enjoy ourselves for a few hours before remembering that our lives were in shambles.

Purple and yellow flowers covered every table with big centerpieces. Small string lights hung across the patio like something out of a movie, and purple candles surrounded a three-tiered cake on one of the tables. The view was the main reason I'd chosen the place. A park was visible on the other side of the lake, where a group played a game of soccer.

For October, it was a bit warmer than usual. The air was mildly humid, a tad too warm in direct sunlight, but under the umbrellas was the perfect temperature.

"Ash, what on earth is this?" Mom asked, putting her hands on her hips with an eyebrow raised at me.

"Okay," I said, holding my hands up in surrender. "Today is a special day."

Sam helped Gary sit at a shaded table before turning to me inquisitively.

"Nora has gone into remission, and we're throwing her a surprise party." I beamed at them, waiting for the news to sink in.

"Oh my god," Angie screeched. "Are you serious?"

I nodded, my smile so wide my cheeks hurt.

"That's wonderful," Gary said before a deep cough erupted from him.

"Is she on her way?" Mom asked.

"Yep, Regina and Nora are on their way. Nora thinks we're just having dinner."

I looked at Sam, expecting to see him happy, but his frown was deep and his eyes glistened with the threat of tears. I had the sense he was feeling the same as me. Happy for Nora, but realizing Gary's chance of remission was practically nonexistent.

While our family discussed Nora, I moved to Sam's side and dragged him to the railing, away from everyone.

"You okay, Angel?"

His lips drew into a tight line, and his gaze shifted to the lake.

"I know it hurts," I whispered, tugging him against me. I kissed the side of his head, wrapping my arms around him. "We can't lose hope. Okay?"

Sam nodded, nuzzling his face in my neck.

"Do you want to talk about it?"

"No. If I do, I'll cry."

"It's okay to cry," I said.

"I don't want to cause a scene." He pulled back, meeting my eyes. "This is supposed to be a celebration."

"Always thinking of others," I whispered, then kissed him.

"Oh," Mom exclaimed. "Nora, honey, come here."

Sam and I turned to find a short head of dark hair with a bright smile emerging from the restaurant's doorway. Nora wore a flowy baby blue sundress with tiny white flowers dotting the fabric. It was the brightest thing I'd ever seen her wear.

Mom rushed to Nora and swooped her into a hug.

"Congratulations. Ash told us the great news," Mom said, pulling away to allow Angie in.

Regina appeared with Izayah on her arm, a wide grin, and a laugh that warmed my chest. "Careful, she's still fragile. Not too rough."

"Stop it, Nana, I'm not glass," Nora grumbled, but she couldn't stop her grin even as she tried to glare.

Gary cleared his throat and beckoned Nora to him. She threw herself into his arms. The sight of them filled my chest with an aching tug. I bit the inside of my lip, holding back the building tears.

"Ash, you could've told me Zay would be here," Angie said before falling against him with a satisfied smile. "You two are sneaky."

Zay laughed, and his deep voice boomed when he said, "Surprises are meant to be sneaky."

"Okay, okay," I said, waving my hands around. "Who wants food? It's all on me tonight, so have whatever you want. The whole patio is ours. We can be here for the next four hours."

"Big baller," Angie said. "I'm getting the most expensive thing on the menu."

Everyone laughed and sat around Gary under a covered table. Conversation filled the air. Boisterous laughter. Noise from the soccer game across the lake. Muted music from inside the restaurant.

It was nice. Something I knew we would remember for a long time.

Sam bumped my shoulder with his and leaned in. "If you need help with the bill, I can. We both know Angie will actually get the most expensive item on the menu." He chuckled.

I smiled at him, running my hand through his hair. "Not to worry. You won't need to pitch in. I've got it covered."

"Oh?" He smiled, backing away. "So, you are a big baller?"

I chuckled. "No."

"Sounds like you are."

"Sammy."

"Looks like I'm ordering the most expensive thing on the menu and maybe I'll see what their most expensive liquor is." He raised his eyebrow and smirked. "What do you want to drink, baby? Whiskey? Top shelf?" He backed away until he reached the table. "Whole bottle?"

I laughed. "God help me and my wallet tonight."

"Let's get a picture before we eat," Mom said, motioning for everyone to move closer.

"I vote Zay takes the picture because he has the longest arms," Angie said.

The guy was probably on his way to seven feet tall. Bald head, with a thick, long beard and a bit of a gut. He was a big dude. Angie called him her teddy bear. It was cute. I hoped things worked out for them.

"Come on," I said, slinging my arm over Sam's shoulder, leaning closer to Gary. "Zay, sit on the end with Angie so you can get us all."

"All right." He held his phone up in the air, positioning it until he found the perfect angle. "One," he said, starting the countdown.

"Wait, wait," Nora said, jumping up from her seat. "I want to be next to Angel." She rushed around the table and slid in next to Sam before holding up her hand with a peace sign. "Ready."

We all laughed, and Zay snapped the picture.

Chapter 32

Sam

"Dad, wait," I said, rounding the back of the van to pull the wheelchair from the trunk. "Stop being so stubborn." I grabbed the folded wheelchair and set it up while Ash tried to keep Dad from getting out alone.

The man could barely walk without assistance, but that didn't stop him from trying. I never knew how stubborn my dad was until he was told he couldn't do something.

He's going to give me a heart attack.

"I still can't believe you've never been to a single zoo," Angie said, rounding the trunk with Nora at her side.

"Mama always said I was too sick to go." Nora's smile wavered before adding, "Then she was gone, and Nana is too old to walk around the zoo."

Angie laughed and grabbed the other folded wheelchair, smiling at me before turning her attention back to Nora. "Good thing we brought her the spare wheelchair, then."

I rolled the wheelchair for Dad around the car and stopped abruptly at the sight of Ash holding my father up against the closed side door. He fought off a smile while scowling.

"Your timing could've been better," Ash said to me.

I chuckled and kicked the wheel locks into place before helping Ash sit my dad in the wheelchair.

"Dad, you could learn some patience."

"I didn't want to be trapped in the car while everyone else left me behind," he grumbled.

"Dad, no one is leaving you behind." I rolled my eyes. "Put your feet up." I pointed to the footrest he wasn't using.

Dad groaned like he wanted to protest but put his feet on the rest and leaned back.

Ash passed behind me with a grin, sliding his fingers over my lower back before heading toward the Zoo's entrance where Jane, Angie, Nora, and Regina were waiting for us.

"Look at that, Dad," I said.

"What?"

"You took so long being a pain that we're the last ones ready."

He pulled a baseball cap from the side pocket of the wheelchair and mumbled something I couldn't hear, sliding his cap over his head to hide the hair loss from the chemo.

Watching my dad's progression with lung cancer had been an experience that was difficult to put into words. A man I pictured like Superman, indestructible and unshakeable, became frail and fearful. My father hid his fears with an attitude and grumpy remarks. He didn't have to explain; the doctors had done enough of that. We simply embraced his personality shift for what it was. Some days, I leaned into it, egging him on until I could get a laugh out of him.

Ash and I had talked about how important it was to make memories like this with Dad. We both knew where it was leading. There was no coming back from this. Dad's doctors had tried to sell us on hope, but we all knew.

And Dad is tired of fighting.

Jane pushed Regina in the other wheelchair, and Angie and Nora walked beside them, pointing at an enclosure with colorful birds and trees covered in deep reds and oranges swaying with the gentle breeze.

November had come too quickly. It was almost Thanksgiving, and I had questioned how we had gotten here. How we had grown close to a random girl and her grandmother. How Ash and I became a couple. How our family could accept it immediately. It all baffled me.

I tried not to go down the *what-if* rabbit hole, but it was difficult. I spent a lifetime too afraid of the unknown, only to discover I could've had it sooner if I hadn't been scared. If I had taken a leap. Voiced my feelings. I could have had this sooner.

Ash's hand landed on my shoulder, and he leaned close, whispering, "Stop thinking so hard. You're going to get wrinkles." He rubbed his fingers over my forehead.

I looked into his eyes and smiled. "You always know."

"Hard not to. You looked all angry at nothing."

"They have lions," Nora shouted, rushing over and bouncing on her toes. "Lions! Can we go see?"

As a group, we peered through the fence overlooking the lion enclosure. A lone lion with a thick mane lay sprawled lazily in the grass surrounded by three lionesses. I had never seen one in person. They seemed big on TV but felt bigger in real life.

"Sammy," Dad croaked, and I bent closer to hear him, "do you remember when we came here to see the lions?"

I shook my head. "I don't"

Much like Ash, my memories from childhood were few and far between. I was lucky to have some memories of Ash, but many of those were missing as well. Ash seemed to have more memories of us as young kids, but mine weren't there until around middle school, and even those were fuzzy or simply gone. I had feelings of what I knew my time with Ash had been like back then. A few memories here and there of watching wrestling on his tiny bedroom TV, curled up together on his single beanbag chair. It was snippets of moments for me. Anything related to my parents didn't exist until I was ten, but many were lost. Gone. Empty.

"Well, you were about seven, and you begged me to come see the lions." He chuckled, causing a string of deep coughs that shook his entire body. When the coughs died down, he continued, "I brought you on a Saturday, the busiest day of the week. It was August, so the temperature was sweltering and humid. I was unprepared, and we had to buy cups of water from the food stand where they charged me three dollars a cup. Damn criminal."

Jane laughed, wheeling Regina closer to listen to Dad.

"I'm telling you, honey, six dollars for water back then is a racket."

"I can't believe you let them get away with that," Regina replied. "I woulda raised hell."

That got a laugh from us all.

"You laugh now. You should've seen me thirty years ago."

"Are you a haggler, Regina?" Ash asked.

"You bet your butt I am," she huffed, shifting her purse on her lap. "Those places cheat you out of hard-earned money."

"So, you paid six dollars for water?" I said, trying to get Dad back to his story.

"Yes, yes," he said, shifting in the wheelchair. "After we got the water, we walked all the way to the lion enclosure. Back then, it was in a different spot than this one. It was all the way at the back of the zoo. By the time we got to the enclosure, Sammy was cranky and wanted to go home because he was hot, but I refused to turn around after all the effort. So, we get to the enclosure, and the lions were nowhere to be seen!"

I laughed. "Where were they?"

"I asked an employee where they were. They said the lions were hot and had—on their own—gone into the building where they had access to fans that blow on them."

"Did we go see them inside?" I asked.

"No! There was no viewing area back there," he said, almost shouting, sending himself into another coughing fit.

"So we didn't even get to see the lions that day?" I chuckled, but a part of me desperately wanted to remember this memory with him. It didn't feel like I had been there. It was like my dad was telling a story about a stranger. I had to keep looking at the positives, or the past would swallow me. "Hey, we're here now, and the lions are right there. How about we take some pictures?"

"That's a wonderful idea," Jane said.

We took pictures of the lions, then of ourselves. Dad and I took a picture with the lions visible in the background. We stood around the lion enclosure for over an hour before wandering through the zoo with no planned direction. Nora mostly led the way, seeing something and rushing off to it with Angie chasing after her.

I hoped I would remember this day for the rest of my life. I wanted to keep my memories. I didn't want to lose any more.

On the way to the parking lot, Ash took over pushing Dad. We walked shoulder to shoulder, not saying anything. I wanted to tell him I enjoyed today, yet the pain in my heart was overflowing.

How many more days would Dad have like this? What was the limit? When would it end?

Rich pink and orange lit the sky, setting a gorgeous sunset over the end of an amazing day.

My family was with me. The people in this world I loved with everything I had were with me.

Maybe the end was coming, but it wasn't here yet. I still had time for moments like this. I had time to make more moments. I had time to replace the memories missing from my past.

I needed more memories. I needed more time.

Chapter 33
Ash

My phone rang from the hotel room nightstand, and I fought through the grog of sleep to find it. When my fingers finally landed on the phone, I grabbed it and rolled onto my back, squinting at the bright screen. Sam's name stared back at me, sending my stomach sinking. The few times I'd traveled back to Raleigh in the months I had lived with him, he never called in the mornings.

I tapped the answer icon, pressed the phone to my ear, and said, "Is everything okay?"

I could hear his shuddery intake of breath before he spoke. "Ash," he said, with a waver in his voice, "we're at the hospital." I held my breath. The sting of adrenaline raced through my veins with a jolt. "Dad couldn't walk. He couldn't get out of bed. He—" Sam sucked in a breath. "He said he was having trouble moving his body. That he was in a lot of pain. I didn't know what to do."

"I'm here," I said, wishing I was standing beside him. I slid off the bed and flipped on a light. "I'm on the next plane out of Raleigh." I grabbed jeans from my travel bag and climbed into them. "I'm leaving my hotel right now." I tugged on a shirt as a soft sob came through the line. "Are Mom and Angie with you?"

"They are," he choked.

"Good. Okay, Angel, I need to get to the airport. Do you want me to stay on the phone with you?"

"Yes," he said, barely a whisper.

"You've got me."

I grabbed my Bluetooth earbuds and put them in before brushing my teeth and tossing everything into my bag. There was no rhyme or reason to how it all went into the bag. Nothing got folded. I shoved it in and forced the bag closed until it zipped.

Within minutes, I ordered a rideshare, checked the room one last time, rushed down to the lobby, and checked out so fast that I probably left the receptionist with whiplash.

When the rideshare arrived, I hopped in, tossing my bag beside me on the seat. It was a carry-on because I hated dealing with the luggage claim at the airport. I was grateful for my choices at that moment. While the person drove, I searched for the next flight to Virginia.

"Sammy," I said, breaking the silence. "You still there?"

"I'm here."

"I have a flight that boards in twenty-five minutes." I clicked on the option to book the flight. "Two hours, Angel. Okay? I'll get a ride from the airport to the hospital."

"Okay," he whispered. "I'll let you go so you can get to your flight."

"I love you, Sam."

"I love you too."

The call ended, and I was left with a pit of ice in my gut. The tumors had spread rapidly even with the chemo. Gary had lost most of his hair. He was skin and bones, deteriorating before our eyes, and there was nothing we could do. When his doctors suggested radiation, he'd denied it. I didn't understand why until I researched radiation treatment and read through forums of people talking about their loved ones going through the treatment. There came a point where one wondered which was worse: cancer or the medicine. I didn't think I would want to do it either. Not with so little hope.

The cancer had moved to stage four. The likelihood of Gary making it through had gone from a minuscule chance to next to none. We were still coming to terms with that news.

The driver pulled up to the drop-off zone, and I jumped out, slinging my bag over my shoulder, and pushed through the crowd. I barely registered the chilly bite of December before I was inside, hurrying to the check-in counter.

It took five minutes to check in before I sprinted to the boarding zone.

When I reached my gate, someone near the door called back the first group. I dropped my bag on the floor and leaned against the wall, gulping air like a fish out of water.

My ride was three minutes away. I quickened my pace, jogging through the airport, dodging people and luggage. When I pushed through the exit, a pristine layer of snow shimmered under the morning sunlight. The crunch of my footsteps cracked through the crisp stillness.

Someone brushed against me, apologizing as they rushed to a taxi waiting at the curb. My phone pinged a notification that my ride arrived, and I hurried down the row of cars parked along the edge of the pickup zone. I hopped into the white SUV, and the driver greeted me before taking off.

I was grateful he didn't want to chat. I was moving with single-minded purpose and couldn't stand the idea of small talk with a stranger.

My phone came to life in my hand, and I answered the call immediately.

"Ash, why aren't you in the office with me right now?"

I forced a laugh through the tension in my throat. "I'm in Virginia. Gary's in the hospital."

"Is he okay?"

"Yes, Tae, Gary is in the hospital and is completely okay."

"You fucker. You know what I meant."

I sighed, resting my head on the window. "I don't know this time. Sam seemed really worried."

"I know the last few months have been hard on you and your family. You know I'm here for you. Whatever you need."

Tae was a good friend. He sincerely cared about me, and that extended to the people I loved. I hadn't had many people in my life like him. I looked through the window, watching the snow-covered trees along the highway pass by in a blur.

It was a beautiful morning.

Would Gary make it to Christmas? Would we share a snowy Christmas one last time? I hoped so.

Gary made holidays a big deal when he and Mom married. When I was a kid, I hated it. Holidays reminded me of my asshole father and his toxic family, but Gary slowly filled my memories with good ones. Christmas mornings by the fireplace and a tree decorated with random ornaments. The smell of pine in the hours before the sun came up. Hot chocolate and muffins for breakfast while we all crowded around the tree, opening gifts.

I was grateful to have those memories. The family I had with him and Sam had probably saved me from a lot of the darkness that chased me when I was younger.

"Hell, even if you asked me to fly up there to help you through it. Business. Contracts. All these things can be finalized and handled by our people. Mari is more than capable." Tae broke through my thoughts, dragging me back to the present. "Actually, I think she would rather you and I disappear and let her run everything."

My chest warmed as I laughed. "She loves me, but you? Yeah, she would kick you out on your ass in a heartbeat."

"He's got jokes now?"

"I've always got jokes, but it's hard to see when you're always blocking me with your big head."

"Okay, okay, asshole," Tae said. "Keep me posted when you can. And if you need time off, let me know."

"Thanks, Tae. I appreciate you."

"We aren't doing that, Ash."

"What?"

"Getting all emotional. Save that for when I'm drunk or unconscious."

"Fucking dick. Go back to work."

"Ah, that's more like it." He laughed and hung up.

The car pulled up to the hospital, and I thanked the driver before grabbing my bag and hopping out. I plucked my keys from my pocket and searched for Sam's car. When I found it, I tossed my bag in the trunk, then headed inside.

The person behind the counter gave me a visitor sticker and half-assed instructions on how to get to Gary's room. It took far too long to navigate my way through the maze of corridors and dead ends than it should've. When I made it to Gary's ward, I found a nurse who could direct me to the waiting room in a corner across from the nurses' station.

The waiting room was stark white, with fluorescent lights harshly casting stale white light across the solemn faces of the individuals in the room. Three of which belonged to me. Mom and Angie sat huddled beside each other, wrapped in each other's arms. Sam stood near them, staring up at a tiny TV on the wall with a home renovation show playing.

I thanked the nurse for their help and approached Mom and Angie, kissing them on the top of their heads. "Hey, girls," I whispered.

"Hi, honey," Mom said, cupping my cheek in her hand. She was warm, and that warmth spread through my body with such comfort that it could be called magic.

I pulled back and neared Sam. He still had his back to me, entirely focused on the TV show, as if it were the only thing holding him together.

"Angel," I whispered, and Sam's head snapped around.

The moment our eyes met, relief flooded his face, instantly warming my heart. He stepped close, his arms enveloping me as he nuzzled his face in my neck.

"Tell me," I said, crushing him against me.

He shook his head, squeezing me tighter.

Kissing the side of his head, I ran my hands down his back and held him until my feet hurt and my back ached. The TV show Sam had been watching had long since changed, and Mom and Angie had fallen asleep. The only other person in the room was an older woman focused on the TV like Sam had been.

"Sammy," I said, my voice cracking. I cleared my throat before speaking again. "Tell me what happened."

His fingers dug into my back when he pulled back, looking me in the eye. "There's a tumor pressing on his spine," he said, choking the words out. "They can't operate because it could do additional harm, but the tumor is so big, Ash, and it's putting pressure on the nerves. He can't walk anymore." Tears ran down his cheeks.

I cupped his face, wiping away the tears pouring from his eyes.

"They said he's progressed so far that no amount of surgeries will be able to help him." He swallowed and a fresh stream of tears poured down his cheeks. "They don't think he has much longer."

I nodded, swallowing. "When they say much longer, what did they give as a timeline?"

He choked down a sob. "Two to three weeks." He bit his lip, gnawing on the skin.

I released a deep breath. Two to three weeks? That's not a long time. Not at all enough time. I drew his face close and kissed his forehead, knowing there was nothing I could ever say to make this situation better. Absolutely nothing.

"Pearce family?" a nurse called from the doorway of the waiting room.

Sam turned toward the nurse, then glanced at Angie and Mom, who were still asleep.

"Angel, we can go. Let them rest."

He nodded, and we approached the nurse.

"You may come back into the room to meet with the doctor."

We followed the nurse back to Gary's room. He was asleep and hooked up to all kinds of machines. The sight had the news sinking in at lightning speed. Two to three weeks. That was a blink of an eye.

We sat beside the bed, and I texted Angie and Mom to let them know we had gone back to talk to the doctor. Sam held my hand while we watched Gary sleep. The steady beep of the monitors was constant, and the blood pressure machine would kick off every few minutes, jolting us from the steady lull.

"Sam," I whispered, and he slowly turned his head to look at me with a frown. "Do you need anything?" He shook his head and went back to watching his dad.

It was hard to see Gary like this. Only a few months ago, we were camping and hiking. We went fishing on Lake Erie. He taught Angie how to do home maintenance in her new apartment. He built custom shelves for her because "those cheap ones from the store are too expensive and not sturdy." The two of them had schemed to get Sam and me back on speaking terms. He had looked so good. So healthy. How could he deteriorate this quickly?

It wasn't fair.

He didn't smoke. He had a few beers a week. He ran a couple miles every morning. He ate healthy most days. Rarely came down with any illness. Gary had been the picture of health.

The doctor finally came in and introduced himself. He stood at the foot of Gary's bed, his eyes softening when he looked at us. "The most recent bloodwork is showing some concerning numbers. We would like to keep him overnight to run some tests, but based on these preliminary numbers, his heart and liver are beginning to fail."

Sam's hand crushed mine at hearing the news. He swallowed a few times, then looked at me like he was pleading for me to take over.

I've got you, Angel.

I asked, "What are we looking at if that is the problem here?"

The doctor frowned. "It's not great, but I can't give anything else until we get through more tests to confirm my suspicions."

I nodded. "Do you think there's a chance of bringing him home, or will he need to be kept here until end of life?"

Sam's head snapped toward me, but I kept my attention on the doctor. I couldn't stand to see the look on his face. It would break the armor I was desperately trying to hold together.

"We'll know more tomorrow, but there are options for at-home nurse care. I can get you the number for a reputable company."

"That would be great. Thank you," I said and shook the doctor's hand. The doctor left the room, and I scooted my chair closer to Sam before wrapping him in a hug.

While my heart cracked to pieces, I swore I wouldn't let Sam see me crumble. He needed me to be strong more than ever, and I would be whatever he needed.

Chapter 34

Sam

Ash and I practically ran through the hospital. Jane and Angie had slept in the room with Dad last night. We alternated days, keeping him company overnight.

Heart failure. Liver failure. Tumors spread through his entire body. They were everywhere.

Dad had been poked and prodded. X-rayed. Scanned. He was a lab experiment for the doctors, but there was nothing they could do. His cancer had progressed too far. The tiny tumors they had removed over the summer didn't even put a dent in the spread. If anything, the tumors were replaced tenfold. In the two and half weeks he had been in the hospital, the one on his spine had completely paralyzed him from the waist down.

I swallowed down the giant ball in my throat and pushed through a door, quickly entering the cancer ward.

Waking up to a voicemail for Ash and me to get to the hospital immediately was not the best start to my day, but the message from Angie had been cryptic. We didn't know what we were walking into.

The door to Dad's private room was open, and the lights were off except for a small strip of light behind his bed that allowed the nurses to see when they checked in on him.

Jane rested her head on the bed beside Dad, holding his hand like she did whenever she was there. The cheap chairs they offered for visitors were anything but comfortable, and spending eighteen to twenty-four hours sitting in one while looking over Dad was getting to us all.

I stopped at the foot of the bed and held my breath, too afraid to move now that I was in the room.

Ash bent over Angie, kissing the top of her head before rubbing Jane's back to wake her. "Ma," he whispered.

Jane stirred and sat up, rubbing the sleep and exhaustion from her eyes. "Hi, boys," she said. Her voice, soft and raspy.

Angie had quit her job to be available to help out. She would cook us meals and clean the house. She did laundry for her and Mom, then would drop into my apartment to help Ash and me with cooking and cleaning.

Ash had talked about taking time off from work, but I stopped him. I didn't want him to ask Tae for extended time off. It would be unfair to him. We were all somehow making it work, and Angie was the sole reason any of us ate every day.

"Ma, what was the cryptic voicemail about?" Ash asked, keeping to a whisper.

Fresh tears streamed down her face, and she shook her head, holding her hand to her lips as if she couldn't speak. Angie's eyes met ours, filled with a sense of hopelessness and defeat.

I held my breath, too nervous to even breathe.

No. No. It can't be now. Not now.

"The doctors," Angie said, choking on her words. Tears rolled down her cheeks. She took in a deep, shaky breath. "They don't think he'll last the night."

The air disappeared from my lungs in a rush, and my knees buckled. I braced myself on the handle at the foot of Dad's bed, staring at Angie like I didn't hear her right. My vision blurred and darkened at the edges.

Ash's voice cut through the pounding of my heart. "Which doctor? Can I speak to them?"

Their voices faded. Everything slowed down. I planted both hands on the end of the bed and stared down at my father. He was hooked up to machines. An IV had been in his arm for weeks. An oxygen tube was taped under his nose. He had a bag attached to him to piss in. He couldn't get out of bed.

I knew this was coming. I knew. They told us. I had a timeline, but I was still hoping. I had hoped that the only family in this world I had left would live through this. That he would fight. He would make it because he was strong and filled with so much life.

We didn't deserve this. He didn't deserve this. He deserved to live a long, happy life with our family. He—he. . . I wanted to have more time. I needed to have him longer. I. . .

I bent over the foot of the bed as the pain in my chest spread, squeezing my chest and throat until it hurt to take a breath. Until I wanted to scream to make it stop. My eyes stung with tears, flooding my eyes until I couldn't see anything. The tears spilled over, scalding my face as they poured down my cheeks. My throat tightened even more, like a hand was crushing it. I couldn't breathe. Everything was being crushed. My heart. My chest. My throat.

I don't want to be alone.

I don't want to live through this.

A powerful hand landed on my back, and Ash's deep voice cut through the crushing weight hanging over me. "Angel," he whispered. His hand trailed up my back and gripped my shoulder, pulling me away from the bed to face him. He cupped my face in his palms. "I'm here." His eyes flicked over my face, capturing me in their hold.

I swallowed past the pain in my throat, holding his gaze, looking into those eyes that had been with me forever. The eyes of the person who always took my pain on as his own. Who protected me and loved me without thought.

His thumbs brushed over my wet cheeks, spreading the tears over my skin. "I'm right here," he whispered, squeezing my face tighter, crowding me with his body. I wrapped my arms around him, clinging to his shirt like he could root me in place.

My lips trembled. I couldn't think of anything to say.

"Breathe," he whispered. "Let yourself feel it and breathe."

I closed my eyes, listening to his steady breaths, matching mine with his until the tightness in my throat subsided.

"Sam," Dad said, sounding like he struggled to speak. Like my name was a strain on him.

Ash pulled back and smiled. "Hey, Gary, it's about time you woke up." He rubbed my face with his thumbs before releasing me. His hand found the small of my back as he faced my dad, gripping the same railing at the foot of the bed I had used to keep myself from dropping to the floor. "Did you get a good night's rest, or have these nurses been keeping you up all night again?"

Dad choked out a laugh. "They won't leave me alone," he said. His voice was croaky and thick.

"I think they've got crushes on you. You're a goddamn catch. That's for sure," Ash said, sounding upbeat and happy.

This was what Ash was good at. He could pretend to be happy in any situation, but I knew he was holding it together for the rest of us.

"Your mom seems to think so," Dad said, squeezing Jane's hand with a smile.

I wiped my tears away, summoning the strength to hold it together, and moved around the bed, sitting on the edge opposite Jane. "Hey, Dad, do you want anything specific for breakfast? Ash and I can grab you some real food and sneak it in."

His eyes lit up. "I'd love one of those breakfast sandwiches from the bistro near the house." He looked at Jane. "You know the one."

I patted his hand before standing. "I'll go get it for you. If the nurses catch us, we can blame it on Ash."

Ash feigned offense and clutched the area over his heart. "Are we finally using me as the bad guy?"

I nodded at him with a slight smile cocked to the side. "You damn delinquent. Sneaking food into a hospital," I said, laughing.

"I've corrupted him, Gary. Call the cops!"

I shoved him and glanced back. "We'll be right back."

When I was far enough away from the room, I fell against a wall and slid to the ground, burying my face in my hands.

Ash sat beside me, resting his arm over my shoulders, and said, "We can sit here as long as you need."

I tugged my bottom lip into my mouth, fighting back my tears, and looked at him. "It came too soon."

He cupped the side of my face, pulling me down until my cheek rested against his shoulder. I nuzzled my face into the soft skin beneath his jaw, feeling his pulse.

"I know, Angel," he croaked.

I sobbed, wanting nothing more than one more day. One more vacation. I wanted to turn back time and relive our camping trip. Go back and relive every moment with my dad. It wasn't enough time. It wasn't enough. I wasn't prepared for this. I didn't know it would end this way.

If I had known, I would've—I would've done more. Spent more time. Cherished every second. Taken more pictures. Asked for more vacations. Said yes to camping more often. I wouldn't have complained about ticks and dirt. I would've gone fishing with him more. Bird watching.

I would've done it all.

All of it.

Why didn't I do more?

Did Dad wish I had been there more? Did I spend enough time with him?

Does he think I was enough?

Ash held me until the tears dried up, and my throat was raw. When I pulled back, I cupped his jaw, sliding my thumb over his cheek where a line of tears had fallen.

"Can we get Dad his sandwich and grab Nora and Regina on the way back? They'll want to say goodbye."

Ash leaned into my touch and nodded. "Whatever you want, Angel."

Nora wouldn't let go of my hand as we walked through the hospital. We carried bags of food from the bistro. We'd ordered nearly the whole menu, wanting Dad to have the choice of anything he wanted. I even snuck him his favorite coffee.

When we entered the room, a nurse, who went by Cookie, eyed the bags in our hands but breezed past us like she didn't see anything.

"Thank you," Ash whispered behind me.

Cookie cackled. "For what, honey? You aren't even here."

Jane and Angie quickly stood, rushing to help us with the food. I grabbed Dad's coffee and snuck it to him.

"We brought some friends and I have your favorite coffee. You have to be quick so the nurses don't see."

Dad chuckled, a rough, airy sound, and pressed the button for his bed to raise him into a better position to eat. "I can't believe you got all this."

We set the food out on two little side tables and along the foot of the bed, creating a buffet spread to choose from.

"Did you buy the whole restaurant?" Jane asked, plucking a blueberry muffin off the bed next to Dad's foot.

"Everything except the building," Ash said, picking up a paper wrapper with a sandwich tucked inside.

"Nana, sit over there," Nora said, pointing to the chair closest to Dad.

The small hospital room flooded with laughter. The smell of food and coffee masked the chemical smells of disinfectant, and the chatter drowned the sounds of the machines.

If this is Dad's last day, I hope this is enough for him to know how loved he is.

"Almost ready?" Ash asked, appearing in the bathroom doorway while adjusting his tie.

I nodded and turned my attention back to the mirror. We were in matching black suits, but my eyes were red from crying. Any other time, I'd crack a joke about how we looked like we were transported right out of *Men in Black*, but I couldn't bring myself to do it. Not today.

"C'mere, Angel. Let me fix your tie for you." Ash grabbed my shoulders and turned me to face him. "Gary would've scolded you for how crooked this is. You can't be embarrassing him on his day." He slid his fingers around the tie, running his warm skin beneath the collar.

I bit my lip, fighting back the tears threatening to start again. "Stop, Ash. I just stopped crying."

His head tilted, and he patted my chest. "All better. Nice and straight." He flashed a smile and added, "Well, the tie, not you." He winked and backed away. "Let's get out of here. We still have to pick up the girls in the sex-mobile that is the Pearce family's minivan."

Ash pulled my Jeep into the driveway and parked out of the way before hopping out and opening the garage door with a code. When I finally found the courage to get out, he was already backing the minivan out of the garage and pulling it up to the front door.

While he parked, I walked into the house.

I felt numb. I was going through the motions. Doing what I was supposed to when I really wanted to crawl into bed and hibernate until this ache in my chest disappeared. Ash had been great to everyone. He was always there to pick up the slack and help where he could. Angie and Jane were still living in the house. Ash would leave me at home to check on them every day. He had even asked Tae to fly out to help with the funeral planning since the three of us were barely functioning.

Jane came down the stairs dressed in a long black dress. She wrapped her arms around me and pressed her face to my chest. I held her, knowing if I tried to speak, I'd cry again. I was tired of crying.

"Angie's almost ready," Jane whispered and released me. She rubbed her finger under her nose and sniffed. "Can we wait outside?"

I nodded and opened the door.

Ash leaned against the hood of the minivan with his arms crossed over his chest. The morning sunlight lit him up in an artistically beautiful way. The sight of him waiting there warmed my heart because while I was feeling alone and losing my dad had crushed me, having Ash at my side supporting me with everything he had—I couldn't help but fall in love with him all over again.

His worried eyes bounced between Jane and me. "Hi, Ma," he said, stepping toward her, wrapping her in a tight hug. "How're you holding up?"

She kissed his cheek and climbed into the van without answering him. The crack in his smile was brief, but I caught it. Ash was in pain like the rest of us, but we'd become so reliant on him being strong that he hadn't taken the time to mourn with us.

"Baby," I said, beckoning him toward me.

A slight smile dimpled his cheek as he approached, climbing the steps until he was mere inches from me.

"What is it?" he asked, placing his hands on my hips.

"I love you." I kissed him, slipping my arms around his neck. "You don't have to sacrifice yourself for us. We'll be okay."

His fingers tightened on my sides, and he pulled me closer. "I'm not sacrificing anything."

Liar.

He kissed my nose, then my cheek. "Where's Angie?"

"Getting ready still."

He tapped my hip and pulled away. "I'll kick her into gear." He dropped another kiss on my cheek and disappeared inside.

Ash parked the minivan in the garage, and we all filed out of the car. Headlights appeared in the driveway behind us, and multiple cars pulled in, packing the driveway so much that a few cars had to park on the lawn.

"I'll get the food set out for everyone," Angie said, disappearing into the house.

The funeral was nice. As nice as it could be for a funeral, and there were a ton of people who showed up. We already had the standard service and reception, but Jane wanted a smaller, more intimate gathering with people who were closer to us.

The group lined up at the front door, greeting each other. Dad and Jane's friends had come. Tae and Lexi had helped with the funeral arrangements and offered to take charge of the catering tonight. Zay, Angie's boyfriend, had pitched in too. I couldn't thank them enough for everything they'd done. Regina and Nora had come by every day since Dad's passing. Regina had been significant in helping us. She cooked food. Nora cleaned and kept our minds busy. They were all there for us, even when we hadn't asked them to be.

Nora approached me, her frown reflecting my own. "Hey, Angel," she said and crashed into me, wrapping her arms around my waist and burying her face in my chest.

I held her, trying not to crumble in front of everyone.

"How are you two holding up?" Regina asked Ash, reaching for his arm in a comforting touch.

"We're doing all right," he said, clasping her hand in his. "We ordered that Italian place again. I know you love their lasagna as much as Gary did." Ash led her up the stairs.

"You didn't order it specifically for me, did you?" I heard her ask as they disappeared through the front door.

"Let's join them, Nora. I'm pretty hungry." I rubbed her back and tried to walk, but she squeezed tighter.

"Angel, I'm sorry you're hurting."

I rolled my lips together, fighting back the tears. "Thanks," I croaked.

"If you want to talk about it, you can talk to me." She looked up at me, resting her chin on my chest with a smile. "Both my parents died in a car accident. I know a thing or two about losing them."

I stroked the top of her head. "Thanks, kiddo."

"Hey, I'm not a kid! I'm fourteen!" She released me from her hug and grabbed my hand, dragging me inside while explaining the difference between a kid and a teenager.

I laughed a genuine laugh for the first time in days. "Well, then, kiddo," I said, pulling her back toward me, "I think you need a refresher on what an old man actually is because Ash and I are not there yet."

She spun, giving me the stink eye. "No, you have it wrong. You're Angel. Ash is old man."

She dragged me through the house to the kitchen, where everyone had crowded around the table to pile their plates with food. Soft music played through the open back doors. Light filtered from the kitchen to the deck, where people sat on the outdoor furniture circling the firepit beneath yellow string lights. Ash and Angie had spent the last few days setting it up. It reminded me of the times the five of us had sat on the deck in the summer, making s'mores over the firepit.

It was oddly comforting to see the house filled with life. There were people around me—around us—who loved us.

I had so many memories I could carry with me. Dad left me a family with Jane, Angie, and Ash that was stronger than anything else I had in this world. When I looked at them, I overflowed with love.

We would be okay because we had each other.

Chapter 35

Ash

I closed my laptop, shutting down for the day before stretching. I couldn't remember the last time I'd moved, but the way my joints were aching, it had likely been a few hours. In the two months since Gary's passing, Sam and I had fallen into a comfortable routine, and his place was feeling like home.

Making my way from the guest room, which we now used as my office, to our bedroom, I looked through the expansive windows, taking in the view of the lake. We shared so many memories in this place. I didn't know when, but the move was coming.

The front door flew open, banging against the wall. "Baby," Sam shouted, excitement clear in his tone. "It's happening!"

I turned toward the door but didn't move from my spot near the window. "What's happening?"

Sam ran down the hall, his heavy footsteps sounding like ten men stampeding through the apartment. He caught himself on the doorframe, huffing as he flashed a smile as bright as the sun.

"Victory X is moving to North Carolina!"

He ran toward me, leaping into my arms.

Squeezing him tight, I said, "Congratulations." He'd spent long hours and sleepless nights ensuring everything was taken care of for the company and his employees.

Any employee who didn't want to move would get a very generous severance, and those who moved with Victory X would have their moving expenses paid. There were additional benefits to following Victory X, which seemed to be going over well with his management teams.

"Does this mean your employees will be told about the move now?"

"Yeah, and I can't wait. I hope I don't lose too many people."

"I'm confident you won't."

He slid from my hold and tugged me into a kiss as his feet hit the ground. "But now, we have to find a place to live."

"That won't be hard. There are plenty of apartment buildings out there."

Sam looked over my shoulder at the view. "How many places in Raleigh have a view of a lake?"

I shrugged, sliding my hands down his sides, resting them on his lower back. "Probably none."

"I'll miss this view. I don't think we'll ever find one like this again."

I shrugged. "I like the view of what's in front of me more than anything else in this world."

His cheeks turned pink in a flash. "I'm serious, Ash. I'm going to miss it here."

I kissed his forehead, holding him close. "Me too."

His gaze raked over my face, and a sly smile dimpled his cheeks. "Wanna make some more memories of the view?"

I raised an eyebrow, drawing him closer. "Always. What did you have in mind?"

He bit his lip, backing me up until my back hit the window. "Wanna take a guess?"

With a groan, I pulled him closer and squeezed his ass, delighted in the sensation of him pressed against me. "I've got an idea."

My phone ringing jolted me awake. The number of times I received phone calls early in the morning had become far too frequent. I rolled over, forcing Sam's arm off me before grabbing my phone and answering it without looking.

"Hello?" I said, the sleep in my voice evident.

The sound of someone sobbing on the other end sped up the process of waking up. I glanced at the caller ID, hit with a wave of concern.

"Nora? Are you okay?" I sat up, reaching over and shaking Sam awake. "Sammy, wake up."

He groaned and rolled away.

"Nora, what's wrong?"

"I—she. . ." the rest of the words were a jumbled mess I couldn't understand.

"Nora, slow down. I can't understand you."

Her sobs were gut-wrenching.

"Sam, fucking wake up!"

Nora's crying had me panicking. I didn't know what was happening, but every worst-case scenario ran through my head. Someone broke in. Someone kidnapped her. Someone touched her in ways that had my blood boiling. My feet hit the floor, and I rushed into the closet to pull on clothes.

"Nora," I said as I slipped my legs into jeans. "I need you to take a deep breath for me. I can't understand you through the crying. Please."

"Nana won't wake up," she yelled before the sobs returned.

My blood ran cold.

"Sam, call the police," I shouted, slipped on a T-shirt, and rushed back into the room.

Sam was finally sitting up, looking confused and groggy.

"Why?" he asked.

"Regina won't wake up, Sammy. We need someone to get to Nora."

In seconds, he had an emergency dispatcher on the phone.

I slid my shoes on and said, "We will be there in fifteen minutes. Go into the living room and wait for the police. Stay on the phone with me until Sam and I arrive, okay? Can you do that for me?"

"Yeah. I can," she sputtered through her sobs.

Sam was up and dressed, talking with the dispatcher on speaker.

"They're on the way," the dispatcher said before asking Sam a series of questions.

While he answered the dispatcher, I kept Nora talking the whole way to the car. I tossed Sam my phone and hopped into the driver's side of the Jeep. The moment Sam's ass was in the car, I took off.

The fifteen-minute drive felt like an eternity. When I turned down the road to the tiny, run-down apartment complex, I swung the car into a parking spot near the rescue teams and police officers and flew out of the car.

I took my phone from Sam and said, "Nora, are you with police officers right now?" Her quiet "yes" broke my heart. "Tell them Sam and I are here and are coming to meet you."

"Okay," she said before speaking to someone else.

There was too much going on for me to hear what was said, so I stopped near an officer waving to get her attention.

"Ma'am," I said, wondering how I could play this without being family.

The officer looked at me like I had interrupted her favorite movie and snapped, "Can I help you?"

My immediate reaction was to be nasty right back, but Sam stepped in, stopping me.

"Hi, I'm the one who called this in. The young girl in that apartment is our family friend. Her grandmother is the one we called in about. We need to get in and see her or take her home. I'm not sure what your regulations are, but the young girl has no remaining family."

The cop eyed Sam like we were a couple of creeps before walking away without a word.

"Nora," I said, trying to get her attention. "Can you hear me?"

"Yeah," she said, sniffling.

"What did the cop say to you?"

"You can come, but they need to find out what will happen to me after this."

I nibbled on my lip. Would they send her to foster care?

The cop returned and let Sam and me through, though she looked unhappy about having to do it.

When we entered the apartment, we saw a scene straight out of a crime scene show. Cops were everywhere, walking in and out. A cop sat on the sofa beside Nora, writing in a notepad.

"Nora," Sam said.

She spun around, climbed over the back of the sofa, and launched herself at Sam. He caught her, holding her tight while she sobbed, burying her face in his shoulder.

Pocketing my phone, I walked over and rested my hand on her back. "We're here."

I wasn't sure how much time had passed, but when two people from Child Protective Services came into the apartment to take Nora away, I wanted to stop them. I wanted to fight for her to stay with Sam and me. But we weren't family in any capacity. We had no leg to stand on to claim her. According to the government, we were strangers to her.

Sam nudged me, then said to the man in charge of where Nora would end up, "Hi, um, could you not leave yet? Would you let my partner and I have a moment to chat about something?"

The guy looked us over for a moment before nodding his agreement.

Sam grabbed my arm and led me to the side of the room. He chewed his lip nervously, so I ran my thumb over his lips.

"What is it, Angel?"

"So, I've been thinking. From what it sounds like, we could get a judge to maybe agree to let us adopt her. Or, at the very least, be her legal guardians."

My heart stopped, and I forgot how to breathe.

I stared at him.

Me, adopt a kid? Me?

"You're serious, Sam?"

He nodded and said, "Yeah. I am. I don't want her to end up in foster care. As weird as it is to say this, I like her a lot. She's a good kid. She's been through hell. How we all met was a weird stroke of luck, but I don't want to see her taken away and passed around the system. What if her cancer comes back? What if someone abuses her?" His expression grew more and more worried with each passing second. "I couldn't forgive myself if we don't try."

"You know I've never wanted kids," I said, running my fingers through my hair.

The worry lines on his forehead dipped further. "She's fourteen. She'll be eighteen in no time, not that I want to kick her out after that. But, Ash, can you honestly look me in the eye and tell me you would rather see them take her away and put her in foster care?"

I chewed my lip because I definitely didn't want that, but I was in no way ready to be a dad. Especially a dad to a teen.

"Think about it, Ash. Please?"

I cupped Sam's face, stroking his cheeks with my thumbs while I played with the idea. I liked Nora; she was a good kid. But my biggest fear was ending up as a parent and turning out like my father. I didn't want to be that kind of man. I was afraid of what I could become.

"Sammy, I don't know if I'm ready for that responsibility."

He stepped closer, grabbing the nape of my neck. "Ash, we can do this. I know we can."

"What if I'm exactly like him?"

Sam slid his fingers through my hair, soothing my fears with a single look. "You could never be like him. You don't have it in you." He chuckled. "And did you see yourself after answering the phone this morning?"

I cocked my head and smiled. "What do you mean?"

"You went all *Dad mode*," he said with a wide grin. "Ordering me around and shit. You looked like your daughter had just called you and told you someone was bullying her. I swear I thought you were going to get pulled over before we got here for the way your crazy ass was driving. Then when that cop—"

"I get it," I said, cutting him off.

Maybe I was more cut out for being a parent than I thought. But a kid is a lot of responsibility that I wasn't anywhere near ready for. Sam was right, though. Nora was fourteen and mostly could take care of herself. It wasn't like she was a young kid where I would need to learn things like changing diapers and bottle feeding.

The idea of adopting Nora was growing on me.

Besides, it was Nora, the snarky teen who bet me fifty bucks I was getting stood up at the airport. The girl who wove her way into our family.

I sighed, glancing at the CPS agent. "You think we really have a shot at adopting her?"

Sam shrugged. "Worth a try, isn't it?"

"Ready?" I asked Sam, lacing my fingers with his.

"More than ever," he replied.

We pushed through the courthouse doors and headed to the room reserved for us. After weeks of back and forth with the State and CPS, we were told our chances of being approved for adoption would be higher if we were married.

Naturally, we agreed.

Mom and Angie stood in the center of the room beside an older man with salt and pepper hair. They were beautiful in their dresses. Mom wore a sky-blue dress with lace accents. She'd done her hair and makeup and looked absolutely stunning. Angie wore a pastel yellow dress with light makeup, and her long hair fell to her waist with cute little curls.

"Our girls look lovely," I said, squeezing Sam's hand as we approached them.

"So, we're telling them about the adoption at dinner, right? Is that good timing?"

I laughed and looked at him. His pale blue eyes shimmered under the crappy yellow lighting, and in his suit, he was as handsome as ever. He was every bit the man I'd loved my whole life, and I couldn't believe we were actually here.

Sam was about to be my husband.

Holy fuck. My husband.

"Yeah, we tell them at dinner."

"They're gonna freak," Sam whispered.

I chuckled and hushed him before we stopped next to the officiant. The guy who would marry us and make it official.

Chapter 36

Sam

I'm getting married.

I'm marrying the love of my life.

I held Ash's hand, focusing on my breathing.

The officiant started speaking, but I had no idea what he said.

I'm panicking. I think I'm panicking.

I'm marrying Ash.

Oh, good Lord. Ash will be my husband in a matter of minutes.

Ash stood in front of me, smiling. God, he was beautiful. His suit hid most of his tattoos. He had his earrings in and a fresh haircut. This beautiful, strong, caring man was about to be mine. Sure, I had him. He was mine for a while now, but this was official. This was legal. It was binding and told the world he was *mine.*

Damn, if that isn't a power trip.

The officiant motioned toward me and said, "Sam, please present your vows."

Oh, God.

My body shook with nerves. Ash's smile was so wide the corners of his eyes wrinkled. It was adorable and sexy.

I swallowed.

This is Ash, the man who has seen me at my worst.

This isn't embarrassing at all.

Please, for the love of God, don't forget the words.

I drew in a deep breath and tried to pretend we were alone.

"Ash, I never thought this day would come. I spent too many years expecting to see you up here with someone else. The moment you looked my way, as I had always wished you would, was both euphoric and horrifying." I glanced at Jane

299

and Angie. "I let fear keep us apart, but I need you to know you're my other half. My perfect puzzle piece. The oxygen I breathe. The ground I stand on. You're with me in my dreams. My waking thoughts. Without you, I'm empty. You protect me. You rescued me in so many ways I could never thank you enough. I always know you'll be there whenever I need you." I paused, fighting through the building tension in my throat. "You're the love of my life," I croaked as tears pricked behind my eyes, threatening to spill over. I reached up and cupped the side of his head, running my thumb over his jaw, loving the feel of his stubble scraping over my skin. "My soulmate," I whispered and swallowed down the tears. "I'll love you for eternity."

Ash's eyes shimmered like he was on the verge of crying, but his smile never wavered. He held my waist, tugging me close like he'd done so many times before, but this was more intense, and the look in his eye reminded me of the camping trip in Ohio. Of that night in the spring when he laid himself bare for me, hoping I would accept him.

His face drew close, and his breath tickled my skin.

"I've loved you for a lifetime, even when I was blind to my feelings. I've loved you since you hopped down from your perch with dirt on your face. I've loved you since you first flashed me that crooked grin." He smiled, pinching my cheek. "You say I rescued you, but you saved me. You're the only reason I'm standing here today."

My heart thundered. I saved him? From what?

"Angel, do you remember what I said when we were standing in that spring next to that beautiful waterfall?" he asked, his voice a rough whisper.

"I remember."

"I choose you today. I choose you tomorrow, and I will choose you until the day I die. And if the afterlife exists, I'll choose you again. If reincarnation is real, I'll choose you in my next life and the life after that because you are my life." A tear slipped down his cheek. "You are my everything. You're the sun and the moon. You own me like the moon owns the tides. You're an angel sent from heaven to give me the strength to live this life."

My chest swelled with joy. I was overflowing with love for this man. The boy I fell in love with became this amazing, caring, loving man in front of me, and he was mine.

I didn't wait for anyone to say anything. I didn't hesitate. I closed the distance and kissed him. I clung to him, tangling our tongues together. Pressing our bodies as tight as we could get. My fingers weaved in his hair, ruining the gel, but I didn't care. I needed to have him. I had waited a lifetime to have him, and I never imagined I could have him as my husband.

The officiant said something I didn't catch, and Jane and Angie giggled, but we kept kissing. I didn't want to pull away from him. I didn't want to stop touching him.

Angie said, "Get a room already."

Ash broke our kiss, chuckling and pulling back enough to brush his nose over mine. "I love you, Samuel Pearce."

"I love you too, Ashton Pearce."

He took my last name.

I fucking love this man.

I finally pried myself away from Ash enough to face our family. Jane sobbed, wiping her nose with a bundle of tissues, and tears streamed down Angie's face. Their makeup surprisingly held together. When those companies said they made it waterproof, they weren't joking.

Ash spread his arms, letting go of my hand, and said, "Bring it in, girls."

Angie rushed to him and crashed against his chest. "I love you guys. I'm so happy for you."

They turned to me, then circled me, wrapping me in their loving hugs.

My heart might have been torn to shreds this past year. I lost friends along the way. Healing would take time, but seeing us together like this gave me hope. I was sure Dad was smiling down, watching us, knowing he left me where I belonged.

After changing out of our suits, we drove to Jane's new apartment. She had sold the house and all the furniture. Anything considered family heirlooms went into a storage facility for Ash, Angie, and me to sort through when we were ready. But she wanted to be out of the house that reminded her of Dad. She had moved closer to Angie, who had found another apartment in Alexandria with Zay.

Today, Ash and I had used the excuse that we wanted to celebrate in private with only the four of us, but really, we were telling them about the adoption plans.

I was a nervous wreck but still riding the high of our ceremony.

"Hey, husband," Ash said as he hit the button for the elevator.

"Yes, husband?" I said and a laugh bubbled up through me.

"You ready to tell them we're gonna be dads?"

I laughed again. "You think they can handle this? We get married and have a kid on the same day?"

He chuckled, gripping the back of my neck to pull me close. "They'll be fine." He brushed his lips over mine as the elevator doors opened. "But I have to say, I can't wait to get you home tonight so I can make love to you over and over." He tugged me into the elevator, hitting the button for the floor before leaning against the wall and pulling me close. "And over." He kissed me. "And over."

"I think that's enough overs."

The elevator jerked to a stop, and we ambled to Jane's apartment. The door was already unlocked, so we walked in.

Angie and Jane were at the kitchen table, and when Angie saw us, she waved. "Hey, lovebirds," Angie called.

"Hi, piglet," Ash said.

I sat at the table while Ash grabbed a bottle of water from the fridge.

My hands were clammy and turning cold with each passing moment.

"So," Ash said, sitting next to me.

I wasn't sure how they would take the news, and I didn't like the idea of dropping this on them and then moving to Raleigh, but Ash and I had planned it out. Since the night Nora lost everything, we'd spent weeks working through our options and planned everything down to a science. We knew what we wanted, and now we were only waiting on word from our lawyer that it would all happen.

"So?" Jane said, eyeing us like we were about to drop bad news on her.

I bit my lip, and Ash leaned forward, resting his arms on the table to play with his water bottle.

"Sammy and I have some news," Ash said, and Jane and Angie exchanged worried looks. "A couple months ago, when Regina passed, Sam and I made a decision, and we've been working toward that goal since." He paused, glancing at me with a devious smirk. "We've been working with the state to adopt Nora."

Angie gasped, slapping her hands over her mouth. "Are you serious?"

"You're adopting her?" Jane asked, her eyes wide with surprise.

"We're trying," I said. "There are many stipulations we have to meet, one being that they preferred us being married." I held up my hand and waved my finger, which now had my wedding band.

"You got married so that you can adopt Nora?" Angie asked. The shock in her voice had me chuckling.

"I mean," Ash said, placing his hand on my thigh, "I didn't need this as a reason, but it sped up the process."

"I'm going to be an aunt?" Angie said, her eyes swelling with tears. "Really?" She grabbed Jane's hand and said, "You lost the bet! I win!"

"What bet?" I asked.

Jane shook her head. "It was stupid."

Angie laughed. "I bet Mom and Dad that I would be an aunt before I turned thirty, and they both said, 'There's no way either of those boys will be parents any time soon'." She mocked Jane too perfectly. "Don't pretend you don't remember Mom!" Angie said, then smacked her hand on the table. "Pay up."

Ash laughed. "What did you bet on?"

Angie leaned over the table, close to Ash's face, and whispered, "The ultra-secret chocolate chip cookie recipe from Grandma."

Ash patted the top of her head and said, "Good job, piglet. Make sure you text me the recipe."

Jane released an exasperated sigh, but her smile was wide, cutting lines on her cheeks. "I'm really proud of you." She took Ash's hand in hers, brought his knuckles to her lips, and kissed him before clasping her hands around his. "I'm so proud of you both." She rested her forehead on his hand.

"Ma, stop," Ash said, stroking her hair with his free hand. "You're gonna make me cry."

"These are happy tears," she whispered. "I'm immensely happy."

I was too. Whatever our future had in store, I knew I wouldn't be alone. I had a family who loved me. A husband who loved me more than life itself. And hopefully, I would have a daughter I could cherish and give everything to.

Epilogue
July Third Three Years Later

Ash

"Nora, hurry up," I called, knowing she could hear me down the hall. "You're gonna make us miss our flight." I was exaggerating, but teenagers were the devil, and Sam was already panicking like we wouldn't make it.

"Am not!" she screeched.

With a chuckle, I dipped into the bathroom, scooping up our toothbrushes and the bag of mini tubes of body wash, and God knows what else Sam squeezed into the stupid travel-approved bottles.

"Baby," Sam said, appearing out of thin air behind me, "have you seen my swim trunks? I swore I packed them, but now I can't find them."

I smiled and dropped a light kiss on his lips. "Angel, if you can't find them, you can simply not wear them. You know I love skinny dipping with you."

"Ash, I'm being serious."

I kissed his cheek and walked around him. "We can buy you new swim trunks."

"We shouldn't have to buy new clothes because they were misplaced," he groaned.

"Sam, we don't have time to tear apart the house to find them." I dropped the toiletries into the travel bag on the bed and turned back to him. "We will buy you new ones." His pout was cute as hell, but it wasn't the time. "Nora, if you aren't ready in five minutes, we're leaving without you."

"Whatever, old man!"

"You're both killing me today," I groaned and zipped the travel bag up, then tossed it inside the large suitcase. "Let's go."

Sam appeared to want to protest, but left the room with an exasperated sigh.

"Nora," Sam said from the end of the hallway, "we have to go."

She grumbled something in return that I couldn't hear.

"I know. He's grumpy because he hates traveling."

"He used to travel every weekend," she screeched.

I rolled my eyes and picked up the two suitcases Sam and I had packed for ourselves before heading down the stairs and yelled, "I drive away in ten minutes."

I passed through the front door and had the suitcases in the trunk before either of them stepped foot outside. I leaned against the tailgate, crossing my arms, soaking up the warmth of the sun beating down on me. The summer always brought back memories of our family. Memories I now cherished with a vibrancy I never thought possible.

Sam and Nora stepped through the front door of our four-bedroom single-family home in North Carolina. Sam and I didn't want anything extravagant. We bought what we needed for the size of our family. We were fifteen minutes outside of Raleigh. The drive to work was easy. Nora was in a great high school.

There had never been a time when I would've believed this would be my future—my ultimate joy. I would've never believed that the pinnacle of my happiness as a human on this earth was watching my best friend and a random girl I met in an airport walk out of my house side by side.

Seeing them filled me with a deep sense of love and fulfillment. It was unexpected and somehow the most welcome feeling ever.

"I see you two could finally find it in yourselves to make it," I said, adding a bite of sarcasm.

Nora glared before shifting to a smile. "Old man," she said, skipping toward me. "We were right on time."

"Mm-hm," I hummed. "Hurry up." I squeezed her tight before pushing off the car and grabbing the bag from Sam. "Get in the car."

"Fine, Dad," Nora said and climbed into the back seat.

Sam smiled, sauntering toward me. "You secretly love it." He kissed my cheek and slid into the passenger seat before I could grumble a reply.

He was right. I loved every second with them.

Nora rushed up to the front door, barreling through before Sam and I could get our seatbelts off.

"To be young again," Sam said, climbing out of the car.

I followed him, walking around to the trunk, and pulled our bags out.

"Come on, we aren't old," I grumbled.

He rolled his eyes and said, "I'll be thirty-two in like two weeks. We're old now."

I laughed and handed him Nora's bag. "If you say so, padre."

"Hey,"—he shoved me—"only Nora calls me that. I'm Angel to you, mister."

"Sure, sure," I sang, walking up the stone steps with our bags. "Get a move on, Angel. I bet they started making s'mores without us. If all of it's gone, it's your fault."

Sam pushed past me up the stairs carrying Nora's smaller pink bag. "It's cute that you think they can finish the s'mores without the s'mores champion."

I chuckled, and he darted into the house with the pink bag over his shoulder. Dad-life suited us. Looking at our lives now, I wouldn't have it any other way.

Before heading to the backyard, I set our bags at the base of the stairs. The sliding door leading to the backyard of Angie's house was open, and the screen door let the summer air into the living room. A high-pitched screech echoed through the house from outside, but it was nothing new. Somehow, my family was loud even when nothing was happening.

I slid the screen door open to a scene of chaos.

Angie's hair was tied back in a high ponytail that kept dipping too close for comfort to the fire pit, and remnants of melted chocolate covered her long, flowy summer dress. A skinny little golden retriever ran around with a large stick hanging out of its mouth. The dog swung the stick in all directions each time someone made a noise or moved. Mom kept chasing the dog away from the fire, and Sam and Zay were curled in on themselves, laughing too hard to help with the disaster unfolding before me.

And, of course, my lovely, responsible, nearly adult daughter was recording the damn scene on her phone.

I wouldn't trade it.

"Okay, okay," I said, walking straight into the chaos. "Nora, get your ass over here and wrangle this damn dog."

"But, Dad, this could go viral!"

"I don't fucking care if it goes viral. Get the dog away from here."

She pouted and tucked her phone away. "Fiiiine." She clapped at the dog and said, "Come here, Peaches. Apparently, no one wants to play with your tree branch."

That comment sent Sam rolling again because the damn stick basically was a goddamn tree branch.

"Ma, sit the hell down before you hurt yourself." I rushed over and grabbed Angie's hair away from the fire. "Piglet, I love you. I adore you, but let's not catch yourself on fire a month before you have that baby."

Angie looked up at me, red from laughing. "Hey, Ash. I see you're a party pooper, like always. When did you and Sammy trade places?"

I kissed the top of her head, careful to avoid the melted chocolate coating her hands and—well—everywhere.

"Call me what you will," I said, plopping on the wicker sofa beside Sam and linking our hands together. "What has everyone been up to?"

Sam

Zay and I each grabbed a side of the giant blanket and spread it over the grass. There had been a time when I didn't care about holidays. Dad loved them, so I always participated, but it wasn't until Dad wasn't here and Ash and I had Nora that I cared more. It was the little things like today that we carried with us. The small gestures. The stolen moments. The laughs. Those were what was most important. I treasured the memories I had with Dad, especially the ones leading up to his passing.

"When do the fireworks start?" Nora asked as she flopped onto the blanket.

"We've got a few hours, honey," Jane said.

Ash's hand slid around my waist, and his lips brushed over my ear. "You remember that year you and I had a sunscreen wrestling match?"

I chuckled, remembering it clearly. We had still been avoiding each other back then. "Hard to forget."

"Want a repeat?"

"What?"

He pulled his hand away, and before I could turn to look at him, my face was covered in sunscreen. Ash's cackles got on my nerves instantly.

I wiped my eyes clean, then said, "Oh, baby, you just started a war." I rushed him, throwing my weight into his stomach, forcing him to the ground.

I climbed on top of him and pinned his hands above his head, then rubbed my face all over him. I wiped the sunscreen wherever I could reach without letting him up. He laughed and kicked beneath me, but I had him locked in place.

"Get a room," Angie called.

"Oh my god, is this some weird kind of foreplay?" Nora asked.

I let go of Ash's hands to stare at my daughter. "What did you just say?"

"You act like I don't know when you guys are flirting. Do you not remember how we met?"

"Well, that—"

I was lifted into the air and slammed onto my back in a rush.

Ash had my hands pinned over my head with one hand and his other over my chest, keeping pressure on me.

We probably looked like fools, and I could see Nora's point because Ash between my legs pinning me down was definitely foreplay material.

"Okay, I see your point, Nora," I said between heavy breaths.

"Glad you understand, padre."

Ash bit his lip and wiggled his eyebrows. He leaned in and kissed my neck before moving close to my ear, "You know, there is a cafe at the bottom of the hill with a very nice restroom and if I remember correctly, they have amazingly private bathroom stalls."

"I cannot believe you suggested that."

"Why? You don't like sharing a bathroom with me anymore?"

I laughed and bucked my hips, throwing him off me. "Later."

He chuckled as he sat up, wiping the sunscreen off his face. "Fine."

After the sun set, we all settled on the blanket to watch the fireworks together. Jane, Nora, and Angie were cuddled up next to Zay. Ash and I sat behind them, leaning back to gaze at the stars.

I leaned in, grabbing the back of Ash's head. "I love you," I whispered, then kissed him.

He mirrored me, sliding his fingers along my neck before gripping the back of my head. "I love you too, Angel."

"Stop being so sappy back there, Dads," Nora said before crawling toward us and settling between me and Ash. "But you know," she whispered, "if we're gonna be all sappy. . . Padre, when Dad called you angel that first time we met, I thought it was the cheesiest thing ever, but you're both my angels. I love you."

"Now look who's being sappy," Ash said, pinching her cheek. "I love you too." He tugged her under his arm, squeezing her against his chest.

I ran my fingers through her hair. "I love you too," I whispered.

The sound of the fireworks shooting into the sky stole our attention. Beneath the sparkling lights and the expansive booms, the most important people in my life surrounded me. I was filled with memories of them.

I looked forward to the memories we would make.

A future filled with stolen moments. Shared pain. Joy.

And most importantly, love.

Afterword

Thank you for reading *Love on a Dare*. Sam and Ash were inspired by a random Reddit story video (Toby and Summer) I saw on TikTok; you know, the ones where someone's playing Minecraft or something, and you listen to these ridiculous stories for a good minute or two. This one was about two friends kissing to cover up one of them pretending to be gay. I can't even remember anymore, and I haven't read the original story. It was specifically the kissing scene that I came across that inspired the whole premise of *Love on a Dare*. It was so long ago that I forgot the actual story, but I liked that scene a lot, and it spun a whole story to life that became this huge thing I *had* to write. So thank you, random Reddit user, for inspiring this story. Now that *Love on a Dare* is complete, I'll have to go hunt the Reddit story down to read it for myself.

I didn't intend this to be a bisexual awakening story, but it turned out that way. I'm actually happy it did because a few months after writing my initial draft of LOAD, I saw some people on Threads talking about wanting to see more older characters having a bisexual awakening. At the start, I had Sam and Ash in college, but after a while, it felt right to age them up, which opened the story to something I had never intended or expected. Their whole story shifted and this weird little slice of life story turned into a big slice of life story that I couldn't stop writing.

I had a lot of fun with Ash and Sam. Even though they have their flaws, to me, they're perfect little bundles of love. I think it's so important to show flawed characters who have been shaped by their past. No one is perfect. Not all of us make "good" decisions. We are all human. We hurt each other. Let fear control us. Worry about the "what-ifs" and fall into pessimism. Sam and Ash have a lot of baggage, but their love for each other runs deep, and while they both hurt each other in the beginning, they were able to move past it and have a genuine, caring relationship built on trust and love.

I hope you enjoyed it as much as I did. Thank you for reading.

Acknowledgements

Geri, my wonderful editor and friend, thank you for your feedback and hard work, for being my sounding board again, and for generously supporting me all the way through. I appreciate you more than you could ever know. I love you so much. Thank you for being in my life. I hope LOAD is the start of something more, and I'm so damn happy we did it together.

Terra, I'm proud of you. Thank you for your support and help. Because of you, I had the strength to explore things I ran away from for too long. Thank you for confiding in and trusting me. I don't have enough words to express what you mean to me. You are a light in my life. May you always burn as bright as the sun.

Dan, lord knows I will forever die of embarrassment every single time you mention my books, but it would take me pages to fully express my thanks. Every moment you spent alpha reading this story is so profoundly appreciated. Your feedback was invaluable. Without your feedback, this story would not be the same. From the bottom of my heart, thank you.

To my mom and sister, I appreciate you supporting me and encouraging me to continue this journey even when it means I overwork myself and respond to texts late. Thank you for being my support system.

J, love of my life, my rock—thank you for supporting me every single day, even when I spend eighteen hours a day at my desk, ignoring you for weeks on end. You're the best partner I could ever hope for.

To my alpha and beta readers, thank you for your invaluable feedback and every moment you spent reading this story. You are profoundly appreciated.

About the Author

Jamie Avery King is an author of paranormal, fantasy, contemporary, and LGBTQ+ romance. They live in the Washington, DC, area and grew up loving everything fiction. Jamie's passion for fantasy worlds and tales of finding love has been channeled into their love of storytelling. When they aren't writing and dreaming up new worlds, they play video games, read, or hang out with their dogs and partner.

Keep up to date with Jamie at jamieaveryking.com

@jamieaveryking (IG & Threads)

@jamieking_author (TT)

@jamiekingauthor.bsky.social

www.ingramcontent.com/pod-product-compliance
Lightning Source LLC
Chambersburg PA
CBHW030640020726
47493CB00006B/1802